By Orson Scott Card

Homebody
Treasure Box
Lost Boys

Ender's Game
Speaker for the Dead
Xenocide
Children of the Mind
*Ender's Shadow**

Seventh Son
Red Prophet
Prentice Alvin
Alvin Journeyman
Heartfire
*The Crystal City**

The Memory of Earth
The Call of Earth
The Ships of Earth
Earthfall
Earthborn

Pastwatch: The Redemption of Christopher Columbus
Saints
Folk of the Fringe
Wyrms
Hart's Hope
The Worthing Saga
Songmaster
Lovelock (with Kathryn H. Kidd)

Monkey Sonatas
The Changed Man
Flux
Cruel Miracles

Stone Tables

*Sarah**

*Forthcoming

ENCHANTMENT

ENCHANTMENT

ORSON SCOTT CARD

THE BALLANTINE PUBLISHING GROUP • NEW YORK

A Del Rey® Book
Published by The Ballantine Publishing Group

http://www.randomhouse.com/delrey/

LIBRARY OF CONGRESS CATALOGING-IN-PUBLICATION DATA
Card, Orson Scott.
Enchantment / Orson Scott Card. — 1st ed.
p.   cm.
"A Del Rey book"—T.p. verso.
ISBN 0-345-41687-2 (alk. paper)
I. Title.
PS3553.A655E495   1999
813'.54—dc21   98-52444
CIP

Book design by H. Roberts Design

Manufactured in the United States of America

First Edition: April 1999

10 9 8 7 6 5 4 3 2 1

For Kristine
All these years after that first kiss,
and still the magic grows

CONTENTS

1

LᴇAVᴇꜱ

 'm ten years old, my whole life you've called me Vanya. My name is on the school records, on government papers as Ivan Petrovich Smetski. Now you tell me I'm really Itzak Shlomo. What am I, a Jewish secret agent?"

Vanya's father listened silently, his face as smooth, weathered, and blank as parchment. Vanya's mother, who was merely hovering near the conversation rather than taking part in it, seemed to be having a little trouble keeping herself from smiling. In amusement? If so, at what? At Vanya? At her husband's sudden discovery of their intense commitment to Judaism?

Whatever the cause of her almost-smile, Vanya did not want to be ridiculous. Even at the age of ten, dignity was important to him. He calmed himself, spoke in more measured tones. "We eat pork," he pointed out. "*Rak.* Caviar."

"I think Jews can eat caviar," offered his mother helpfully.

"I hear them whispering, calling me *zhid*, they say they only want to race with Russians, I can't even *run* with them," said Vanya. "I've always been the fastest runner, the best hurdler, and yesterday they wouldn't even let me keep time. And it's my stopwatch!"

"Mine, actually," said Father.

"The principal won't let me sit in class with the other children because I'm not a Russian or a Ukrainian, I'm a disloyal foreigner, a Jew. So why don't I know how to speak Hebrew? You change everything else, why not that?"

Father looked up toward the ceiling.

"What is that look, Father? Prayer? All these years, whenever I talk too much, you look at the ceiling—were you talking to God then?"

Father turned his gaze to Vanya. His eyes were heavy—scholar's eyes, baggy and soft from always peering through lenses at a thousand hectares of printed words. "I have listened to you," he said. "Ten years old, a boy who thinks he's so brilliant, he rails on and on, showing no respect for his father, no trust. I do it all for your sake."

"And for God's," offered Mother. Was she being ironic? Vanya had never been able to guess about Mother.

"For *you* I do this," said Father. "You think I did it for me? My work is here in Russia, the old manuscripts. What I need from other countries is sent to me because of the respect I've earned. I make a good living."

"Made," said Mother.

For the first time it occurred to Vanya that if he was cut out of school classes, Father's punishment might be even more dire. "You lost your place at the university?"

Father shrugged. "My students will still come to me."

"If they can find you," said Mother. Still that strange smile.

"They'll find me! Or not!" cried Father. "We'll eat or not! But we will get Vanya—Itzak—out of this country so he grows up in a place where this mouth of his, this disrespect for everyone that doesn't measure up to his lofty standards, where they will call it creativity or cleverness or rock and roll!"

"Rock and roll is music," said Vanya.

"Prokofiev is music, Stravinski is music, Tchaikovski and Borodin and Rimski-Korsakov and even Rachmaninov, *they* are music. Rock and roll is smart boys with no respect, *you* are rock and roll. All the trouble you get into at school, you will never get into university with this attitude. Why are you the only child in Russia who doesn't learn to bow his head to power?"

Father had asked this question at least a dozen times before, and this time as always, Vanya knew that his father was saying it more in pride than in consternation. Father liked the fact that Vanya spoke his mind. He encouraged it. So how did this become the reason for the family to declare itself Jewish and apply for a visa to Israel? "You make a decision without asking me, and it's *my* fault?"

"I have to get you out of here, let you grow up in a free land," said Father.

"Israel is a land of war and terrorism," said Vanya. "They'll make me a soldier and I'll have to shoot down Palestinians and burn their houses."

"None of that propaganda is true," said Father. "And besides, it won't matter. I can promise you that you will never be a soldier of Israel."

Vanya was scornful for a moment, until it dawned on him why Father was so certain he wouldn't be drafted into the Israeli military. "Once you get out of Russia, you aren't going to Israel at all."

Father sighed. "What you don't know, you can't tell."

There was a knock at the door. Mother went to answer.

"Maybe here in Russia you aren't in class for a while," said Father. "And this nonsense of running, you'll never be world champion, that's for Africans. But your mind will be quick long after your legs slow down, and there are countries where you will be *valued*."

"Which other countries?" asked Vanya.

Mother was letting somebody into the apartment.

"Maybe Germany. Maybe England. Canada, maybe."

"America," whispered Vanya.

"How do I know? It depends where there's a university that wants an aging scholar of ancient Slavic literature."

America. The enemy. The rival. The land of jeans and rock and roll, of crime and capitalism, of poverty and oppression. Of hope and freedom. All kinds of stories about America, from rumor, from the government press. It was 1975 and the Vietnam War had ended only a few years ago—America had bloody hands. But through all the propaganda, the rivalry, the envy, one message was constant: America was the most important country on earth. And that's where Father wanted him to grow up. That's why Mother's Jewish relatives were suddenly the only ones who counted, they and Father's grandmother on his mother's side. To get them to America.

For a moment, Vanya almost understood.

Then Mother came back into the room. "He's here."

"Who's here?" asked Vanya.

Father and Mother looked at him blankly.

"He's called a *mohel*," said Mother finally. Then they explained what this old Jewish man was going to do to Vanya's penis.

Ten seconds later, Vanya was down the stairs, out on the street, running for his life, running in despair. He was not going to let a man take hold of his member and cut bits of it off just so he could get on a plane and fly to the land of cowboys. By the time he came home, the *mohel* was gone, and his parents said nothing about his abrupt departure. He took no false hope from this. In Vanya's family, silence had never meant surrender, only tactical retreat.

Even without the *mohel*, though, Vanya continued to take solace in running. Isolated at school, resentful at home, cut off from romping with his friends, he took to the streets again and again, day after day, running, dodging, leaving behind him ever-grumpier mutters and shouts of Slow down! Watch your step! Show some respect! Crazy boy! To Vanya that was part of the music of the city.

Running was the way he dreamed. Having never been in control of his own life, his idea of freedom was simply to break free. He dreamed of being at the mercy of the wind, carried aloft and blown here and there, a life of true randomness instead of always being part of someone else's purpose. Father's earnest, inconvenient plans for him. Mother's ironic vision of life as one prank after another, in the midst of which you did what was needed. What I need, Mother, is to kite myself up in the air and cut the string and fly untethered. What I need, Father, when you're setting out the pieces for your living chess game, is to be left in the box.

Forget me!

But running couldn't save him from anyone's plans, in the end. Nor did it bring him freedom, for his parents, as always, took his little idiosyncrasies in stride. In fact they made it part of *their* story; he overheard them telling some of their new Jewish friends that they had to be patient with Itzak, he was between realities, having had the old one stolen from him and not yet ready to enter the new one. How did they think of these glib little encapsulations of his life?

Only when Father underwent the male ritual of obedience himself did Vanya realize that this Jewish business was not just something they were doing to their son. Father tried to go about his ordinary work but could not; though he said nothing, his pain and embarrassment at showing it made him almost silent.

Mother, ever supportive, said nothing even to refer to what the *mohel* had done to her husband, but Vanya thought he detected a slight smirk on her face when Father asked her to fetch him something that ordinarily he would get up and find for himself. He wondered briefly if this meant that Mother thought the whole enterprise of believing in God was amusing, but as Father's wound healed and life returned to what passed for normal these days, Vanya began to suspect that, despite her irony, it was Mother who was a believer.

Perhaps she had been a believer all along, despite slathering the tangy, bacony lard on her bread like any other Russian. Father's discovery of his Jewishness was part of an overall strategy; Mother simply knew who ran the universe. Father was forcing himself to act like a believer. Mother showed not a doubt that God really existed. She just wasn't on speaking terms with him. "Six million Jews died from the Fascists," she said to Father. "Your one voice, praying, is going to fill all that silence? When a child dies, do you comfort the parents by bringing them a puppy to take care of?"

Mother apparently believed not only in the idea of God, but also that he was the very same God who chose the Jews back when it was just Abraham carting his barren wife around with him, pretending she was his sister whenever some powerful man lusted after her.

That was a favorite story for Vanya, as Father insisted that they study Torah together, going over to the apartment of a rabbi and hearing him read the Hebrew and translate. As they walked home, they would talk about what they'd heard. "These guys are religious?" Vanya kept asking. "Judah sleeps with a prostitute on the road, only it turns out to be his daughter-in-law so it's *all right* with God?"

The story of the circumcision of Shechem was Vanya's turning point. Dinah, the daughter of Jacob, gets raped by the prince of Shechem. The prince wants to marry her and Jacob agrees that this would make everything all right, only Dinah's twelve brothers are more interested in repairing the family's wounded honor than in getting their sister married to a rich man with a throne in his future. So they tell the prince that he and all the men of his city have to be circumcised, and when the men are all lying there holding their handles and saying Ow, ow, ow, the sons of Jacob draw their swords and slaughter them all. At the end of that story, Vanya said to his father, "Maybe I'll let the *mohel* do it to me."

Father looked at him in utter consternation. "*That* story makes you *want* to be circumcised?"

Vanya shrugged.

"Is there any hope that you can explain to me why this makes sense?"

"I'm thinking about it, that's all," said Vanya. He would have explained it, if he could. Before the story he refused even to think about it; after the story, it became conceivable to him, and, once he could conceive of it, it soon became inevitable.

Later, running, he thought maybe he understood why that story changed his mind. Circumcision was a foolish, barbaric thing to do. But having the story of Shechem in Torah showed that God himself knew this. It's barbaric, God seemed to be saying, and it hurts like hell, but I want you to do it. Make yourself weak, so somebody could come in and kill you and you'd just say, Thank you, I don't want to live anyway because somebody cut off part of my privates.

He couldn't explain this to his father. He just knew that as long as God recognized that it was a ludicrous thing to do, he could do it.

So for a few days Vanya didn't run. And it turned out that by the time the circumcision healed so he *could* run again, they took the city out from under him. The American Congress had antagonized the Russian government by tying most-favored-nation status to Russia's upping the number of Jews getting visas, and in reply the Russians cut the emigration of Jews down to nothing and started harassing them more. To Vanya's family, this had very practical consequences. They lost their apartment.

For Father, it meant no more consultations with students, no more visits with his former colleagues at the university. It meant the shame of being utterly dependent on others for food and clothing for his family, for there was no job he could get.

Mother took it all in stride. "So we make bricks without straw," she said. All his life Vanya remembered her making enigmatic comments like that. Only now he was reading Exodus and he got the reference and realized: Mother really is a Jew! She's been talking to us as if we were all Jews my whole life, only I didn't get it. And for the first time Vanya wondered if maybe this whole thing might not be *her* plan, only she was so good at it that she had gotten Father to think of it himself, for his own very logical, unreligious reasons. Don't become a practicing Jew because God commands it, become one so you can get your son a good life in America. Could she possibly be that sneaky?

For a week, they camped in the homes of several Jews who had no room for them. It couldn't last for long, this life, partly because the crowding was so uncomfortable, and partly because it was so obvious that, compared to these lifelong followers of the Law, Vanya and his parents were dilettantes at Judaism. Father and Vanya hacked at Hebrew, struggled to keep up with the prayers, and looked blankly a hundred times a day when words and phrases were said that meant nothing to them.

Mother seemed untroubled by such problems, since she had lived for a couple of years with her mother's parents, who kept all the holidays, the two kitchens, the prayers, the differentiation of women and men. Yet Vanya saw that she, too, seemed more amused than involved in the life of these homes, and the women of these households seemed even more wary of her than the men were of Father.

Finally it wasn't a Jew at all, but a second cousin (grandson of Father's grandfather's brother, as they painstakingly explained to Vanya), who took them in for the potentially long wait for an exit visa. Cousin Marek had a dairy farm in the foothills of the Carpathian Mountains, in a region that had been part of Poland between the wars, and so escaped Stalin's savage collectivization of the freehold farmers of Ukraine. Because this hill country was remote, strategically unimportant, and thinly populated, Communism here was mostly window dressing. Technically Cousin Marek's dairy herd was merely a portion of the herd belonging to the farflung dairy collective; in actual practice, they were his cows, to be bred and cared for as he wished. A good portion of the milk and cheese they produced didn't quite make its way into the state-run dairy system. Instead, it was bartered here and there for goods and services, and now and then for hard Western currency. Cousin Marek had the room, the independent attitude, and enough surplus to take in a few hapless cousins who had decided to become Jews in order to get to the West.

"The country life will be good for you, Vanya," said Father, though the sour expression on his face suggested that he had not yet thought of a way that the country life would be good for *him*. What Cousin Marek did not have was a university within three hours' travel. If Father was to lecture, he'd have to find a subject matter interesting to cows.

As for Vanya, though, Father was right. The country life *was* good for him. The chores were hard, for though Cousin Marek was a pleasant man, he nevertheless expected that everyone on the farm would work every day, and give full measure. But Vanya got used to labor quickly enough, not to mention the country food, the whole milk, the coarser, crustier, more floury bread they made in this part of Ukraine. The farm was good; but what he came to love lay beyond the farm. For in this backwater, some remnant of the old forests of Europe still survived.

"This is the *rodina*, the original homeland," Father told him. "Where the old Slavs hid while the Goths passed through, and the Huns. And then they were gone and we fanned out into the plain and left these hills to the wolves and bears." Our land. Father still thought like a Russian, not like a Jew.

What did Vanya care, at his age, about the original Russia? All he knew was that the country roads went on forever without traffic, and with grass growing where the wheels didn't make their ruts; and the trees grew large and ancient in the steep-sided hollows of the hills where no one had bothered to cut them down; and birdsong didn't have to fight to be heard above honking cars and roaring engines. Someone had spilled a milkpail of stars across the sky, and at night when there was no moon it was so dark you could bump into walls just trying to find the door of the house. It wasn't really wild country, but to Vanya, a city boy, an apartment dweller, it was a place of magic and dreams, like the paintings of Shishkin; Vanya half-expected to see bear cubs in the trees.

This was the place where all the fairy tales of his childhood must have taken place—the land of Prince Ivan, the grey wolf, the firebird; of Koshchei the Deathless, of Mikola Mozhaiski, of Baba Yaga the witch. And, because he came here about the same time as his first reading of Torah, he also pictured the wanderings of Abraham and Jacob and the children of Israel in this green place. He knew it was absurd—Palestine was hot and dry, the Sinai was stone and sand. But couldn't he picture the sons of Jacob coming back from herding sheep in these hills, to show their father the torn and bloody many-colored coat? Wasn't it from these hills that Abraham charged forth to do battle for the cities of the plain?

He couldn't fly here, either, but he could run until he was so exhausted and lightheaded that it felt as if he had flown. And then he grew bolder, and left the roads and tracks, searching for the most ancient and lost parts of the forest. Hours he'd be gone, exploring, until Mother grew worried. "You fall down a slope, you break your leg, nobody knows where you are, you die out there alone, is that your plan?" But Father and Mother must have discussed it together and decided to trust in his good sense and perhaps in the watchfulness of God, for they continued to allow him his freedom. Maybe they were simply counting on the visa to come and get him back to some American city where they could hide in their apartment from the gangsters' bullets and the rioting Africans that they always heard about.

If the visa had come one day earlier, Vanya wouldn't have found the clearing, the lake of leaves.

He came upon it in the midst of a forest so old that there was little underbrush—the canopy of leaves overhead was so dense that it was perpetually dusk at ground level, and nothing but a few hardy grasses and vines could thrive. So it felt as if you could see forever between the tree trunks, until finally enough trunks blocked the way or it grew dark and murky enough that you could no longer see beyond.

The ground was carpeted with leaves so thick that it made the forest floor almost like a trampoline. Vanya began loping along just to enjoy the bouncy feel of the ground. Like walking on the moon, if the Americans really had landed there. Leap, bounce, leap, bounce. Of course, on the moon there were no tree limbs, and when Vanya banged his head into one, it knocked him down and left him feeling weak and dizzy.

This is what Mother warned me about. I'll get a concussion, I'll fall down in convulsions, and my body won't be found until a dog drags some part of me onto somebody's farm. Probably the circumcised part of me, and they'll have to call in a *mohel* to identify it. Definitely the boy Itzak Shlomo—on your records as Ivan Petrovich Smetski. A good runner, but apparently not bright enough to look out for trees. Sorry, but he was too stupid to go on living. That's just the way natural selection works. And Father would shake his head and say, He should have been in Israel, where there are no trees.

After a while, though, his head cleared, and he went back to bounding through the forest. Now, though, he looked up, scouting for low limbs, and that's how he realized he had found a clearing—not because of the bright sunlight that made the place a sudden island of day in the midst of the forest twilight, but because suddenly there were no more branches.

He stopped short at the edge of the clearing and looked around. Shouldn't it be a meadow here, where the sun could shine? Tall grass and wildflowers, that's what it should be. But instead it was just like the forest floor, dead leaves thickly carpeting the undulating surface of the clearing. Nothing alive there.

What could be so poisonous in the ground here that neither trees nor grass could grow here? It had to be something artificial, because the clearing was so perfectly round.

A slight breeze stirred a few of the leaves in the clearing. A few blew away from the rise in the center of the clearing, and now it looked to Vanya as if it was not a rock or some machine, for the shape under the leaves undulated like the lines of a human body. And there, where the head should be, was that a human face just visible?

Another leaf drifted away. It had to be a face. A woman asleep. Had she gathered leaves around her, to cover her? Or was she injured, lying here so long that the leaves had gathered. Was she dead? Was the skin stretched taut across the cheekbones like a mummy? From this distance, he could not see. And a part of him did not want to see, wanted instead to run away and hide, because if she was dead then for the first time his dreams of tragedy would come true, and he did not want them to be true, he realized now. He did not want to clear the leaves away and find a dead woman who had merely been running through the woods and hit her head on a limb and managed to stagger into the midst of this clearing, hoping that she could signal some passing airplane, only she fell unconscious and died and . . .

He wanted to run away, but he also wanted to see her, to touch her; if she was dead, then to see death, to touch it.

He raised his foot to take a step into the clearing.

Though his movement was ordinary, the leaves swirled away from his foot as if he had stirred a whirlwind, and to his shock he realized that this clearing was not like the forest floor at all. For the leaves swirled deeper and deeper, clearing away from his feet to reveal that he was standing at the edge of a precipice.

This was no clearing, this was a deep basin, a round pit cut deeply into the earth. How deep it was, he couldn't guess, for the leaves still swirled away, deeper, deeper, and the wind that had arisen from the movement of his leg carried them up and away, twisting into the sky like a pillar of smoke.

If that *was* a woman lying there, then she must be lying on a pedestal arising from the center of this deep hollow. Women who bumped their heads into tree limbs did not climb down a precipice like this and climb up a tower in the middle. Something else was going on here, something darker. She must have been murdered.

He looked at her again, but now many of the leaves that had blown up from Vanya's feet were coming to rest, and he couldn't quite see her face. No, there it was, or where it should have been. But no face now, just leaves.

I imagined it, he thought. It was that leaf—I thought it was a nose. There's no woman there. Just a strange rock formation. And a pit in the middle of the forest that had filled with leaves. Maybe it was the crater from an old meteor strike. That would make sense.

As he stood there, imagining the impact of a stone from space, something moved on the far side of the clearing. Or rather, it moved *under* the far side of the clearing, for he saw only that the leaves began to churn in one particular place, and then the churning moved around the circle, heading toward him.

A creature that lived in this hollow, under the leaves like a sea serpent under the waves. A terrestrial octopus that will come near me and throw a tentacle up onto the shore and drag me down under the leaves and eat me, casting only my indigestible head up onto the center pedestal, where it would eventually lure some other wanderer to step off into the pit to be devoured in his turn.

The churning under the leaves came closer. In the battle between Vanya's curiosity and his morbid imagination, the imagination finally won. He turned and ran, no longer bounding over the forest floor, but trying to dig in and put on speed. Of course this meant that his feet kept losing purchase as leaves slipped under them, and he fell several times until he was covered with leafmold and dirt, with bits of old leaves in his hair.

Where was the road? Was the creature from the pit following him through the forest? He was lost, it would turn to night and the monster would find him by his smell and devour him slowly, from the feet up . . .

There was the road. Not that far, really. Or he had run faster and longer than he thought. On the familiar road, with the afternoon sun still shining on him, he felt safer. He jogged along, then walked the last bit to Cousin Marek's farm.

Vanya never got a chance to tell about his adventure. Mother took one look at him and ordered him to bathe immediately, they'd been searching high and low for him, there was almost no time at all to get ready, where had he been? The visas had come through suddenly, the flight would leave in two days, they had to drive tonight to get to the train station so they could get to Kiev in time to catch the airplane to Austria.

Eventually, when they had time to relax a little, sitting on the plane as it flew to Vienna, Vanya didn't bother to tell them about his childish scare in the woods. What would it matter? He'd never see those woods again. Once you left Russia there was no going back. Even if you had left a mystery behind you in the ancient forest. It would just have to live on in his memory, a question never to be answered. Or, more likely, the memory of a childish scare that he had worked himself into because he always imagined such dramatic things.

By the time the plane landed in Vienna and the reporters flashed their lightbulbs and pointed TV cameras at them and the officials inspected their visas and various people descended on them to insist that his parents go to Israel as they promised or to inform them that they had the right to do whatever they wanted, now that they were in the free world—by this point, Vanya had persuaded himself that there was never a human face in the clearing, the pit was not as deep as he imagined, and the churning of the leaves had been the wind or perhaps a rabbit burrowing its way through. No peril. No murder. No mystery. Nothing to wonder about.

No *reason* for it to keep cropping up in his dreams, haunting his childhood and adolescence. But dreams don't come from reason. And even as he told himself that nothing had happened in the woods that day, he knew that something *had* happened, and now he would never know what the clearing was, or what might have happened had he stayed.

2

TRUE LOVE

 o Father's plan had worked after all. When they arrived in Vienna, it was a matter of a few hours' paperwork to confirm his appointment as a professor of Slavic languages at Mohegan University in western New York, where he would join a distinguished language faculty, the Russian jewel in a polyglot crown. Soon the family was established in what seemed to them a spacious house with a wild garden that led down to the shore of Lake Olalaga—which quickly became the familiar Olya, the common nickname for *Olga*, and sometimes, in whimsical moods, Olya-Olen'ka, as if the lake were a character in a folktale.

Raised on stories of America—and especially New York—being a jumble of slums and pollution, Vanya found the woods and farms and rolling hills of western New York to be a miracle. But none of the woods was half so ancient or dangerous-seeming as the forest around Cousin Marek's farm, and Vanya soon found that America might be an exciting place to arrive, but living there could become, in time, as boring as anything else.

Yet his father was satisfied. Vanya reached America young enough to become truly bilingual, quickly learning to speak English without a foreign accent, and taking to the way Americans pronounced his name—Íван instead of Iván—**eye**-vun instead of ee-**vahn**—so readily that it was soon the name he used for himself, with *Vanya* surviving only as his family's nickname for him.

His father and mother were not so linguistically fortunate—Father would never lose his guttural Russian accent, and Mother made no effort to progress beyond American money and the names of items at the grocery store. It meant that Mother's world barely reached beyond their house, and, though Father lectured at other colleges and enjoyed his students, he, too, centered his life around his son.

Ivan felt the pressure of his parents' sacrifice every day of his life. They did not speak of it; they didn't have to. Ivan did his best to take advantage of the opportunities his father and mother had given him, working hard at his schoolwork and studying many other things besides. They had no cause to complain of him. And when he was tempted to protest their sometimes heavy-handed regulation of his life, he remembered what they had given up for him. Friends, relatives, their native land.

Ivan's respite from his parents' expectations was the same one he had found in Russia: He ran. And when he got old enough for high school athletics, he not only continued with long-distance running, he also took up all the games of the decathlon. Javelin, hurdles, discus, sprints—he was sometimes the best at one or another, but what set him apart from the rest of the track team was his consistency: His combined score was always good, and he was always in contention at every meet. He lettered three years at Tantalus High, and when he began to attend Mohegan University, he made their track team easily.

His parents and their friends never understood his need for athletics. Some even seemed to think it was funny—a Jewish athlete?—until Ivan coldly pointed out that Israel didn't bring in Christians to fill out its Olympic team. Only once, near the end of Ivan's junior year in high school, did Father suggest that the time wasted on athletics would be better spent refining his mind. "The body goes by the time you're forty, but the mind continues—so why invest in the part that cannot last? It isn't possible to divide your interests this way and do well at anything." Ivan's reply was to skip a day of finals while he ran all the way around Lake Olya. He ended up having to do makeup work that summer to stay on track for graduation; Father never again suggested that he give up sports.

But Ivan was not really rejecting his father. During Ivan's years at the university, he gravitated to history, languages, and folklore; when he entered graduate school, he became his father's most apt pupil. Together they immersed themselves in the oldest dialects of Ukrainian, Bulgarian, and Serbian. For one year they even conducted all their conversations in Old Church Slavonic, lapsing into Russian or English only when the vocabulary didn't allow a modern thought to be expressed.

Everyone could see how proud Father was at Ivan's exceptional performance—several papers published in first-rate journals even before he entered the graduate program—but what they never were was close. Not as Ivan imagined American fathers and sons were close. Ivan did not speak to his father about his dreams, his yearnings, his frustrations, his hopes. He certainly never mentioned that he still had nightmares about a circular chasm in the forest, where some unnameable creature stirred under the leaves.

Nor did Ivan speak much more readily to Mother—but Mother seemed to know most of his feelings anyway, or guess, or perhaps invent them. When he was in high school he would come home smitten with love for this or that girl, and Mother would know it even though he said nothing. "Who is she?" she'd ask. When he told her—and it was always easier just to tell—she would study his face and say, "It isn't love."

The first few times he insisted that it was *too* love, and what did she know, being old, with true love long since replaced by habit? But over time he learned to accept her assessment. Especially when, now and then, she would say, "Oh, poor boy, it *is* love this time, and she's going to hurt you." To his grief, she was never wrong.

"How do you know?" he demanded once.

"Your face is an open book to me."

"No, really."

"I'm a witch, I know these things."

"Mother, I'm serious."

"If you won't listen to my answers, why do you ask me questions?"

Then, when he was twenty-four, the Berlin Wall came down. The family watched everything on television. As he switched off the set, Father said, "Now you can go back to Russia to do your research for your dissertation."

"My dissertation doesn't require research with sources inside Russia."

"So change your topic," said Father. "Are you crazy? Don't you want to go back?"

Yes, he wanted to go back. But not for research. He wanted to go back because he still saw a certain leaf-covered clearing in his dreams, and the face of a woman, and a monster in a chasm; and for the same reason, he did not want to go, because he was afraid that the place didn't exist, and because he was afraid that maybe it did.

So he spent the rest of the year finishing up his classwork and passing his comprehensives. Then another year of groundwork research for his dissertation and it was late July of 1991, only six weeks before his ticket back to Kiev. Naturally, that was when he met Ruth Meyer.

She was the daughter of a doctor in Ithaca, a couple of lakes away in western New York. They met at a Presbyterian wedding—the groom was a friend of Ivan's from the track team in college, the bride a roommate of Ruth's. They reached for the same hors d'oeuvre on a plate and within a few minutes stood outside on the porch of the house, watching a thunderstorm come in from the southwest. By the time the rain came they were holding hands.

"Say something to me in Old Russian," she said.

Old Russian was too modern for him. In Old Church Slavonic, he said, "You are beautiful and wise and I intend to marry you."

She closed her eyes as if in ecstasy. "I love it that you speak a language to me that no other woman will ever hear from you."

"But you don't understand it," he pointed out.

"Yes I do," said Ruth, her eyes still closed.

He laughed; but what if she *had* understood? "What did I say?"

"You told me that you hoped I'd fall in love with you."

"No I didn't." But his embarrassed laugh was a confession that she had come rather close to the mark.

"Yes you did," she said, opening her eyes. "Everything you do says that."

After the wedding, Ivan came home to his mother and sat down across from her in the living room. After a few moments she looked up at him.

"Well?" he said. "Is it love, or is it nothing?"

Her expression solemn, Mother said, "It's definitely *something*."

"I'm going to marry her," he announced.

"Does she know this?"

"She knows everything," he said. "She knows what I think as I'm thinking it."

"If only she knew *before* you thought it, you'd never have to think again."

"I'm serious, Mother," he said.

"And I'm not?"

"Don't tease me. This is love."

By now Father was in the room; there's something about the mention of marriage that brings parents, no matter what they were doing. "What, you fall in love now, when you're about to leave the country for a year?"

"Maybe I can postpone the trip," said Ivan, knowing as he said it that it was a stupid idea.

"That's good, marry now when you don't have a doctor's degree," said Father. "Her father plans to support you?"

"I know, I have to go. But I hate waiting," said Ivan.

"Learn patience," said Father.

"In Russia you learn patience," said Ivan. "In America you learn action."

"So it's a good thing you're going to Russia," said Father. "Patience is useful much more often, and you especially need to learn it if you plan to have children."

Ivan laughed giddily at the idea. "I'm going to be such a good father!" he cried.

"And why not?" asked Mother. "You learned from the best."

"Of course I did," he said. "Both of you. You did the best you could with a strange kid like me."

"I'm glad you understand," said Mother. That wry smile. Was it possible she wasn't joking? That she had never been joking?

During the weeks before he flew to Kiev, he spent more time in Ithaca than in Tantalus. His mother seemed sad or worried whenever he saw her, which wasn't often. One time, concerned about her, he said, "You're not losing me, Mother. I'm in love."

"I never had you," she said, "not since you escaped from the womb." She looked away from him.

"What is it, then?"

"Have you told her your Jewish name?" she asked, changing the subject.

"Oh, right, Itzak Shlomo," he said. "It hasn't come up. Does it matter?"

"Don't do it," she said.

"Don't what? Tell her my Jewish name? Why would I? Why shouldn't I?"

She rolled her eyes. "I'm such a fool. Now you will, because I asked you not to."

"When would it come up? Why does it matter? I haven't used the name since we came here. Our synagogue is Conservative, so is theirs, nobody cares if I have a gentile name."

Mother gripped his arms and spoke fiercely, for once without a smile. "You can't marry her," she said.

"What are you talking about? We're definitely *not* first cousins, if that's what you're worried about."

"You remember the story of the Sky, the Rat, and the Well?"

Of course he did. It was a tale she had told him as a child, and he studied it again in folklore class. A not-so-nice rabbinical student rescues a young woman from a well, but only after she promises to sleep with him. Once she's out of the well, she insists that he promise to marry her, so that they are betrothed. Their only witnesses are the sky, the well, and a passing rat. Back home, he forgets his promise and marries someone else, while she turns down suitor after suitor until she finally pretends to go mad in order to make them go away. Then his first two children die, one bitten by a diseased rat, the other from falling down a well. He remembers the witnesses to his betrothal and confesses to his wife; she does not condemn him, but insists that they divorce peacefully so he can go and honor his promise to the young woman. So that's how it happens that he ends up keeping his word after all. The moral of the story was to keep your oaths because God is always your witness, but Ivan for the life of him couldn't figure out what she was getting at.

"I'm not betrothed to anyone else but Ruth," he said.

"You think I don't know that?" she said. "But there's something."

"Something what?"

"I dreamed about that story."

"This is about a dream?"

"You were the man and Ruth was the one he never should have married. Vanya, it won't work out. This is not the right girl for you."

"Mother, she *is*, you just have to trust me on this." Impulsively he bent down and kissed his mother's cheek. "I love you, Mother," he said.

When he stood straight again, he saw that tears dripped down her cheeks. He realized that it was the first time he had kissed his mother in years, the first time he told her he loved her since—maybe since he was eight or nine. Or younger.

But she wasn't crying because of his kiss. "Do what you do," said Mother softly. "When the time comes, you must trust *me*."

"*What* time? What is this, a game of riddles?"

She shook her head, turned away from him, and left the room.

Of course he told Ruth all about the conversation. "Why shouldn't I know your Jewish name?" asked Ruth, shaking her head, laughing.

"It's not like it was my real name," said Ivan. "I never even heard it until we were about to emigrate. We aren't very good Jews, you know."

"Oh, I know," she said. "As I recall, at Denise's wedding you were reaching for a shrimp."

"So were you," he said. "But I'm the one that got it."

She raised an eyebrow. "I was reaching for *you*," she said. "So I got mine, too."

He laughed with her, but he didn't really like the joke. Their meeting was pure chance, or so he had always thought. But now she had raised another possibility, and he didn't care for it. Was I set up? If she manipulated that, what else might she have plotted?

No, no, that was complete nonsense, he told himself. It was Mother's weird objection, that's what made him suspicious. And besides, what if she *had* plotted to meet him? He should be insulted? Beautiful, intelligent girl maneuvers to meet awkward, penniless grad student—how often did *that* happen? Oh, all the time—in grad students' dreams.

Mother was so eager for him to get out of New York—and away from Ruth—that for the last week he had to keep asking her for clothes each morning because she had already packed everything. "I don't need to take all my clothes with me," he said. "I'm a student. Everyone will expect me to wear shirts for several days between washings." She shrugged and gave him a shirt—but from her ironing, not from his luggage.

All of Ruth's family came to the airport at Rochester to see him off, and so did Father. But Mother wasn't there, and that made Ivan a little angry and a little sad. All these years, he had thought that Mother's amused smile was because she was secretly smarter than Ivan or Father. But now it turned out that she was superstitious, troubled by dreams and folktales. He felt cheated. He felt that *Mother* had been cheated, too, not to be educated better than that. Was that something she picked up from her Jewish grandparents? Or was it deeper than that? Not to see her son off on a trip that would take at least six months—it wasn't right.

But he had other things to worry about. Being jovial with Ruth's mother and father, saying good-bye in restrained and manly fashion to his father, and then prying Ruth away as she clung to him, weeping, kissing him again and again. "I feel like I've died or something," he said. She only cried harder. That had been a stupid thing to say, as he was about to board a plane.

After all her mother's remonstrances and her father's patient instructions to let the boy *go*, it was Ivan's father who was finally able to lead her away so Ivan could get on the plane. He loved Ruth, yes, and his family, and her parents, too, but as he walked down the tube to the plane, he felt a burden sliding off his shoulders. His step had a jaunty bounce to it.

Why should he feel like that, suddenly lighter, suddenly free? If anything, this journey was a burden. Whatever he was able to accomplish in his research would be the foundation of his career, his whole future. When he came back, he would become a graduate and a husband, which meant that his childhood was truly over. But he would still be hanging fire until he became a professor and a father. That was when his adulthood would begin. The real burdens of life. That's what I'm beginning with this trip to Russia.

Only when he was belted into his seat and the plane pulled back from the gate did it occur to him why he felt so free. Coming to America, all the burden of his parents' hopes and dreams had been put onto his shoulders. Now he was heading back to Russia, where he had not had such burdens, or at least had not been aware of them. Russia might have been a place of repression for most people, but for him, as a child, it was a place of freedom, as America had never been.

Before we are citizens, he thought, we are children, and it is as children that we come to understand freedom and authority, liberty and duty. I have done my duty. I have bowed to authority. Mostly. And now, like Russia, I can set aside those burdens for a little while and see what happens.

3

CHASM

n these heady days of revolutionary change, it was hard for Ivan to concentrate on his research. The manuscripts had been sitting for hundreds of years in the churches or museums, the transcripts and photocopies for decades in the libraries. They could wait, couldn't they? For there were cafés springing up everywhere, full of conversations, discussions, arguments about Ukrainian independence; about whether Russian nationals should be expelled, given full citizenship, or something in between; about the low quality of the foreign books that were glutting the market now that restrictions had eased; about what America would or would not do to help the new nation of Ukraine; whether prices should remain under strict control or be allowed to inflate until they stabilized at "natural" levels; and on and on.

In all these conversations Ivan was something of a celebrity—an American who spoke Russian fluently and even understood the Ukrainian language, which was patriotically being forced into duty even in intellectual discussions that used to be solely the province of Russian. He had the money to pay for coffee, and often paid for stronger drinks as well. He didn't drink alcohol himself, however—as an athlete, he had ostentatiously *not* acquired his father's vodka habit. But no one pushed it on him; he could drink or not drink as he pleased, especially when he was paying.

Not that these conversations were at a particularly high level. They were just neighborhood chats and gossip and rants and diatribes.

But that was the point. At the university, he would still be his father's son; in the cafés, he was himself, listened to for his own sake.

Or was it for the sake of his money? Or his Americanness? Or just good manners? Did it even matter? After enough weeks of this, Ivan began to weary of the constant conversation. No one's opinions had changed, nothing important was being decided, and Ivan was sick of the sound of his own voice, pontificating as if being American or a graduate student gave him some special expertise.

He began to spend more time with the manuscripts, doing his research, laying the groundwork for his dissertation. It was a mad project, he soon realized—trying to reconstruct the earliest versions of the fairy tales described in the Afanasyev collection in order to determine whether Propp's theory that all fairy tales in Russian were, structurally, a single fairy tale was (1) true or false and, if true, (2) rooted in some inborn psychologically true ur-tale or in some exceptionally powerful story inherent in Russian culture. The project was mad because it was too large and included too much, because it was unprovable even if he found an answer, and because there probably was no answer to be found. Why hadn't anyone on his dissertation committee told him that the subject was impossible to deal with? Probably because they didn't realize it themselves. Or because, *if* it could be done, they wanted to see the results.

And then, in the midst of his despair, he began to see connections and make reconstructions. Of course his reconstructions might be merely a projection of Propp's thesis onto the material, in which case he was proving nothing; but he knew—he *knew*—that his reconstructions were not nonsensical, and they did tend to coalesce toward the pure structure Propp had devised. He was onto something, and so the research became interesting for its own sake.

Bleary-eyed, he would rise from the table when the library or museum closed, stuff his notebooks and notecards into his briefcase, and walk home through the dark streets, the gathering cold. He would collapse into bed in his tiny room, sublet from a professor of Chinese who never intruded on his privacy. Then he'd rise in the morning, his eyes still aching from the concentration of the day before, and, pausing only for a hunk of bread and a cup of coffee, return to the museum to resume again. The harder he worked, the sooner he'd be done.

That was how the autumn passed, and the winter. Shortages of coal and oil made the bitter cold even harder to bear, but, like Bob Cratchit, Ivan simply bundled up and scribbled away regardless of the chill in every building in Kiev. He was so immersed in his work that sometimes he didn't even read his mail from home—not from Mother, not from Father, not from Ruth. It would sit in a pile until finally, on a Sunday when the library opened later, he would realize how long he'd gone without contact from home and open all the letters in a binge of homesickness. Then he'd scribble hurried and unsatisfactory answers to all of them. What was there to say? His life was within walls, under artificial lights, with row on endless row of Cyrillic characters in old-fashioned handwriting shimmering in front of his eyes. What could he possibly tell them? Ate bread today. And cheese. Drank too much coffee. A dull headache all day. It was cold. The manuscript was inde-cipherable or trivial or not as old as they claimed. The librarian was friendly, icy, flirtatious, incompetent. The work will never end, I wish I could see you, thank you for writing to me even when I'm so unfaithful about writing back.

And then one day it wasn't cold. Leaves were budding on the trees. Ukrainians in shirtsleeves flooded the streets of Kiev, taking the sun, carrying sprigs of purple lilacs with them in celebration of spring. How ironic. Just when the season was about to make life in Kiev worth living again, Ivan realized he had accomplished all that he needed to do in Russia. Everything else could be worked out on his own, without further reference to the manuscripts. Time to go home.

Funny, though. As soon as he thought of going home, it wasn't Tantalus he thought of, or the shores of Lake Olya, or his mother's face, or sweet Ruth's embrace.

Instead he thought of a farm in the foothills of the Carpathians, with wild forest just beyond the cultivated fields. The face he saw was Cousin Marek's, and what his body yearned for was not the loving em-brace of a woman, but rather to hold the tools of the farm and labor until sweat poured off him and he could fall into bed every night physi-cally spent, and rise in the morning to face a day filled with a thousand kinds of life.

Even as memories of the place flooded back to him, Ivan realized that there was key information he had never known as a child. The name of the town where he would have to transfer from train to bus, and from bus to whatever ride he could get on the road to . . . what vil-lage? He had no idea how to tell a driver his destination. He didn't even know Cousin Marek's last name.

Oh well. It was just a whim.

But it was a whim that wouldn't go away. After months of barely writing to them, it was absurd to call his parents over this unscheduled side trip. But he picked up the phone and talked and waited his way through the half hour it took to make the connection.

"You want to go back *there*?" asked Father. "What for?"

"To see the place again," said Ivan. "I have fond memories."

"This must be a new meaning of the word *fond*. I still have backaches from that place. The calluses haven't healed yet."

"Mine have," said Ivan. "I wish they hadn't. Sometimes I think I was freer on that farm than . . . well, no, I guess not. Anyway, I haven't spent that much on food or whatever, so I've got plenty of money left for a trip. Does Marek have a phone?"

"Not that I know the number anymore," said Father.

"Then ask Mother, you know she'll have it squirreled away somewhere."

"Oh, yes, I'll love that conversation. 'So, Vanya is all done with his research but he's not coming home, he's going to visit his cousin while his mother languishes. What should I expect from a son who doesn't write to his parents? We can't force him to love us—' "

Ivan laughed. "Mother's not a whiner, Dad."

"Not to *you*," said Father. "*I* get a solo performance. And Ruth, she'll be glad to hear that you *can* wait to see her—because you have to say hello to some cows."

Ivan laughed again.

"You seem to think I'm joking."

"No, Father, I just think you and Mother are funny." Wrong thing to say. Father didn't like to think he was amusing. "Sometimes," Ivan added.

Unmollified, Father replied, "I'm glad to provide you with entertainment. Our ratings are low—one viewer—but the reviews of our performance are good enough maybe we'll be renewed for another season . . ."

"Come on, Father, I want to pay a call on Cousin Marek. He took us in when we needed help, should I be this close and not make the effort?"

"Close?" said Father. "As close as New York is to Miami."

"You've got the scale wrong," said Ivan. "More like from Buffalo to Syracuse."

"Tell me that again after four hours on the bus."

"Call me back when you have the information?"

"No, Mother has it right here in the book." Father gave him all the information and they said good-bye.

They refused to sell him a ticket at the train station until right before departure—inflation was too high to be able to lock in the price even the day before. Nor could they guarantee him that the bus would even be running. "Capitalism now," said the ticket agent. "They only run the bus if there are enough passengers to pay for the fuel."

That night, after half an hour of trying, he got through by telephone to Cousin Marek.

"Little Itzak?" Marek said.

"I use *Ivan*, mostly." Ivan was a little surprised. Cousin Marek had always called him Vanya. Ivan didn't remember that Marek had even known his Jewish name. But that was a long time ago, and perhaps the old farmer had been amused at this family of Russian intellectuals who suddenly decided to be Jews and then took up residence on a farm.

"You eating kosher?" asked Marek.

"No, not really," said Ivan. "I mean, I avoid pork, lard, things like that."

"No lard!" cried Marek. "What do you put on your bread?"

"Cheese, I hope," laughed Ivan.

"All right, we'll go out and pluck a few from the cheese tree." Marek laughed at his own joke. "Come ahead, we're glad to have you. I'll find out when the bus is coming in and I'll be there to meet you. I'm afraid all the cows you knew are long since knackered."

"They didn't like me anyway."

"You weren't much of a milker."

"I'll be no better now, I'm afraid, but I'll do whatever you need. I . . . pole vault rather well." It took him a moment to think of the Ukrainian word. Marek laughed.

That night, when Ivan was through packing, he was still too full of springtime to sleep. He went outside for a walk, but even that wasn't enough. He began to jog, to run, dodging through the streets as he used to do as a child. When he was a child he had never been allowed outside to run at this time of night, and it surprised him how many people were still out and about. But it might not have been like that, before. Had there been closing laws for drinking establishments? Or a curfew? He wouldn't have known, not at his age, or if he knew, he forgot.

In school in America he had picked up the American idea of life in the Soviet Union, even though he had lived there and knew it wasn't all terror and poverty. But his memories of life in Kiev had faded, or retreated out of sight, anyway, to be replaced by the American version. And it was true, partly—the high-rises were all hideously ugly slabs of concrete with only the most slapdash attempts at aesthetics, as if socialism required that beauty be expunged from public life.

But the older parts of the city still had grace to them. He headed for the Staryy Horod, the old part of the city, and stopped only when he reached the Golden Gate, built in 1037. He touched the stone and brick columns, which had once stood in ruins but now were restored to something like their original form. When the Golden Gate was first built, and the little church atop the arch was still sheathed in the gilded copper that gave the gate its name, it was the center of Kiev, and Kiev was the center of the largest, most powerful kingdom in Europe. He imagined what it must have looked like then, with the stink and noise of medieval commerce in these streets. The trumpets blaring, and Prince Vladimir the Baptizer or Yaroslav the Wise riding with their retainers through the cheering throngs.

Ivan had no romantic notions of chivalry, of course—Russian legends, history, and folklore had never had an "Arthurian" period of anachronistic dreaming. The people lived in squalor and filth, by modern standards. The difference between the aristocracy and the lower classes was entirely expressed in the quality of clothing and the quantity of food. By his clothes a man was known; wealth was worn on a man's body, and on the bodies of his womenfolk. So the cheering throngs would be wearing plainer colors, the traditional weave of these grasslands, while the prince and his people would be wearing silks from the East, looking for all the world like Oriental potentates—even though the princes were Scandinavians from the north, not Oriental at all. The wealth of Rus'—ancient Russia—was in trade, and the trade was in the fabrics and spices of the East.

So of course it would not be just the smell of dung and sweat and rotting fish and vegetables—there would be whiffs of the heady aromas of cinnamon, pepper, cumin, basil, savory, paprika. Ivan breathed deeply and almost believed that he could sense some lingering traces of the ancient days.

And with those breaths he was ready to move on. He ran down the hill into the Podil district, the area where he had grown up. Some old churches and monasteries remained, but most of the buildings dated from the 1800s. Running along these ever-more-familiar streets felt like coming home, and soon enough he found himself in the street where he had lived as a child. What came to him then was not history, but memory, and not memories of oppression or want, but rather of happiness with his parents, with his friends. Here was the postbox, here the spot where old Yuri Denisovich sat to take the sun every bright afternoon, and here was the place where Mother always came to bring treats to Baba Tila, an old Armenian or Georgian woman, somewhere foreign and mountainous and exotic, anyway. Every day or so, a little treat to the old lady. Did she still live here?

Ivan slowed, stopped in front of the building. His first thought was that he had no idea which room belonged to the old lady, since they had never gone inside. Baba Tila was always at the stoop, wasn't she? No. She sat at the window right beside the stoop, so Mother climbed three steps and then handed the treat to Baba Tila through the window. Treats, Mother called them, but as often as not they were just leaves. For tea, Mother said, so that was a treat. But once it was dirt. Mother only looked at him with disgust when he laughed about it. "Baba Tila grows plants in her window box," she said.

"But it's just dirt. That's not much of a treat, is it?"

He couldn't remember how Mother answered. Perhaps she hadn't. Perhaps she simply closed the box, took his hand, and went out for the walk. How old was he then? Three? Five? It was hard to remember. The visits to Baba Tila stopped when he went to school. Or no, probably they didn't—Mother simply went without him, while he was in school.

A man of perhaps forty came up the street, just a little ahead of himself in the night's drinking. He climbed the stoop, then paused at the door and looked back down at Ivan.

"You want somebody?" he said. "It's late."

"I used to know somebody who lived here," he said. "Baba Tila. An old lady. That apartment, right in front."

"Dead," said the man.

"You knew her?"

"No," he said. "But after she died nobody would rent the place. It was a pigsty, had a smell to it or something. It was empty when I moved in, but they didn't even show it to me. I asked, too. Ground floor front—I could have used that. Stuck me three flights up in back."

"Doesn't matter," said Ivan. "Childhood memory, that's all."

"Just so you're not one of those damned burglars. Cause if I catch you breaking in I'll shatter your bones, I hope you know that."

"I'm an American student," said Ivan. "No burglar."

"American," scoffed the man. "And I'm Chinese." He went inside.

Ivan was flattered. He hadn't lost his native accent, not a bit of it, if a suspicious man refused to believe he was a foreigner. Cool.

Ivan walked away, began to break into a jog, and then turned and went back and looked up again at Baba Tila's window. He remembered that a couple of times when Mother brought him here, Baba Tila had not been home. Those times, Mother had left her gift on the window-sill, and then had reached up and taken something—he never saw what—concealed in the stones on the near side of the window, just out of sight from the steps. Remembering this, he had to reach up and feel the place where things had been concealed, touch the stones his mother had touched. And yes, of course there was the faintest tinge of a hope, a thrill of possible discovery: What if there was something hidden there for Mother after all these years, that he could bring home to her?

Ridiculous; but he could not resist the impulse. He stood on the top step and leaned over. It was an easy-enough reach—he was taller than his mother, after all, and she had not had to strain. His fingers skimmed along the surface of the stones that rose up the left edge of the window, then probed again into the cracks, into the gap between wooden window frame and stone wall.

And there was something. In a gap between, about where Mother's hands had always reached, he felt a corner of something. He stroked it with his finger, once, twice, each time drawing the corner of it a little farther out. The third time, it emerged enough that he could grasp the corner, draw out the whole thing. A folded slip of paper. Damp, stained and weathered, mottled and rippled and warped by the reshaping of winters—how many of them? All the winters since Baba Tila died? Or all the winters since Mother had stopped coming to see her? Was this paper a message to Mother? Or to some other visitor who took Mother's place?

He opened it. The writing was unreadable in the faint light available to him. It might not be readable at all. He refolded it and put it in his pocket, then jogged away, heading for his apartment.

There, under the bright light in the kitchen, he opened the note again, and found he could read it well enough, despite the streaking and staining of the paper. It was simple enough:

Deliver this message.

Simple, but recursive to the point of meaninglessness. Nothing else was written on the paper, so the instruction to deliver the message apparently *was* the message. But to whom was he to deliver it? And was he the intended message-bearer, anyway? Hardly likely. Maybe the paper had been attached to some other paper that had slipped farther back into the crevice. Or maybe it was part of a larger message which had been removed long ago, this little instructional note having been overlooked. But even as he thought of this, he knew it wasn't true. If there was another message with this one, containing the message itself and the name of the person to whom it should be delivered, why would this cover note be needed? When one addresses an envelope and puts a stamp on it, one hardly needs to then attach a note to the envelope saying, "Deliver this letter." One gives it to the postman and he does his job.

Who was the postman? What was the message? One thing was certain: Whoever was meant to be the messenger, whoever it was who might have made sense of this recursive note, had not picked up the message for many years. Indeed, all meaning was now utterly lost, and all that remained was this brief writing which might as well have been in Minoan Linear A for all the luck he would ever have in deciphering it.

But it was found in the place where Baba Tila left things for Mother, and Mother would want to have it. Ivan took the note and tucked it into his luggage, an inside pocket of the carry-on bag. Even if he forgot it, it would be there when he got home, he'd find it again as he was unpacking, and he'd take it to Mother. Maybe she'd explain to him then who Baba Tila was and why she brought her gifts. Maybe she'd tell him what this message meant. Though, more than likely, Mother would simply go enigmatic on him, give him one of her inscrutable smiles, and tell him that if he didn't already understand, he never would.

Women always said things like that, and it made him crazy. It's as if every conversation with a woman was a test, and men always failed it, because they always lacked the key to the code and so they never quite understood what the conversation was really about. If, just once, the man could understand, really comprehend the whole of the conversation, then the perfect union between male and female would be possible. But instead men and women continued to cohabit, even to love each other, without ever quite crossing over the chasm of misunderstanding between them.

And I'm marrying Ruthie?

Well, why not? She loved him. He loved her. In the absence of understanding, that was as good a reason as any for living together and making babies and raising them up and throwing them out of the house and then going through the long slow decline together until one of them died and left the other alone again, understanding as little as ever about what their spouses really wanted, who they really were.

Was that tragedy? Or was that comedy?
Was there really any difference?

The semester had just ended, and Ruthie was over for a visit. Esther Smetski had liked her son's fiancée from the start, but she hadn't enjoyed spending time with her ever since she realized that Vanya mustn't marry the girl. It wasn't Ruthie's fault, was it? Something Vanya had done. Something that happened to him that the boy himself didn't understand, but he was encumbered, he wasn't free to marry, and here was this girl with his ring, with a right to come to the Smetski house and cluck her tongue over what a bad correspondent Vanya was.

"My mother keeps saying, 'He doesn't act like a young man in love,' and I have to keep explaining to her that he's doing research, he's buried, he spends all day writing and reading and he hardly wants to do more of it when the libraries close." Ruthie's voice sounded almost amused by the whole thing, but by now she had delivered this speech often enough that it no longer seemed to conceal wounded feelings. She really didn't mind that much that Vanya didn't write.

Piotr nodded and smiled mechanically. Esther knew from years of experience that Piotr only barely tolerated small talk, and when the small talk had already been said many times before, it was all he could do to keep from getting up and stalking out of the room and doing something productive. But for Vanya's sake he smiled. He nodded.

"But he must write to *you*, Piotr," said Ruthie. "About his research."

Piotr. What a name for a Jew. Of course he had his Jewish name, taken when he converted, but his academic reputation had been established under the name Piotr Smetski, and he wasn't about to make people switch to calling him Ruven Shlomo.

"No, not often," said Piotr. "I'll have plenty of time to hear about it when I look at drafts of his dissertation." He smiled wryly.

As they talked for a few minutes about the work Vanya would have to do when he came home, Esther tuned out their conversation and thought about Vanya, about how strange it was that this other woman, this girl-child, should speak of her son so possessively, should speak of his future as if it were her own future. When I held him in my arms, when I whispered his true name into his ear for only God and me to hear and understand, I did not do it just to hand him over, a scant two decades or so later, to this American girl, this doctor's daughter, this child of money, of imitation country clubs. There was majesty in the child, and only banality in this marriage.

Fool! she said to herself. Marriage is about banality. Its *purpose* is banality, to create an environment of surpassing safety and predictability for young children to grow up in, the foundation of life, the root of inner peace. What do I want for him, a troublesome, restless woman? A *queen*? She almost laughed at herself.

"Was that funny?" asked Ruthie, feigning perplexity.

"I'm sorry," said Esther. "My mind wandered for a moment, and I was thinking of something else. What are we talking about?"

"Whatever it is, it looks like what *you* were thinking was more entertaining," said Ruthie. "Tell us!"

"Yes, please," said Piotr, his irony only barely concealed; what he meant was, please save me from having to talk to this person. Was this girl so stupid she couldn't hear it? Piotr, you must not be snide in front of her. We'll be listening to her for many years, unless Vanya acquires a sudden rush of wisdom.

"It's hard for me sometimes," said Esther. "Listening to English. I have to work so hard."

"I wish my Russian were a little better," said Ruthie.

"You have no Russian," said Piotr, surprised. "Have you?"

"I can say *palazhusta*."

"*Pozhalusta,*" Piotr corrected her. "Please."

Ruthie laughed. "See? Even that I can't get right. I'm afraid our children won't be bilingual."

But at the mention of children, she got a faraway look and glanced toward the window.

Something wrong with talking about children. Esther felt an alarm going off inside her. Suddenly the girl doesn't want children. This is how God orders things. In all the old stories, when a man married a woman he had no right to marry, the marriage was barren. In the old days, the woman tried but couldn't conceive or bear a child. These days, though, the woman can *decide* to be barren. But it amounts to the same thing, doesn't it? Vanya must not marry this girl. If only he would listen to his mother.

"The way children talk these days," said Piotr, "you'll be lucky if they're lingual at all."

Esther leaned forward a little in her chair. Ruthie at once focused on her. She might not realize it consciously, but the girl knew she had let something slip, and she knew Esther had picked up on it. That was the way communication was among women, most of the time; few women realized it, but they all depended on it. "Women's intuition" wasn't intuition at all, it was heightened observation, unconscious registration of subtle clues. Ruthie knew that her mother-in-law didn't want the marriage, and knew that somehow she had just given fuel to that cause; Ruthie knew this, but didn't realize that she knew it. She simply felt uncomfortable, on edge, and she noticed more when she was conversing with her future mother-in-law. Esther didn't need to be told any of this. She knew, because she had trained herself to know these things. It was a school at least as rigorous as any university, but there was no diploma, no extra title to add to her name. She simply knew things, and, unlike most women, knew exactly why and how she knew.

"Ruthie, you know you aren't planning on having a lot of children," said Esther. At once she softened the remark with a more general observation. "American girls don't want so many children these days."

"You only had the one," said Ruthie, still smiling, but definitely on the defensive, with a remark like that.

Esther let her own ancient sorrow rise to the surface a little; her eyes watered. "Not for lack of desire," she said. The emotion was real enough; choosing to show it at this moment, however, was entirely artificial. And it worked.

"Of course you wanted to fulfil your traditional role as a Jewish wife and mother," said Ruthie. "That's the religion of scarcity. You feel the obligation to produce sons to become rabbis, and daughters to give birth to more sons in the next generation."

"Oh, is that all it is?" asked Esther.

"Of course there's the biological imperative toward reproduction," said Ruthie.

"Such big words," murmured Esther. Piotr wasn't entirely unobservant. He caught the irony in Esther's voice and grew more alert to what Ruthie was saying.

"But in the feminine Judaism, in the loving Bible, you have only as many children as you need. Like Eve, with only two sons, and bearing a third only when one of the first two died. She was free, not cursed at all—the curse was from the other Bible."

"Other Bible?" asked Piotr.

"Two Bibles, conflated, one hidden inside the other," said Ruthie. "The Bible of scarcity is the book with the curses in it. Adam earns his living by the sweat of his face; Eve bears children in sorrow and is ruled over by her husband. A zero-sum game where it's all right to drive the original inhabitants out of Canaan and keep their land, where if a man can't pronounce the word *shibboleth* it's all right to kill him because he's an outsider. That's the Bible of killing and hatred and a jealous God who wants all idol-worshipers killed—struck by lightning at Elijah's bidding or slaughtered by the swords of the Levites when Moses gave the command."

"You're quite the scholar," said Piotr.

"Not me," said Ruthie. "But my class in Feminist Judaism this semester really opened my eyes."

"Ah," said Piotr.

"A woman's value doesn't come from childbearing and obedience. It comes from her boldly making decisions—like Eve's decision to eat the fruit and *know* something. It was Adam who followed *her*; she was the rebel, he was the follower. And yet what is it called, 'the Fall of *Adam*'!"

"That's what the Christians call it, anyway," said Piotr. His bemusement was growing.

"It's the Bible of scarcity that makes Jews think they have the right to displace the Palestinians. In the feminine Bible, the lamb lies down with the lion."

"Lions are always glad when lambs act like that," said Piotr. "Saves all that energy wasted in hunting and chasing."

"Now you're teasing me," said Ruthie, reverting from feminist lecturer to sweet little thing when the latter seemed like the best way to win. And sure enough, Piotr at once began to backpedal.

"Of course, I know you didn't mean it that way, I was joking," he said.

"You must think I'm some kind of radical or apostate or something," said Ruthie.

No, thought Esther. I just think you're a girl who has seized upon the philosophy that will allow you not to bear children to my son, whom you're not supposed to marry.

"Of course not," said Piotr.

"But Esther does," said Ruthie.

There it was, the gauntlet thrown down.

"I'm sure it was an interesting class," said Esther. "But you know how hard it is for me to follow English."

Ruthie got the faintest smirk on her face. "Ivan says you understand English fine except when you don't want to."

So the boy was more observant than she had thought. "Is that what Vanya says?" Esther answered, letting herself sound a little hurt. "Maybe he's right. When I'm upset, it's harder to concentrate on listening to English."

"So I did say something to upset you," said Ruthie.

"I'm upset that my boy should be so heartless as to postpone coming home to his fiancée. It must be breaking your poor heart. Not having your young man, now *that's* scarcity, *nu*?"

The conversation returned to safer ground, and after a few more minutes Ruthie announced she must head home to see her parents.

"You mean you came here first, before you saw your own mother?" asked Esther. "You're so sweet."

"She was hoping for word from our son the nonwriter of letters," said Piotr.

With a laugh and kisses all around, Ruthie left.

" *'Nu'?* " asked Piotr as soon as Ruthie was gone. "Are you suddenly taking up Yiddish?"

"I hear it from women in the synagogue, I pick it up," said Esther.

Piotr switched to Russian. "And here I believed you when you told me your family had been Jews living in Russia even before the Goths came through, long before Yiddish was invented in Germany."

"You never believed that," said Esther mildly. "You read it in a history somewhere that Russian Jews all migrated in from Germany and so you know my family tradition can't be true."

"Why not?" he said. "Does it matter? What it means is that you keep your own set of rules. Jews so ancient that they don't think the Talmud deserves all the authority it gets. Jews who can make a sandwich of beef and cheese."

"But not *ham* and cheese," she said, smiling.

"That Ruthie," said Piotr. "Do you think she really believes that feminist nonsense about the nice feminine Bible hidden inside the nasty masculine Bible?"

"She does for now," said Esther. "But like most college feminists, she's not going to let the theory stop her from marrying."

"And you're an expert on this?"

"I hear the women at synagogue talking about their daughters." She imitated them in English. " 'Oy! The younger generation always knows more than the older! Two thousand years Jewish women have more rights than Christian women ever had, but suddenly we're oppressed, and it takes my daughter to tell me?' "

Piotr laughed at her take on the matrons of the synagogue. "You know what I was thinking? She got so excited when she was spouting this ahistorical countertextual nonsense, and I caught myself thinking, 'What an idiot her teacher must be,' and thinking about her teacher made me realize—the kind of excitement she was showing as she mindlessly spouted back the nonsense she learned in college, that's just like the excitement some of my own students show. And it occurred to me that what we professors think of as a 'brilliant student' is nothing but a student who is enthusiastically converted to whatever idiotic ideas we've been teaching them."

"Self-knowledge is a painful thing," said Esther. "To learn that your best students are parrots after all."

"Ah, but students who fill their heads with my ideas and spew them back on command, they are at least saying intelligent things, even if they all come from me."

"Especially if they all come from you."

"It's my mission in life." He kissed her. "Filling empty heads."

"And mine is filling empty stomachs," she said. "Now that she's gone, we can have supper. I only had two pork chops, I couldn't have shared with her."

He looked at her sharply for a moment, then realized she was joking. "Really, what's for dinner?"

"Soup," she said. "Can't you smell it?"

"The house always smells like good food," said Piotr. "It's the perfume of love."

Over supper, they talked of many things and, sometimes, talked not at all, enjoying the comfortable silence that comes from long friendship, from shared life. Only when she was rising from the table to carry dishes to the sink did Esther broach the subject that was most on her mind.

"Do you think there's any chance that Vanya's lack of letters to Ruthie means that he doesn't want to marry her after all?"

"No," said Piotr. "I think he isn't thinking about her. He's thinking about his work."

"And when you're working, you don't love me?" asked Esther.

"We're married," he said, "and you're here."

"And if you were in Russia like Vanya, you wouldn't write to me either?"

He thought for just a moment. "I wouldn't go without you," he finally said.

"Very carefully chosen words," she said.

"I wouldn't be without you," he repeated. "Without you, I wouldn't be."

She kissed him and then washed the dishes as he returned to reading and grading student papers.

Cousin Marek was as good as his word, sitting there in one of the village trucks waiting for him. "Everyone's glad you're back," he said. "All grown." Marek laughed. "A Jewish scholar is supposed to have glasses and clutch a book."

"I do my share of book clutching. Can't help it that my eyes are still good."

"I was teasing you. Because you have shoulders. Seeing you as a boy, who would have guessed?"

The pole vault, the discus, the javelin, putting the shot, that's what had given him shoulders like a blacksmith. Sprints and hurdles, those were the cause of his thighs. Mile after mile of endurance running, that was what kept him lithe and lean. And all of this would sound foolish, Ivan knew, to a man whose massive muscles all came from the labor of farming. Ivan's body had been shaped by competition and meditation, Marek's by making the earth produce something for other people to eat. It didn't feel right to Ivan, to talk much about athletics. So he turned the subject back onto Marek himself. "You must still be carrying that calf up the stairs."

Marek looked puzzled.

"American joke," said Ivan. "A tall tale. The story is, a farmer carried a calf up the stairs every day. His wife asked him why, he says, 'I want to be strong enough to carry him when he's a bull.' "

Marek thought for a moment. "Bull won't let you carry him up the stairs, even if he'd fit."

"That's why it's a joke."

Marek burst out laughing and punched Ivan heavily on the arm. "You think I don't get this joke? Only it's a Ukrainian joke, Ukrainians must have carried this joke to America!"

Ivan laughed and tried not to rub his arm. He might have muscles, but it wasn't as if he'd ever boxed or wrestled or anything. He wasn't used to getting punched. He wondered if Cousin Marek had punched Father a lot when he lived here. That would explain why Father wanted never to come back.

It was after dark when they got to the farm. The place seemed strange, until Marek explained the differences. "New henhouses over there," he said. "There's more of a market for eggs now, so we grow them, ship them straight to L'viv in refrigerator cars. Capitalism! And everything looks so bright because we have enough electricity that you can turn on the lights in every room in the house at once."

"But you never actually do that," said Ivan.

"No, no, of course not," said Marek. "There are two of us, so there should never be more than two lights on at once, and only one when we're in the same room. Now you're here, sometimes *three* lights!" He laughed again.

Marek's wife, Sophia, had incredible quantities of food waiting for Ivan—crepes filled with cottage cheese and topped with sour cream, meat-filled cabbage rolls, broth with beads of fat floating on the surface, dumplings filled with fruit, mushrooms stewed in sour cream. He knew enough to plunge in and eat until he felt sick. There was nothing else he could do, unless he wanted to offend them his first night. "I never eat this much at home," he explained. "You can't fix so much food for me in the future, I'll get sick."

"Look at you, all skin and bones, complaining about too much food," said Sophia. She pinched at his arm, expecting apparently to find it as slender as when he was a boy. Instead, she found herself having to use two hands to span his upper arm. Marek roared with laughter. "Not so skinny," said Marek.

"Hitch up the old oxplow," said Sophia. "As long as he's here to pull, we don't need to use the tractor."

They had prepared the same bed he had slept in as a boy, but everyone had to laugh when they realized that it was like trying to play a piano sonata on an accordion. He wasn't going to fit. So he ended up sleeping in the bed his parents had shared.

He didn't sleep well, however. The bed was softer than what he was used to, and it was a strange place; or maybe it's because it wasn't a strange place, but rather a familiar one from a time of great stress in his childhood, but whatever the cause, he kept waking up. Finally, just at dawn, he woke up needing to pee so badly that he couldn't lie in bed any longer. Tired as he still was, sore from tossing and turning, he had to wince his way out of bed and into some clothes. Here in the foothills, spring wasn't so far advanced, and it would be cold, heading for the outhouse.

Once he was outside, though, hugging himself against the cold and peering through a cloud of his own breath in the faint dawn light, he realized that the outhouse wasn't where he remembered. The henhouses were there now. He began to circle the house, looking for a well-worn path that would show where the outhouse was now. He made a complete circuit of the house, and then, thinking he must have overlooked the building in his weariness and the dim light, he began another circuit. It was only Cousin Marek on the porch, laughing at him, that made him realize his mistake.

"You never heard of indoor toilets, boy?" asked Marek. "Where did you pee last night?"

"I peed at the station," Ivan answered. "I ate and just fell into bed and slept when I got here."

Marek pointed out the add-on structure on the gable end of the house. "One bathroom upstairs, one downstairs, just like America," he said. "Cost me a whole year's profit plus half a beef each to the plumber and the electrician, but Sophia says it's worth it, not having to trudge outside all winter long."

"Lead me to it," said Ivan, "before I explode."

Breakfast threatened to be as heavy as dinner, from the sounds Sophia was making in the kitchen. Ivan couldn't keep eating at that pace. So before he went out for his morning run, he stopped in the kitchen and gave Sophia a hug and greeted her and then said, "I'll only stay until I've eaten enough food to equal twice my body weight. At the rate you're cooking, that means I'll be heading out sometime tomorrow afternoon."

She laughed as if it were a joke.

"Sophia, I beg you." He got down on his knees. "I'm an athlete, I run, I can't eat so much."

"Eat what you want, nobody's putting a gun to your head," she said.

"I'm afraid of seeing your frown, if I take small helpings. I'm afraid of hurting the feelings of the greatest cook in all Ukraine."

"What do I care about *her*?" she demanded. "You won't hurt *my* feelings, because I take no pride in my cooking, I know it's plain food, you must have much better food in America."

Ivan laughed and kissed her, but he knew he was doomed. If he didn't want to spend his whole visit hearing how much better American food must be compared to the miserable Ukrainian fare that she did such a bad job of cooking, he would eat copious helpings of everything.

So he'd better get in a good long run today, and plenty of work. Though what work there might be for him he couldn't guess—the farm must be fully mechanized by now, and Ivan had never driven a tractor in his life. He wouldn't know how to begin plowing or planting.

He jogged to the road, stretched against the stiffness of his joints and the cold of the morning, then took off at an easy loping pace that he knew he could keep up half the day, or longer. To survive Sophia's copious meals, he would have to have a good long run every day. Maybe two.

The roads had been improved a little, too. Not much, for these last few years hadn't been easy in the Soviet Union. Not a lot of money for capital expenditures or infrastructure maintenance. Yet the roads were smoothly graded. Maybe the locals got together and did it themselves, not waiting for government to come in with money. That's how government began, wasn't it? Collective labor. And then somebody got lazy and hired a substitute, and pretty soon it was all taxes instead of the sweat of your back. But it began here, on roads like these, villagers with axes cutting down trees, with picks and spades and prybars pulling out stumps, with sledges and scrapers leveling the road. That's work even I could do, thought Ivan. But it's already done.

Then, abruptly, he realized where he was. North through those trees, and then bearing a little to the northwest, he'd find the trees growing tall and massive, with a canopy so thick that no underbrush grew. And then a clearing in the middle, a circular chasm filled with leaves, and something moving within the leaves.

He couldn't understand his own fear, but there it was. He half-expected to see some huge creature, the guardian of the chasm, leap out of the woods and slap his head right off his shoulders, as if it had been waiting for him all these years to punish his intrusion. Irrational, he told himself. Pure foolishness. It never happened anyway, it was a dream born of my fears and anger in that time. No chasm, not even a clearing, and certainly no creature swimming in a lake of leaves, an airshark circling and circling, rustling the detritus of ancient trees as it kept watch for the next curious trespasser to topple down within reach.

Ivan shook his head and laughed at himself, his voice too loud in the suddenly bright light of sunrise, sounding a little forced. Whistling past a graveyard, wasn't that the saying? He ran on, staying with the road, another mile or two, pretending that he wasn't thinking any more about that childish nightmare, pretending that he wasn't remembering the face of a woman becoming visible, a woman lying on a bed on a pedestal surrounded by dangers.

Since Ivan was currently leaning toward the idea that fairy tales converged because they satisfied innate psychological hungers, he couldn't help but wonder what fairy tale he had constructed for himself, with this dream. What kind of inner hungers had stirred him as a child, to make him invent a place like that, a woman so beautiful, a danger so ineffable and dreamlike? Was he the hero, torn from his home, and so now he needed some goal for his quest? Or some monster hiding in the leafy deep to do battle with? All of it designed to give meaning to the meaninglessness of his parents' decision to uproot him, not just from his home, but from his name, his identity, his native language, his friends. Or maybe it was just a way of making concrete the nameless dread that all those changes caused in him. In that case it had served its purpose, this dream. All his fears could be placed under the leaves in that forest, and then be left behind when he boarded the airplane and left Russia behind him. Safe at last, the monster forever trapped under a distant bed.

Now that he was a happy, well-adjusted adult, he should have no more need for such a tale. Yet he could not stop thinking about the woman, the chasm, the guardian that stirred the leaves as it passed. So there was something else going on here, some hunger that was still unsatisfied. Ah, yes. It wasn't just the monster that made the dream haunt him. It was the woman on the island. He had been just the age for such inexplicable dreams when he first thought up this personal myth—the hormones of puberty were flowing, but no physical changes had yet begun, so he had all kinds of desires but no idea yet what the object of those desires might be. A chaste princess on an island in the forest! Dry leaves instead of water in the moat. The princess on a pedestal, covered by dead plants, which swirl away from his feet as soon as he tries to cross the meadow-chasm to save her.

Now, as an adult, he could laugh at his own fantasies, pretend to be amused at his younger self. But he was not good at fooling himself, not deliberately, anyway. He was still afraid. More afraid than ever. Coming back down the road he had to pass the same place, and tired as he was, he sprinted past it. Let nothing leap from the woods, except to find me already running as fast as the wind to get away from it.

Soon enough, he was home, sweating and hungry, to join Marek at the breakfast table. Only Marek wasn't there.

"Still milking?" asked Ivan.

"Oh, no, he's plowing," Sophia explained. "He takes bread and cheese and sausage with him. Can't waste a moment getting the ground ready for planting, once the soil thaws in the spring."

Ivan looked at the table, covered with bread, fritters, a bowl of kasha, open-faced sandwiches, canned peas. "So you and I have to eat this huge breakfast between us?"

She laughed again. "Oh, I don't even eat breakfast anymore, just tea and a nibble of bread."

"This is for *me?*"

"Only as much as you want. I know you eat so much better every day, fine hamburgers and milkshakes, but—"

"Don't talk about that vile American food when I have *this* to eat!" Faking gusto, he sat down and began to wolf it down. No doubt about it, he was going to have to get Marek to take him to the fields tomorrow. He might not be any good at plowing, but he couldn't take another breakfast like this.

After breakfast, Ivan tried to help with the housework, but was met with stubborn refusal. Sophia was not going to have a man doing women's work in her house. It was against nature. So, using his nonexistent woodman's skills, Ivan went out to the tractor shed and followed the trail of the heavy equipment until he found the field that Cousin Marek was plowing that day. Sure enough, there was the tractor, in the middle of a half-plowed field, and yonder was Marek in the shade of a tree, eating bread and cheese and sausage. Marek saw him and waved to him, called to him.

Ivan utterly refused the offer of food. "I just ate enough breakfast to feed Napoleon's army. If he'd run across your wife, Cousin Marek, he would have taken Moscow and history would have changed utterly."

Marek laughed. "You think Sophia cooks too much food? Wrong, my young friend. She cooks exactly the amount of food needed by a man who works himself to the point of exhaustion every day. The problem is not to get her to cook less. The problem is to work hard enough that her meals are exactly right for you!"

"There isn't that much work in all the world."

"You say that because you read so many books, so you think that thinking is work."

"I notice *you* didn't eat breakfast this morning."

"Because I was going to sit on a tractor and drive it around all day."

"So give me some job to do that will use up this food that sits like a lump in my belly!"

Which is why Ivan found himself repiling all the hay in the barn, miserably hot work with periodic stops for sneezing fits. At the end of the job, he was dripping with sweat and too filthy and itchy to stand it for another moment. Yet when he got to the back door of the house, Sophia wouldn't let him in. "You think I want all that hay in my house?" she said, looking him over. "Get those clothes off and leave them in the laundry shed. I'll run a bath for you. I remember you always came home filthy as a child, too. Sweating like a pig. And stinking like a goat!" But she said it all so cheerfully that Ivan could only smile his agreement and obey.

Just as Marek had predicted, the day's work really had earned out the breakfast Ivan had eaten. He wasn't terribly hungry at dinnertime, but at least he didn't still feel bloated from breakfast. And when he kept dozing off during the meal, he realized that he had finally earned the right to refuse to eat without giving offense. "You poor thing," said Sophia. "Get to bed before you fall asleep in your cabbage rolls."

He woke again at dawn, just like the day before, and even stiffer in his joints and muscles. His back ached from his labor with the hay fork. His hands were sore despite the work gloves he had worn. His first impulse was to roll over and go back to sleep. But he knew that would lead nowhere. He had to get up and work the stiffness out of his body.

He thought of running another way, down toward the village, perhaps, instead of toward the forest. But in the village he would have to talk to people—it wasn't Kiev, where strangers let strangers pass without a conversation. And at this hour of the day, he preferred solitude. Besides, was he going to let his own private myth keep him away from the most beautiful part of this countryside?

So he ran to the place where the path led into the woods, and passed it by without a second look. And when he came back, he didn't especially hurry, either. The place had lost its power over him.

Yeah, right. That night, despite an exhausting day spent at the filthy job of cleaning out chicken coops, he kept waking up from one long dream. The same dream as before. And when he woke up in the morning, he knew something that he hadn't understood before.

When Mother told him he mustn't marry Ruth because of her dream, he had thought it was just foolishness on her part. But now he wondered. She knew him better than anyone, didn't she? Maybe she knew something she couldn't put into words, something she didn't really understand. Maybe she understood what it was in his life that made this imaginary place so important to him. The Jewish folktale she had dreamed of was about encumbrances that made a marriage impossible. Well, couldn't Mother have understood, at some deep level, that Ivan was somehow encumbered in a way that kept him from being free to truly give himself in marriage? That's why she dreamed the dream she did, and why he dreamed his own dream of this woman who was definitely not Ruth, this woman who was unattainable, protected by a monster in a moat. Maybe he had to overcome this fear before it was right for him to marry Ruth. Maybe that was why he had conceived this impulsive desire to come back to Cousin Marek's farm. Precisely because he could not go home and become Ruth's husband as long as that monster still prowled in the chasm around the unattainable sleeping woman.

But if this was all psychological, how was he going to resolve it?

Maybe the first step was simply to go to the place and satisfy himself that it didn't exist. Oh, there might be a meadow, but it wouldn't be perfectly round, there wouldn't be a woman in the middle, and the leaves would lie on ordinary ground, and not a chasm at all. Maybe he had to see that his memory was false in order to begin the process of mending this tear in his psyche.

So on this morning, he headed straight for the path in the woods, and instead of hesitating, he boldly, fearlessly jogged into the forest and made his way among the trees.

The path was not clearly marked, and his memory of the whole journey through the woods wasn't all that clear. If the place didn't really exist at all, not even a meadow, then how would he know that he had found where it *wasn't* in order to prove to his unconscious mind that the monster wasn't real, that the imprisoned woman did not exist and therefore did not depend on him for rescue?

He needn't have worried. Though the run was long, he recognized the way the underbrush cleared and knew he was getting closer. The climax forest with its massive trunks and lack of underbrush, that turned out to be real, so that running here was like taking a jog through an endless Parthenon, column after massive column rising out of sight to some pale-green vault of unimaginable hugeness. He was getting closer, closer . . .

And then he was there. The clearing in the forest. Perfectly round, covered with leaves. Exactly as he had seen it for all these years in his dreams and memories.

Real.

But of course it was real. The *meadow* was real. But there was no woman in the middle, just a slight rise in the ground. And no chasm, either, for when he stepped closer the leaves did not swirl away from his feet and reveal a—

The leaves swirled away from his feet. He stood on the lip of a chasm, just like the one he had remembered so well. Not imaginary at all.

And there on the far side, movement under the leaves, churning it up like a gopher eating its way under the lawn, only faster, faster, heading right for him.

When he came here before, that movement had made him run away in blind panic. But he was older now, more confident of his own abilities. If he outran this thing as a child, then he could certainly outrun it now. And maybe there was no need to run. Maybe it was trapped in the chasm and could not get out.

So he stood and waited for it to come to him.

4

KISS

 he creature under the leaves came to the edge of the chasm and stopped. Then, slowly, the movement of the leaves showed that it was backing away.

For a moment, Ivan was relieved. He had half-expected it to bound out of the chasm and attack him. Instead, like a good watchdog, it was backing up to wait for him to make the next move.

A sudden rustling, as if the creature were furiously engaged in some task under the leaves. After a few moments of this, stillness.

What now? thought Ivan. He turned to take a few steps along the edge of the chasm.

The leaves churned and something flew out of the pit, narrowly missing Ivan's head. By reflex he recoiled from it and fell to his buttocks as he heard a loud *thwack!* He looked over and saw a stone about the size of a nine-pound shot embedded in the quivering trunk of an ancient tree. What was down there, a howitzer?

Another churning in the leaves. Ivan immediately fell flat and rolled. Another stone whistled out of the chasm. Ivan scurried around and stood behind a tree, peering around to look at the place the stones were coming from.

That's why the creature backed up toward the far side of the chasm—it wanted to get a clear shot at him. Apparently it could see through the leaves.

Ivan's first impulse was to head back for Cousin Marek's farm. Who needed this?

His second thought was that Cousin Marek would probably have some kind of gun. Not that Ivan knew how to shoot, but how hard could it be?

Only then did he realize that he must be out of his mind to think of any such thing. This place wasn't one he wanted to explain to Marek or anyone else. It was his own madness that made it so real.

No. Not madness. It *was* real. He had found this place as a child, had run from it. But he hadn't been able to forget it. It haunted him, and now that he was here as a man, it was time for him to do whatever needed doing. *He* would have to do it, and no one else. If this place was meant for Cousin Marek, he would have found it long ago. There *was* a woman on the pedestal surrounded by the chasm, and it was for her that he was brought here.

Brought here, yes, but to die? To have his head stove in by a stone?

He darted to another tree. The creature under the leaves moved to position itself directly between him and the woman. Ivan darted again, and this time only paused a moment and began to jog to the next tree. The creature followed. Ivan moved out from the trees and began to jog along the edge of the chasm, following the circle. He kept his eyes on the ground under his feet, as leaves scurried up and out of his way with every step. It wouldn't do to lose his footing and slip down into the chasm where the watcher would have him at its mercy. Either it had a very powerful stone-hurling weapon, or it had thrown that rock by hand. A creature who could put a shot with such force wasn't one he wanted to tangle with. So he jogged until he had made a full circuit. Only then did he dodge behind a tree and look to see what the creature was doing.

It had followed him, and at such a speed that the leaves churned up by its passage were being caught by the breeze and blown out of the chasm. In fact, the level of leaves in the moat had fallen by about a foot, so the edge of the chasm was clearly marked all the way around. Ivan wondered how many leaves could be blown out of the moat that way, and so, before the creature could draw even with him, Ivan took off running again—and it was a real run, not the jogging pace he had set before. He did not have to study the ground so carefully, since the leaves were mostly gone from the path he was running, and the lip of the chasm was clearly visible.

As he completed the circuit again, he didn't even pause, just kept running, for he could see that ahead of him the level of leaves was even lower. It was working, and sometime soon the creature was bound to become visible. When he could see it as well as it could see him, then he might have some idea of what to do next. So he kept running, even faster now. Around the chasm, again, again, again. The track wasn't that long, and he was only beginning to settle into his pace when he realized that he was leaving the creature far enough in back of him that he was coming up on it from behind. If he ran just a little faster, he'd be able to see it, especially now that the leaves were down from the edge by six feet. The creature had to be tall enough to be visible now above the leaves, or it wouldn't have been able to hurl a stone with such a low trajectory.

With a burst of speed he was able to catch a glimpse, then more than a glimpse of a broad expanse of fur, long arms churning as the creature lumbered on two legs, then fell to all fours and ran, stubby tail bobbing up. A bear. A *huge* bear, for when its arms were outstretched it seemed it could touch either wall of the chasm, just by lurching a little to the left or a little to the right. With walls at least twenty feet apart, that meant an armspan of fifteen feet, maybe more. No chance of prevailing in a wrestling match. No Beowulfish battle was going to take place *here*, even if Ivan had fancied himself some kind of warrior.

Ivan stopped running as the bear continued rambling out of sight around the pedestal. Most of the leaves had now drifted from the pedestal, and he could clearly see that there was indeed a young woman lying on a low wooden bed, her hands clasped across her waist, her eyes closed.

From this distance, in this light, she seemed ethereal, at peace, an icon of beauty. How many tales had he read that recounted this moment? It was almost perfunctory, the way the tales had it. The hero sees the woman and from that moment his entire life is changed. Whatever she needs, he will obtain for her; whatever barrier stands between them, he will overcome. But never did the tales explain why.

Now Ivan knew. In fact, he had really known ever since he was ten, ever since he glimpsed that luminous face for a single moment and then never forgot it, so he had to come back. He had thought it was the creature under the leaves, his fear of it that haunted him. But seeing her face again, recognizing that profile, feeling how the sight of her stabbed him to the heart—now he knew why this place had haunted his dreams, why he hadn't been able to let the memory go. Not the bear. Not the strange place. Her. It was always her.

Apparently the bear had caught on to the fact that Ivan had

lapped him, for now it emerged from behind the pedestal and immediately reared up on its hind legs, roaring and showing a formidable set of teeth. It had jaws like a crocodile, or so it seemed to Ivan.

The teeth weren't Ivan's primary danger at the moment, however, for the bear fell to all fours, then came up with a large stone between its forepaws. Balancing the stone on its left paw, it drew back its arm like a javelin thrower. This was no regular bear, that was for sure, and Ivan decided that it was time to run.

The stone must already have been in the air by the time Ivan got himself turned around, and the bear's aim was good, for even as Ivan launched himself to run the other way, the stone caught him high in the back, toward his left shoulder, and sent him spinning and sprawling right at the edge of the chasm, one arm hanging over into the pit.

The air was knocked clean out of him, and for a split second he blacked out. It took a moment for him to understand what had happened, and what the loud rushing, rustling sound might be. Oh, yes. A bear in the leaves. Running . . .

Toward me.

Ivan opened his eyes to see the bear not six feet away, one great arm already swinging toward him, claws ready to rake his arm and drag him down into the pit. He rolled away just as the bear's paw struck; he felt the wind of it, felt the ground shudder a little with the impact. He kept rolling, despite the pain in his back, then struggled to his feet. His left arm hung useless. Broken? No, but numb. As he ran among the trees, he tried to think what this meant. Nerve damage? Spinal injury? Permanent paralysis, or temporary trauma that would heal? His left arm, gone—the thought left him sick with dread. What was he thinking, toying with an animal like this? If it could be called an animal, a bear living fifteen years at least under the leaves protecting a woman who lay uncorrupted on a pedestal. And it wasn't just fifteen years, Ivan knew that. It had to be longer. Centuries.

After all the fairy tales he had read and studied, the one possibility he had never entertained was this: That they might be true, or have some basis in truth. That the world might actually admit such possibilities as giant magical bears that could throw stones, as enchanted women who could lie forever in a coma waiting for . . .

For a knight. That's what this woman needed, a knight in armor, preferably with a *very* long lance, suitable for killing bears from a distance. In all the tales, the hero had a magic sword, or a magic sack from which he could draw everything he needed, or a magic helper who would do the impossible task for him. All Ivan had to help him was the limited wit of a graduate student so foolish as to be pursuing studies in a field that guaranteed him a lifetime of genteel poverty, and whatever strength and agility remained in the body of a college decathlete three years out of shape. In other words, he had nothing, and she needed miracles.

"One-armed Ivan and the Magic Bear"—it didn't sound like fairytale material to him, especially the part about how Ivan hightailed it out of there, holding his useless left arm and wailing about how unfair it was, him against the bear, just him alone against a magic bear.

He stopped and leaned against a tree, then looked back toward the chasm. He could see leaves drifting through the air, settling like snowflakes down into the pit in the ground. He knew that not one of the leaves had been lost. They would all float back, and soon the moat would be filled again, the leaf-covered meadow smooth and level except for that one slight rise in the middle. That woman who lay waiting.

What is she to me? I don't know her. She clearly has enemies more powerful than I am, and why am I suddenly her friend, anyway? Why me?

But even as he wished to be free of this impossible task, the thought of someone else coming to this place, reaching that pedestal, bending over her, kissing her, waking her up—it was unbearable.

I'm here, now. I'm the one. No one but me.

And yet in the rational part of his mind: This is why so many knights have died. This is why Troy fell, for a woman like this.

He wiggled his left hand. His fingers moved.

OK. So it was temporary, the numbness. The soreness in his back, that would probably heal, too, though right now the pain wasn't sending any such message.

The woman was waiting. The leaves were coming back again. The bear thought it had won, with a single stone on the back of a wouldbe hero who was running away.

What if he ran the circuit again, only not so fast this time, so he wouldn't overtake the bear? Maybe he could keep the beast running around and around until it wore out.

Of course, it was quite possible that magical bears didn't get tired. But with a bear this big, how magical did it have to be? It used claws, not spells, to try to tear his flesh into bacon strips. Nor were the stones hurled in some magical way, either. Yes, the bear was smart—for a bear—able to figure out about stone-throwing—he had never seen *that* behavior on the Discovery Channel. But it hadn't cast a spell on him or anything. What did he remember about bears in the fairy tales, anyway? Eaters, all of them. And talkers, some of them. But spells were for devils and demons, witches like Baba Yaga and great wizards or godlings like Mikola Mozhaiski—though old Mikola was more likely just to give advice. Bears, however, even magic ones, were still bears.

He jogged back toward the chasm. The bouncing pace hurt his back, so he changed to a loping stride that took him much faster and felt smoother. Soon he stood again on the brink. The moat had already half refilled with leaves. He heard the rustling, saw leaves flying from the far side of the moat, where the bear had sensed his return. Ivan waited until it was in sight, then began to run again along the lip of the pit, this time checking to make sure the bear could always see him, that it was always chasing him from behind.

Around and around and around, circle after circle, until the moat was utterly empty of leaves, the last of them blown away. Now he could see that the base of the pedestal—the inner wall of the chasm—was smooth stone, sloping in and out a little, like an apple core. There would be no climbing that surface.

So why bother dealing with the bear, then, if he couldn't get up that wall to the woman anyway? Tests within tests, and he probably wasn't going to pass any of them.

The bear showed no sign of weariness, while Ivan's back and shoulder were getting sorer and sorer. No help for that. It was finish out the task right now, or he'd have to start again from the beginning another day, for he knew he could not walk away for another decade or so. He wasn't a child anymore, he was a man, and a man sees it through, if he can.

So far, I'm still doing what I can. No more, but no less either.

The sun was at full noon, a warm day. Ivan took off his sweater as he ran, tossed it aside, under the trees. A while later he unbuttoned his shirt. He wished for better shoes than these—he had left his best running shoes in America, not thinking he'd need them, and these were broken-down old shoes, good enough for light running in Kiev but not for a serious marathon like this.

One foot after another, just like a marathon, but not covering any ground. He began to know each tree trunk far too well, recognizing every feature on them until he stopped caring and they all became one tree whirring past on his left, again and again. Why hadn't he run counterclockwise, like any good racer? He wasn't used to turning right, right, right. He thought of stopping, hiding in the trees until the bear caught up, then running the other way, but he drove the thought from his mind. If he was going to tire out the bear, he had to use his one advantage—an athlete's endurance, the strength of a long-distance runner. Bears weren't horses. They weren't used to running all day.

And sure enough, by midafternoon the bear was beginning to tire. Shambling along on all fours, it was going slower and slower, and never stopped now to growl at him. Its head hung lower, too. It was unflagging in the relentlessness of its pursuit, but it was running out of stamina. It was not an omnipotent bear. Ivan smiled. So far so good. Except for the part about knowing what to do next.

On every circuit he had passed the tree that had been struck by the bear's first stone. He long since stopped noticing the round shape of it, stuck like a diadem about nine feet up. But now he remembered it, slowed to look at it when it came around again. Not deeply embedded. Probably easy enough to dislodge.

On the next pass, Ivan put on a burst of speed, left the edge of the moat, and ran straight for the tree. Planting a foot low on the trunk, he let his momentum carry him up until the stone was in reach. It dislodged far more easily than he had expected, hitting him on the chin and chest as it fell. It was heavy and it hurt, but it was nothing like the injury to his back. His hand came away a little bloody when he touched his chin, but he could feel that it was just a scrape, not a cut, and he'd just have to live with it until he could get some disinfectant. He winced to remember the painful disinfectants of his childhood. None of that babyish American anesthetized stuff for tough *Russian* children!

As if he could count on even getting back to Cousin Marek's house, not with the foolish trick he planned to try.

He bent over and picked up the stone, then jogged to the lip of the chasm.

As he expected, the bear had caught up, was already getting a large rock between its paws. No sense in waiting, Ivan decided. He balanced the nine-pound stone on his right hand in best shot-putting style. This wasn't the standard competitive shot put, unfortunately. In track meets, the goal was to put the shot as far as you could, not to hit a target with it. Especially not a target that moved back and forth like the bear's head.

He'd just have to give it a try and see what happened. If he missed with this stone, the bear had thrown others; he'd just have to find those and try again.

He turned, spun, launched the stone. It sailed out over the chasm. He could see at once that he had overshot—it was going to hit the smooth stone wall behind the bear.

But at that moment, the bear rose to its feet, clutching a stone between its paws. It rose so quickly that it placed its own head directly in the trajectory of the stone Ivan had hurled at exactly the moment for it to catch the bear on its left eye, knocking it backward so its head struck forcefully against the stone of the pedestal.

With a whimper the bear slid down to sit like a curbside drunk, canted to one side, blood pouring from the empty socket of its left eye. The eye itself was smeared down its bloody cheek.

What have I done? thought Ivan, his heart immediately filled with pity for the injured animal.

What am I thinking! he demanded of himself, remembering his own injuries, the stones launched at his own head.

But I'm the intruder here, he thought, his sense of justice insisting on being heard.

But the woman is held captive here because of that bear, he reminded himself.

The woman. How long till the bear woke up, angrier than ever? How long did he have to figure out a way to get to the pedestal?

If he couldn't climb up the smooth stone wall, there was no point in climbing down into the chasm where even a one-eyed bear could make short work of him.

Many of the trees around the moat were tall enough that, if he had any way of felling them, they would easily span the chasm— indeed, some of them could have spanned the whole meadow. The trouble was that some limb of the tree would almost certainly strike the woman. He could easily imagine that between magical sleep and being crushed to death by a huge tree limb, the woman would undoubtedly vote for the coma.

How far was it across the moat to the pedestal? Twenty feet? He had long-jumped as much as twenty-four feet, not world's-record jumping but enough to win some meets. But he hadn't done any long-jumping since his undergraduate days. And what if it wasn't twenty feet? What if it was twenty-six feet? Or why not twenty-nine feet eleven inches? Just far enough to be a new world's record if he made it. Still, it wouldn't have to be a neat landing—there were no judges to disqualify the jump if a hand dangled or his butt swung in too low. On the other hand, if he missed and dropped into the chasm, the bear would kill him even if the fall didn't. And he wasn't going to do any world's-record jumping, not with his back injured as it was.

With his toe he drew a line representing the outside edge of the moat, then another line representing the distance of the pedestal. Had he made a good estimate of the distance? He paced it off. Twenty-two feet. But what did that prove? He had no way of knowing if he had been accurate at all in the way he drew the lines. Nor was pacing a distance all that accurate, either. He never got precisely the same count twice.

The bear gurgled and stirred.

No time for practice jumps. If he was going to get to the middle and waken the princess, he had to go now.

He walked back into the woods, pacing off a clear, straight path, making sure there were no obstructions. He gave himself one practice run-up—his life depended on his getting a good launch. He could hear the bear moaning in the pit as he began the real run, faster, faster. He planted his foot and pushed off, soaring over the chasm, remembering only in that moment that there was no room on the pedestal for any kind of run-up to make the jump back. Even if he made it to the pedestal, that's where he was going to be staying, unless there was some kind of instruction manual.

There were more immediate worries, however, because in mid-jump it also became clear to him that either it was a longer jump than twenty-two feet or his injury had weakened his jump, because his feet weren't going to land on top of the pedestal. He had time enough only to tuck his legs a little so he didn't rebound; then he sprawled onto the grass of the pedestal's crown, his trunk mostly on the pedestal, his legs dangling.

He began to slip downward, just as he heard the bear growl angrily. Gripping the grass with one hand, clawing for purchase with the other, he ignored the shooting pain in his left arm as he struggled to draw himself farther up out of the pit. He tried to swing his heels up, out of reach, as a searing pain in his left leg notified him that the bear was on its feet and quite able with only one eye to aim a raking blow at him. His fingers found purchase on the leg of the low wooden bed the woman was lying on. He dragged himself up, out of the bear's reach, his legs now safely up on the cool grass.

Grass. The leaves were gone now even from the pedestal.

He looked down at his leg. His left trouser leg was in tatters. The bear's claws had made two gaping tears in the side of his calf. They were bleeding copiously, but neither injury was pumping blood. No arteries had been torn. He pulled his pants off, tore the damaged leg into strips, and wrapped them around his calf to close the wound and keep it from bleeding so profusely. Now there was no hope at all of jumping back, or climbing either, or outrunning the bear, or any other foolish plan he might have thought of. He had reached the woman, but what good would that do if he woke her only for them to die here together?

The bear was still roaring down in the chasm. Ivan stood to look down at him, but the pain and loss of blood made him dizzy. He staggered; for a moment he thought he would fall down onto the waiting bear; he leaned the other way, stumbled back, fell against the bed, and found himself sprawled beside her, his hand on the cool but living flesh of her bare arm.

Now, at last, he could look at her. Dressed in the imported Oriental silk of a wealthy woman of the Rus', she had the high-cheeked features of a Slav; but he was not so American that this looked alien to him. Indeed, he could see that by any standard of beauty she was a lovely woman, young and smooth-skinned, her hair a lustrous brown with many lighter hairs that caught the waning sun of afternoon and shone like fine gold wires. Love poems had been written with less provocation.

But Ivan didn't love her. Ivan didn't even know her. Or rather, he didn't know her as a person, or even as a woman; he knew her as an icon, as the princess of the fairy tales. She was asleep because of some evil charm placed upon her by a jealous rival, a powerful witch who hated her. Had her finger been pricked by the sharp point of a spindle? Who knew which details of the old stories might be true? The only thing wrong with this was that apparently all the princes and knights had missed their chance. Maybe, upon examination, there'd be an array of rusted armor and old gnawed man-bones down in the bear's lair, but the fact was that the age of chivalry hadn't brought this woman back to life, and now here it was the 1990s, and far from being a prince or knight, her rescuer was a kid who liked to run and jump and throw things but who wasn't going to be much of a champion when it came time to fight the bear, which was how this tale must surely end. He would have to fight the bear, or distract it, anyway, long enough for Rapunzel here or whatever her name was to drop down to the bottom of the pit, preferably without breaking her legs, and then climb laboriously up the other side—for which task that lovely silk gown would be particularly slick, voluminous, and unhelpful.

I don't know you, ma'am, and apparently I'm expected to die for you.

He toyed with the idea of leaving her asleep and trying to figure out how to save himself.

Then the loss of blood and the exhaustion of running all day claimed him. He lay back on the grass beside her bed, closed his eyes, and as the sun dipped toward the horizon, he fell asleep.

He woke in the darkness to find something cold and dry on his face. A leaf. Leaves. He brushed them away. The faintest light of pre-dawn was glowing in the east, beyond the trees. He remembered at once where he was. Had he slept the whole night here? Cousin Marek would be worried. Would be searching for him—he hadn't thought of that. Marek might find his trail, might find him.

Ivan sat up. The meadow was again smooth and covered with leaves. If Marek showed up now, he might fall into the chasm. At this moment he might be running through the trees, searching, shining a flashlight to left and right, never seeing until it was too late how the leaves swirled away from his feet and the pit yawned before him—

"Go back! Stop!"

Ivan's own voice shocked him, coming in the silence of morning. Of course Marek wasn't coming. If he were, Ivan would see the lights, would hear the footsteps.

Almost at his left hand there came a violent rustling in the leaves, which whirled away, revealing the bear clinging to the side of the pedestal, its paws clawing at the grass, its mouth silently open. Now that it was revealed, though, the silence ended. It roared, slavered, gnashed its teeth at Ivan. He sprang backward, tripping on the woman's bed. The bear reached farther up onto the grass. Those great arms were going to make it. The bear was going to join him here. And it would be no good jumping down into the chasm, for he'd never get out of there again. He had no choice but to prevent the bear from climbing up.

Don't kick at its head, he told himself. Those jaws are quick and they won't let go.

Instead he clambered up onto the bed and jumped with all his strength down onto the bear's arm.

It accomplished nothing except to send pain shooting up from his left leg as the wound reopened and blood seeped out onto his crusted ankle. He groaned in pain. The bear roared again, and got the other paw farther up onto the grass.

Ivan rolled down and knelt beside the bear's claw—was it this one that had torn open his leg?—and pulled to try to get the bear to fall backward into the pit. Instead, the bear lunged upward, snapping at his hand with its great teeth. He recoiled, bounded away, over the body of the woman.

What will the bear do to *her*? he wondered, filled with a new dread. But then he realized that if the bear were going to harm her, it would have made this climb long ago. She was safe enough. Only he was in danger.

Well, if he was going to die, she was going to watch him do it. There would have to be one witness, at least, to how much he gave for this woman who meant absolutely nothing to him except that she had haunted his dreams since he was a boy.

As the bear heaved its chest up onto the pedestal, Ivan knelt beside the bed, leaned down, and kissed the woman's lips.

They were soft and alive. She kissed him back.

Her eyes opened. Her lips parted. She gave a soft cry, drew her head away from him.

He knelt up to look at the bear. Its hind legs were now scrabbling for purchase on the pedestal.

She stammered something in some language. A Slavic language, but very oddly pronounced. He knew he should understand it.

After a moment, it registered on his brain. Though the accent was unfamiliar, she had to be speaking a dialect of proto-Slavonic, closely related to the Old Church Slavonic that he and his father had spoken together so often.

"What did you say?" he demanded in that language.

"What?" she asked back.

Speaking slowly, trying to emphasize the nasals and bend his pronunciation toward the accent he had heard from her, he repeated his question. "What did you say?"

"Prosi mene posagnõti za tebe," she said slowly, each word separated. He understood now—easily, in fact: Ask me to marry you.

This was hardly the time for romance, he thought.

But her gaze was fixed on the bear. It towered over them, its arms spread wide, its mouth open as it brayed out its triumphal cry. Ivan realized that she wasn't proposing a romantic relationship, she was telling him how to vanquish the bear.

"Proshõ tebe posagnõti za mene!" he shouted in Old Church Slavonic. Will you marry me!

For a moment she hesitated, her face a mask of anguish.

"Ei, posagnõ!" she answered.

The bear was gone, even as the last echo of its roar rang in the air.

Ivan rose to his feet, walked to the edge of the chasm. No sign of the animal. No sound of it, either, snuffling along the bottom. Nor were the leaves returning. They were gone, all the leaves that had filled the moat only moments before.

But there was something new in place. A bridge, a span of smooth white stone reaching across the chasm to the other side.

"Thank God," he whispered. He walked to the bridge, stepped on it, tested it. Firm and true. He took two more steps.

The woman cried out. He looked back at her. She gazed at him in awe, perhaps even in horror.

"You walk in air!" she cried.

"No, on a . . ." He wanted to say *bridge* but he didn't remember the Old Church Slavonic word. He tried it in Russian, Ukrainian. She only shook her head. Then she pointed to the opposite side of the chasm.

"This way," she said. "Here is the bridge."

He recognized the word at once when *she* said it, because it wasn't that far from the Russian word after all. So she must have understood him.

He watched in shock as she stepped off the edge of the chasm and walked three steps out into the middle of the air.

"Wait!" he cried. It was clear she was being held up by something—he just couldn't see it. Yet seeing her there, standing in midair, made him tremble to the groin in fear. She was falling, she had to be falling.

"Come," she said. "You are my betrothed, and I must take you home."

"I can't," he said. "You see a bridge, but I see nothing here. The only bridge I see is on the other side."

She took the few steps back to the pedestal, reached out her hand to him. "Though you are only a peasant," she said, "you are the one who broke the curse on me, and you are the one whose offer of marriage I accepted."

A peasant? He looked down at his clothes. Knights didn't dress like this, but peasants didn't, either.

"Or did the bear take your sword from you?" she asked. "Did you take off your mail to climb?"

"I never wore mail," he said. "Nor used a sword. I *am* a peasant." *Smridu,* that was the word he used. Worker. Commoner. But a free man, at least. She hadn't taken him for a slave. That was something.

"The bear had lost an eye," she said.

"I threw a stone at its head," he answered.

"Then you vanquished the bear. The only reason he didn't kill you as you bent over me was because he kept trying to see you through the missing eye."

"No, the only reason he didn't kill me was because you agreed to marry me."

"You talk so strangely," she said. "Are you a Roman?"

She must think he came from the Byzantine Empire, the lands still ruled by the last vestige of the empire of Rome.

"My parents live in a faraway country. Far over the sea."

She relaxed. "And you came to find me?"

"I flew here to study ancient manuscripts, actually, but—"

She had stopped cold on the word *flew* and was covering her mouth in fear.

"I don't mean that I can actually fly myself," he said.

"What are you? What kind of wizard?"

"No wizard," he said.

"You carry no weapon, you speak a strange language, yet you flew here, you threw a stone that blinded the Great Bear. What star will wink out now, because of your stone?"

"Oh, do you call that—" He meant to say, Oh, do you call that constellation the Great Bear, too? But he didn't know the word for *constellation* in Old Church Slavonic.

She was not going to wait for him to finish. "Whatever you are, you will be my husband," she said. "Even if you cannot see this bridge, hold my hand and I will take you across."

She reached out to him. He took her hand.

The moment they touched, he could see the bridge she was standing on. It was very different from the bridge he saw. Where his was like a natural formation of stone, hers was of wood, ornately carved and decorated, with gilding on the upper surfaces. He recognized the workmanship. From sometime before 1000 C.E. Like her clothing.

Where did her bridge lead? What would he find there?

"I'm betrothed to someone else," he murmured.

"Not now," she said, looking horrified that he could even think that such a thing might matter. "If you don't marry me now, then all is lost, and the Widow will devour all my people, all this land."

"The Widow?" he said.

"Even in your land you must know of her," she said. "The evil widow of old King Brat of Kiev, who was driven from his throne by the Rus' and ended up ruling a little kingdom called Pryava. Since he died, she brutally took over other lands until her kingdom borders ours. She claims to be the bride now of an even greater king. She consumes nations and spits out nothing but bones."

"And she's the one who put you here?"

" 'Until Katerina finds a husband,' she told my father, 'then I, Ya'— I mean, she said her name—'I am heir to all these lands.' Then she had the Great Bear pursue me. He drove me here, where I could run no farther. I fell asleep, and he guarded me, until you came and gave me your oath, setting me free of him. Now I must get home to my family."

" 'Ya,' " said Ivan, echoing her. "Ya-*ga?*" Was it possible that this evil queen was the witch of the fairy tales? "*Baba* Yaga?"

She gasped and put her hand over his mouth. Her hand was callused from work, and she was stronger than he expected. But he liked the feeling of her touching him, though there was only fear and annoyance in the gesture.

"Are you a fool, to say her name right out? Even here. Even in this place." So it *was* Baba Yaga. If unconsciously he was looking for fairy tales, he had stumbled onto the mother lode.

She took her hand away from his mouth.

"Sorry," he said. "For saying her name, and I'm sorry about your kingdom, too. But . . ."

"But what? We have no choice but to marry. Forget this other woman. Take her as a concubine after we are wed."

"But it's been a thousand years," he said. "More than a thousand years that you've been lying here."

She looked at him as if he were crazy. "No thousand years," she said. "It is *today*. This morning is *today*."

She pulled at his hand, drew him onto the bridge, and led him to the other side.

Piotr and Esther lay in bed at the end of the day, watching Johnny Carson because Piotr enjoyed the program; Esther barely understood it. Even when she caught the meaning of the English, she rarely knew why everyone was laughing. But she watched because Piotr wanted to watch. Carson was wearing a turban and holding envelopes to his head, then saying things that made people whoop and laugh.

Piotr also laughed. She could feel the bed shaking.

Then, suddenly, it was as if she were falling; her stomach lurched within her. No, it was as if a baby kicked in her womb. No, no, it was as if her baby did not kick. It was as if she were carrying a baby and suddenly knew that it was dead and would never kick again.

"He's gone," she whispered.

"What?" asked Piotr.

Esther began to cry.

Piotr turned off the television, concerned. "What is it, my love? Are you sick? What's wrong?"

"He's gone," she said. "My little boy. He's gone. He's left this world."

Piotr put his arms around her. "Hush, hush, my love, that can't be so, that can't be true. How would you know it, anyway, so far from him? You're just afraid for him, a mother's worry, but don't be afraid, he's with Cousin Marek, he's safe, he's safe."

His words, his tone, they were meant to be comforting, but she took no comfort from them, only from the arms he wrapped around her, only from the warmth of his body next to hers. We made only one baby out of our love, Piotr, only one baby, one little boy, and he is gone.

BABA YAGA

Yaga was busy when Bear came back. She was in the midst of a tricky extraction of the living eyes of a merchant who had failed to bring anything interesting to sell, but who had the most fascinating silver-tinted irises that might have some unpredictable effects in spells of vision and illusion. The fellow was trying to persuade her, in his halting foreign speech, that perhaps she could make do with only one of his eyes, while she concentrated on popping out the left eye without bursting it, when Bear gave a great roar just outside the room.

The merchant jumped in surprise, which of course caused him even more pain than he was already in, as the cords that bound him cut more deeply into his throat. Choking, he managed to croak out, "What was that?"

"My husband," sighed Yaga. She was grimly determined not to show how bitterly his return disappointed her. Not that she had really expected to keep him tied up guarding the princess forever—for one thing, there were some very useful spells that she could only cast when he was close at hand. Still, she had thought that by putting both Bear and the princess in a place cut loose from time she would gain more than the few months that had passed for her during the princess's enchantment.

The real disappointment, however, was the knowledge that the princess had somehow managed not only to wake up but also to get the person who woke her to propose marriage to her. The whole point of putting her there had been to make sure that whoever kissed her would be some stranger from another time and place who wouldn't speak a word that she could understand, so that Bear would have plenty of time to eat him from the head down before there was any betrothal possible. And here was Bear, showing that her plan hadn't been foolproof after all.

"Do hold still," she said irritably.

"Sorry," croaked the merchant.

Out popped the eye.

"Here we come," said Yaga.

The merchant sighed and whimpered.

Yaga reached back with her long, thin blade to sever the optic nerve and blood vessels as close to the back as possible—must get the maximum strength from this eye, considering how much the fellow who grew it for her was going to miss it. "There," she said. "Want to see it?"

The man groaned. Taking this for a yes, she held up the eye with its dangling cord. "Now your eye will see for *me*," said Yaga. "Which will give it a much more interesting career than it would ever have had in your head."

"Please," whispered the man. "Let me keep the other."

"Don't be stingy," said Yaga. "Didn't your mother teach you to share?"

The door flew open.

"My darling husband," said Yaga. "Didn't I tell you to knock first?"

The answer was a roar. Bear shambled into the room on all fours, then stood to his full height and roared again.

"Hungry?" asked Yaga. "I'm almost done with this head, if you want it."

"Who is that eye for?" demanded Bear.

"Why, do *you* want it?" Whereupon Yaga looked up and realized that yes, indeed, Bear *could* use an eye, for the very good reason that he had only the one, while his other socket was bleeding. "Did you save the eye?" she asked. "Did you think to bring it back to me?"

"It was crushed," said Bear savagely. "The bastard threw a boulder at me."

"Aren't gods like you supposed to be able to, I don't know, regrow anything that falls off or out?"

"It didn't fall," said Bear. He sounded downright hostile. "And it wouldn't have happened if you hadn't trapped me there without any powers beyond the natural strength of a bear."

"I was using your powers here, my love," said Yaga. "I couldn't very well let everything fall apart at home just because you're out playing with some princess."

"I want to kill you," said Bear.

"No you don't," said Yaga. He couldn't possibly. The spells that bound him assured that his love for Yaga would be unflagging.

"Well then I *want* to want to kill you."

"Bear, meet . . . what's your name?"

The merchant murmured something.

"Do you have to play with your victims like that?" said Bear. "Why can't you kill them first and then take their parts?"

"Things start to corrupt when the body is dead. So I have to take the best parts when they're at their freshest." By now she had finished packing the first eye in clean white ashes. She closed and sealed the box, and set to prodding at the other eye. "You will be a dear and break open the head for me, won't you? I want to get the brain whole, if I can."

In answer, Bear lurched over, grabbed the man's head between his paws, and tore upward so violently that the cords cut right through his throat. With a twist, Bear pulled the head off the spine and dashed it to the stone floor. It split open with such force that the brain was splashed all over Yaga's feet and the rugs as well.

"You clumsy, insolent—"

"Don't start with me!" roared Bear.

For a moment she was afraid of him, for he still carried himself with the power of a god, and she wasn't *completely* sure that her binding spells would be utterly irresistible, if he got angry enough. Gods were dangerous creatures to enslave. Who knew how deviously they might manipulate the reality around them?

But in a moment, she could see that he really wasn't angry— anger being forbidden to him. The roaring and acting up were the result of pain, and after all, the poor dear had lost an eye. "I should scold you for killing him before I got the second eye out," said Yaga, "but I think your wound is making you cranky and I forgive you."

"Give me the eye you took from that man."

"It wouldn't fit," she said. "And you'd start seeing like a man, which would do you no good at all." She popped the second eye out of the head. Since it was already dead, it wasn't so important to pack it in ash. In fact, she might as well dry it to be powdered later—there were plenty of uses for it yet. "You did waste the brains, you know. I can't even tell which part is which."

Bear stepped in the midst of the pile of brains and twisted his paw.

"Don't be spiteful," said Yaga.

"Kill the girl and take the kingdom if you want it," said Bear. "Forget all this song and dance. You have the power. Or rather, *I* have the power."

Yaga sighed. "I don't want just to take it. I want to keep it. The high king at Kiev—"

"Is your sworn enemy. The Rus' drove your late husband from the throne of Kiev, didn't they? Stuck the two of you out here in this backwater kingdom of Pryava, didn't they? What do you care what the king of the Rus' thinks of your claim to the throne of Taina?"

"I don't want a war with the Rus'," said Yaga. "And you know why."

Bear roared in frustration.

"Ah, yes, my love. You thought you could trick me, didn't you? But I know that as god of this land and all its people, you're god of the Rus' as well, and if the high king went to war against me, it would weaken my hold on you. Everything must be done legitimately, my pet. Including my conquest of Taina. You're their god, too, aren't you?"

That was a sore point between them, since the king of Taina had converted to a religion that refused to recognize the power of Bear.

"We're really on the same side in this, my love, remember that," said Yaga. But as she looked at his matted fur, his blood-soaked muzzle and chest, she couldn't help but think: If this winter god, this walking rug, this one-eyed whining bear is the magical guardian of Russia, then Russia is going to have a very troubled future. "Tell me all about the knight who threw the rock at you."

"He wasn't a knight," said Bear. "He was practically naked."

"Come here and let your Baba Yaga put something on that wound."

He shambled over and put his head in her lap. She began to clean around the wound and apply a salve to it.

"He carried no weapon. He didn't really fight. He just ran and ran."

"How did he get to the princess?" asked Yaga. She had to know, because there was always the fear that somehow Bear had got himself free of her bindings enough to throw the contest against her.

"Jumped the chasm," said Bear. "Which you said no man could ever do. You said any man who tried would end up in the pit where I could take his head off." He scooped up a pawful of brain and ate it sloppily while she worked on his eyesocket.

Bear winced at the salve, as well he should, since she had deliberately left the pain-deadening herbs out of the mix.

"I can't be right about everything, can I?" said Yaga. "After all, *I'm* not a deity."

"Yaga, Yaga, Yaga," he said, as if she had made a foolish joke.

How she hated that nickname! And yet the name had stuck, until now it was the name she used for herself.

Her late husband King Brat had given her the name when he brought her to Kiev as his twelve-year-old bride. That was the pet name he murmured to her tenderly as he raped her immature body, and again as she pretended to weep over the grave of the first baby he sired on her. His dear Yaga, his sweet pet Yaga, Yaga the loving mother who pressed the face of his greedy slurping spawn into her breast long after it stopped struggling for breath and then, wailing, laid his first-born son in the very lap that had forced it on her. It was a message, though Brat never understood it, dense heavy-armed warrior that he was, a message that people understood *now*, with him deposed from his throne and then dead of a withering disease, and his widow married to a husband who at last *looked* like what every human husband secretly was, a hairy stinking drooling beast. A simple message: If you make Yaga do what she doesn't want to do, you won't like the result.

And maybe the message had changed over the years, and now it was more along the lines of: If you try to stop Yaga from doing what she wants to do, you and everyone you ever liked will be destroyed. But in spirit, in origin, it was really the same message. If she had to leave the gloriously beautiful coastland of her childhood and then the bustling traders' town of Kiev to live in this crude woodland, at least she would control all the kingdoms around her and run things her way.

The only drawback was that she always had to have some husband with the title of *king*, or no one would take her seriously. Well, she showed all those suitors who pursued her after Brat died. They thought they could get her and her late husband's kingdom, too. But she wouldn't settle for any of these petty princes. Her consort would be a god.

So Brat's precious "Yaga" was Bear's wife now, and no one even remembered that she had once been Olga, a hopeful young princess in a lovely kingdom on the south shore of the Baltic Sea. And now that she happened to be getting on in years, they were starting to call her *Baba* Yaga—grandmother, of all things! Of course it was ironic. A term of endearment, used for someone they hated and feared so much? The accusation that she ate babies was so widespread that she was tempted to cook one up and taste it someday, just to see what all the fuss was about. Grandmother, indeed.

She got up from her place beside Bear and carried the dead eye to her dressing table, where she could see herself in the mirror. Of course she had marked the mirror with several wards, so no passing spirit could leap out of the mirror and harm her. There was so much envy of her power and beauty.

"I don't look like a grandmother," she said.

"Yes you do," said Bear. "You know those spells don't work on me."

"I don't care what *you* see," she said.

"I've never seen the point of using magic to fool yourself."

"I have to live surrounded by beauty," she said. "Even in the mirrors."

"So you're going to make me *seem* to have both eyes?" he murmured.

Yaga ignored his self-pity. "About the princess Katerina."

"You know the story. He kissed her, she woke up, and they walked over the bridge."

"*Which* bridge?"

"Her bridge. I thought you were so sensitive you'd feel it when she came back into the world."

"I did feel it," said Yaga. "I thought it was gas." *Had* she felt it? No. What went on at that place was undetectable to her. But as soon as Katerina left the place and returned to Taina, then Yaga would know her every movement.

"Well, now you've got Katerina awake and headed for Taina with a husband who runs very, very fast and hurls a mean stone."

"He's not a husband yet," said Yaga.

"You mean to cast a spell to make a eunuch of him? He fell in love like any dog when he saw her, lying there giving off her love smell like a bitch in permanent heat."

"Sometimes I regret having given you the power of speech."

"So take it away again," he said. "I'd never miss it. Not like an eye."

"I don't need a spell to make a man into a eunuch," said Yaga.

Bear murmured something.

"I heard that."

"No you didn't," he said.

"Well, I know what you meant to say, anyway, and it wasn't funny."

"We'll see what the servants say when I repeat it to them."

"Go ahead," she said. "I'll just have to kill every one of them you tell."

"You should only kill what you intend to eat," he said. "It catches up to you, in the end, all this murdering."

"It's not murdering, it's my life's work," she said. "Besides, *you* killed this fellow."

"Yaga, Yaga, Yaga," he said.

"Shut up," she murmured sweetly, and sat on his lap. "I'm glad to have you back, darling."

"Are you?" he said. "It occurred to me, as I was running around and around in the moat, trying to stay between the peasant and the princess, it occurred to me that your plan could only be for no one to ever kiss the girl, in which case your loving husband would be trapped in the chasm forever."

"Don't be silly. As soon as her father died I would have brought you home."

His huge claws caught at the cloth of her dress and delicately shredded it right off her body without so much as scratching her skin. Then his paws rested firmly, tightly, crushingly against her belly and chest, pulling her so closely against him that she could hardly breathe.

"I don't think you should send your loving husband on any more permanent errands," he whispered in her ear.

"Well, why would I, anyway?" she wheezed, struggling for breath. "Do remember how much you love me, my *pet*."

His arms relaxed. She sucked great gouts of air into her lungs.

"Not killing you," he said, "is just an old bear's way of saying I love you."

"I love you, too," she said.

If only she knew some way to break down the last barrier and take his magic whole, so she didn't need him at all. Take his immortality, his godly powers, and then be rid of him the way she was rid of Brat. But if there were spells for emptying and discarding a god, she hadn't found them yet. Maybe the Christians should be encouraged. Maybe if everyone stopped believing in these forest totems, they'd lose their power.

In the meantime, Bear was hungry and needed feeding. Then he'd void himself wherever he felt like it, all over the house. It had taken her all these months to get the stink out of the house while he guarded the sleeping princess. Now the odor would be back in force. If only she could . . .

If only, if only. No matter how much power she had, there was always something else to wish for.

5

NAKED

 van stepped off the bridge onto the grassy meadow and
his clothing disappeared.

Startled, he let go of Katerina's hand and tried to
cover himself, then realized how pathetic he looked,
clutching his genitals, and turned his back on her.

"What are you doing?" she asked. "Peeing?"

Since all his sphincters were firmly clamped down, that wasn't
likely. "I'm naked," he said. "What happened to my clothing?"

"I don't know," said Katerina. "Your skin is very smooth. Like a
baby's."

It bothered him that she didn't seem bothered by his nudity. He
sidled toward the bridge. "Maybe if I cross over to the middle again, I'll
get my clothes back."

"They'd just disappear again the minute you came back here,"
said Katerina impatiently.

If I come back, Ivan thought.

"Your skin is so smooth," she said again. "And white. Have you
been sick?"

Her comment annoyed him. He was proud of having a decathlete's body. She was looking at him as if he were . . . what? Unmanly.

But there were worse things to worry about than her rude assessment of his body. The bridge was invisible again, and he couldn't
remember quite where it had been.

"Take my hand again so I can see the bridge," he said.

"No," she said.

"I need my clothes."

"You can't have them," she said.

"I don't like being naked in front of you."

"I already saw," she said. "You don't have to hide your deformity."

Deformity?

It took him a moment to realize what she meant. In America practically everyone in the locker room had been circumcised. But to Katerina's people it would be rare. Nudity, however, must be common. Well, it wasn't common to him.

"I need to wear something," he said.

"I know, it's cold. Too bad you couldn't get the skin off that bear."

"Give me your . . ." He tried to think of the Old Church Slavonic word for *hoose*, but if he ever knew it, he didn't know it now. "Your clothing. Robe. Coat." That about exhausted the approximations he could think of.

No answer.

He looked over his shoulder at her. She was, finally, blushing.

"What, I can be naked and you can't part with one piece of clothing?"

"Are you trying to shame me?" she whispered.

"I'm trying *not* to shame us both," he said. "I can't walk into your parents' house naked."

"Better naked than wearing women's clothing," she said.

"I'm not going to wear it like a woman," he said. "Now give it to me before I freeze to death standing here."

Sullenly she dropped her hoose off her shoulders, then leaned down to pick it up from the ground. She looked away as she handed it to him.

True to his word, he didn't put it over his shoulders—since it was open-fronted, it would hardly have served his purpose that way. Instead he wrapped it around his waist and tucked it like a bath towel.

"Good," he said, facing her again. "I'm covered."

But she who had stared frankly at his nakedness would not look at him now.

"I'm wearing it like a soldier's kilt," he said.

"When people murmur that the husband of the queen once wore her clothing, I will be able to say, I never saw him wear any such thing, and I can swear to it by the Holy Virgin."

"Are you telling me that it's better for me to come to your parents' house naked?"

"It would be better for you to come to my parents' house dead than wearing women's clothing."

"Well, here's an idea. How about if I don't come to your parents' house at all? Give me your hand so I can see the bridge, and I'll be on my way."

She whirled around to face him, to clutch at his hands. "No, no, wear whatever you want. You can't leave, you *must* come to my house, you have to marry me or we lose it all. After everything, after you fought the bear, after you woke me, to leave now would be worse than if you had never come!"

He held her hands. "Listen, I understand that wearing women's clothing is a . . ." He struggled for a word for *tabu*. "A sin. When we get near the village, I'll wait in the woods until you can bring me men's clothing." Gingerly he removed the hoose and handed it back to her.

She looked at him with disgust, refusing to touch the garment. "Do you expect me to wear this now that it's been around your loins?"

"No," said Ivan. "No, I see that you can't wear it now." He reached out and dropped the hoose into the chasm. "It's gone."

Her disdain was undiminished. "Nothing is gone," she said. "You just gave the hoose to the Widow."

"I was just down there," he said. "She wasn't there."

"*She* makes the rules, not you," Katerina said. "I have to marry you, but you're a fool. She must have picked you out herself."

That really pissed him off. "Maybe you have to marry me, but I don't have to marry *you*."

"Naked in the woods, a deformed peasant who wears women's clothing and speaks like a stupid child, it's not as though you had a lot of choices."

Her taunt was so ridiculously myopic that he had to laugh. He thought of Ruth back in New York, waiting for him. All this magic, these dreams of childhood, the evil monster he had beaten, the princess he had kissed, what were they? Foolishness, he could see that now. He didn't belong here. The rules made no sense to him. Clearly she expected him to go through with a real marriage. Like the rules in a china shop: You break it, you bought it. Only in this case, you kiss her, you've married her.

Well, he didn't like the rules. He didn't like the idea of marrying someone who thought he was a deformed cross-dressing peon, and even less did he like the idea of getting caught up in some kind of struggle with a mythical witch from the nightmares of fifty generations of Russian children. He'd done his part. He woke her up and set her free. The prince didn't have to stay. Especially when he wasn't a prince.

"Look," he said.

"I've already seen enough," she said.

"I mean listen."

"If you mean listen, say listen," she said. "Why do you talk so funny? Twisting all the words around?"

"Because I'm not from here!" he said. "Your language isn't my language." To prove it, he burst into modern Russian. "You speak a language that is already dead, that is hinted at only in fragments of ancient manuscripts, so you're lucky I speak any language you can understand at all!"

She looked at him now with dread. "What kind of curse was that? You spoke of death. Did you curse me to die?"

"I didn't curse you," he said in Old Church Slavonic. "I spoke in my own language."

But then he wondered what language was his own. Russian was the language of his parents' home, but the language of his childhood was Ukrainian. But all these years of thinking, speaking, writing in English—didn't that make English his language, too? When he was married to Ruth, wouldn't English be the language of their children? For that matter, didn't Old Church Slavonic have as much claim to be one of his languages? However badly he might speak it, it had been the private language he and his father once shared. And now, could he really pass up the chance to learn a dialect of proto-Slavonic, the true spoken language, after all these years of knowing and using the shadow of it that had survived?

Yes, he could. He had a life, and this wasn't it. He had done what he came to do—he cleared away the leaves, defeated the beast, crossed the chasm, woke the princess. That was as far as the stories ever went. None of the stories included shivering naked between forest and pit, the princess scorning you as a peasant, sneering at the symbol of your childhood covenant with God and loathing you for daring to try to cover your nakedness.

Well, actually, that wasn't true. Western stories ended with getting married and living happily ever after. And Russian fairy tales went far beyond that—to betrayal, adultery, murder, all within that romantic marriage that the wanderer stumbled into. The old tale of Sleeping Beauty might end happily in French or English, but he was in Russia, and only a fool would want to live through the Russian version of any fairy tale.

Ivan dropped to his knees in the grass and crawled along the edge of the chasm, reaching out with his left arm to try to feel the invisible bridge.

"What are you doing?" she said.

"Going home," he said.

She sighed. "You won't find it."

He stopped probing for the bridge. "Yes I will."

"You've already put your hand through it several times," she said. "It isn't there for you."

"You mean it only *exists* when you're holding my hand?"

"It exists all the time," she said. "For me."

"So I can't get back home without your help."

"Why would you want to leave, anyway?" she said. "When you marry me, you'll be a prince. Heir to the throne. Someday you'll be king of Taina."

"I've never even heard of Taina," he said. "I don't want to be king of anything. I want a doctorate and tenure at a university and a wife and children who love me." Of course he used the modern Russian words for *doctorate* and *university* and the English word for *tenure*, since he'd never had to say it in Russian and wasn't sure how.

She was baffled by the strange vocabulary, of course, but tried to make sense of it. "So you're on a quest?" she said. "To find this . . . *tenure*?"

"Yes, exactly," said Ivan. "So if you'll be so kind as to help me back over the bridge, I'll find my own way home from there."

"No," she said.

"Listen, you owe me. I woke you up."

"Yes," she said, "and because of that there's no one else I can marry. After the wedding you can go search for your *tenure*."

"Listen," he said. "I'm betrothed to someone else."

"No you're not," she said coldly.

"I assure you that I am," he said.

"You are betrothed to me," she said. "If you were betrothed to someone else, I would not have woken up when you kissed me. The bear would not have gone away when I agreed to marry you."

"And how would the bear know?"

"The bear didn't know. The spell knew. The universe knows when an oath is being made, and when an oath is broken."

"Well, the universe just slipped up, because I was engaged to Ruth before I—" He heard his own words and stopped.

Before? What did *before* mean now? He was in her world—had been in her world since he reached the pedestal in the middle of the chasm. And by her clothing and her speech he was pretty sure her world was medieval, maybe 900 C.E., maybe earlier. So at the moment in time when he kissed her, he and Ruth hadn't even been born yet.

But that was ludicrous. Because *he* was there, as a man in his twenties who had definitely given his word, earlier in his life, to marry Ruth. Therefore it was a betrothed man who kissed the princess.

But he kissed her centuries before his betrothal.

Round and round it went. What good were the rules of time when the rules of magic contradicted them?

Mother had told him that there was something wrong, some impediment to his marriage with Ruth. Was it this? Even though he hadn't yet come here and fought his way to the princess, had this moment already happened centuries before? Did objective time—the flow of centuries—override subjective time, the flow of his own life?

There was no way he could even begin to discuss such concepts with Katerina. Even if he had enough Old Church Slavonic to speak these thoughts, he doubted she'd have the philosophical background to understand them. Just as he didn't have the background to grasp the way things worked here. Bridges that existed for one person and not for another. Bears that lived for centuries in leaf-filled pits. Witches who put spells on princesses. It was great to read about these things, but living with them wasn't half so entertaining. And he had a feeling that before he was done with all this, he'd like it even less.

"So I'm trapped," he said.

"Yes," she said coldly. "Poor you, a peasant boy trapped into marrying a princess so you can become a king."

"I don't want to be a king," he said. "And I'm not a peasant. Or a boy."

"You're certainly not a knight."

"I must be a knight," he said. "Or else how could I get past the bear?"

"You're too weak and soft and young to be a knight."

No one had ever called him weak and soft, and he was older than she was. Almost by reflex he tensed his muscles, feeling them bulge and move under his skin. "How can you call me weak?"

In reply she took hold of his right forearm between her hands. Her fingers overlapped considerably. "This arm has never raised a sword." She gripped his left upper arm. "Could this arm hold a shield for more than five minutes?"

"I've never needed to," said Ivan. "But I'm hardly a . . ." He struggled to think of a word that would mean *weakling*.

"Smridu," she said. Peasant.

"I'm not a smridu. I've never farmed in my life. I don't even know what farmers do."

"No, I can see that," she said. "You have the manners of a peasant, but those thighs would never get you through a plowing season. They'd break like twigs."

Her cold assessment of his naked body infuriated and shamed him. He had never tried to bulk up like a Schwarzenegger, he had tried for genuine all-around athleticism. Her scorn was so unfair, so culturally myopic—and yet he knew it would be pathetic to defend himself. "In my country I'm considered strong enough."

"Then your country will soon be conquered, when real men see their opportunity. What are you, a *merchant?*" She glanced down at his crotch, continuing her assessment of his body. And then, suddenly, her eyes grew wide.

"What?" he said, fighting the urge to cover himself or turn away.

"I heard about this. The Jews do this."

"Yes, that's right," he said. "I'm a Jew."

Her gaze grew stony and she muttered an epithet that he didn't understand.

Great, that was all he needed. Anti-Semitism, too.

"If you think you can sell the daughter of a king into slavery, think again," she said. "My father will ransom me, and then he'll come and hunt you down and kill you anyway."

"Slavery!" he cried. "What does my being a Jew have to do with slavery?"

Her fear eased. "If you're not a peasant and you're not a knight, then I thought you might be a trader, and then I thought of the Jews who traffic in slaves, carrying people west to sell them to the Franks."

Ivan remembered his history. In this era all the traders dealt in slaves.

"Traders don't steal slaves, they buy them. War captives. Debtors."

"But the bishop says that—"

Of course. No sooner are these people converted to Christianity than the Church starts in with the calumnies against Jews. "The only thing the bishop knows about Jews is the lies the Christians made up about us."

Her face flushed. "How dare you say that Christians are liars. *I'm* a Christian and I never lie."

"Well, I'm a Jew and I never captured a slave in my life. Or bought or sold one either. And I never met a Jew who did."

She glared at him. "What a lie," she said. "I have watched my father buy slaves from Jews himself!"

"Well if you *buy* the slaves, what right do you have to criticize a Jew for selling them?"

"In my father's kingdom, Christian slaves earn their freedom by fifteen years of work."

"Oh, but Jewish slaves would stay slaves forever?"

"All our slaves convert to Christianity."

"Of course they do!" cried Ivan, exasperated. "If Christians are the only ones you set free!"

"But Jews sell Christians into slavery," she said.

"And who do you think they sell them *to*?" he demanded. "Christians like your father. I can't believe we're even having this conversation. Dealing in slaves is evil when Jews do it, but perfectly all right when Christians do it, is that the rule?"

"Why should I argue with a boy?" she said.

"You shouldn't argue. You should listen and learn the truth. I'm a Jew and I'm not a prince and I don't want to marry you, I want to go home and marry Ruth. According to you I also wore women's clothing. Nobody's going to want me to be king, so let's forget the whole thing. Let me go back across that bridge."

She was adamant. "The man who kissed me is the man I have to marry," she said, "or the Widow rules over the people of Taina."

"So you'd even marry a slave-stealing Jew?" he said.

"Now you admit it!" she cried triumphantly.

"No, I don't admit it!" he shouted back. "The only thing I admit is that I don't want to marry you!"

"You gave your word!"

"There was a bear!"

She squared on him like a trapped badger. "And there will be another bear, or worse. I will marry you for the sake of the people. Maybe you don't care about them, maybe you *have* no people, maybe you come from a land where other people's suffering means nothing. But in my land, even a peasant would die for his people, would stand against Hun or Saxon if it would save the life of even one child. Because in my land, even the peasants are *men*."

He looked at her, and remembered how she had looked to him before he kissed her, the ethereal beauty, the perfection of her. Well, that was gone. But there was a different kind of beauty now. Or perhaps it wasn't beauty at all. Nobility. She made him ashamed.

"They're not my people," he murmured.

"But they're *my* people, and if I'm to save them, I have to marry you, even a man who wears women's clothing and lies to my face."

"Is the Widow so terrible?" he asked.

"Terrible enough to choose you as the one she let past the bear to wake me."

"Hey," he said. "Nobody *let* me past that bear! I *beat* him."

"You hit him with a rock," she said scornfully.

"I set you free of that spell."

"Someone else would have eventually."

"When? It was already more than a thousand years from your time to mine." The language she spoke was at least that old.

She gasped. "A thousand years! But . . . in a thousand years . . . my people . . ."

She turned from him, gathered her skirt, and plunged into the woods.

He ran after her, which worked fine on the grass but immediately became quite uncomfortable in the forest, with harder ground and nuts and stones among the fallen leaves. "Wait!" he called out.

"They're all dead by now!" she cried.

"You don't know that!" he called after her. "In all the stories, the king and his people slept while the princess did!"

She heard him; she slowed, but not enough.

"Slow down, you have to wait for me! I don't know the way!"

She stopped and watched him pick his way gingerly along the broken ground. "You walk as if the ground were on fire."

"I usually wear shoes," he said. "My feet aren't used to this."

Another scornful look from her.

"Excuse me for not living up to your image of manhood."

"Jesus Christ is my image of manhood," she said coldly.

He realized that he had used the word for *icon*, for that was the word he and his father had adapted to mean *image* or *concept*. But to her it would still have only religious connotations. She had no idea of who he was and what his world was like. It was childish of him to be angry at her for her ignorance. He at least had studied her world; she could not possibly imagine his.

"The land I come from," he said, "leaves me ill-prepared to live in yours. I need your help."

Her expression softened. She was beautiful again. "I'll help you. Will you help me?"

"I'll do what you need," he said. "I've come this far. I might as well see it through."

The English idiom became a meaningless phrase in Old Church Slavonic. Ivan and his father had done a lot of that, translating idioms word for word as they developed their own version of the dead language. It began as an anachronistic joke, but then became a habit of speech that he would find hard to break.

"I don't understand you," she said.

"Nor do I understand you," he answered. "But I'll do my best to help you save your people from the witch. After that, I can't promise anything."

"After that," she said, "it doesn't matter what you do."

"You'll take me back here and let me go home?" he said.

"I'll lead you across the bridge," she said. "You have my word on it."

In the bottom of the chasm, the hoose rose from the ground as if a woman's body filled it, though it was empty. It turned around and around. Dancing. Then the spinning grew faster, faster. The skirt of the hoose spread wider, until the hoose lay flat in the air, rotating like a helicopter's blades. Leaves began to drift into the chasm, then get caught up in the whirling of the hoose, until a tornado of leaves rose up from the pit.

It lasted for a few moments, then dissipated, the leaves settling back down in the meadow around the chasm.

And down in the pit the hoose clung to the outside wall, hanging from a dozen knives that stabbed through the fabric into the earth. From each knifepoint a black oily liquid flowed. And out from behind the fabric, first one, then dozens of spiders scurried, spreading across the face of the wall.

The most important thing that Katerina had to figure out was whether this boy was her rescuer or just another vile trick from Baba Yaga. There was plenty of evidence for the latter. The strange clothing he was wearing when he kissed her—pantaloons like a rider from the deepest steppe, boots so low and flimsy he couldn't wade through a stream; yet a fine, tight weave and astonishingly expensive colors. His strange language—intelligible yet accented, and laced with new and foreign words whose meaning she couldn't begin to guess at; how could she tell conversation from incantation and spell casting? The chopped-up body of a Jew, though his head was uncovered. The smooth, white skin of a boy who had never worked or fought in his life, and yet a posture of utter boldness, as if he had never met an equal, let alone a superior. His face had the peace of someone who had never known hunger or fear, and though he hadn't the forearms of a warrior or the thighs of a plowman, he wasn't scrawny, either. And he was so strangely clean and odorless, except for the tang of sweat from his recent exertion. There was a beauty to him that for just a moment had stirred in her a kind of recognition, perhaps a desire; the thought passed through her mind, Is this how angels look, beneath their robes, shed of their wings? Certainly in the proud, commanding tone of his voice there might be the authority of an angel; it was plain he considered himself as regal as she. And yet he was so oblivious to shame that he would take clothing from her body and put it around his own.

It was possible to imagine him touching her, his clean young body possessing hers, yes, even with that strange maiming of a Jew. She would not shudder at that part of her wifely duty. But it was impossible to imagine such a man being king.

But he was just the kind of strange, perverse seducer Baba Yaga might try to force upon the kingdom of Taina.

Was he sent by the witch Baba Yaga? It seemed so unlikely, for hers was not the only power, or even the greatest one, in this shifting high-stakes chess game. If there were no governance upon her, Baba Yaga would simply have killed Father long ago—and Katerina, too, no doubt—or, failing simple assassination, she would have brought her army to Taina where her brutal slaves and vicious mercenaries would no doubt have brushed aside Father's army of ardent but relatively unskilled farmer-soldiers.

No, the witch was still bound by rules, such as they were. Some said that Mikola Mozhaiski still watched over the land and people of Taina, though he had not been seen in years, and that he would not permit Baba Yaga to violate the deep, underlying law. The person of the king was still sacred, and no magical spell could take a royal life or sever the kingdom from its rightful ruler unless he acted in such a way as to lose the right to rule. And since her father, King Matfei, had always acted honorably as king, taking nothing from his people but what he needed to bring about their own good, and giving to them all that was required for their safety and sustenance, his right to the crown was unassailable. Baba Yaga could not brush aside the natural order of the universe. Not yet, at least, although they said that she had harnessed to her will the terrible power of a god.

Father, however, was convinced that it was not Mikola Mozhaiski who kept Baba Yaga in check, but rather his conversion to Christianity and his ordination as king by Father Lukas. "The same authority by which the Great Imperator sits upon the throne of Constantinople," he often told her. She never spoke disrespectfully to her father, and so her answer remained unspoken: If Christian ordination had the power to keep a throne attached to a man's buttocks, so many Great Imperators would not have been deposed or killed in years past.

The Holy Trinity created the heavens and the earth, she believed this absolutely; but she *knew* that it was Mikola Mozhaiski to whom the power had been given to protect sailors from the dangers of voyaging and kings from the dangers of politics. And unlike God, you couldn't pray to Mikola Mozhaiski, you couldn't curry favor with him, he asked of you neither baptism nor mass. You either kept to the rules or you didn't. If you did, even a witch like Baba Yaga had no power to destroy you, and if you didn't, he had no help for you.

So if it wasn't Baba Yaga's little trick, how did Katerina end up with this naked bumbler crashing barefoot through the woods behind her? He had already managed to lose the path several times even with her leading the way—he had no sense of the forest at all. How did he survive childhood without falling in a pit or getting bitten by a snake? Why didn't some merciful wolf run across him as a lost child—he must surely have spent half his childhood hopelessly lost—and send him on to heaven? Well, not heaven. He *was* a Jew.

How in the world did a man like this get past the bear?

She asked him.

"I jumped across," he said.

Jumped across. A chasm that wide and deep?

That gave her pause. A magical bear was sure to stop an ordinary knight. But a man so light that his body was like a boy's, and yet so strong that he could leap over the bear's head, fly across the chasm like a bird, like an angel . . .

Was his very boyishness the reason he was chosen? In that case, was it not a virtue to be admired, and not a failing to be despised?

She stopped and looked at him again. After a few moments of pushing branches away so they wouldn't scrape him as he passed, he finally looked ahead and noticed that she wasn't moving. That she was looking at him.

He became shy again at once, turning his body sideways, as if that would hide his genitals instead of displaying them in profile. A biting fly distracted him—he slapped himself. The movement was very quick. The man was agile. His body was so tightly muscled that no part of him, not even his buttocks, quivered after the sudden movement. This was the only sort of body that could have overleapt the bear and woken her with a kiss. And in the marriage bed, wouldn't he lie more lightly upon her than any of the hulking knights who had looked at her with covert desire?

"What?" he said.

"I was waiting for you to catch up," she said. "We're almost there."

The main village—Taina itself—was unchanged. It surprised her a little. No new lands had been cleared because the old soil was worn out. Even the houses were all in the same places, with only a few new ones for couples who had been married since she pricked her finger on the spindle and fell into the dream in which the bear chased and chased her until she could run no more and fell exhausted on the stone, to lie there watching as the earth all around her collapsed and the bear leapt into the chasm, and then to sleep. A dream in which she fell asleep. And yet it was no dream, was it? For there was the chasm when she woke again, and there the bear. And here was the kingdom of her father, the land that she lived to serve.

She stood at the edge of the wood, surveying the familiar scene, when her newly-promised bridegroom finally came to stand beside her. His baby-tender skin was scratched and raw from pushing through bushes and brambles. He could have used the protection that a length of cloth might have given him. She felt a pang of guilt for having shamed him into casting away the hoose—though such feelings were irrational, she knew. Better to have a thousand scratches than to offend God.

"What's wrong?" he asked.

"A thousand years have passed, you said," she said scornfully. "But it's been no more than a few months. The same fields are still being planted, no new ones have been cleared. And so few new houses— Dimitri, Pashka, Yarosz—they were all betrothed when the Widow's curse caught up with me. And none of the old ones abandoned or burned."

"Those are houses?" asked the oaf.

"What do you think they are, hayricks?" How stupid was he?

"I just mean they're—small."

"Not everybody is as tall as you," she said. "I don't imagine you could even lie down straight in a regular house. Not without sticking your head out the door and your ass in the fire."

"You have such a pretty way of talking," he said. "Like a princess."

"Of course I talk like a princess," she said, baffled that he would say such an obvious thing. "Since I am one, however I talk is the way a princess talks."

He raised his eyebrows in obvious mockery. What right did he have to be so hateful? She couldn't help thinking back over the conversation to see what he could possibly have thought was unprincesslike in her words. Was it because she had spoken of a man lying down? She hadn't said anything about lying down *with* somebody, had she? Wherever he came from, they must be such prudes, to be so fussy about a man's nakedness and take offense at mere words.

She felt the warmth of exertion radiating from his body. His bare skin was so close to her, and yet he hardly smelled at all. And he was taller than she had realized. She was uncommonly tall for a woman, and she didn't even come up to his shoulder. In fact, she was almost eye-to-eye with the nipples on his chest. Which, she noticed, were shriveled with the cold. The breeze was picking up, too, and his skin was mottled and seemed to have a bluish cast. Again she thought of the clothing she had denied him.

She reached down, took hold of his hand, and started leading him into the village.

At once he pulled back, fighting her like a donkey that didn't want to carry its burden.

"What?" she demanded.

"I'm naked!" he said.

"Yes, you stone-skulled ninny, that's why I'm taking you to my father's house, so you can get out of the wind!"

"Can't you go fetch clothes for me?"

"Am I your servant? You're my betrothed—would you leave me to enter the village alone, with you cowering in the woods, not even seriously injured?" She yanked his arm and began dragging him on. She glanced over her shoulder and saw, to her shame, that he was cupping his genitals with his other hand like a toddler who had just learned to play with himself. Was he really *that* determined to make himself utterly ridiculous?

"Stop that!" she hissed at him. "Stop handling yourself!"

He rolled his eyes in obvious exasperation, but he obeyed and uncupped himself. But he also pulled his hand away from hers, and walked beside her, refusing to follow her or to be dragged along. Good—he was asserting his right as her husband to walk beside her, without claiming to be her lord and walk ahead.

As soon as she was recognized, women began coming out of their houses and children began to gather in the lane, shouting and cheering and jumping up and down. Some of the more eager boys and girls ran on ahead to her father's house, so her father was waiting for her at the door when she arrived.

Tears streaming down his face, King Matfei embraced and kissed her. Only after many such hugs and kisses did he finally give any notice to the naked man beside her.

"King Matfei, my father, here is the man who crossed the chasm and blinded the bear and kissed me to waken me from the spell."

If Father noticed that she had used the word *mozhu* instead of *vitez—man* instead of *knight*—he gave no sign of it. He simply took the cloak from his own back and placed it over the man's shoulders.

Naturally, the oaf began shivering almost at once. Naked, he doesn't shiver; put a warm cloak on him, and he acts like it's snowing. Was he determined to look like a fool?

"Come inside, come inside," said the king. "The man who brings me my daughter from the Widow's power will always be honored in my house. But you must tell me your name before you come inside."

The man hesitated, as if he didn't even know his own name, before finally saying, "Ivan."

Ivan, the name of the Fourth Evangelist, the one beloved of the Lord. What was a Jew doing with a name like that?

"Ivan," said Father, "you have brought joy to my house and hope to my people here today. Come inside, for this is now *your* house and *your* kingdom; as God is my witness, you shall have nothing but good from me and mine."

"Thank you, sir," he said. Did he not know a guest-pledge was expected from him in return?

But Father paid no heed to the lapse in courtesy, and led the man inside.

Katerina paused for a moment at the threshold of her father's house, and turned to face the gathered crowd. "Soon I will have a husband," she said to them, "and then Taina will be safe from the Pretender."

A momentary hush fell over the crowd. Of course she had not said the name of Baba Yaga, but they all knew whom she meant.

Then they erupted in cheers. King Matfei and his daughter Katerina would keep them safe from the baby-eating monster who turned all men into slaves and was married to a bear. The witch's curse had been overcome. All was right with the world.

*   *   *

You get used to being naked, that's the first thing Ivan discovered. Crashing through thick brush with branches snagging at your bare skin, you stop worrying about who's looking and spend your time trying to keep yourself from being flayed alive. He got shy again when they entered the village, but once he decided simply to let the gawkers gawk, he found himself much more interested in what he was seeing than in what they were.

He hadn't realized it till now, but he came to this village with two sets of expectations. As a scholar, he had a very clear idea of what a medieval Russian village should look like, and what he saw was pretty much what he expected. The houses of skilled tradesmen attached to the king's household were bunched up like a town, close to each other and close to their work sheds. There were stables and pigpens with all the smells that one might expect. And just beyond the king's town the forest opened up into many stump-dotted fields, each with its little hut for the family that farmed there. Other plots were fallow, going back to woodland, with saplings rising among the ancient stumps, all trace of farming subsumed in the grasses being grazed by sheep and cows.

What Ivan hadn't expected was the sheer numbers. A village like this was supposed to have only a tenth of the population that this land obviously sustained. Ivan remembered the professor who scornfully dismissed the stories of vast armies ranged together for battle: "The whole population of Europe at that time could not have assembled an army that large." Well, if Taina was any guide, it was the medieval writer and not the modern professor who knew what he was talking about. The fields went on and on, and other villages and manor houses could be seen, or at least guessed at from the smoke rising from unseen cook fires. Taina was no Paris or London, but then, there were more students at Mohegan University than there were citizens of either Paris or London in the 800s C.E.

The king of Taina was no tribal chieftain. This was a settled land, and the king could field a sizeable army if he needed to—many dozens of knights, if each manor house supplied one or two, and hundreds of armed villagers for infantry. No wonder Baba Yaga was resorting to subterfuge instead of conquest. And with the land so bountiful, feeding such a large population, it was no wonder Baba Yaga coveted it. Ivan wondered if this land was so productive and well-populated even today.

Yet even as he recognized and admired the medieval village he had expected, Ivan had to wrestle with a completely different set of expectations, courtesy of Walt Disney. Wasn't it Sleeping Beauty he had kissed? Then where was the magnificent palace? Never mind that

Disney's movie version of the story was set in some weird combination of the sixteenth and nineteenth centuries—Ivan couldn't help being let down at seeing—and hearing, and smelling—such a coarse reality instead of a magical dream.

The king didn't live in a palace at all, or even a castle. His house was made of timbers instead of sticks, and was large enough to enclose a banquet hall and many rooms, but it was all one story in height, thatch-roofed and completely unfortified.

For defense, there was a nearby hill-fort of pre-Roman design—earthworks with a palisade of wooden stakes at the top, designed with plenty of gaps for bowmen to shoot through. And in the middle of the fort, a tall watch tower arose, allowing several villagers to stand and watch out over the whole surrounding forest—but also allowing an approaching enemy an easily visible landmark to march for.

No palace, no castle, no stoneworks of any kind. Everything was built of wood, easily susceptible to fire. But why not? There were plenty of trees to rebuild anything that might burn. And defense came from the strength of arms and, Ivan supposed, whatever magic the local people might know how to wield. And since magic worked here, perhaps they could count on the protection of their gods.

Gods? Only at that thought did Ivan notice what he should have spotted first of all. Just down the slope from the king's house was a wooden chapel with an Orthodox cross above the door.

That's right, Katerina had spoken of Christ. Yet this land was so far north and west—there was no record of a missionary journey that resulted in the conversion of this kingdom in the foothills of the Carpathians.

The reason was obvious, of course. Such a missionary journey would only have been recorded if the kingdom itself had survived. The very fact that Ivan had never heard of the conversion of Taina—indeed, had never heard of Taina at all—suggested that it got swallowed up in a kingdom that was *not* Christian, its identity lost, its brief flirtation with Christianity forgotten. Whatever cultural influence the Byzantine priests might exercise here would amount to nothing. This place was doomed—the cross on the chapel was a sure indicator of that.

With that doleful thought in mind, Ivan stood behind Katerina as she embraced her weeping father and then introduced him, in all his splendid nudity, shivering from the cold and bleeding from a hundred scratches. When the king took the cloak from his own shoulders and wrapped it around Ivan, he was moved by more than the graciousness of the gesture. This man will lose his kingdom, Ivan was thinking. The story of the sleeping princess will survive and spread all over Europe, but the witch will have her way with this kingdom after all, and waking the princess from her slumber would turn out to be no blessing to these people. Ivan thought of this place in flames, and shivered, even though now, with the cloak around him, he was not so cold.

When King Matfei asked his name, Ivan almost blurted out "Itzak Shlomo." What was he thinking? It took a moment even to think of his Russian name. And then to decide against the familiar *Vanya* and use the formal *Ivan*. And then to remember to pronounce it the Russian way, instead of like an American. "Ivan," he finally said. He decided against giving a surname, since family surnames were not in use at this time, except for royal dynasties. Besides, Ivan was in a fairy tale now, wasn't he? And in the fairy tales, Ivan was always Ivan, just as in the English tales Jack was always Jack.

With a gracious speech and promise of hospitality, the king brought Ivan inside. Behind him, he heard Katerina address the crowd, but did not linger to listen to what she said. He was more interested in the room surrounding him. It was smoky from the large fire in the center; the hole in the center of the roof drew most of the smoke upward, but left enough behind that Ivan's eyes stung. A deer's carcass was sizzling and spitting over the fire as a servant lazily turned the spit.

King Matfei sat, not on a throne, but on a large chair at the head of the banquet table, while Ivan was shown to a seat at his right hand—the place of honor. Still, except for the cloak, no clothing had been offered to him, but as Ivan's eyes got used to the interior darkness he realized that he was not the only naked or nearly-naked man here. A goldsmith working at a second fire in one corner of the great room wore nothing but his apron, and now Ivan realized that most of the smoke that was irritating his eyes came from the goldsmith's hearth. It took only a moment for Ivan to understand why this craftsman was laboring in the king's house instead of his own work shed—this was the king's gold the man was working with, and it didn't leave the king's house. There were also two boys of perhaps eight or ten years who wore nothing at all as one of them swept the floor of old straw and the other strewed new straw behind him. Slaves—that's who went naked here.

The king had shouted instructions to his servants from the moment he entered the house, and Ivan was no sooner seated than bread and cheese and mead were set out in front of him. Moments later, a steaming bowl of borscht was added, and, lacking a spoon, he picked up the bowl and drank from it eagerly. It was a rich broth, beefy and strong.

The crowd was cheering outside and shouting the names of Katerina and Matfei, as Katerina herself made her way into the great room and took her place at the king's left.

"So," said King Matfei. "You saved my daughter!"

"Yes, sir," said Ivan. He drank again from the soup bowl. Borscht dribbled from the sides of his mouth, down his chin and onto his chest. The bright red dripping broth would look for all the world as if he had bitten into the raw, warm heart of a fresh kill in the forest and let the hot blood run. For a moment he felt like a savage indeed, who had triumphantly brought back the prize from the teeth of the bear.

"He wants you to tell him the story," said Katerina. Her tone of voice added an unspoken epithet: *idiot.*

"It was nothing," said Ivan. "Really."

Matfei and Katerina looked at him as if he had just peed on the table.

"Saving my daughter was *nothing*?" asked King Matfei.

"No, no, Father," said Katerina, glaring at Ivan. "My beloved Ivan is merely waiting until your other knights have gathered, to tell the glorious tale of his triumph over the Widow's fiendish and hideous bear."

Ivan realized his mistake at once. He knew this from his studies. Modesty wasn't valued in this culture. A man boasted about his exploits and won extra points if he told the story well. What else was he forgetting?

Ivan tried to cover his faux pas by taking another draught of borscht, draining the bowl entirely.

"Then let's gather them all," said King Matfei. He called out to the naked boys who were sweeping and strawing. "Run and summon my boyars!"

The boys dropped broom and straw where they might fall, and took off for the door.

"Won't they be cold?" asked Ivan.

Katerina rolled her eyes. "You see how compassionate my rescuer is?" she said to her father. "He even cares for the comfort of slave boys, as if he were forgetting they would stay warm by running."

"You talk funny," said King Matfei to Ivan. "Are you a foreigner, or are you simple in the head?"

"Simple in the head," said Ivan at once.

Katerina glared at him. "He jokes."

"On the contrary," said Ivan. "Your daughter has made a great effort to tell me just how stupid I am."

King Matfei turned to face the princess, and for a moment she seemed to wither under his gaze. Then he laughed and smiled and hugged her close to him. "How can I think for a moment you would be ungracious to your rescuer!" he cried. "The man is jesting!"

"You'd be amazed at all the funny things he does," said Katerina. Her smile could freeze steam.

"I speak differently," Ivan explained to the king, "because I learned another dialect of your language as a child, and there are many words I don't know. I promise to learn as quickly as I can."

"Katerina will help you," said King Matfei. "She knows *all* the words!" With that he roared with laughter, and hugged Katerina even tighter.

She smiled and hugged her father back. Such a happy family, thought Ivan. What the hell am I doing here?

This is the first day of happily ever after, that's what I'm doing.

And, when he made the effort to see past his own fear and his resentment at the way Katerina had disdained him, he had to admit that Katerina and her father really *did* seem happy. King Matfei teased her, but treated her as someone to be proud of, someone to like as a person, not just as a property to be married off. Apparently women were not so oppressed as they would become in later centuries.

"I was so afraid for you, my daughter!" said the king. "I thought I might never see you again. All my boyars went in search of you, and found no track or trace or rumor. The dogs found no scent, and the prayers of Father Lukas went unanswered. I was going to set them all again to searching—or praying—but here you are, rescued, betrothed, and sooner than I could have hoped."

"I was enchanted only a few months," said Katerina. "Though Ivan thinks it was a thousand years."

"How could it be a thousand years?" asked King Matfei of Ivan.

"To you it seems only a few months," said Ivan, "but I assure you that in my land we know of a thousand years of history that passed while she slept. I think that your boyars couldn't find the princess Katerina because the Widow did not merely hide her in the forest, but hid her in the centuries as well."

"It makes no sense to me."

"Such are the ways of witches," said Ivan.

"I know nothing of the ways of witches," said King Matfei, "except they are of Satan and must be resisted with all our power."

"I am even more ignorant of them than you are," said Ivan, "for up till the day I fought the bear and freed your daughter, I did not believe that they existed."

"Well, that was stupid of you," said King Matfei.

"Yes," said Ivan. "I see that now."

"You weren't joking, then, when you said you were simple in the head."

"There are many things I don't understand," said Ivan. "I hope that you'll give me time to learn."

"Are you so clumsy that no one gave you any work to do?" asked the king. "Look at your arms and shoulders—I don't know if you could lift a basket of flowers."

"I lifted the stone that blinded the bear," said Ivan, getting a little annoyed.

Katerina looked concerned. "My father is teasing you," she said.

Ways of showing humor must have changed a lot over the centuries, then. It sounded to Ivan like he was being insulting.

"In my land," said Ivan, "I'm regarded as a . . ." He had no idea how to say *athlete* in Old Church Slavonic. It wasn't a concept likely to be useful in the liturgy or histories. "As a good runner."

The king's face went white. "They say this to your face? That you run?"

Ivan had to think frantically to guess at what he had said wrong. Then it dawned on him. "Not running from battle," he said. "Running races. Two men side by side, then they run and run and see who arrives first."

"We have slaves carry our messages," said the king.

"Then I suppose no one but the slaves will run races with me," Ivan said, chuckling. But he found himself chuckling alone. So much for humorous banter. Apparently the jokes would only go one way around here.

"I'll bet you're not Christian, either," said the king.

"No, sir," said Ivan. Was there any defect that he lacked? Whether he could father children had not yet been tested.

"He's a Jew," said Katerina. Trust the princess to come up with another flaw—though to her credit her lip didn't curl and her tone didn't curdle when she said it.

"Never mind," said King Matfei loudly. "Father Lukas will teach you of Christ and you can be baptized in plenty of time to marry my daughter."

"I'll be glad to speak with Father Lukas," said Ivan. "But if there's some way around this marriage idea—"

"What he means," said Katerina, "is that all of this is new to him and he will learn *everything* that is required of him." Her eyes made it clear to Ivan that this was not a good time to throw the marriage into question.

King Matfei whispered to his daughter again. He apparently believed that no one but her could hear him, though of course his harsh whisper was audible in every corner of the room. "How did somebody as stupid as this defeat the Pretender's bear?" And then, in a voice even softer, though still clearly audible: "Are you sure he isn't sent by her as a trick?"

"For the answer to that," said Katerina softly, "you'll have to ask Mikola Mozhaiski."

"Yes, well, he hasn't been by here in years. Not since you were little. I don't know if he even remembers I exist. After all, I'm only a king." Looking up into the beams of the thatched roof above his head, Matfei bellowed, "Does Mikola Mozhaiski talk to anyone but the gods?"

Ivan thought he was joking, and smiled a little. Matfei saw his expression and twisted in his chair to face him square on. "Is that funny to you?"

"I've never met Mikola Mozhaiski," said Ivan. "I don't know anybody here."

"You know my daughter," he said. It sounded like he wasn't pleased about it.

"She doesn't like me," Ivan said, determined that some of the truth, at least, would come out.

The king roared with laughter. "What does it matter if she likes you! She's going to *marry* you! You're getting more than any other man will have!"

It was in that moment of surpassing banality, sitting at the dining table, surrounded by the stink and noise of a medieval hall, the king himself showing complete disregard for the fact that his daughter might not like the man who was supposed to marry her, when it dawned on Ivan that he wasn't going to be able to beg off the way he might have done in back in Tantalus, politely turning down an invitation to have dinner with a new acquaintance or attend the Mormon pageant at Palmyra. If the king decided Ivan was going to marry his daughter, turning him down was going to be a little tricky. And as for getting baptized, well, history was littered with the bodies of people who didn't find quite the right way of saying *no thanks* to a fervent evangelist with a sword.

It was like the moment when a war correspondent realizes for the first time that the bullets whistling around him don't notice or care that he is a noncombatant with a notebook or a tape recorder or a steadycam. And, like that imaginary war correspondent, Ivan wanted nothing more than to hug the ground and shout to someone in a hovering chopper, "Get me out of here!"

But Ivan kept his poise and showed no sign of his moment of panic. He must concentrate on the details of the moment. Whatever else happened, he was still a scholar getting field experience like no other grad student in history. He must live in the moment and forget the future. He spread lard on his bread and ate it, smiling at the king. He didn't insist that he was already engaged to someone else. He didn't mention his disinclination to become a Christian. He didn't burst into tears and call for his mother. He just chewed and swallowed, hoping that the knot in his stomach wouldn't cause him to throw up.

He wasn't getting out of here without Katerina's help, which she wasn't likely to give. There'd be no ticket home. He wasn't even on standby.

Was this going to be his life? To marry this beautiful barbarian woman and spend his life eating pork and crossing himself? Sure, until the day he had to face some knight in combat using a sword he probably couldn't even lift. Or until the day Baba Yaga sent an extremely resentful one-eyed bear to do the job right this time.

Death was the least of his worries. Looking around, he realized that long before someone got around to killing him, he would have to deal with a thousand much more tedious afflictions. He was bound to be infested with fleas—he could almost see them hopping around in the straw on the floor. And what of the unsanitary water? He would definitely stick to alcoholic beverages here, trying to strike some balance between drunkenness and dysentery. And what would happen to him, living on a diet from the era before refrigeration and flavor? Already he was wishing for a simple chocolate-vanilla swirl from TCBY, with just one scoop of chocolate sprinkles.

Never again.

The boyars were gathering, and the knights of King Matfei's *druzhina*. There were women present, too, wives or relatives of these men of high station. The slaves brought out more and more food, and the guests ate with gusto. This was the king's table, and what he had to provide for the lords and knights who were loyal to him was a free lunch.

Of course their table manners were shocking—slabs of bread were their plates, knives and fingers their only utensils. The women ate with as much gusto—and as much splashing and dripping and dropping—as the men. Ivan noticed that even though they all conversed with each other, few could look at anything but him, sizing him up, wondering why he was naked except for the robe over his shoulders. No doubt they were as disappointed in his physique as Katerina and her father had been. If only he knew the local idiom for "beggars can't be choosers."

The king had been conversing with some of the boyars seated nearby, but now turned again to Ivan. "My future son seems distracted," said the king. "You can't be drunk on the little bit of mead you've had."

"I'm sorry," said Ivan. "I don't always understand what you're saying."

"Believe me, we don't always understand *you*, either!" said the king with a laugh.

But at that moment Ivan realized that one of the women on the other side of the room might be choking. She sat rigidly, her eyes wide with fright yet also glazing over, her fingers scrabbling at the table's surface as if she were trying to get a grip on it. No one around her noticed.

Ivan rose to his feet, toppling his stool, and would have rushed to her around the outside of the tables except that too many slaves and diners were crowded there. So he stepped up onto the table and jumped off the other side, the robe falling from his shoulders as he did. He strode through the open space in the midst of the tables until he stood opposite the choking woman. She didn't even see him, she was so far gone in her silent agony. He swung himself over the table, upsetting several cups. Ignoring the protests of those whose mead he had spilled, Ivan squatted down, reached his arms around the woman's waist and clasped his hands just under her sternum. There was no rigid underwear to interfere with the Heimlich maneuver, so he dragged her to her feet, held her body close to him, and gave one swift inward jab with his hands.

A piece of half-chewed meat flew out of her mouth and out into the middle of the floor. The woman gasped and sobbed for breath, leaning over the table as Ivan let go of her.

At once several rough hands seized her, and Ivan was surrounded by shouting men, one of whom gripped him by one arm, tore him away from the others, and flung him against the wall. His head spinning, vaguely aware of splinters in his face and his naked shoulder, Ivan had no idea who had attacked him or why, but it was clear from the iron grip on his arm that the business wasn't finished yet.

It would have ended badly if the king himself had not roared a command. "Stop, you fool! What are you doing to your future king!"

From the man who gripped his arm Ivan heard an answering growl. "No man, naked, may lay his hands upon my brother's wife in such a way as that!"

"He saved her life, you blithering fool!" cried the king. "Are you blind? She was choking, didn't you see it? And whatever he did—look, out in the middle of the floor, the bit of meat that was going to be your sister's death!"

The grip on Ivan's arm did not relax.

The woman, finally recovered enough to speak, turned around to face her brother. "Don't hurt the man, Dimitri," she said. "He held me only around the waist, as if we were dancing. And then he—popped the food out, and I could breathe again."

"But he's naked," said Dimitri.

Dizzy and frightened as he was, Ivan couldn't help but notice the irony that this was the first person who seemed to agree with him that his being naked was a very bad idea.

"He saved my life. While you, brother Dimitri, sat beside me making jokes. You would have kept joking until I dropped dead on the floor!"

"Why didn't you tell me you needed help?"

"Because I was choking, my wise brother!"

By now the king had made his way through the throng to stand beside Ivan. "Dimitri," said the king, "instead of ripping my guest's arm from its socket, would you please let go of him and thank him for saving your sister's life?"

It was couched as a request, but Dimitri interpreted it, correctly, as a command. "Sire," said the knight. "I serve you always." He let go of Ivan's arm—the blood rushed painfully through the too-long-constricted veins—and now Ivan could turn to see the man who had seized him and tossed him so easily into the wall. Dimitri was built like . . . like Popeye. Like Alley Oop. His forearms were unbelievably muscular, his shoulders as massive as a bull's. Was *this* what Katerina had been comparing him to? Was this what a "man" was to her? Ivan was taller than Dimitri, but in no physical way would he be a match for him. For the first time in his adult life, Ivan felt downright frail.

This man could snap my bones like twigs.

And it was clear that despite the king's words, Dimitri wasn't really mollified. His apology, while it sounded sincere enough—the king was watching, after all—clearly wasn't what he wanted to say. "O guest of the king, I'm sorry I threw you against the wall. I'm also sorry you laid hands upon my sister. If you had told me she was choking, I would have saved her."

Oh, sure, I'll bet you would, the Heimlich maneuver was done all the time in the ninth century or whenever this is.

But Ivan decided that it was best to pretend to accept the apology and avoid antagonizing this man any further. "Sir, I would have told you, but I'm a stranger here and I don't speak your language very well. I did not know how to say that she was choking. I only learned the word when it was said just now. So instead of speaking, as I should have, I thought it was better to act."

"Of course it was better," said King Matfei. "And you were fast—over the tables and across the room faster than a stooping hawk." He turned and addressed the whole company. "Have you ever seen a man bound over a table like that? By the Bear, if I only had a hound that could leap like you!" Then the king realized what he had said. "That is, not by the Bear, of course, but by the Lord's wounds."

"Amen," said a few of the more pious.

Katerina approached now, holding the robe she had picked up from where it fell. Not taking her eyes from Ivan's face until she moved behind him, she placed the robe onto his shoulders. Gratefully he gathered the cloth around his waist. Katerina took her place beside him. "Do you see what a man the Lord has brought to me? Two women he has saved this day, Lybed and me, but I am the fortunate one who will have him as my husband."

The hall rang with cheering.

"Lucky for you the princess got your promise first," said Dimitri's sister, Lybed, her eyes alight with something more than mead. "For I'm a widow, and I would gladly have thanked you well enough to wear you down to a stump."

The company whooped at the ribald boast, King Matfei among them. Even Katerina smiled.

But Dimitri did not smile. Instead he took his sister by the arm and pulled her away. "We've eaten enough," he said. "I'm taking you back to your children before you're too drunk to walk."

"I'm not drunk," Lybed protested, but allowed herself to be led away.

"Well, now," said the king. "We've seen with our own eyes that you're a worthy champion, even if you do seem a mere lad. What you lack in strength you'll make up for in liveliness, I'll swear! So come back to table and have whatever you want!"

Ivan saw the opportunity and took it. "King Matfei, forgive me, but what I want most is a bed. I ran with a bear all morning."

The king could take a hint. "What kind of host am I! The man rescues my daughter and brings her home, my kingdom will be saved from the great Bitch, he even saves the sister of my master-at-arms, and I don't even think to give the man a bed! In fact, I'll give him *my* bed!"

"No, no, please!" Ivan protested. "How could I sleep, lying in the bed of a king?"

King Matfei laughed. "So what? When you marry my daughter, you'll be sleeping in the bed of a princess."

Ivan glanced at Katerina. She showed no sign of noticing her father's reference to the presumed consummation of their marriage. But this was a woman who knew how to speak her mind. About the marriage, she had nothing to say. She would do her duty, but she didn't have to relish it.

He had always thought that he would marry for love. Instead, it looked like his bride was going to take him out of grim duty.

Please, yes, let me go to bed. If I sleep, perhaps I'll wake up back in Cousin Marek's house, or in Kiev, or back in Tantalus in my own room. That's how these mad dreams end, isn't it?

The bed, when they led him there, offered no redolence of home. It was clearly a place of honor, a bedstead a full three feet off the ground. But the mattress was straw in a tick, the room was cold and stank of old sweat and urine, and it wouldn't get him any closer to home. There might be magic in this world, but none of it was in this room, and none of it was Ivan's to command.

It took Esther a day of shopping, but she found it in a mall in Syracuse: a clay basin, made in Spain, plain dark blue inside, brightly decorated on the outside. She bought it and brought it home, arriving after dark. Piotr asked her where she had been, but she answered him in one-word sentences that let him know this was not a good night for chat.

Out in the back yard, she set up the basin on a lawn table, out in the open where moonlight fell directly on it. Then she took the garden hose and filled it to the brim with water. Using blades of grass and twigs from the lawn as shims, she finally got the bowl exactly level and perfectly full, so that the water in the basin was poised to brim over, held in place all the way around by surface tension alone. The last few drops she added with an eyedropper.

The water trembled from the last drop, shimmering for a long time as if to the echo of a distant drumbeat. She sat and watched, cupping her hand over her mouth and nose lest her breath disturb the water. The night was still, but she did not trust it. She murmured words to keep breezes away from this spot, ancient words in a language she didn't really understand, and for good measure included the incantation that would keep the eager insects of spring from seeking out this pool of water for egg-laying.

At last the water was perfectly still. Carefully, she rose to her feet. Holding her clothing close to her body, so nothing would touch the basin and disturb the water, she looked directly down into the deep dark blue of the pool, the water as expressionless as night, and whispered, over and over, the true name of her only child.

6

NEWCOMER

 hile Ivan slept, Katerina and her father took a walk up to the hill-fort. The sound of mock combat came from the yard within; because Katerina wanted to talk in privacy, she held back, and her father waited with her outside the gate.

Father knew what she wanted to talk about. "Well?" he asked. "What kind of king will he be?"

"King?" She shook her head ruefully. "He knows nothing of kingliness."

Father smiled slightly and looked off in the distance. "I'm sure you're right."

"Which means that you're not sure," she said, laughing.

"All through the dinner, I thought, the Pretender must be rejoicing to see this awful creature my daughter brought home. And then he saves a stranger from choking."

"And provokes Dimitri—"

"Oh, of course, he does everything wrong, Katerina. But he does have the *heart* of a king. When he sees someone in need, he does not hesitate to act. He does not measure the cost, he does not fear criticism—"

"But if there's anything you taught me, Father, it's that a king *must* measure the cost! And he must act in a way that will be above criticism."

"I did not say that this Ivan has the *mind* of a king. Only that he has the heart."

"What good is the heart without the mind?"

"Better than the mind without the heart," said Father.

"And what good are his personal qualities, if the people will not accept him? Look at him, Father. Who would follow him into battle?"

"You know, this whole idea of hereditary kingship has never sat well with me," said Father. "We always elected our kings, in the old days, to lead us in war."

"Yes, but that law of succession is the only thing holding the Widow back," said Katerina.

"No one would vote for her, either."

"If they feared her enough, they would," said Katerina. "So I have to succeed you, and my husband will be king, and I gave my word to Ivan, and he to me."

"We can fight the Widow," said Father. "Choose another man. I'm sorry for this good-hearted boy, and grateful to him for saving you from the Widow's curse, but choose another husband and we'll fight. Our men are courageous."

"One man with courage is no match for ten men with blood lust upon them."

"God will fight with us against the powers of darkness. He fought for Constantine, didn't he? 'In this sign, you will conquer!' "

"Maybe that story is true, and maybe it isn't."

Father looked at her in horror. "Do we not have the word of Father Lukas for it?"

"He wasn't there, Father."

"He wasn't at the resurrection, either."

"Father, I'm a Christian and you know it. But the armies of Rome have been defeated many times since they converted to Christianity. Maybe when God has some great purpose, like converting an empire, he gives victory to his followers. But Christians can die. I don't want Taina to be a nation of martyrs."

"So you marry him because that's what the Widow forced us to promise in order to get you back, and then we're so weak, having this man of twigs for a king—did you see his arms? I don't know if he can even *lift* a sword. If he were a tree he'd fall over in the first wind."

"But he has the heart of a king, you said. If there's time enough, can't he learn all the rest?"

"So you like him," said Father.

"He freed me. You didn't see the bear. He was the god of bears, I swear it, Father. Terrifying. But Ivan faced him. Stayed with me and didn't attempt to flee even as the bear climbed the pedestal. Did what I asked him to do to save us."

"Obedience is not a quality of kings."

"He did what was needed. In the moment of danger. Afterward . . . I don't know, perhaps he really does come from a land where everything is crazy and the sun shines at night. But if the people would follow him, I don't think he would disappoint them. Especially if he has time to learn."

"But he may not have time. And they may not follow him."

"They *would* not follow him," said Katerina. "Not now. Not yet."

"Maybe this is the man God brought us," said King Matfei. "In my heart I want to have faith. Father Lukas says that Christ said that God works through the weak things of the world to achieve his great purposes. But can I bet on this boy Ivan, when my people's lives are at stake?"

"More to the point," said Katerina, "do we have any other choice?"

"If only *you* could lead them in battle."

"Do you think I haven't thought of that, Father? But I am no soldier. I can govern, I can hold the kingdom together and give justice to the people, but who would follow *me* into battle?"

"Put Dimitri in charge, in your name—"

"Then Dimitri would be king," said Katerina. "The king is the war leader. The war leader is the king."

"Not if you're the one giving them the orders. Making the plans. You will be the king, Katerina, even though you can't lead them into the fray."

"No, Father. They have to see the king putting his life at risk, fighting alongside them. They have to see the king's arm fall upon the enemy and rise up soaked in blood and gore. There's no escaping that. You're a man of peace—you would have turned away from battle if you could. But you did what your kingdom required."

"Katerina, you're smarter than ten sons. You're right, though. You can't lead men into battle. You will stay home and have babies—lots of them, mostly sons, so our kingdom will never be left without a male heir again!"

"Ivan's sons," said Katerina.

"*Your* sons," said Father. "Maybe we'll be lucky. Maybe he'll marry you, get you pregnant with a boy, then take sick and die."

Katerina gripped her father's arm. "How can you say such a

thing?" she whispered harshly. "It's the sin of David, to wish for the death of a loyal man."

"Get Father Lukas to read you the story again, Katerina."

"I can read it myself."

"King David's sin wasn't wishing, it was *doing*."

"Would you wish my child fatherless?"

"I would raise the baby as my own, if this Ivan were to die. But have no fear—the Pretender will probably use every spell she knows to keep him healthy. He's too useful to her and too destructive of all our hopes for her to let him come to harm."

"Don't despise him, Father," she said. "*Teach* him. Make a man of him."

"Of course I'll teach him," he said impatiently. "And I don't despise him, I told you that. I admire his heart. But those weak arms—what were his parents thinking?"

"I think they were raising him to be a cleric."

"Good for them. They should have taught him that when clerics see princesses lying enchanted in a place of power, with a huge bear as guardian, they should go away and let her be until a *real* man arrives to have a go at the task!"

"He *is* a real man, Father. In his heart."

Father put his arm around her, held her close. "Who am I to stand in the way of love?"

Katerina grimaced. Father kissed her forehead, then led her into the fort. In the yard, some of the older men were training boys with wooden practice swords. Katerina came up beside her father and added a parting shot to their argument. "If they can teach boys, they can teach Ivan."

Father rolled his eyes, but she knew he would try to make this betrothal work. He would do it because that was the only hope for the kingdom.

At the verge of the forest, Nadya was returning to her hut to get back to her weaving—so much work left to do, and never enough time, now that the days were getting so short. She had tried weaving in the dark, once, but nobody would have worn the cloth that resulted, so she pulled it out and did it over and never tried such a mad experiment again. Everything had to be done in the precious hours of daylight. Everything except make babies. Another reason to get done with her work as early as she could. Even though all but one of their babies had died after only a few days, it didn't stop her husband from trying. And with each pregnancy, Nadya had new hope.

But she was getting on in years now. More than thirty years old, and her body wearied of more pregnancies. Their only living child, a son, was a cripple, deformed from birth and then the same leg injured in childhood, so what was already withered became even more twisted and stumpy. Others muttered sometimes that there was a curse on Nadya and her family, but Nadya paid them no mind. She did no harm to anyone—who would put a curse on her? She did not want to start thinking of her neighbors that way.

Not even the strange little old lady who stood leaning against the wall of Nadya's hut. She came in from some distant, lonely forest hut. Nadya always shared food with her and treated her civilly, because you never knew who had the power to curse and because if her husband died before her, Nadya herself might be left on her own, hungry and alone, since her only living child was not likely to earn much bread— still less any to share with her, since her boy had given himself to the Christians and spent all his time with Father Lukas.

"Good evening to you," said Nadya.

"New and news!" cackled the crone.

"You have tales from abroad?" asked Nadya. "Come in, and I'll give you bread and cheese."

The old woman followed her into her hut. "News from Taina!" said the old lady. "The princess is back!"

"I know it," said Nadya. "I was there in the village when she returned with that naked fellow."

The old lady sniffed, clearly offended that Nadya didn't need her gossip.

"But I'm sure you know more about it than I do," said Nadya.

The old lady softened. She took a bite of dry black bread with a nibble of cheese. "I hope you have a bit of mead to keep my throat open."

Nadya handed her a pot of mead. The old lady quaffed it off like a man, then giggled in a way that made Nadya think of some chattering animal.

"He's not *much* of a fellow, this man she brought back to marry," said the old lady.

"He saved her from the Widow's evil trap. Isn't that enough?"

"You think so?" asked the old lady. "You really think that's *all* that matters?"

"He saved Lybed, too, they say. Though Dimitri beat him for it afterward. Isn't that a mean trick?"

The old lady smiled mysteriously. "He might have deserved the beating after all. For another reason."

"Why? What do you know about him?"

"I know he was wearing *this*," said the old lady. She reached into her bag and pulled out a tattered, stained hoose. Nadya recognized it at once as being of fine weave, with a delicate pattern woven into it. Her own work. She had given this hoose as a gift to the princess, and Katerina had been wearing it when she pricked her finger on the spindle and was carried away in her sleep.

"*He* wore it?"

"He demanded it from her. So he wouldn't get scratched up walking through the forest. But the cloth had no comfort for him—see how the fabric tore to let the branches through so they could scratch him anyway? That's why he cast it away. Because a Christian woman's clothing will not bear the insult."

"But—he put it on? He *dressed* in it?"

"Ask him. Ask Katerina if he had this girded about his loins, playing at being a girl. Ask them both, and see if they tell you the truth."

"How do you know this?"

"Didn't they walk right past me, not seeing me, overlooking me as folks always do?"

"*I* don't," Nadya reminded her.

"He cast it away, and I picked it up and brought it here. Because I think the people of Taina should know what kind of wickedness is in the heart of the man who thinks he can marry the dear princess."

"But . . . she wouldn't marry him if he were that kind of man," said Nadya.

"She would, if she thought that's what it took to keep Taina free of the great and powerful Pretender."

"May I—may I keep this? To show?"

"Go ahead," said the old woman. "I have no use for it." Her supper finished, she arose to go. "But I fear the vengeance of this stranger, if it's known who told his secret."

"I don't fear him," said Nadya. "He doesn't look strong enough to lead a dog on a leash."

"You're a brave one indeed," said the old lady. "You think that because you're virtuous and kind, and your son is a priest, and your husband a—"

"Sergei's only a scribe, not a priest," Nadya said.

"As if it matters."

"You were saying?"

"I was just telling you that you're not as safe as you think," said the old lady. "There are some people so malicious, so delighted in evildoing, that even when you treat them kindly, they answer with a curse."

"I hope I never meet such a wicked person." But Nadya entertained a moment's concern that perhaps the old lady was telling a secret about herself. Could this woman possibly have been the cause of the death of each of her babies? Of Sergei's crooked leg? Of the fall from a tree that ruined it further?

She searched her visitor's face. The old lady looked back at her, unblinking, bearing her gaze, showing no sign of guilt or shame—nor of malice or triumph. Only a look of genuine concern. Impossible to imagine that this woman had ever done her harm. It was wicked of Nadya even to have entertained the thought.

Nadya held up the tattered hoose. "Is it wrong of me to tell of this?"

"I don't know what's wrong or right," said the old lady. "The princess seems not to mind. But what of the men who might follow this . . . person into battle? Will God fight on their side, with such a man as king?"

Nadya thought of her husband. Of the vicious combat that stopped Baba Yaga's army when they first attacked. How defeat looked certain, until King Matfei cried out for his men to have courage, and then plunged headlong into the thick of the battle, beating down every sword raised against him. They could not let such a king risk his life for them, not without companions fighting with equal fervor at his side. It was the king who gave them heart.

What heart would this stranger give to anyone? How many lives would be lost, with him at the front of battle? God forbid there should ever be another war, of course, but if the choice was between war now, while Matfei still ruled, or war later, when this weakling was on the throne, better to fight it now. Let there be no marriage, and let Baba Yaga come in claiming to rule by right; the swords of the men of Taina, led by King Matfei, would show them what Baba Yaga's claims were worth.

"I might tell Father Lukas," said Nadya. "I might show this to my son."

"Might?"

If she did tell, Nadya knew, it would break Matfei's heart, and would shame Katerina. After all, if the princess chose not to tell it, then there must be good reason, mustn't there? Who was Nadya, to speak when the great ones kept silent?

"Maybe," said Nadya.

"Well, do what you will with it," said the old lady. "You've always done right by me. I imagine you'll do right by the people of Taina."

"I'll try," said Nadya.

Ivan woke to see a hooded face looming over him. He cried out and shrank into a corner of his bedstead. Almost at once, though, he realized that his visitor was a young priest. Or monk. Or something.

"Father Lukas?" asked Ivan.

"What?" answered the man.

Ivan realized that he had spoken in Russian. But proto-Slavonic wasn't *that* different. "Are you Father Lukas?"

"No," said the man. "I'm Brother Sergei. Not a priest at all."

That would explain his native-sounding speech. "I thought all priests came from Constantinople."

"I couldn't be a fighter or a farmer, not with this leg." Sergei lifted his gown to reveal a mismatched pair of legs, the one normal—or perhaps stronger than normal—and the other wizened, twisted, and several inches shorter. "Father Lukas made me his scribe."

"So you read and write? You have the Greek for that?"

Brother Sergei nodded vigorously. "He taught me the letters. Not Greek though, I can't read *that*."

Can't read Greek? "You mean you read in your own language?"

"Father Lukas taught me the letters."

"What letters? Can you show me?" It was impossible—nobody was writing in Old Church Slavonic, not this far north and west. The Cyrillic alphabet had either just been invented or was about to be, far away at the borders of the Byzantine Empire, and the Glagolitic alphabet was nearly as new and was never that widely used. So what alphabet was Father Lukas teaching?

Brother Sergei collapsed into a sitting position and began to write with his finger on the earthen floor. Impossible as it was, Ivan recognized the figures immediately as the earliest known form of the Cyrillic alphabet.

"A man named Kirill invented those letters," Ivan said.

"I know," said Sergei. "Father Lukas was his scribe." Sergei grinned. "I'm the scribe to the scribe of the great missionary Father

Constantine—he only took the name Kirill a little while before he died. Father Lukas says that by serving him as he served Father Constantine, I am only two steps away from holiness."

"Closer than most men, then," said Ivan. But he trembled at the thought: The priest in this place was, or at least claimed to be, personally acquainted with Saint Kirill himself. Which meant that whatever writing was done in this place would be, if Ivan could only take it away from here back to his own time, the oldest Cyrillic writing any man of the twentieth century had ever seen. Not only that, but it was the definitive answer to the historical question of whether it was Kirill himself who invented that alphabet, or his followers who did it after he was dead.

If Ivan could take it back, so many questions could be answered. That was just one more unbearable irony.

"You speak our tongue much better than Father Lukas," said Sergei. "But you still pronounce it funny."

"I grew up speaking a different form of the same language," said Ivan. "Father Lukas grew up speaking Greek."

"So where are you from?"

"Kiev," said Ivan.

Brother Sergei laughed aloud. "I've heard traders from Kiev. They don't talk like that."

"Oh?"

"Most of them are Rus' and speak North-talk anyway, nothing like our language."

"There are a lot of people in Kiev," said Ivan, "and a lot of ways of speaking."

"It must be a wonderful thing, to live in a great city."

"The wonderful thing," said Ivan, "is to be here in Taina."

"Of course it's wonderful to *you*," said Sergei. "You're going to be king."

Ivan grimaced. "Not much of a king. I'm a poor choice for that."

Sergei shrugged. "There's some who say so. Though one never knows who'll be a good ruler until he wears the crown."

"Well, anyone who thinks I shouldn't be king is right."

Sergei got a sick look on his face. "So it's true, then?"

"What's true?"

"About you wearing Katerina's hoose?"

Ivan could hardly believe word of that had already spread. "Does *she* say that?"

"She says nothing," said Sergei. "But an old woman found this tattered hoose and showed it to my mother, and my mother recognized it as one that the princess had worn. She didn't feel right about telling anyone but me, not until you had a chance to deny it or admit it." Sergei laid the stained and tattered remnant of Katerina's hoose on the bed.

Ivan didn't know what to say. A flat lie might be the best course, but for all he knew Katerina was behind the story, telling it to discredit him so she would not be forced to go through with the marriage. It wouldn't do any good to deny the story outright; no one would believe Ivan over Katerina.

"Brother Sergei," said Ivan, "I come from a faraway land. I was born in Kiev, but I lived the past ten years in a place even stranger and farther off. And in that land, when a woman takes off her clothing, then it ceases to be women's clothing or men's clothing, it's just cloth. Whatever a man wears is men's clothing while he's wearing it, and whatever a woman wears is women's clothing while she's wearing it. Do you understand?"

Sergei thought for a moment, then shook his head. "You mean that this is a *man's* hoose?" His tone was scornful.

"I mean that it's nothing but a piece of cloth, stitched in certain ways, and now torn. Though it wasn't torn at all when I last saw it."

Sergei said nothing.

"Sergei," said Ivan, "if I reached out and tore that cross from your neck, that would be theft, wouldn't it? Stealing a cross! What kind of wicked fool would I have to be, to commit such a sin as that?"

Sergei waited, listening but not willing to concede anything.

"But what if I came upon the cross in the forest. Or under a stone. Then to find a cross would be . . . what, wouldn't it be a miracle? A gift from God?"

"Are you saying you found this hoose and didn't know what it was?" asked Sergei.

"I'm saying that if a man doesn't know something's a sin, and does it, and as soon as he finds out it's a sin, he stops doing it, then is he a sinner?"

Sergei leaned back against the timbered wall. "I'll have to think about that," said Brother Sergei. "I'll have to ask Father Lukas."

Ivan leaned down and wrote his own name in the dirt, in Cyrillic characters. Then he wrote: "never wanted to be king."

Sergei studied the writing for a moment. Then he rubbed out the name and wrote his own in its place, and erased "king" and replaced it with the word "scribe." He looked up at Ivan, and when he was sure

Ivan was looking back at him, he touched his own crippled leg. "When the things you want are taken from you, then you do the things that are left for you to do."

"If you tell this story, of my wearing women's clothing, will it change things so I don't have to marry Katerina?"

Sergei shrugged. "If Jesus came tomorrow, would he heal my leg?"

"I think he would," said Ivan, "if he could."

"But I think he's not coming," said Sergei.

So, what did *that* mean? That Sergei wasn't going to tell about the hoose?

"Come with me," said Sergei. "Father Lukas wants to teach you in preparation for your baptism."

Ivan reached down and erased Sergei's name and the word "scribe," and replaced them with "Ivan" and the word "Christian."

Sergei grinned, erased "Ivan" yet again, and again replaced it with his own name. But he let the word "Christian" stand.

Ivan shook his head ruefully. "We don't get to choose the world we live in, do we?" he said to the scribe. Only later did he realize what a stupid thing he had said. For he *had* chosen this world. Not knowing the consequences, it's true, but still he took Katerina's hand and followed her across the invisible bridge to Taina, instead of returning home over the bridge that he alone could see. That was more choice than Sergei ever got. But this young man was making the best of it.

"Will you help me learn what you have learned?" asked Ivan.

"You already read and write," said Sergei. "Though you make some of the letters oddly."

There was no point in explaining further. "Take me to Father Lukas, then." He stood up to leave and only then remembered that his only clothing was the king's cloak. "Except that I'm naked," he said.

Sergei pointed to a pile of cloth at the foot of the bed. "They must have brought it in while you slept."

Ivan pulled the robe of a monk over his head. Not how he would have expected them to dress a future king, or the fiancé of a princess. But just right, if they thought of him as a cleric. Was the clothing an insult? Or merely the only thing they had that they could be sure would fit a man so much taller than any of the others in this place?

Father Lukas's church was not large, but it was solidly built, and there was room enough inside it for at least a hundred villagers—standing, for no space was wasted on benches in Orthodox churches—

and a tiring-room behind and to the right of the altar. There were two old women kneeling before an icon on a side wall, but whether they were praying or whispering to each other Ivan could not begin to guess. Another thick peasant woman was lighting a candle before another icon. She was not the first—the place was aglow with the flames of faith. No sign of Father Lukas.

Brother Sergei motioned for Ivan to wait while he went in search of the priest. No sooner had Sergei disappeared into the tiring-room behind the altar, however, than the thick-bodied peasant woman turned away from the candle she had been lighting, glanced up at Ivan, and immediately ducked her head and hurried away.

Just as she was leaving, a middle-aged priest with a natural tonsure entered the church, noticing her hurry with amusement. Then he saw Ivan, and instead of looking away, the priest surveyed him coolly, looking him up and down as if trying to determine what he weighed. There was no question that he knew immediately exactly who this new parishioner was.

"I understand you're supposed to teach me to be a Christian," said Ivan.

"If it can be done, Christ can do it," said Father Lukas. His accent was very thick. It was hard enough for Ivan to catch all that the native speakers said; Father Lukas butchered the pronunciation enough that Ivan had to think a moment to be sure he had understood. And even when he knew he had parsed everything Father Lukas said, Ivan still wasn't sure what he meant. Was Christ supposed to teach him? Or was he talking about something besides teaching?

Father Lukas drew him toward the tiring-room; just before they got there, Brother Sergei burst through, almost crashing into them before he realized they were there. Sergei apologized profusely as Father Lukas put on an air of patient tolerance. Ivan could almost hear him saying, "These natives. What can you do?" Father Lukas's attitude immediately increased Ivan's sympathy for Brother Sergei, who doubtless had to put up with Lukas's thinly veiled sneer all the time. But it was more than sympathy for Sergei in particular. Seeing Father Lukas look down on the local Slavs made Ivan feel a powerful surge of solidarity with the people of this village. However dirty the place may be, however primitive, it was no more primitive than anywhere else in Europe, except for Constantinople itself, and for all the airs Father Lukas might put on, Ivan knew there was a day when Slavs would put men in space before the people of any other nation. Chew on that one, you decadent Greek.

So quickly does nationalism surface in the heart of a man who thought he was above such tribalism.

"Oh, you found each other," said Brother Sergei.

"Come, sit with us," said Father Lukas. "I might need you to interpret. This future king has trouble understanding my speech, though his own language also sounds rather strange to my ears."

They went in and sat down. Almost at once, Father Lukas opened a book, leaves of vellum bound at one edge between leather-wrapped wooden covers. The handwriting was in the Cyrillic alphabet, not the Greek that Ivan had half-expected.

"A Bible?" asked Ivan. "In this language? Not Greek?"

"The Gospels only," said Father Lukas. "But you are a man of letters, I think? To know which language the book is written in?"

"What year is this?"

Father Lukas seemed not to understand the question.

"Anno Domini?" asked Ivan.

The Latin surprised Lukas even more. But he was willing to try that language. In halting Church Latin the priest asked some question that Ivan could not begin to understand.

"No, no, I don't speak Latin, I only want to know what year it is. Since the birth of Christ."

"Eight hundred and ninety years have passed since the birth of the Blessed Savior," said Father Lukas.

A book of the Gospels written in Old Church Slavonic before 900 C.E. Ivan wanted to kiss the book. He walked to the table where it lay and gently, carefully turned the leaves. He read it easily enough, despite the lack of punctuation and the early form of the letters. So many speculations and hypotheses about the orthography and the grammar of Old Slavonic were answered by this precious book; nothing this early had survived to Ivan's own time.

"So Saint Kirill died only twenty-one years ago?"

"And his brother Methodius five years ago," said Father Lukas. "But you are too young to have known Father Kirill—Father Constantine, as I knew him." Then he realized what Ivan had actually said. "*Saint* Kirill? You presume what no man knows yet."

Ivan waved off the temporal faux pas. Of course Saint Kirill had not been canonized yet, but from what Sergei had said earlier, Father Lukas revered the missionary to the Slavs. "You were his scribe?"

"Only in the last year of his life," said Father Lukas. "I served Father Methodius for five years after that, and then was sent forth on my own mission among these people. Father Methodius gave me this copy of the Gospels. It was the one that Father Kirill made for him with his own hand, the last copywork he did before he died."

"Not Father Kirill's first copy, then."

"Of course not," said Father Lukas. "That was long since given to the Patriarch of Constantinople for safekeeping, so that more copies could be made from it, endlessly."

So it had been in safekeeping in the Hagia Sophia—no doubt until it was taken by the Turks in 1453.

"But this was copied from it? In Father Kirill's own hand?"

"Part of it," said Father Lukas, smiling a little sheepishly at the near-deception he had almost practiced. "I should have said that from the start. He gave it to Father Methodius to finish. I think half of Saint Mark and all of Saint John are actually in the brother's hand. I served them both well. That is why I was given this precious book."

Ivan thought, uncharitably, that perhaps Father Lukas protested too much. That perhaps after he left on his own missionary journey, Father Methodius spent the rest of his life wondering what in the world ever happened to that book of the Gospels that Constantine and he had copied out.

What has happened to me? Ivan wondered. Because I dislike his attitude toward Sergei, though it is hardly a surprise given the time and place, I immediately assume him capable of all sorts of perfidy. Why shouldn't the book have been a gift?

Ivan began to read on the page where the book had chanced to open. "Whoever says to his brother, I will kill you, is in danger of judgment, and whoever says, Thou fool, is in danger of hellfire."

Brother Sergei gasped in admiration. "Father Lukas, he is already a Christian."

"Being able to read the words of Christ doesn't make one a believer in the Word," said Father Lukas. There was scorn in his voice; or at least Ivan thought he heard scorn.

"Brother Sergei has never known a man who could read and write who was *not* Christian," said Ivan. "So his mistake is understandable."

Ignoring Ivan's defense of the scribe, Father Lukas looked at him shrewdly. "How many of us are there who know this alphabet?" he asked. "How did you learn it?"

"My father taught me," said Ivan. Though, when he thought about it, it was much more likely that his mother had given him his letters. He had entered school already able to read and write, and had no conscious memory of ever learning; but it was impossible to believe that his father would have had the patience to teach a toddler to read and write. Never mind; it would be hard enough for them to believe he learned from his father, let alone from a woman.

"Who is your father, then? He has to have learned it from someone I know."

Why evade, when his answer cannot possibly be checked anyway? "Piotr Smetski."

"His *name* is Piotr?" Father Lukas leapt to the obvious conclusion. "So he was baptized Christian, and took that name upon him. And yet you are a Jew."

"Whatever I am, I'm here now, to be taught by you," said Ivan.

"And what do you expect me to teach you?"

"How to be a Christian. So I can be baptized and marry Princess Katerina so that Taina can be saved from Ba—from the Widow. I think that's the whole story, isn't it?"

"That is not a reason to become a Christian. It is only a reason to go through the empty forms of conversion, with greed in your heart, lust in your loins, and a lie on your lips." Father Lukas leaned close. "I can't stop a man from lying to God, but I can at least make sure he has every chance to be telling the truth when he confesses the name of Christ."

"So this won't be quick and easy," said Ivan.

"The only books written in this barbarian tongue are the Gospels and liturgy," said Father Lukas. "Therefore you must have learned to read from the words of the evangelists, and yet they were not sufficient to convert you. What can I say more, that they have not said?"

"And how do you know that I was not converted?" asked Ivan, getting peeved at the thought of having to go through an exceptionally rigorous course of study in the Orthodox version of Christianity. He hadn't even decided he was going to accept conversion in the first place. Though a sophistry had already arisen in his mind to excuse it. Since he wasn't circumcised until the 1970s, and he would be baptized in the 890s, clearly his circumcision took place *after* his supposed baptism. Therefore whatever rite he went through here to become a Christian would be obliterated nearly eleven centuries later. So it was as if he never converted at all. Wasn't it?

"Were you converted?" asked Father Lukas.

"As much as Brother Sergei here," said Ivan.

Father Lukas snorted. "Brother Sergei has as much faith in Christ as I have in Brother Sergei."

Suddenly Lukas's disdain for Sergei had to be seen in a new light.

Was it possible Lukas disliked Sergei because of his hypocrisy, and not because of his barbaric culture?

"Brother Sergei has never spoken false to me," said Ivan.

"He takes communion and eats damnation to his soul," said Father Lukas. "Nevertheless, he is the only man the village can spare, and he does read and write well enough, and does passable copywork. So . . . I make use of what God has given me."

"As do we all," said Ivan.

"I don't know why you say these things, Father Lukas," murmured Brother Sergei. "Christ has no stronger follower than me."

After the words escaped Sergei's mouth, they all realized what he had just said—that he, a cripple, was the strongest of Christ's followers. But instead of being offended, Father Lukas merely laughed. "At least your infirmities can be seen on the surface, Brother Sergei," he said. "As can your lack of faith. How many of these women piously pray and confess their sins every day, only to turn around and practice black magic in their own homes, inviting the devil to curse their neighbors and calling on heathen gods like Mikola Mozhaiski to bless them?"

"Old ways are hard to let go of," said Ivan.

"Especially when they work," murmured Sergei.

"What?" demanded Father Lukas.

"May I return now to my work?" said Sergei. "He reads better than either of us. You won't need me to interpret."

"Go, tend to your vegetable garden, or whatever work you have found to do. But make sure I see you at vespers! Do you hear me?"

Brother Sergei nodded, smiled, crossed himself, and left.

Father Lukas sank down onto his stool. Ivan took the other and sat beside him, where both could see the book easily.

"You touched the book with reverence," said Father Lukas. "Is Sergei right? Do you already love Christ?"

"I love this book," said Ivan. "With all my heart."

"Then perhaps the job of converting you is already half done," said Father Lukas. Then he drew a deep breath, as if gathering the courage to say what must next be said. "In confession, someone has spoken of a rumor so foul that I can scarcely believe it, but I must know the truth before I go on. Are you disposed to wearing the clothing of women?"

Ivan sighed. Apparently Sergei's decision to keep silent on the matter hadn't extended to others. How many knew about the damned hoose? It's not like he wore it for more than a few seconds. But he might as well have branded a scarlet letter on his chest.

"I did not dress after the manner of women," said Ivan, "or out of the desire to appear to be a woman. I was cold, and took up what would give me warmth."

"You did not know it was women's clothing, then?" asked Father Lukas sharply.

"I knew, but my thought was that it was nothing but cloth, when a woman wasn't wearing it, and when I put it on, that made it men's clothing, for a man was wearing it."

Father Lukas rolled his eyes. "That's the best you can come up with? Even the Pharisees did better."

"Doesn't the blood of Christ wash away sin?" asked Ivan, struggling to remember the scraps of Christian doctrine he had picked up over the years. "If I sinned, it was only the once, and I'll never do it again. Won't the water of baptism cleanse me?"

"It will," said Father Lukas. But he seemed uneasy. "But once you *are* baptized, you must forgo such things, or the penalty is severe."

"As I told you," said Ivan, "I did as Adam and Eve did, when they covered their nakedness."

"A hoose is not a fig leaf."

"Both hoose and fig leaf were the nearest things at hand, to cover a man who was ashamed to be naked."

"Very well," said Father Lukas. "I see that you are a man torn between humble repentance and a desire to justify his sins. The former man must be encouraged, the latter one smothered to death as quickly as possible."

Ivan didn't like the imagery, but beggars couldn't be choosers. "First, though, may I ask you a question?"

Father Lukas waited.

"Do you believe in the power of the Widow?"

"You mean Baba Yaga? Oh, don't be surprised. There is nothing to fear from speaking the name of a witch in the house of God."

"But outside this church, you do believe she has power?"

"I've seen her soldiers in action. I've seen the tortured bodies of some she's punished. Oh, yes, she has power—the power of the jackal, to tear and kill and devour."

"I spoke of the power to enchant Princess Katerina, and leave her guarded by a huge bear for a thousand years."

"It was only a few months," said Father Lukas, "and I have no idea where Baba Yaga might have hidden her, or what poisons might have been used to keep her asleep. As for magic, if Baba Yaga has enlisted the devil into her cause, she will find that Christ is more than a match for him, and he will betray her at the final moment, as he betrays all who trust in him."

From this speech Ivan decided that Father Lukas wouldn't be a good one to trust with the truth about his problems. He didn't want to imagine what would have happened had he faced the bear armed with a cross instead of a large stone or Katerina's quick-witted fulfillment of the terms of the enchantment.

Too bad. But at least, in studying with the priest, Ivan would have a chance to get his hands on the oldest Cyrillic manuscript that anyone in the twentieth century had ever seen. In fact, anything that Ivan wrote while he was here, if it survived, would automatically be the oldest surviving Cyrillic manuscript.

Ivan imagined writing an account of his life here, using local inks and parchment, and hiding it up for future generations to find. What consternation it would cause, to have such an obvious modern forgery that was undeniably written on ancient parchment, which could be carbon-dated to the ninth century.

Consternation? It would be a disaster. Even if someone else saw Ivan writing in the modern, fully developed Cyrillic alphabet and changed the shape of their letters even slightly to adapt to his style, it would falsify the archaeological record and make nonsense out of scholarship forever. With a sinking feeling Ivan realized that the one thing he could never do while he was here in Taina was write with his own hand.

"What is it, my son? I saw your face filled with pain."

"It was my keen awareness of the awfulness of my sins."

Lukas searched his face. "Are you converted so quickly?"

"To know my sin is not the same as being converted," said Ivan. "Do those who suffer the torments of hell not know their sin? And yet the atonement of Christ has no power over them, because they rejected the works of righteousness."

How easily the words came to his lips. He wasn't sure if he was aping the radio and television preachings of Protestants or dredging up some half-remembered morsel of the rumors of Orthodox preaching that one could learn here and there in a Kievan neighborhood. Or was it some question on *Jeopardy*? Whatever the source of his Christian theology, translated into Old Church Slavonic it apparently sounded convincing enough to Father Lukas. Ivan thought that "works of righteousness" was a nice touch, because in European history in high school he remembered that the Protestants were big on grace, the Catholics on works, and presumably the Orthodox were in the works camp, too.

Why had he dodged the seminars dealing with the Church in Russia? Irrelevant, he had thought at the time. The Church was the influence that had made the chronicles of early Russian history so utterly useless, as every chronicler twisted the record to make it seem that Orthodoxy had prevailed at every point. Now he was going to have a crash course in Christianity whether he liked it or not, ending with baptism. The Orthodox didn't do it by immersion, did they? No, surely they were sprinklers.

If only he could get home again, he'd never have second thoughts about marrying Ruth again. The hoops she made him jump through were nothing compared to this.

And yet . . . he remembered Katerina's beauty as she lay asleep on the pedestal. And again, later, when she entered Taina with a bold, regal bearing. None of this highfalutin royal-wave nonsense like the Queen of England, dignified and aloof. No, she was a princess who knew her people and strode among them without pretense, the first among equals. Not like a politician, desperate to be liked, either. She was as untainted by pleading as by arrogance. She was a formidable woman, and he was supposed to get a baby into her as quickly as possible. It was an intimidating thought. But not an entirely unpleasant one.

That is, as long as he had no choice anyway. And as long as he could stay persuaded that he wasn't being false to Ruth, any more than he was being false to Judaism. It still felt like sophistry to him, to claim that his engagement to Ruth was a thousand years in the future.

"Your mind wanders," said Father Lukas.

"I'm tired from the journey," said Ivan.

"Then tomorrow we'll meet again."

Do we have to?

Ivan wisely kept the thought to himself. But then he thought of a way that perhaps he could avoid spending so much time in Father Lukas's company. "I hate to keep you from your ministry," said Ivan. "Perhaps if Brother Sergei could teach me the basics, and then I could come to you for examination."

"Sergei?" asked Lukas with obvious distaste. "Shall the blind lead the blind?"

"May a man, coming out of darkness, not spend a moment blinking until he is able to bear the light of the sun?"

"I have only the vaguest notion of what you mean, and even that vague notion smacks of Plato rather than Saint Paul. Nevertheless, since Brother Sergei performs his work at best sloppily and at worst not at all, I doubt you would be doing the work of the Church serious injury if you took him from his duties."

"You are very kind, sir."

"Call me Father," said Lukas.

"Father," said Ivan.

Esther saw her son in the still water. His was the only face the water could have shown her, for what other living person was linked to her by blood and love? My Itzak, my Vanya, what is happening to you?

He was dressed in the robe of a medieval monk, and behind him loomed the figure of an old man in priests' garb. Vanya moved his lips. In Russian he said the word *Father*.

Then an owl flew over the water, inches from her face. Such was Esther's concentration that she did not move, did not screech, though the startlement made her heart race. Nevertheless, the flapping of the owl's wings caused a momentary breeze over the water, rippling the surface. The image disappeared.

She wanted to weep in fury that his face was gone.

In a moment, though, she calmed herself. No need for anger. She knew that he was alive. Wasn't that the purpose of her search? He was not in this world, but he was in some world, and if he was in the hands of Christians, at least it did not seem he was being mistreated. And he was asking for his father. Almost as if he knew someone was watching him, and he wished to speak. She would look again tomorrow night.

7

CONSPIRACIES

ing Matfei had wished more than once that his father had not happened to be king when the edict came out of Kiev that from now on only a son of a king, or a grandson through a daughter, could inherit a throne among the East Slavs. He and his father knew this law for what it was, a means for the king of the Rus' to steal the thrones of their neighbors, one by one. They were patient, these Rus'. They had come out of the north, blond men with goods to sell and savage punishment to mete out on those who would not let them travel, buy, and sell as they would. Where the Rus' traded, they settled; where they settled, before long they ruled. And now they would wait, generation after generation, for a king to be childless or daughtered, and there they would be, ready to pounce, ready to claim that the high king of Kiev had the right to appoint a new king—invariably a kinsman of his own—or to succeed to the throne himself.

Matfei's father had been elected to lead his people in war, as kings always were in the old days among the Slavs. If someone else had been king when the law changed, then Matfei probably would *not* have been elected. Too many other men in Taina were stronger, bolder, wiser. When the new law made him king without election, at first he feared resentment. But the people had been oddly quiescent about the change. As if they were rather proud of having a hereditary king instead of an elected one. Then Father Lukas came along, proclaiming that God chose which men would be born to kings and which to peasants, and therefore it was God who made men kings, giving each king exactly the sons—or the lack of sons—that he deserved. Thus the matter was settled.

Or would have been, had Matfei's sons not died in infancy. Murdered, some claimed, through sorcery. But Matfei had seen their weak bodies, how small they were: one that turned blue and died, having never breathed; one with a twisted spine. Maybe they were killed by sorcery. Or maybe they were just born weak or deformed. Matfei didn't understand such things. It seemed to him that much of what was called sorcery was merely the working of nature. A cow died—did anyone think that cows would live forever?—yet the whispers invariably arose about some old woman gone simple with age who mumbled something that might have been a curse, or some jealous neighbor who might hold a grudge. And so there arose stories about his sons. Nothing was proved.

Though with Baba Yaga as an enemy, the rumors were not hard to believe. Ill things happened before she married King Brat and came to Kiev to infect the world with her malice. She could not be blamed for every bad thing that came along since Brat lost his kingdom and she ended up in Pryava, so perilously close to Taina. But once Baba Yaga had set her heart on getting Taina, the bad things that happened were dire indeed. The failure of the copper mine. Two years of drought. And then his daughter, ensorceled and spirited away, hidden from all eyes until she came home with . . .

If Matfei hadn't been king, he wouldn't be standing here now in the practice yard of the fortress, watching this long-limbed stranger make an ass of himself with sword and broadaxe alike, knowing that he was appointed by some cruel fate—or merciless enemy—to be the father of Matfei's grandchildren and the leader of his people in war.

O Jesus, what did I do to offend thee, that thou breathedst life into this pile of twigs and sentest it to me as a man? Mikola Mozhaiski, have you no better care for your land than this, to shame us before our enemies like this? Are the Slavic people so poor in the eyes of all the gods that they are not to be given the power to rule over themselves, but must have foreigners rule over them? Must all the old laws be done away? Must the trickery and nastiness of women become the power of this land, instead of the forthright strength of men?

And yet . . . it could be worse. At least the boy had a king's heart and felt responsibility keenly. Bad as he was at it, he *was* trying to learn to use these weapons. He would no doubt do his best. His pathetic, useless, doomed best.

He dressed in women's clothing without a second thought, and said that this was common in the land he came from. And this is what must be the father of my grandsons? Ah, Mikola Mozhaiski, my vanished friend. O Jesus, whom I have chosen as Savior of my people. And thou as well, Holy Mother, whose womb held and nurtured God. Why must I like him, this stranger whose very existence now endangers my people?

Dimitri Pavlovich, obedient to Matfei's request that he put aside his anger, was trying to teach Ivan how to absorb a broadaxe blow with his shield and twist the weapon out of the enemy's hands. But Ivan would have none of it. He kept leaping backward, dodging the axe entirely, then whacking Dimitri on the back with his practice sword. Oh, how clever it seemed to Ivan, this dancing. But what Ivan did not understand, could not grasp in his feeble foreign mind, was that in battle there would be a man to the left and right of his enemy, who would see the sudden gap in the line as Ivan leapt back, and he would never have a chance to leap forward again to make his clever blow. Instead, he would have to retreat farther yet, and if the men to either side of him did not fight his battle for him, soon the enemy would come pouring through the gap, and the day would be lost. A man had to stand his ground, giving no inch to the enemy, bearing his blows and striking back harder, forcing the other man to give way. This seemed beyond Ivan's comprehension.

Was this how Jesus Christ rewarded Matfei for letting Father Lukas set up his church and baptize all who wanted? For changing his own name to a Christian one? What kind of god was Jesus Christ, after all? A god who let himself be crucified, and his leading followers stoned to death or burned or crucified. And all those dead and tortured saints. It did not bode well for the future of his followers.

Crucifixion would look merciful compared to what Baba Yaga did to those who opposed her. Hadn't they seen it when, newly widowed, she had the leading men of the Drevlianians impaled or flayed alive as her way of answering their king's marriage proposal? The one survivor, blinded and castrated, was sent back to report what his eyes had last seen, and to give his own genitals to King Mal in a little box as her answer to his words of love. What would she do to Matfei's people when, with Ivan as the war leader, her troops easily overpowered them?

Something had to happen to free them of this burden. Some miraculous deliverance. For instance, Ivan's glorious martyrdom for the sake of Christ. Provided that he had first fathered a son on Katerina.

That was the most important matter. That Katerina be filled with a son, so the succession would be secure and Baba Yaga would lose her legal pretext. After that, Ivan would be quite expendable.

Not that Matfei would do anything himself to harm the man who would be, after all, his son-in-law. What kind of monster was he, even to think of such a thing? God forgive me, he murmured to himself. It is for thee alone, in thy infinite mercy, to deliver us from this burden.

Finally, Ivan understood the instructions and tried to stand his ground. But when Dimitri's blow landed on the twig-man's shield, it knocked him down, shield and all. In his fury at the man's utter inability, Dimitri took a step forward to offer the killing blow, though of course he would make it fall to the side. But Ivan chose that moment to bring his booted foot up under Dimitri's kilt and into his crotch, causing him to fall writhing on the ground.

Matfei jumped to his feet, roaring. "It's a practice, you bone-headed fool!"

"Tell him that!" cried Ivan. "He was about to kill me!"

"It's a practice axe!" shouted Matfei. "It has no edge!"

"It's heavy! It would have crushed my head!"

"He wasn't going to hit you!"

"How was I supposed to know that?"

"Because he's a true knight and you're betrothed to the princess! That's why! Now look at what you've done."

"Isn't that what I should do to an enemy?"

"An enemy will be wearing a solid steel plate with a point, to catch and impale the shin of any man who tries such a maneuver in battle. What, you think you're the first to come up with the idea of kicking a man in the groin?"

"Nobody told me," said Ivan.

"Why should I have to tell you? Do you think your enemy is going to be as stupid as you?"

"You all grew up fighting and talking about fighting. In my homeland we used none of these things."

"Your homeland must be a nation of women!" cried Matfei.

Only after saying it did he realize that, apart from his voice, there was no sound on the practice field. Everyone had stopped to hear the argument. And now these words, this deadly insult, had shamed Ivan in front of all the men and given credence to the rumors that had been flying for the past week, about how readily Ivan had put on women's clothes. Rumors that Katerina had reluctantly confirmed to King Matfei in private.

"One soldier of my land," said Ivan icily, "could kill every man here in five minutes or less."

Keeping his voice down, Matfei nevertheless could not leave such an empty boast unanswered. "Then why don't you show us this amazing process?"

"Our soldiers use weapons that you don't have."

"Make one for us! Or show us how it's made, and we'll make our own!"

"It takes better iron than you have. No smith could make it here."

"Easy to brag about what you cannot show us."

"Easy for you to shame a man who comes from another land, with different customs. If you came to my land, you would be as unskilled as I am, in the things that matter to my people."

"Perhaps that's so," said Matfei, keeping his voice low but unable to hide the fury he felt. "But I am not in your land. You are in mine. You are engaged to my daughter. My people need you to lead them into war."

"I agree with Dimitri—I'll never make a soldier," said Ivan. "As for your daughter, I release her from—"

Matfei punched him in the mouth before he could utter the words that would have opened the door for Baba Yaga to come in. Ivan staggered backward, holding his face. Blood poured from his nose and his lip, which had torn against his teeth.

"What did you do that for?" the boy asked, gasping.

"Are you a fool?" said Matfei. "If you break off this engagement, then all is lost!"

"All of what is lost?" asked Ivan. "All my blood? How's that for a beginning?"

"Are you such a coward and a weakling?" Making no effort to hide his scorn, King Matfei turned to help Dimitri rise from the ground. Dimitri leaned on Matfei's shoulder and limped gingerly to a grassy place where he could lie down to recover.

"Father Matfei," said Dimitri—for he had earned the right in battle to address his king so familiarly—"I have borne many things for you, and will bear anything you ask, but I cannot teach this fool."

"For God's sake, try," whispered Matfei.

Dimitri spoke more quietly. "He goes to it with a will, but he hasn't the strength in him. Everyone has seen how badly he fights. No one would follow him."

"For *my* sake, try," said Matfei. He helped Dimitri stretch out on the grass. Their heads were very close together.

"You should have let me marry her," whispered Dimitri.

"The Widow's curse—"

"Hang the old bitch," said Dimitri. "If the people chose, they'd choose me."

"We face a witch," said Matfei. "She has powers your sword can't fight. Maybe God sent this boy to us for a reason."

"What can he possibly do that we can't do better? He knows nothing. He can do nothing."

How could Matfei argue with him? All he had was a faint hope—hope in a miracle. "Maybe we'll be lucky," said Matfei, speaking the thought that had crossed his mind earlier. "Maybe this boy will father a child and die."

He spoke wryly, meaning it as a joke. But the moment the words passed his lips, Matfei knew he had crossed a chasm, and there was no turning back. For Dimitri had heard the king speak of Ivan's death as a desirable thing and even name the time when it would be most convenient for it to occur. No matter how Matfei might protest in the future that he never meant it, he could not have found a clearer way to sentence young Ivan to death. If not Dimitri himself, some other man would find a way to rid the kingdom of this interloper. And his blood would be on Matfei's hands.

"I didn't mean it," Matfei said, knowing that Dimitri would not believe him.

"I know you were joking," said Dimitri. But it was in his eyes that he did not take it as a joke. "Still, we need an heir, and soon. There are ways to make sure that a child is conceived at once, and that it's a boy."

"And have the baby born ensorceled?" asked Matfei. "We might as well hand the baby over to the Widow herself. I don't want my grandsons to die as my sons did."

"I thought you didn't believe that it was magic killed your boys."

"I believed that seeking vengeance for it would do no good. Nor will killing this young man. He saved my daughter from the witch. He saved your sister."

"And no harm will come to him from me," said Dimitri. "You can be sure that if he dies, it will be an accident."

"An accident that you and I will do all in our power to prevent," said Matfei.

"Our vigilance will be marvelously complete," said Dimitri. "At least until we know the baby is a boy."

Matfei could see now that no matter how sincerely he might plead with Dimitri to spare the stranger's life, he and all the knights of the druzhina would know that Matfei's original reasoning was sound: Only with a child conceived and the father dead would the kingdom be better off than it was before Ivan rescued the princess.

Matfei rose to his feet and returned to where Ivan was whacking futilely against the wooden dummy with his practice axe. Oh, Lord Jesus, what have I done? thought Matfei. The boy has a king's heart. He's trying to learn. God brought him to us. And I have betrayed him and God.

Or have I? My people matter more than this one young man. It was my mouth that asked for him to die, and I am the one who will stand before the judgment bar of Christ to answer for it. Let the sin be on my head. If Jesus damns me for saving the life and freedom of my people at the cost of one life, then I'll damn him back. Let me burn in hell—I'll burn there knowing that I did what my people needed, and that is the duty of a king, however he might pay for it later. I, too, have a king's heart.

I'm no King David, killing a man so he can hide the shame of stealing his wife. When I kill, it is for the good of others.

But I'm still a murderer, Matfei told himself, refusing to hide from what he had done. I have killed with my mouth. There is no mercy in me. What difference now, between me and Baba Yaga?

There *is* a difference, something inside him shouted. Please, Jesus. Please, some god, some wise man, show me what it is.

Sergei didn't like the way people were talking about Ivan. Mother swore that she told no one but Father Lukas in confession, and Sergei knew that Father Lukas never betrayed the secrets he learned that way. Yet the rumor was abroad, that Ivan was a man who dressed in women's clothes. No one quite believed it, or something would have happened already. But no one completely disbelieved the story, either. Not even Sergei.

No, that wasn't so. Sergei knew that Ivan was strange—but it had nothing to do with him prancing around in the princess's hoose, as the old lady had told Mother. Ivan's strangeness was something else. He didn't care about the things that mortal men cared about. With Baba Yaga panting to invade Taina, with a wedding coming up with the beautiful Katerina, with Father Lukas trying to probe his soul, with all of Christianity to learn in a few days, Ivan acted like these things didn't even matter. All he wanted to do was study the manuscripts. And not the Gospels, either. Ivan insisted on studying the working papers, the lexicon that Father Lukas had brought with him, the one written by the hand of Kirill. It was as if Ivan thought Kirill was Christ, as if these papers were a sacred relic. He only touched them by the edges. He refused to let Sergei fold the parchments, or even roll them up. "Store them flat," he said, or tried to say, stammering in his strange language until Sergei finally got what he meant and taught him the right words. He was careful with the Gospels, too. But he wasn't any more careful with them, and they contained the words of Christ. It made no sense.

But nothing about Ivan made sense. When they were supposed to be studying Christian doctrine, Ivan would listen for a few minutes, then begin to ask Sergei to tell stories. And not stories about Jesus and the apostles, either. He wanted stories about witches and sorcerers. About Baba Yaga. About Mikola Mozhaiski. About kings and queens, about lost children and wolves in the woods. Stories that grandparents told to frighten children on winter nights. Stories that mothers told to frighten their children into staying indoors at night, or to keep them from wandering into the woods by day.

And now, in the middle of Sergei's feeble effort to tell him that bad rumors were being spread about him, Ivan interrupts as if he didn't even care, and he says, "I need you to write these down."

"Write what down?"

"These stories. The story you just told me. About Ilya of Murom."

"But . . . these stories aren't true. At least, not in the same way that the Gospels are true."

Ivan shook his head. "But the stories are important. In my land, these stories are different. Changed. Lots of things about Mongols and Cossacks and tsars."

These were words that Sergei didn't understand. Except *tsar*, which was the title of one of the high officials of the Roman Empire, but why would stories about tsars have anything to do with Ilya of Murom?

"So your version of the story, it's older," said Ivan. "It's . . . clean."

"But why write it down? Everybody knows this story."

"Not in my land."

"Then *you* write it down."

"I can't."

"You write faster than I do."

"Sergei, if I write it down, people in my land will think I made it up. But if it's in your hand—"

"Father Lukas says I have a bad hand. He won't let me copy anything on parchment, he says it's a waste of precious lambskin."

"But I say your handwriting is excellent for what I need. Not fine copywork like the Gospels. But a simple telling of the tale. It does need to be parchment, though."

"Where will I get parchment? I have no flock of sheep, and if I did, I'd need the skins for clothing, not for writing."

"If I get you the parchment, you'll write the stories?"

"If Father Lukas lets me."

"He won't let you," said Ivan.

"If you already know that, how can you ask me to do what my priest forbids?"

"He hasn't forbidden it."

"But you said—"

"I haven't asked him."

"Then he might allow me."

"Do you think he would?"

"No."

"Then why ask?"

"You mean . . . keep it secret from him?"

"Yes."

"Lie to him?"

"Has he ever asked you whether you write down the stories of the villagers?"

"No."

"Why would he now?"

"I can't think why he would."

"Then you'll never have to lie to him."

Sergei thought about this. "It doesn't feel honest."

"These aren't Father Lukas's stories," said Ivan. His voice grew intense now, though softer. "These are *your* stories, and the stories of your family, your neighbors, your friends."

"I don't have any friends," said Sergei. "They've never liked me."

"But it's your village."

Sergei shrugged.

"I can tell you, Sergei, that unless you write these stories down, the priests will have it all their way. Only the histories they want to write, and never the true histories, either. Always twisted to make every king look like a Christian, and every defeat look like a victory. Your people will be forgotten. No one will even know there was a land called Taina. But if you write these stories, I can promise you that your land will never be forgotten, these stories will live forever."

"But I'm with the Church now, Ivan," said Sergei. "You can't ask me to oppose the writings of the priests."

"Not *oppose* them, Sergei. What you write won't erase a single word of their chronicles."

"Where would you get parchment?"

Ivan laughed. "I'm betrothed to the princess. Do you think I can't get parchment if I want it?"

Sergei could hardly understand what he meant. "What difference would that make? Being betrothed to the princess?"

"I can ask the king for parchment. He won't deny me."

"But . . . where would he get parchment?"

Ivan looked as if he couldn't comprehend the idea. Yet the words were simple, weren't they?

"He's the king," said Ivan at last.

Sergei couldn't think of what this might mean.

"He can do what he wants," said Ivan, explaining.

"We can all do what we want," said Sergei. "But killing a lamb or a kid and using the skin for parchment—you have to have something very important to write."

"Even the king?"

Now it began to dawn on Sergei what Ivan was assuming. "Oh. In your land, kings can do whatever they want. Like the emperor in Constantinople."

"We don't have kings."

"Then why don't enemies invade your land and take it away?"

Ivan laughed, but there was no mirth in it. "We have armies. We just don't have kings."

"If you have armies," said Sergei, "why are you such a bad soldier?"

Ivan looked surprised.

"Well, *that* can't be kept secret," said Sergei. "Everyone sees how you can hardly swing a sword. How thin you are."

"I was never in the army," said Ivan. "There are many people in my land, and only some of them become soldiers. I was . . . one who reads."

"And that's all?"

"And sometimes I write about what I read."

"So you copy manuscripts?"

"No, I write *about* them. I describe them."

"Why would you do that? If someone can't read the manuscript, how can they read your description of the manuscript?"

"It doesn't matter what I did in my land. I can't go back, can I?"

"Which is why it makes no sense for me to write these stories. You can't take them to your land, so how will they get there?"

"We'll bury them."

"*Bury* them?"

"Bury them very carefully. In a way that will keep them dry. So that someone can dig them up in a thousand years."

"I don't understand anything you say," said Sergei. "Burying a parchment in my land won't get it any closer to yours."

"You'd be surprised."

"Unless your land is underground," said Sergei.

Ivan laughed. "No, Sergei, I'm not from hell."

"Then from where? Heaven?"

"I'm no angel, either."

"I wondered. Your skin is so smooth. You have hands like a baby."

Ivan looked at his hands as if for the first time. "I wish I could fly, though. That would be convenient."

"You're not a saint, either?"

Ivan rolled his eyes.

Sergei realized something, having seen Ivan look at his smooth hands. "You've never even helped with a harvest, have you?"

"No. In my land we . . . we have . . . I don't know the words. But very, very few people help with the harvest."

"It must take them forever to scythe the grain."

"No, no, you see, the scythes run by themselves."

"So you're a sorcerer!"

"No, it's not sorcery at all, it's more like . . . when you pull a cart, you don't have to pull each wheel, you pull the whole cart and the wheels come with it. We just have better carts. They pull themselves."

Sergei had to laugh. "Now you're just lying to me to make fun of me."

"No," said Ivan. "My land is strange, though, compared to here. But another way of looking at it is, Taina is strange to *me*. All the years I was growing up, it never occurred to me that there might come a day when my life might depend on how I handled a broadsword or a battleaxe."

"We're alike, though," said Sergei. "I'm a terrible soldier. All I'm good for is reading and writing. And washing up."

"And I can't even do that."

"You can, though. Write all you want."

"No," said Ivan. "I make my letters wrong."

"I saw you make some letters I'd never seen before. Like this one."

With his finger, Sergei drew the letter Щ on the table. At once Ivan seized his hands and held them tightly.

"Don't ever make that letter again," he said.

"How could I? I don't even know how it sounds."

"Just don't use it. You shouldn't. It would change everything. It would make the record unclean. Forget it. Put it out of your mind."

Sergei nodded his understanding. So . . . he had inadvertently learned a powerful rune from a land of sorcery. He would have to keep this in mind. Someday he might have to use this rune. For despite Ivan's warning, Sergei was not about to forget something that was so dangerous and disturbing. In all his life, Sergei had never known how to do anything that would frighten anyone. It was an interesting feeling. He liked it.

For a while, Katerina was able to fool herself into believing that things were going well—that Ivan was earning the respect of the knights and other men by his hard work on the practice field, and that Ivan's obvious decency and concern for others, as exemplified by saving Lybed from choking, had won the hearts, or at least the patience, of the women of Taina. But gradually she realized that the absence of negative comment about Ivan did not mean there was approval or even tolerance. Instead, it meant that no one was talking to *her* about Ivan. It was a bad sign, not a good one. People had never shut her out before. She had assumed that she could bring him into the community; instead, he might well be dragging her out.

But what point was there in discussing this with Ivan? She couldn't think of a thing he could do more than he was already doing. She knew he didn't want to become a Christian, but he was preparing to do it. She knew he had no interest in being king, let alone soldiering, but he was working hard at it every day. If she told him her fears, it would only discourage him, and she'd have to listen to more insistence that she take him back to the enchanted place and lead him across the bridge so he could go home.

She tried to imagine what it would be like to be in his place, cut off from family, trapped in a situation not of her devising. In fact, that's precisely what had happened to her when she was chased by the bear and ensorceled into sleeping for however many months or centuries it was. But of course she had slept through it, while Ivan had to be awake through his time of estrangement. And her exile had ended with return. Would his?

It was to avoid such a conversation with him that she found herself avoiding any conversation with him apart from dinnertime, when nothing private could be discussed. But this silence between them could not go on forever, she knew; she was not surprised when, one afternoon in her father's house, she heard him in the great room, asking a slave which bedchamber was hers.

The slave was no doubt trying to guess which would cause more trouble, to tell or not to tell, and then would have to decide whether to make trouble or not, which was probably the more difficult decision. Slaves were so untrustworthy. And yet life would be impossible if you had to do all that work yourself. When would she have time to look after the people, if she had to spend her time down at the river, washing clothes, or out in the kitchen, preparing dinner?

Anyway, she spared the slave the burden of making a choice. "In here," she called out to Ivan.

He actually stopped to thank the slave, as if the girl had done anything or even meant to do anything to help him. He was still a stranger, would always be a stranger.

Whatever it was he wanted to talk about, she knew she didn't want to discuss it with him. So she preempted him by leaping to a conclusion she knew was false. "I hope you're not thinking of claiming some privilege of intimacy because we're betrothed."

He did not rise to the bait. "Your purity is safe. I only came to ask how I could get some parchment."

Why would he come to *her* for a parchment? Did he think she had a secret hoard of lambskins and kidskins? "Why would you ask *me*? Father Lukas asks for the skin of a lamb when he needs something to write on. If he doesn't claim the skin, then it's used by others."

"I know that," said Ivan. "Sergei explained that."

"Then why did you come to me?"

"So you could tell me how I could go about getting a parchment. Or tell me who could teach me how to make parchment out of lambskin."

"And why would you waste time on something like that?" It would hardly raise the knights' opinion of him, if he spent hours parching lambskin.

"Because there's something I want to write down."

Was he serious? "Do you have any idea what you're talking about?" she asked.

"I know how to read and write, if that's what you mean."

"You weren't brought here to be a cleric! Father Lukas will find his own young men and teach them. Like Sergei, who has no other usefulness. But you . . . to spend your hours writing or making parchment . . ."

He had been ingratiating up to now, but his temper had apparently been stretched too thin. "What am I supposed to do, then?" he demanded. "Spend all day in the practice field, hearing Dimitri taunt me and watching all the others snicker behind their hands?"

"It takes time, I know."

"It takes years to put on that kind of muscle. I ache all over, and while I'm getting better, I'm a long way from good. It won't hurt anybody if I spend a little time doing things that I'm actually good at."

"But you aren't good at making parchment, if you don't even know how."

"I want to write something."

"Use birchbark. You just peel it off the trees and soak it and press it flat."

"Birchbark doesn't last."

"Neither will you, and neither will Taina, if you don't work at soldiering."

"I know how long it takes to train my body. I've been running all my life, but I was training for the decathlon—"

"The what?"

"A contest. Running, jumping, throwing the . . . spear. The discus. The . . . stone. It took years of training until I was competitive. Someday, a few years from now, I might be good enough with the sword to hold my own with the best of them. But not next week or next month."

"But they have to see you trying. They have to see you getting better at it."

"They refuse to see it," said Ivan. "No matter what I do, they laugh. Fine, that's their privilege. But if you think they're going to respect me more by watching me fail, day after day—"

"You're giving up?"

"I just want to write something down!"

She didn't like him speaking to her with such exasperation. As if she were an unreasonable child. "Don't shout at me."

"And what will you do to punish me? I'm already in hell."

"Taina is the most beautiful place, filled with good people!"

"They may be good to you, but all I get from them is resentment and scorn. I didn't ask to be here. You *demanded* that I stay, for your sake and for theirs. Well, I stayed, and I've tried to do what you asked—no, what you commanded—but now that it's clear that I'm not going to live up to your expectations, let's just agree it was a mistake and let me go home!"

"No," cried Katerina.

Calmly Ivan began removing his clothing.

"What are you doing!" she demanded. "I told you not to expect to claim any marital privileges—"

Ivan stopped. "I don't want *your* body, I want mine. I'm here as a slave, so I'm going to dress like one."

"You're not a slave! You're my fiancé."

"No, I'm sorry, that's simply a lie. A fiancé would be your equal, a man you loved, a man who was going to be your husband. But you don't even speak to me, you avoid me and everyone sees it. I'm shamed after every meal, when you go off and leave without a word to me. I'm not here because you want to marry me, I'm here because I'm the tool you need to hold on to your kingdom. I'm like a milk cow, only I'm not giving enough milk. So what do we call a man who is forced to work against his will at tasks he hates, to benefit someone else while he's treated with contempt by everyone around him? If he's a captive and he can't escape and has no hope of ever getting his freedom? What is he, but a slave?"

"I didn't choose you," said Katerina. "You chose yourself."

"So my mistake was saving you, is that it?" he said softly. "You'd rather have waited another thousand years asleep than be stuck with me, is that it?"

"We could have waited a few months more."

"You should have posted a sign," said Ivan. "Don't fight the bear and kiss the princess unless you're very good with sword and battle-axe. Oh, but wait, a sign would have been useless. The kind of man you want wouldn't know how to read anyway."

He said it with such scorn that she realized: He feels contempt for people who can't read.

"*I* know how to read," she said. "But I haven't yet thought of a way to make the Widow's army disappear by reading them to death."

"In my land, it is Taina that has disappeared. Utterly forgotten, because no one wrote a word about it. I want to write the story of this land, and hide it somewhere that someone will find it in the future, and read it, and know that this land existed, and who you were. I'm trying to save Taina from oblivion."

"You fool!" she said. "We don't want to be remembered! We want to *survive*."

"And I'm no help to you, am I," he said coldly. "So take me back. Let me cross that bridge to my own world."

She could see how miserable his situation was. And how little she had done to make it better. But she could not let him leave. Not yet. "As soon as we're married."

"How can I say this without breaking your heart, Fair Princess? I don't want to marry you."

This was the conversation she had been trying to avoid. These were the words which, if he acted on them, would ruin everything. She flailed about for some way to turn him away from this decision. "If you didn't want to marry me, you shouldn't have asked me."

"There was a bear," he reminded her. "And you told me to ask you."

"You asked me and I said yes. It was an oath. Are you a man of no honor?"

"Ask the knights who mock me, the women who laugh at me behind their hands. I have no honor here for keeping my word."

"A man like you *has* no word to keep," she said.

She regretted the words as soon as she said them. His face closed off, as if he had moved beyond anger. "You know nothing at all about men like me." He turned and left her room.

She wanted to call after him, to say, "There *are* no men like you!" But she would not shout like that in her father's house. Besides, she wasn't even sure what she meant by it. That he was not a man? No. He *was* a man, she knew that, a man to be admired in many ways—just not in the ways that mattered to the people, not when judging a man who might be their king.

What a stupid, miserable way to start a marriage. Where was the respect she owed to her husband? The slaves had heard the argument, and no doubt dozens of others as well. Word would pass through Taina and the people would scorn Ivan even more, for the princess had set the example of showing him disrespect under her father's roof.

Why had she behaved that way? All her life she had cultivated iron self-control, to keep silence when others shouted, to say nothing when others rattled on, to be content with stillness even when no one else was speaking, and all eyes turned to her. But this man provoked her beyond endurance.

And why is that? she wondered. Why does he have such power over me? I should despise him for being a weakling when I needed a kingly man. But instead I'm angry because he doesn't . . . because he doesn't love Taina as much as I do. Because he doesn't want to be king. Because he doesn't want to be my husband.

Because I want him to respect me and love me, and all he wants is to get away from me and my kingdom. The one man in the world who wouldn't like to be married to someone like me, and he's the one God brings to me. A husband who thinks he's being treated like a slave.

And he's right. He's a captive here, and instead of trying to win his heart, his loyalty, I've hidden from him. As a result, I have only his fear and resentment. I've worried because the people are not accepting him as their future king, but *I* haven't accepted him, and he has not accepted me. I've said the words of the promise, but haven't acted as if he were going to be my husband. But *he* has kept *his* word, doing his best to accomplish all the tasks I set for him.

Who is the one without honor?

Dimitri's scorn for Ivan on the practice field and her own disrespectful attitude were surely playing into Baba Yaga's hands. Indeed, *that* was the sort of thing that Baba Yaga loved to do—to sow seeds of discontent and dissension among her enemies, so no one trusted anyone, so people hated those they should follow and clung to those they should hate.

Katerina resolved that she would from this moment forward treat Ivan with respect. Where he was ignorant, she would simply teach him, without letting anyone see her surprise or dismay at what he did not know. And she would do her best to help others see his virtues.

She would talk to Dimitri, too, and persuade him to work more respectfully with Ivan. Though how she would soften that tough old bird, she had no idea. Dimitri had been a figure of awe in her life since her childhood. When her aunts had told her about Baba Yaga's curse, Katerina asked them, "Who will save me from my enchanted sleep?" and Tetka Retiva answered, "The strongest knight," and Tetka Moika said, "The wisest man," and Tetka Tila said, "The purest love." Katerina thought the purest love must have been her mother, who was dead, and the wisest man was her father the king, or perhaps Father Lukas, neither of whom, upon waking her, could wed her.

But the strongest knight, everyone knew, was Dimitri, and so she half-expected to find herself betrothed to him one day. That was the perspective from which she viewed him for many years, each year growing more sure that it would be a very hard thing to have Dimitri as a husband, for he acted bravely, and never delayed for such irrelevancies as thinking through the consequences or wondering if he had the right to decide. She had expected, when the bear chased her to the stone where she lay down weeping, knowing she would sleep either forever or until her future husband awoke her, that if she ever saw another human face again, it would be Dimitri's, bending over her, his lips still cool from the kiss that wakened her, ready to speak the question to which her answer had to be yes.

And in that moment, she had prayed, O Mikola, O Tetka Tila, O Lord Jesus, O Holy Mother, let the purest love awaken me, or the wisest man, but not the strongest knight. Then she realized that she had prayed to Jesus third, not first, and when she spoke to the Holy Mother, it was not so much the Blessed Virgin as her own dead mother to whom she prayed. No doubt this was damnation, and she sank down into sleep, into despair.

Then she awoke, and it was this strange boy bending over her, who was not a knight at all, and not terribly wise either, as far as she could tell. But perhaps his was the purest love.

But she did not have his love. She had only his promise, and that given under duress, and kept reluctantly. Lord Jesus, did I offend thee with my prayer? Forgive me, and let me have the husband who will save Taina from the witch. Even if it is Dimitri. I will do whatever my people need me to do.

And yet this thought also, this prayer at the back of her mind: Art thou not the God of miracles? Then is there not some miracle thou canst bring about to turn this boy Ivan into a knight, and somehow make him wise, and a man, and let him love me?

Ivan sat alone in the tiring-room. Father Lukas was out among the people, doing whatever it is that priests do. Sergei was cleaning out the priest's chamber pot and then washing the priest's clothes, hopefully not in the same water. Ah, how Ivan longed for the twentieth century at times like these. The lush melodies of a flushing toilet—the rush, the swish, the gurgle, the gulp, and then the lingering aftertones, the whispering hiss, and then ... silence! The glorious rhythm of a washing machine with an out-of-balance load, knocking and pounding its way across a laundry-room floor! The bucolic life had lost its charms for him somewhere between the fleas and the itchy woolen clothing.

His little plan to record the stories of the people of Taina had come to nothing, foiled by the simple fact that cheap paper hadn't been invented yet, or at least hadn't yet reached Europe, while the birchbark they used for jotting notes on decayed about as quickly as toilet paper. Ivan wracked his brains to remember how and when papermaking had made its way west from China. Would it be three or four centuries he'd have to wait?

Connecticut Yankee in King Arthur's court, my ass. American

ingenuity amounted to squat in this place. These people needed a very specific kind of man, and he wasn't it. Katerina was beautiful, but she hated him, which didn't bode well for the marriage. And Ivan simply wasn't interested in living the life that this time and place offered.

There must be other men of his temperament here. What did they do? The men who had no wish to do violence. The men who wanted to learn, to know the answers, to solve mysteries. The men who quickly lost interest in any physical activity that didn't let them think their own thoughts.

The men who hadn't yet grown up.

That's what Ivan had to face about himself. The life he had chosen was a cocoon. Surrounded by a web of old manuscripts and scholarly papers, he would achieve tenure, publish frequently, teach a group of carefully selected graduate students, be treated like a celebrity by the handful of people who had the faintest idea who he was, and go to his grave deluded into thinking he had achieved greatness while in fact he had stayed in school all his life. Where was the plunge into the unknown? Where was the man who would stand against all comers to protect his family, his people?

Easy to say that he was lucky enough to live in peaceful times, that he was never called to war. He was called now, wasn't he? And here he was slacking, avoiding practice with the weapons of this time and place. He was stronger than he let them see; finding himself unskilled when he was used to being a contender, resenting their scorn, he had backed off, had stopped trying. Like a kid who would only try when he knew he could win.

It wasn't childish to follow in the footsteps of a distinguished father, was it?

But his father hadn't stayed in the cocoon. Years before anyone guessed that the Soviet Union would collapse, Ivan's father had decided he had to get his family out. So he declared himself a religious man, let them slice him up, lost his home and his job, risked years of deprivation and harassment, and finally won, taking his family to a new land of freedom. But to do it, Father had given up the idea of ever teaching another class in his native tongue, of ever walking the streets of his native city. Afterward the world changed, so some of these things might be possible again—but Father hadn't known it would happen.

Compared to that kind of risk, what am I? I took the leap, yes, but I didn't like the ledge where I landed—I fought the bear, I kissed the princess, but now I don't want to be king. Well, where in the fairy tales did it ever say that Cinderella had to like being queen, or that Jack got to choose whether to marry the king's daughter or whatever it was that happened to him after he killed the dragon or the giant or whatever the hell he did? When Father got the family to Austria, he didn't say, "Never mind, too scary, let's go back."

OK, so Father couldn't turn back. Neither can I. I've got to do it, so maybe I should get my ass in gear and do it for real.

Ivan stood up, closed the book of the Gospels, and set it aside. Then he took the single parchment sheet of the lexicon and turned it over and set it on top of the other pages Father Lukas had been given by Saint Kirill . . .

The lexicon was blank on the other side.

And most of the other sheets also had at least some space on the back. Room for a lot of writing, if it were small enough. Room for Sergei to do all that Ivan wanted him to do.

Except for one small problem. How could Sergei hide it from Father Lukas, if it was written on Father Lukas's own papers?

By dinnertime, Ivan had come up with an answer. As usual, King Matfei listened carefully to the concerns of the boyars before giving the rest of the meal over to the singing of a minstrel slave who had recently been given to him as payment of a debt from another kingdom over the mountains to the west. Ordinarily, Ivan would have listened carefully to the song. But tonight, he leaned to the king and said, "I'm ready to be baptized."

King Matfei raised his eyebrows. "Father Lukas says not."

"Father Lukas judges that I'm not ready to be a priest, and he's right. But am I ready to take the covenant of baptism and confirmation as a Christian? I think so. What more is needed than that I believe in Christ?"

"That's precisely the point on which Father Lukas says you are lacking."

"And I say that I believe well enough for baptism," said Ivan. "Am I a liar, or is he mistaken? I am the only fit judge of what is in my heart, I think."

King Matfei looked off into space, bemused. "A complicated question, now that you put it that way."

"Until I'm married to Katerina," said Ivan, "the kingdom is in danger. What is to stop the Pretender from sending assassins?"

"The high king in Kiev would not allow her to take possession if it were known she had murdered to get the kingdom. More important, though, there are spells that my late wife's sisters added to the curse. If the witch raises a hand against the royal house of Taina, then the curse falls upon the witch herself."

"Until I'm married to Katerina, killing me would not be killing a member of the royal house."

"Then why aren't you already dead?" asked the king, reasonably enough.

"Because she knows what a terrible soldier I am, that no one would follow me into battle. She thinks the marriage would work to her advantage. When I'm discredited completely *and* married to Katerina, she'll be content."

King Matfei looked at him strangely. "*You* say this?"

"I am not going to be a terrible soldier forever. I'm going to work very hard until I *can* wield a sword and be useful in battle."

If King Matfei had an opinion of the likelihood of this ever happening, he kept it to himself.

"If the Widow gets word that I'm improving," Ivan continued, "then it will be in her interest to kill me. I want to be baptized and married. Let's get on with the journey and see where the road takes us."

"Father Lukas won't baptize you until he thinks you're ready."

"I will continue my studies," said Ivan. "In fact, I want to. But let it be here. Let Sergei bring the books and papers into your house and train my mind here, during meals and before bedtime, so I can spend all the daylight hours training my body to be a soldier."

"I'll think about it," said King Matfei.

The next day, Sergei showed up soon after dawn with a dozen parchments and the book of the Gospels in a basket. "Father Lukas is furious," said Sergei. "But your baptism will be day after tomorrow. And here I am, living in the king's house!"

Within moments, Ivan had shown him all the blank spaces on the parchments.

"Write on *these*? The very parchments written by the hand of Kirill?"

"And then we'll seal them all up and hide them to be found in a thousand years," said Ivan.

"You're serious about this," said Sergei.

"It's the second most important thing I'll ever do here in Taina."

"And what's the most important?"

"I have to learn to be a knight, so I can be a king, so I can be a husband." He did not add aloud the most important point: So I can go back home.

BABA YAGA

Yaga found her husband tearing at a human thigh. It was disgusting, the way he let blood drool onto his fur, making a mess of everything. On the other hand, the ligaments and tendons and veins stretched and popped in interesting ways. It made Yaga wish that Bear hadn't disassembled the body. She liked to see how everything connected with everything else. And Bear absolutely refused to eat humans while they were still alive, with the feeble excuse that when they weren't dead they made too much noise and moved around too much. To Yaga, that was just another proof of Bear's laziness. Godhood was assigned to the most unworthy people.

Still, he *was* pleasant company, much of the time, and he was more or less permanent—he was the only male she'd ever slept with that she couldn't kill no matter how much she sometimes wanted to. As a result, he stayed around long enough for them to develop something akin to friendship.

"How are you with the broadsword?" Yaga asked her husband. "Or has losing an eye made it impossible for you?"

"Having no thumb makes it impossible for me." He talked with his mouth full, of course. "I've never needed a sword. I knock swords out of men's hands. I bite off the ends of their spears. I roar at them and they shit themselves and run stinking into the woods."

"This bridegroom of Katerina's—you know, the fellow who put your eye out—he didn't shit himself, did he?"

Bear cocked his head to remember. "He ran."

"But not away. I distinctly recall that he ran around and around until he made you stupid. Oh, wait—you started that way."

"We're not in a good mood today, are we, my love?" said Bear.

"He's practicing with the sword. Doing exercises. Hours a day, till he staggers back to Matfei's squalid little hut of a palace and falls asleep. Lifting bags of stones on a yoke to make his thighs and back stronger, directing the fletchers to make light javelins with hard metal points and teaching the boys to throw them. He might make something like a king out of himself after all. He's becoming a nuisance."

"Poor Baba Yaga." Bear let the bone drop on the floor. Later, one of the servants would pick it up and give it to the cook to add to the stew for the prisoners and slaves. Still, it annoyed Yaga that he was so untidy. And sarcastic, too, as he added a little jab. "I thought you said that telling the people he wore a dress would undo him."

"It will," said Yaga, feeling surly but knowing that the dress thing hadn't worked out quite as she hoped. "It still might. But they seem to have let the rumor wash over them. Maybe they're waiting for him to make some stupid mistake, and then they'll say, We knew it all along, after all, he wore a dress."

"Is Queen Yaga learning a bit about human nature?"

"Bestial nature. They scarcely deserve the name of human."

"I'm sure they feel the same about you."

"*Nobody* thinks of *you* as human."

"To my enormous relief."

"If this unmanly foreigner becomes a real king, then he's lost his usefulness to me."

Bear finally got it through his head what she was asking. "If you think I'm going to go roaring into Taina and bite his head off, think again. I heard what you said about javelins. This fellow aims projectile weapons far too well."

"Are you a coward?"

"I lost an eye for you already. Must I die for you?"

"You can't die, you fool. You're immortal."

"Yes, well, I thought my eye would grow back, too, but it hasn't."

"You've lost faith in yourself! Isn't that rich? A god who has become a self-atheist!"

"You don't even know what it means to be a god. The burden of it."

"You should have remained a weather god like your father. Taking on a totem only subjected you to the pains of mortality. Without even the release of death."

"The whole father-son thing doesn't have the same meaning in my family," said Bear. "We don't breed true. Weather god was never my option. This people didn't need a sky god. They needed a god to keep winter under control. Like any *good* king, we respond to the needs of the people. We become what they need us to be."

She understood the thinly veiled criticism of her own kingship. "Did they need you to be a one-eyed cowardly old fart?" She poured him a dish of mead. "To help settle your meal."

He looked at the dish but didn't lap at it immediately. "I should never have let you seduce me," he said.

"I didn't seduce you, I enchanted you. There's a world of difference."

"Bears have no business marrying women. We're unfaithful by nature."

"But *you* kept your word, you sweet hunk of bear, you."

"Hera let Zeus dally."

"Hera was weak," said Yaga. "She deserved what she got. And in case you're thinking of going about betraying me with other women, I've put a charm on you. Try it and your balls fall off."

"If Hera couldn't do that to Zeus, I doubt you can do it to me. You're not even a goddess."

"Try it and see."

"Don't worry. I'm done with human women."

"Good. Stick to swans and heifers or whatever it was that Zeus had a taste for. Or she-bears. But as far as humans go, you're mine."

"Why this charade of marriage? You only want my power. You don't even think about me except when I come into your room."

"I think about you all the time, my love," she said, pretending to feel hurt.

"I'm not going to go kill that boy, not in the middle of Taina, surrounded by soldiers. He and I will have an accounting about this empty eyesocket of mine, but not now. Certainly not at your behest, my love, since *you're* the one who sent me into that pit to fight with him."

Yaga silently went back to combing her hair. They both knew, of course, that he would do whatever she told him to do, and if he tried to resist, she could make things very uncomfortable for him. A binding is a binding, and the one who is bound is bound. Anything else was just talk. When the time came, when she really meant it, Bear would kill whomever she wanted dead.

Apparently mistaking her silence for patience, Bear went on. "Do you have any idea how sad it is, to see you comb those few scraggly grey hairs of yours as if they were long luscious tresses? I can see your sallow scalp right through it, the hair's so thin. I've seen bald men with more hair."

She sighed. "*I'm* combing thick reddish hair tonight. Sorry if you don't love me enough to see that."

"And your dugs hang down to your knees."

"Only when I'm sitting and leaning forward to see into my mirror."

"I don't have eyes enough to waste them looking at lies."

"Since the truth can never be known," said Yaga, "a wise woman learns to become a connoisseur of lies, choosing only the best and most satisfying to surround herself with. I sink into my lies like feather-beds, and they keep me safe and warm." She got up and danced a little through the room.

"So you plan to kill the boy yourself?" asked Bear. "Won't that cost you any chance for the throne?"

She shrugged and kept on dancing. "I'll find other hands to do it for me. I always do."

She began to sing a melody. The rhythm of it had nothing to do with her twirling steps. Bear lost interest. He lay down on the floor and fell asleep.

"I've *got* to find a faster-acting spell," Yaga murmured. "It took you forever to fall asleep."

Bear opened his one eye. "I didn't take your damn potion," he growled. "The stuff stank so bad I could hardly tell that it was supposed to be mead in the dish. You can't poison a bear, you silly bitch."

"I'll try it again sometime when you have a cold!"

Bear snarled at her and went to sleep again. Or seemed to.

Living with a god is not what it's cracked up to be, thought Yaga. They think their women should be grateful just to have them around.

She looked into her mirror again, but this time she shook into her palm a bit of dust out of a bag made from a ram's scrotum. Then she blew across her hand. The dust flew toward the mirror, then clung to it as if it had been glued there.

"Bring me the sleeping warrior," she whispered to the mirror, careful not to blow any dust from the mirror's surface.

The face of King Matfei appeared in the mirror, shimmering.

"Not the king, the warrior. The mighty Dimitri."

Nothing happened; the mirror went blank.

He must not be asleep, the fool.

Quickly she pulled a small wooden carving of a man's head from a box near her dressing table. She anointed it with a dab of bearfat—

a supply she replenished from time to time without particularly mentioning what it was to her husband—and then whispered the name of Dimitri over it, naming it so that whatever she did to it would be done to Dimitri. Then, laying it on the table, she poured out a thin trickle of sleeping sand onto the head.

Within only a few minutes—but it felt like tedious eternities—the mirror shimmered again, no longer empty. There lay Dimitri asleep. At this time of night he should have been asleep long ago. But perhaps he had lain awake with worry about the kingdom he served. Well he might.

Yaga reached out, her fingers extended toward the mirror. Then she plunged her hand into the glass. It hurt; it always hurt to have part of her body in one place, and part in another. But one had to endure many hard things in order to achieve great ends. With her hand she toyed with a lock of Dimitri's shaggy hair, then caressed his hairy cheek.

"Do not wake, O great one. Do not wake, O king who is yet to be. The interloper will marry thy bride, to fulfil the terms of the curse, but in the moment of the marriage, he is the heir. Therefore all is fulfilled. Wait thou not for the conception of a child, for such a child would be as weak as the father. Once wedded and bedded, Katerina will hold the kingdom by widow-right, as Baba Yaga did, and her new husband shall be king beside her, and the sons he makes in her body shall inherit after them. Be thou that man, O great one. Thy bright herald tells thee what the Winter God most surely desires of thee."

Then, grimacing, she rose from her stool and plunged her head through the glass. It felt to her as if she had been beheaded, or at least as she imagined such a thing might feel; but even so she managed to put a loving smile on her face and kiss the cheek of the sleeping man. Then, wincing from the pain, she pulled herself back through the mirror, first her head and then her hand.

Slumping down into her stool, she rested a moment, panting. Then she carefully wiped the precious powder from the mirror with a dry cloth. There was no retrieving the powder to use it again on glass, but the cloth was charged with it now, and thus had within it the power to carry any item, like a box and all its contents, across an infinite distance. Baba Yaga was very economical with her spells. Anything that could be reused in any way, she kept. It made for a cluttered house, but it was worth it.

She scooped the sleeping sand from the table and restored it to the little box in which she kept it. Then she took the wooden head, used a bit more of the bearfat, and named it as No Man, so it would be ready for the next use.

In the morning, Dimitri would wake up with a clear memory of a bright and terrible dream. A divine herald came to me, that's what he would whisper to himself. A bright messenger, so beautiful of face. The smell of the Winter Bear on her. And she kissed me.

Don't laugh at what my mirror shows, Bear, until you understand just how and when I do the showing.

8

WEDDING

 imitri awoke trembling from his dream. He felt as if he had not slept at all that night, though the sky was already grey with dawn. Over and over again he felt the caress on his cheek, heard the words of the herald, then shook with ecstasy as the kiss came, again, again, again. I am meant to be king through widow-right. The Winter Bear has conceived of such a plan for me!

Though why God should choose him, Dimitri had no idea. He had never converted to Christianity, having accepted baptism only as a courtesy to his king. He still did all the old rites, including calling the Bear back to the world in the spring, which Father Lukas had expressly forbidden. But they couldn't very well let the world languish in winter, could they? The soil had to thaw so they could plow. And now he had learned that apparently the Christian God had not replaced the old gods. Father Lukas was full of lies. And the Winter Bear was full of promises.

Dimitri had loved Katerina ever since she was old enough to draw the eye of a good man. Everyone knew that he was the one who, had the old laws prevailed, would have been elected king, and then any girl would have been proud to be his bride, or even a concubine, just for the hope of having the strength of a king in her babies. Yet the new laws were in force, and so only by marrying this one girl could he claim what would have been given to him freely had the people chosen. Thus he knew his destiny: to marry Katerina. She grew up pretty and clever and good—marrying her would not be a hard price to pay.

But even of that he had already been cheated without knowing it, by Baba Yaga's curse and the efforts of Katerina's aunts to weaken it. When Katerina pricked her finger and ran off and disappeared, a grieving King Matfei told everyone about the terms of the curse. Dimitri went forth the moment that he understood, searching high and low for her. But he never found her, though he taught three dogs to search only for the scent of her from her clothing. It was as if she was no longer in the world. That was what he told the king, though he meant to keep searching.

Then, as he was about to set out again, she came back with this weakling fool who insulted his sister and couldn't lift a sword. Dimitri despaired then, bowing to the humiliation of having to try to teach this mutilated woman-dressing half-man how to wield the sword of a knight. His only consolation was how slowly the fool progressed at it. Easier to teach a pig to sing or an ass to dance. But that was his fate. The gods hated him. And hated Taina, for that matter, to serve them up so ripely to the witch.

Now, after this dream, he wondered: How could he have lost hope? The Winter Bear loved the people of Taina after all, and would give them the king they needed despite the curses of Baba Yaga.

When the word spread through Taina that the wedding would be hastened, Dimitri smiled and rejoiced more than anyone. They thought he showed good spirits and true loyalty—and so he did. The sooner she was married, the sooner he could help Ivan to his accidental demise and so liberate the kingdom from Baba Yaga's interference. He would marry the widow and become king of Taina after Matfei died. He would be a good king, too, especially if the messenger came to him again and taught him how to please the Bear. Then just as the great Emperor Constantine became a champion of Christ after seeing the cross in the heavens promising him victory, so would Dimitri make sure that in his kingdom and in every other kingdom where he might have influence, the name of Bear would be on every man's lips, and every knee would bow to the Lord of Snow.

On Thursday Ivan was baptized. It was a simple ceremony at the river. Father Lukas was annoyed and showed it. King Matfei, Katerina, and Sergei were the only witnesses. It took all of ten minutes, including immediate confirmation, and there he was, soaking wet and a Christian.

Sort of a Christian. A Christian who knew that almost eleven hundred years later he would be circumcised to fulfil the covenant of Abraham. But for now, Christian enough to marry Katerina.

King Matfei embraced him and kissed him after the ceremony.

Then he took Katerina's hand in one of his and Ivan's in the other, and beamed. "Well, now, there's nothing more to wait for. Let's have the wedding!"

Katerina smiled—but it wasn't heartfelt, or so Ivan imagined. He kept a grave demeanor himself, and nodded. "As you wish, Your Majesty," he said.

"It will take a couple of days for preparation. Shall we say Sunday at nones?"

"*This* Sunday?" asked Ivan.

"I think it would be unfair to ask the seamstresses to have the dress ready for Saturday," said Katerina. "But if my bridegroom is impatient, I can forgo the dress." From her tone of voice, it was clear she had no intention of forgoing anything.

"No, no," said Ivan. "Sunday will be fine."

The preparations for the wedding were both more and less than Ivan had expected. Certainly the event was the only thing that mattered in the village during the two days of preparation. And yet, when all was ready, it wasn't that much. Katerina's dress was extravagant, by local standards, but there were no jewels, real or fake, and apart from her dress and the paraphernalia surrounding the priest, there were no decorations. Fresh straw on the floor; a huge feast waiting for the guests so that Ivan's memory of the wedding would always be redolent of roast boar and stewing cabbage and beets; a crowd of people inside and outside the king's house; and Katerina's dress.

By now he knew to keep his comments to himself. The feast was a considerable portion of the year's calories. The dress was prepared in record time, considering it was hand sewn; later he would learn that it was really a remake of a dress that had belonged to her mother, or it would have been impossible to complete it. The food, the dress: that was labor enough to account for the frantic busyness of the two days between the decision to go ahead and the wedding itself.

So Ivan's new program of working hard at improving his fighting skills didn't have enough time to show any meaningful results, except that he ached all over. The days of agonizing repetitions led to nights of exhaustion and soreness and mornings so stiff he could hardly rise out of his bed. Marathoner and sprinter he might be, but he had never used his body so brutally. He knew that a certain amount of muscle tearing was necessary for the bulking up he needed, but since he had done little in the way of weight training and nothing of swordplay, he had no experience of his body under this kind of stress. He wasn't sure whether he was doing too much, whether he should back off.

Dimitri was downright cheerful in all Ivan's practices, praising him now, telling him he was going to be a wonderful soldier. But Ivan was pretty sure that the king must have told him to be more encouraging, because Ivan could see for himself that he was no more skillful with a sword now than he had been before, or, if he was making progress, it was almost imperceptible. Nothing happened by reflex yet. There was always a time lag while he thought of the next move. Dimitri could have chopped him to bits. But instead, he moved more slowly and never laid a blow on Ivan. He was almost . . . nice.

He smiled way too much.

Well, fine. Dimitri was a resource, a teacher—what mattered was what Ivan did, and the only judge Ivan needed to please was himself. As when he was an athlete in college, he had his own standard of excellence, his own goals to meet. Let Dimitri think it all had to do with the pace he set; Ivan would learn as quickly as possible. His life—and perhaps more lives—depended on it, and he was determined to disappoint nobody, least of all himself.

Meanwhile, every night Sergei showed him what he had written on the backs of Saint Kirill's parchments. Ivan cared nothing about the quality of the prose or of the penmanship, but it happened that in language and in lettering Sergei was simple and clear. Indeed, the first thought Ivan had upon reading what Sergei wrote was: How authentic!

Authentic, and yet he felt more than a little unease about the project. Sergei would never have written this document if Ivan had not virtually bullied him into it; Sergei didn't even see the sense in it. Ivan almost had to shake him to get Sergei to refrain from writing some introductory apology for presuming to deface these precious documents by writing stories of the silly country folk upon them, his only excuse being that Prince Ivan forced him to do it. Then Sergei wanted to have his first story be that of Ivan and Katerina and the fight with the bear. Even worse! It would have spoiled everything! No introductions, no explanations, no references to Ivan's existence. Certainly nothing to show that this was a directed project. Let it be itself.

For even though Ivan had caused Sergei's accounts to exist, they were still genuine. The stories were untainted by Ivan's expectations. Sergei's language was all his own. Not a letter shaped by Ivan's hand would appear on the page. It was real.

The trouble was that Ivan had no idea how to preserve these manuscripts so they would be found. If he buried them, the parchment would rot away. If he left them out to be preserved in the church, like all the other ancient manuscripts, some cleric would think it was nothing but working papers or scrap and would throw it away. No one would think of recopying it. There was almost no reasonable chance of it reaching the tenth century, let alone the twentieth. He had to hide it in such a way that it would be preserved . . . but what if he hid it too well? Even if it didn't rot, it would do no good unless someone found it someday.

If only he could carry the manuscripts across the bridge with him. But he couldn't even be sure the bridge would ever be there for him. The problems of this little kingdom were real. Why would Katerina ever let him go back home? When would it ever be convenient?

Besides, carrying it home would do no good at all. The manuscript had to pass through the eleven intervening centuries. If he crossed the bridge and presented it to the world in 1992, scholars and scientists would look at it and say, What a wonderful replica, how cleverly done, but please don't ask us to believe that something so obviously new is a genuine product of the ninth century.

To put it in its simplest terms, there had to be eleven hundred years of radioactive decay of the carbon-14 molecules in the parchment. And the only way to get that was for it to sit somewhere for eleven hundred years.

If only he had a nice big Ziploc bag.

Wrap it up in cloth inside a box of sand to keep it dry, inside tightly stitched leather, inside another layer of sand, inside another box, inside a case of stone; hide it all in a hole in the side of a hill where there'd be good drainage and the hillside would erode away at exactly the rate to make a corner of the box appear in 1992 . . .

And then find some way to be back in his own time so he and no one else could discover this most precious find. Not because it would make him famous and be the foundation of a brilliant career. Or not *just* because of that, but also because these stories were truer of this time than anything that had passed through the centuries of illiteracy to be written down only during the folktale movement of the 1800s. Too many more-recent events and cultures had impinged on the tales since then.

Even now, studying what Sergei wrote, Ivan began to recognize even older tales underlying these. What would eventually be fairy tales still had redolences of god-stories and myths. Traces of the god who leaves and must be called back—the tale of the Winter Bear was clearly such a one. And in the Winter Bear were echoes of the Weather-god of the Hittites, of Zeus, of Jovis-pater, of Woden. The ancient Indo-European ancestors were still whispering in these tales. Priests once shed blood to make the tales come true. What Sergei could not guess, what Father Lukas would utterly deny, what Ivan himself had not been sure of until now was this: These tales were also a kind of holy book and deserved to be treated as such by scholars. People once lived by these tales as surely as they lived by the tale of Moses and the burning bush, of Abraham and the ram in the thicket that took the place of his beloved son, of the loaves and fishes that fed a multitude, of the God who put his blood into a cup and his flesh into bread and served them to those who loved and followed him.

These stories must survive to a time that is sorely in need of them. If I could only bring them forth and lay them before the people— not the scholars, they'll study them and argue and equivocate—but the people, the Russian and Ukrainian and Moldovan and Belorussian people, who have lost their way because for seventy-two years they were in thrall to a religion that gave them gods and priests who killed and imprisoned and cheated and betrayed them, the people then found that when this nightmare religion fell, the only new religions offered to them were the old Christian one that had been a tool of tsars for centuries and a whimpering dog kicked around by the Communists for another and the religion of brutal free-market capitalism, the worship of money, which the Americans insisted had to be the established church of all the newly freed countries, even though they did not really practice it themselves. Let the East Slavs, the freed slaves, find their ancient soul in the Ivan tales and the tales of Mikola Mozhaiski and Ilya of Murom and Sadka the minstrel and the Winter Bear. Before the great Saint Kirill gave you your state religion, before the Scandinavian Rus' put their name on your nation and your language, before the Tatars got you used to the yoke and a foot on your neck, before envy and admiration of the West led you to remake yourselves over and over again in their image, you had a soul of your own. The root of it is here.

He laughed at himself, thinking these thoughts. What have I become? A prophet of some ancient druidlike Slavic religion? I give too much weight to this. But my people have lost their way, and this is a small, faint whisper of a memory of ancient dreams that once bound us together.

My people? Am I not an American boy? I thought I was. Even during these months of my return to Kiev, I still thought of myself as an American visiting in a land that used to be my own. But now that I've lost Ukraine again, I think of it as my homeland, my people; now that I have no one whom I can speak Russian to, I think of it as my own tongue. I have lost them, perhaps forever, and these manuscripts are the only gift I can send to them, and I can't even be sure of doing that.

Four feverish days thus passed, in exhaustion on the practice field, exhilaration as he read over Sergei's work, and then lying sleepless and aching in his flea-ridden bed, pinching the damned insects between his thumbnails so he could burst their miserable tough carapaces and thinking grandiose thoughts of accomplishments that would remain forever out of reach.

So he was not in the best of shape when the day of his wedding began, and the king himself rousted him out of bed and insisted on the two of them going down to the river together to swim in the bitterly cold water. No doubt this, too, had its roots in some ancient, culturally potent ritual, but when it came to swimming, Ivan was a great believer in heated and chlorinated pools.

But when he and the king came out of the water, shriveled and shivering and stamping their feet, while dozens of men stood by laughing and making obscene catcalls about how disappointed Katerina was going to be when she saw her husband's cold-withered hilt, for the first time it dawned on him that this was the day of the irreversible steps. To marry Katerina was not just a show, not just a courtesy, a favor to a pretty woman who was in a bit of trouble the other day. If he made these vows, he was promising to be her husband. She was promising to be his wife. She would bear his children. They would raise them together.

He wasn't ready.

It didn't matter. Ready or not, he realized, here I come.

Sergei sat in Ivan's room, trying to remember all the details of the tale of the Bear's gold ring before committing any words to paper—there was no room for errors on the remaining parchment. Ivan was somewhere, probably with the king, getting dressed out in garments fit for a boyar's wedding; it would not be right for him to dress as a prince until after the wedding, and even then modesty suggested he might wear slightly humbler clothing. Only when he became king would the distinction disappear. To jump from peasant garb to boyar's clothing was shock enough.

Sergei valued such solitary time at a writing desk. Father Lukas so disdained Sergei's copywork that he rarely gave the young man much of anything to do that used his skill with letters. Until now, Sergei had not thought he had any. But over these days of furious writing, he could see how his hand had become smoother, tighter, more regular.

He could also see how much more fluidly the language came from him. Looking over the first tales he wrote down, he saw that not only were the letters too large and ill-shaped, but also the language was awkward and sometimes confusing. What he was writing now, however, was in letters much smaller and yet more, not less, legible.

The trouble was, all the blank space on the backs of the parchments was nearly full. Sergei hated to see the project end. Though he had chosen the best stories to write down first, there were so many more yet to write; and when the work ended, what would there be for Sergei then, except more slavelike labor at the church? Father Lukas would not know how Sergei's hand had improved. He would have him hobbling about emptying slops, sweeping up, carrying things. Sergei had never understood why, if his malformed body made him so unfit for the physical labor of the village, they determined to give him to the priest—to perform his physical labor. Perhaps they felt that Father Lukas did not need to have his menial work performed quickly or well. Or perhaps they expected him to be more patient with Sergei's slowness and clumsiness. If so, they were mistaken. Well, not entirely. Father Lukas did not yell at him to hurry, or curse him when he spilled or broke something. But the look of beatific patience in Father Lukas's eyes as he mumbled a prayer—of course it was a prayer, he was a priest, wasn't he?—could stab deeper than the shouts of the village men and women ever had.

A message to a faraway land, to be wrapped and double wrapped and saved for a thousand years in the earth. It was surely an age of miracles, that such things were possible. Christ himself never buried a message.

Thinking of Christ in the context of stories made Sergei remember the parable of the stewards with their talents. It occurred to him that he, Sergei, was the steward with the single talent, and he was indeed planning to bury his talent in the earth. But how could he do otherwise? These stories were already had among his people—he could hardly show them his writings, for they would say, "We all know the story, Sergei, why would you write it down?" There was nothing to do but bury it. Still, it made him uneasy, to know that he was like the foolish steward in this way. But perhaps he was misinterpreting the parable. Or at least misapplying it. If only he could ask Father Lukas about it.

Out in the corridor, Sergei heard voices for a few moments before they came near enough for him to make out what they were saying. Two men.

"Of course she'll try to disrupt the wedding. This is a disaster for her."

"It's the child she'll go after, when a boy is conceived. What's the wedding to her?"

"The wedding is everything. She must respect widow-right, even without children, because she herself holds her kingdom by widow-right alone."

"Less widow-right than sheer terror. Who in her benighted land would dare stand against her? Only a few of them have even enough courage to flee."

"She will move against the wedding, and we must be prepared."

"If you say so. It costs nothing to be vigilant. Katerina and Ivana will have our protection."

The use of the female form of the name *Ivan* struck Sergei hard. He had not heard anyone speak so offensively against Ivan. Or perhaps he had, but now he knew Ivan better and so it bothered him more.

"As for the twig-man, the vigilance ends after he's bedded her."

The other chuckled. "I see now why you care so much for widow-right."

"Let's just say that it's to the Pretender's benefit to kill him before the wedding; afterward, we're the ones with the most to lose if he stays alive."

"He's such a clumsy fellow. Everyone knows it."

"He might fall into the river and get swept away."

"Or he might tumble from a cliff."

"He might even fall on his own sword."

"That's as clumsy as you can get."

Chuckling grimly, the two men parted.

If Sergei had ever been permitted at the practice field, he might have known the voices. Neither could possibly be the king—that was a voice he knew. He could also rule out Father Lukas and Ivan himself. But most of the other voices Sergei knew well were those of the women who came to pray and confess at the church.

A plot to kill Ivan, but the plotters were not known. Still, they were men who felt responsible for vigilance during the wedding. Not common peasants, then, but men of soldiering age and with the responsibility of boyars or of the king's own druzhina, the knights who stayed always under arms and under the orders of the king. If the king's own druzhina were plotting against Ivan, what did that mean? Either they were not obedient to the king, or they were. If they were, then the king was a murderer like King David of old; if not, then the king's authority was in danger, for his men were contemplating a great crime against the king's will.

Sergei must tell someone. But whom? Ivan, even if he knew, would be powerless to protect himself—he was the only man of such an age in Taina who handled the sword as feebly as Sergei himself. The king? Well and good if the king were not in the plot, but if he was, then what good would it do to tell him?

Who is wise? Who can tell me what to do?

Father Lukas had grave misgivings about the marriage, just as he had had about the baptism. But as Kirill had told him more than once, a priest has no right to withhold the rites of the Church, even when the person receiving them is clearly unworthy. Let God damn whom he damns; it is our business to try to save all who come before us. Especially the marriage, Father Lukas knew, for there was no law requiring that a Christian priest give his blessing to a marriage. The old customs still had full force, and if he declined to marry this foreign pretender to the Christian princess, the marriage would happen anyway, but the priest would be seen by all as the enemy of the king and the people in their effort to stay free of Baba Yaga.

Thus did the compromises begin. He had seen a thousand such compromises with political power during his years in Adrianople, where bishops constantly had to bend to the will of the political and social leaders of the city. In Lukas's opinion, as a young cleric, bending to political pressure had become so habitual as to be automatic, even in cases where a good Christian should have resisted. Yet now that he himself had to weigh the needs of the Church in this place, where the foothold was yet so fragile, he could clearly see that it was more important to preserve the kingdom that preserved the Church, than to insist on utter rectitude when it might put the survival of the Church in danger.

So he put the best face on it, even refraining from complaint that Ivan had appropriated his one assistant. Truth to tell, he rather hoped Ivan would keep Sergei, thus putting King Matfei in a position where he would have to give Father Lukas a new assistant—preferably one who wasn't clumsy and stupid, and who wasn't deformed in mockery of the creation of God. How could anyone be expected to keep their minds on worship and holiness with the clump clump clump of Sergei's passage from room to room? A little boy would be preferable—they never talked back, or if they did, you could whack them a couple of times and get them in line. You could beat Sergei, too, of course, but it did little good. Sergei had never changed his mind through beatings—the man was stubborn beyond belief. A stump would respond better to teaching. At least stumps never talked back to their master.

Father Lukas went outside to greet the people gathering at the bower., Old pagan custom, this collection of greenery and flowers. Homage to some god whose name Lukas did not even wish to know. Well, the technique for dealing with that nonsense was well known to every priest. He would declare the flowers to be in homage of the Word of God, the ineffable Son, who made all things that grow upon the earth, and for whom palm fronds were laid down to cover the ground at his coming.

Oh, of course. Now that all the work is done, here comes Sergei. Father Lukas refrained from turning away in distaste. Let the man come. He was no worse a burden than the horsehair shirt Lukas wore under his tunic, where other men wore linen. The constant rashes and raw patches from the horsehair kept his flesh mortified before God; if God then chose to mortify the spirit as well, that was his holy business.

As he held still, waiting for Brother Sergei, the women who had been working on the bower came up to ask him for approval.

"Yes, lovely, lovely. God will be pleased that you did such work in his holy honor."

There. Now even the unbaptized among you have served God, without even meaning to.

"Oh, look, there's my boy."

It was Sergei's mother who spoke; but she was not speaking to Father Lukas. Instead, she was half-dragging a bent-over old lady along with her to intercept Sergei as he headed for Lukas. "Sergei, look who's come to the wedding!"

Sergei greeted the old lady with deference but without recognition. "You know, Sergei," said his mother. "The one who gave me the . . ." Her voice fell to a whisper. But Lukas knew what she was saying: The old woman who gave her the hoose that Ivan had supposedly worn. A troublemaker and a gossip, thought Father Lukas. A king by his conversion and example could create a church; old women with their gossip and nastiness could destroy one.

It was just as well that the old biddy was ignoring Father Lukas. Indeed, she ignored Sergei, too, after a perfunctory greeting. Apparently she wanted to talk only to her sisters in crime, the gossips of the bower.

Sergei quickly got away from his mother and closed the rest

of the distance between him and Father Lukas. "Father, I need your counsel."

"Really? I thought only Ivan was your teacher now."

"I'm *his* teacher," said Sergei, somewhat resentfully.

"Let's not argue about who is teaching whom," said Father Lukas. "What did you want my foolish counsel for?"

"I overheard something in the king's house. Two men speaking, plotting to . . ." Sergei looked around.

So did Lukas. The old woman who had come with Sergei's mother was still loitering nearby. Listening? Lukas took Sergei's arm and led him into the church. He could see the old woman wandering off, around the church in the other direction. Well, let her listen. What could an old woman hear through walls?

"Speak quietly, we have an eavesdropper," Lukas murmured.

"A plot to kill Ivan, Father," said Sergei. "Two men in the corridor. Speaking of how there should be an accident after the wedding."

"More fools they," said Father Lukas. "They'd better await the birth of a son."

"Widow-right," said Sergei. "Have you heard that word before?"

"In whispers, lately," said Father Lukas. "But there *is* no widow-right. That's Baba Yaga's invention, to justify her continuing to hold her late husband's throne and forbidding a new election to replace him. Baba Yaga's law will never work to the benefit of Taina."

"Then perhaps at the wedding, if you say something to that effect . . ."

"There's no part of the ceremony where the priest, acting in the place of God, warns the guests not to murder the bridegroom because it might jeopardize the succession."

"You'll do nothing?"

"I'll do what I can. But to pollute the wedding with charges and accusations, especially when they're only vague ones about two men overheard and perhaps misunderstood through walls and doors, that I will not do, because it would do no good."

"That's why I came to you for counsel, Father. Because you would know what to do."

Cheerful now, Sergei bustled out of the church.

Father Lukas sat down on a bench and thought about what Sergei had told him. A plot to kill the bridegroom. It should have been foreseen. Indeed, Lukas had foreseen it—but not so early. Someone had lied to these conspirators and told them that there was no need to wait beyond the wedding night.

A great tumult arose outside. Cheers and laughter. The arrival of the bride.

Lukas went out to greet Katerina and bring her and the ladies who had sewn the dress onto her into the church.

"One last confession before the wedding," said Katerina.

Father Lukas led her to the one bench at the front of the church. In most churches it would have been reserved for the king and his family, but King Matfei insisted that old men and women use it while he stood during mass. Now, though, it was available for hearing confession. He seated her so that she would be facing the icon of Christ the Judge on the wall. "Keep your voice low," he reminded her.

Her confession was simple and rather sweet, as always. Father Lukas did his best to remain dispassionate during confessions, but it was hard to keep from being judgmental. The people whose confessions were always lies made him tired; others, though, made him seethe with the small-mindedness of their view of sin, or with their ignorance of their real sins. Some even spent their confessional time confessing the sins of others—always couched, though, as confessing the sin of "wrath" at this or that person, followed by a recital of all the awful things the person did to provoke their poor victim to sin. Wake up! he wanted to shout.

But never with Katerina. Her confessions were pure, laying no blame on anyone but herself. For instance, Father Lukas was well aware of how annoying—nay, disturbing—this Ivan fellow could be, yet not a word of complaint from Katerina. Rather she confessed to having neglected him, and failed to help him; by the time she was through Father Lukas was persuaded that indeed she could have done better. This was disturbing to him because he was quite aware that he himself had done much worse. It wasn't a pleasant thing, when the priest was guiltier of a sin than the parishioner who confessed it to him.

Which is perhaps why, when he had absolved her with advice about how to do better—but no further penance—he then unburdened himself to her. He told her what Sergei had overheard, and the obvious danger that Ivan was in.

"But that's so foolish," said Katerina. "There is no widow-right under the new law. If they're looking to the Widow to behave consistently with her own situation, it's in vain. If they kill Ivan before I have his child in me, they will have done the witch's work. It will give her the pretext she needs."

"Perhaps Sergei misheard them."

"Perhaps," she said. "He truly has no idea who the plotters are?"

"It could be anyone, though it's likely to be knights of the druzhina, or perhaps a few boyars." A conspiracy among boyars was less likely, if only because they were scattered on their manors throughout the kingdom, while the druzhinniks were always together in such a manner that conspiracies could grow like mushrooms, overnight.

"What can we do?" she asked. "If I ask men to guard him, then in all likelihood I'll be inviting at least one of the conspirators to protect against himself."

"I foresee the real danger on the practice field," said Father Lukas. "I hear that Ivan is working very hard now—but accidents can happen during practice, and who could prove it was anything else, should a passing blow inadvertently pass through his throat."

She was about to come up with something else, but at that moment the shouting began outside.

"Fire! Fire!"

Father Lukas rose to his feet and walked toward the door. "What a time for one of the kitchen fires to get out of hand," he said. "I hope it's not at your father's house."

"No," said Katerina. "I think it's here."

Sure enough, the flames were already licking in at the windows and crackling along the ceiling. The church was entirely of timber, with almost no daub in it at all, and it was bone-dry. The fire might have started only two or three minutes ago, and already it was almost too late to get out of the church.

"Run!" shouted Father Lukas as he headed for the door. By the time he got to it and held it open, Katerina had her skirt hitched up and was ushering toward him the old ladies who had been praying in the church. The slowest of them she finally picked up and bodily carried out the door. Only when they were all outside did Father Lukas remember that the precious books and parchments were all in the tiring-room.

"O God, help me!" he cried as he headed back into the church.

"No!" cried Katerina. "It's too late! Come out! I command it in the name of the king!"

What was the king's word at a time like this? thought Father Lukas. It was the authority of the fire itself that stopped him, for he wasn't two steps inside the church when the roof collapsed over the altar. The tiring-room was gone. Father Lukas barely made it back to the door before the rest of the roof gave way, and as it was, flames shot out the door after him so fiercely that his robes caught on fire. He fell to the ground and several of the people fell upon him, to smother the fire with their own clothing and bodies. Except for the singeing of his hair, he wasn't even burned. But the church was gone, his books and papers were gone, even his robe was in ruins.

There was no kitchen fire close to the church. There was no lightning to spark a flame. It had to have been set. Who would set a fire?

As if in answer to his unspoken question, Sergei's mother let out a wail. "She's dead, she's dead, she's dead!"

Who? The old lady, Father Lukas soon learned, the one who lived out in the forest, the one who had brought the hoose to her, which she had so carefully related to him in confession—another of the ones who so gladly confessed other people's sins. Lukas expected to see a corpse, though the old woman was so dried-up that it was just as likely she had burned instantly to a single sheet of grey ash that wafted up into the breeze and was gone.

Gone, that was where she was. There was no body.

"I say she set the fire," said one of the men. Father Lukas looked around. It was Dimitri, the master-at-arms. "Who else? She's not here, she didn't burn, this fire was set."

"Why would she do it?" asked Sergei's mother.

"Are you that stupid, not to see it?" said Dimitri. "No wonder your son's such a dunce. This old woman from the woods, who else is it but the Widow herself? And you took her into your house!"

Father Lukas sighed inwardly at the way Dimitri refused to say Baba Yaga's name outright.

"She ate at my table," said Sergei's mother. "Would an evil witch do that?"

"She'd do it if it got her close enough to burn down a church," said Dimitri.

"It's no use arguing about this," said Father Lukas. "The building may be gone, but the Church itself cannot be destroyed by fire. If it could, the devil would be laying fires all over Christendom. What was taken by fire can be built again by sweat."

"Well said, Father Lukas!" cried Sergei. But Father Lukas was under no illusions about the reason for his enthusiasm. Anything to ease the blame that was bound to come to Sergei's mother for having brought the old woman here—especially if it really was Baba Yaga in disguise.

"Father Lukas," said Katerina, "what matters now is this: Shall we postpone the wedding?"

"Whatever you wish," said Father Lukas. "We could easily post-pone the marriage to another day."

"No!" roared Dimitri. "Every day that passes brings more danger! Don't you see that the fire was set with Princess Katerina inside? This wedding must go on, so that the curse is swept away at last and Taina can be free of the Widow's claims!"

"If only it were that easy," replied King Matfei as he strode toward the group, Ivan jogging along behind him. They both went directly to Katerina, and Father Lukas was pleased to see that Ivan did look genu-inely concerned for his bride, taking her hand and looking her up and down to make sure that she had not suffered harm from the fire.

"My lord," said Dimitri, "every moment we delay plays into the Widow's hands. I say we proceed with the wedding without delay!"

"Your kind suggestion is well meant, and I thank you for it," said King Matfei. "But let us take at least a moment to assess the damage that was done here."

Flames still burned hotly in the ruins of the church. There was no approaching it, the heat was so intense. King Matfei walked around it, Father Lukas following close behind. Only when they reached the end where the tiring-room had been did Lukas realize that not all the books and papers would have been destroyed. "Sergei!" he cried out. "Sergei, the book of the Gospels that you took up to the king's house! The manuscripts you were using to teach Ivan!"

Sergei's face brightened, but then almost at once he grew sad, and then began to weep. "Ah, Father Lukas! This morning Ivan told me to bring the parchments back here to the church, and I did it."

Father Lukas whirled on Ivan. It could not possibly have been his fault, and yet Father Lukas was filled with an entirely unjustified rage against him. "Could you not have studied for one more day!"

Ivan blushed. "Father Lukas, what study would I do on my wed-ding day? We thought to bring them here as the safest place to store them."

Father Lukas had not wept in the aftermath of the fire, but to have his hopes raised and then dashed again was too much for him. "Ah, God, I have been an unworthy servant, to let thy Gospels perish in the flames of hell."

"Not the Gospels," said Sergei. "I left the Gospels there in Ivan's room, because he was still reading them. It was all the parchments that I brought back."

"The book is saved?" Impulsively Father Lukas embraced the crip-ple. "God bless you, my son."

"A happy day, then, after all," said King Matfei.

"Let all see the wisdom in this," said Katerina, "that the priest cried, not for the wood of the church, but for the words of the Gospels. The Church is in the words, not in the wood!"

A cheer went up at those words. Most were cheering for the heartening sentiment; Father Lukas, who was now going to have to go back to working out of a peasant hut, at least for a while, joined in the cheering, but his approbation was for Katerina's cleverness in making a homily out of a church burning, and a lesson out of his own tears. She was very, very good at leading the people. A shame she had to have a husband at all.

"I wish I had been a more dedicated student," said Ivan sadly, "and had not caused Sergei to return the parchments." He turned to Sergei. "Go at once to my room and make sure the book of the Gospels is secure."

"No need," said King Matfei. "After the wedding is soon enough. Dimitri is right! Let there be no more delay. If this was the work of the Widow's hand, then let her get no satisfaction from it! Father Lukas, to the bower we go!"

After all the tumult, the wedding was an anticlimax. With the bonfire still crackling and popping its way through the timber of the church, there was a sense of the end of the world in the ceremony, as if they were getting married in the midst of the ruin of civilization. Which is not far from the truth, thought Ivan. These people wouldn't live to see it, but in historical terms, they would not have long to unite under the king of the Rus' in Kiev before the Mongols would burst across the steppe, toppling kingdoms and bringing all under the sway of the Golden Horde. The soul of Russia would be fatally compromised then, with no king able to survive in resistance. When all rulers must be quislings, cooperating with the conquerors to wring taxes and tribute out of the people, then the people have no reason to regard any government as legitimate. Here, though, Ivan could see what the Golden Horde stripped away from the Eastern Slavs. In the way the people revered King Matfei and adored Princess Katerina, in the way these two royals lived right among the people, serving readily and leading boldly, without pomp and pretension, Ivan could see how it used to be, what was lost. A government with true legitimacy. Rulers that the people know and, more important, that know the people. What tsar ever went out and sweated through the harvest with the smerdy? What princess ever called all her subjects by name, and laughingly bore their wedding-night jests?

In this moment, Ivan loved these people and this place. Not the way Katerina loved them, because she knew each one and all their stories from childhood on; Ivan loved them as a whole, as a group, as a community. Maybe Cousin Marek had such a sense of belonging, but no one had it in Kiev, not even among the Jews, who did a better job than most of holding themselves together. And if this is community, he thought, then America has no communities, or none that I have ever seen.

Was it smalltown life, then, that made the difference? Perhaps. But we could have kept it, had we valued it, this feeling of belonging, of being known. Instead we have a century and a half of American literature harping on the evils of smalltown life. How everyone is always in your face and knows your business, about how the guardians of virtue are imperfect themselves and so have no right to judge. Those poor elitist fools—they hated community but had no idea of the emptiness of life after community had been killed. Here it was, the people in each other's faces, the gossip as vicious as ever when the knives came out, no doubt the average number of plots and intrigues, hypocrisies and self-righteousness. But all that paled in the face of the great power of the place: that everyone knew who everyone else was.

Even Sergei. Everyone knows what he is and it's not a good thing to be. Yet where else could he go? Who would he be in another place? Americans love to pick up, move on, start over. But instead of being somebody fresh and new, they become somebody lonely and lost, or, far too often these days, they become nobody at all, a machine for satisfying hunger, without loyalty or honor or duty. And with the death of Communism, that's what my own people in Russia are becoming, too.

There it was again, that thought of the Russian people being his own.

The Orthodox ritual was strange to him. He had been too young to be aware of religion when he left Ukraine—if, indeed, his family had known anybody who would seek out a church wedding under the Communist regime. And since returning to Kiev, he had not known anyone who was getting married. He knew the American and English Protestant services through watching old movies now and then. The showy Catholic wedding in *The Sound of Music*. Greek Orthodox services didn't show up much.

Father Lukas said his parts; Ivan and Katerina said their parts, with some prompting, at least for Ivan. Then they drank wine from the same cup, and it was done. The crowd cheered. Father Lukas beamed upon them. His smile was only skin-deep, though. He was not happy. And, if Ivan was any judge of character, neither was Katerina.

Relieved, yes, she seemed to be relieved. As if one great hurdle had been passed. But Ivan knew that this was nothing to her but a marriage for reasons of state. She had grown up knowing such a thing would be needed. He had not. He always expected to marry for love, or at least by his own choice. He had hoped for a bride who would be proud to say the vows with him. This was dismal indeed, to know that she was merely doing her duty to king and country, to God and Daddy.

And tonight. Oh, that was going to be the scene from his dreams. To bed a woman who was only doing it because her people were being held hostage. How is this going to be distinguishable from rape? Ivan had tried reading Ian Fleming once; a friend had lent him *You Only Live Twice*. In one of the early chapters, Fleming had written that "all women love semi-rape." Ivan was only fourteen at the time, and still not sure that he understood all the nuances of English. But the idea seemed so loathsome to him that even if it were true, he did not want to know it. He gave the book back to his friend unread. To sleep with an unwilling woman—Ivan was not even sure he would be able to perform. That was one difference between the sexes that women never really understood: A woman could just lie there, and the job would get done. But if the man was put off his mettle, so to speak, there was no way to sleepwalk through it.

Can't wait for tonight.

He just hoped that Sergei had the sense to head for Ivan's room the moment the wedding was over, and get those parchments hidden. Fortunately, King Matfei was conferring privately with Father Lukas, so if Sergei hurried, he could come back with the book of the Gospels before the priest thought of going to Ivan's room to get it himself.

It had been clever of Sergei, to think of using the fire as a means of convincing Father Lukas not to look for the parchments. Now Ivan and Sergei had more time to conceal them, and would never have to hear Father Lukas raging at their having defaced the precious manuscripts he was given by Kirill himself.

The surprise was how readily and convincingly Sergei was able to lie. He had to be a practiced liar, to do it so naturally, without a breath of embarrassment. It was a good thing to know about Sergei.

Of course, come to think of it, Ivan had not hesitated to join him in the lie. So much for their being Christians. Though, come to think of it, there was a good long tradition of Christians lying when the need arose, and often when it didn't. Ivan couldn't think of a religion that was any damn good at making utter truthtellers out of its practitioners. Maybe the Quakers were truly plainspoken at one time, but even they managed to squeeze out a Richard Nixon after a few hundred years of suppressing their human propinquity for untruth.

Sergei, if you're going to lie, I'm just glad you're on my side, and good at it, and smart about which lies are worth telling.

Then it occurred to Ivan: Who told the bigger lie today? Sergei, when he said that the parchments burned up in the fire? Or Ivan and Katerina, when they spoke as if what they were doing was actually a marriage?

He still held her hand in his. Her skin was cool. One of them was sweating so much that their hands were slippery against each other. Ivan was reasonably sure that it wasn't her.

9

HONEYMOON

owhere was the difference between the ninth century and the twentieth century clearer to Ivan than when it came to the little matter of the wedding night. Americans in the eighties and nineties had prided themselves on their openness about sex, but to Ivan those open-minded Americans seemed like prudes compared to the ribald—or downright lewd—comments, gestures, and charades that surrounded him and Katerina as they led a huge troop of villagers to the king's house.

Nor did an R or PG-13 rating seem to be much in evidence, for seven-year-old boys were making obscene suggestions and movements right along with their elders. There was so much of it that after a few minutes Ivan couldn't even bring himself to be shocked. He was numb.

Numb—that's just the feeling you hope for on your wedding night.

With all the discussion of his and Katerina's marriage as an antidote for Baba Yaga's curse or as a strategic move in the struggle to keep Taina free of the witch's rule, it all came down to this: Ivan was supposed to perform. But perform what? How? Like any other male American of even minimal alertness, Ivan knew that he was expected to be both masterful and sensitive, that the worst sin he could commit would be to finish before starting—in all the comedies people acted as if it were only slightly less awful than throwing up on the salad—and the second-worst sin would be to find himself unable to start at all.

Or maybe the worst sin of all was this: Ivan had no idea how it was supposed to go. Beyond what you got in health class and dirty jokes and bad movies, he simply had no serious hands-on experience.

All the statistics suggested that the only males who hadn't had sex by age sixteen were either quadriplegics or insufferable geeks. Ivan was neither—in fact, he was an athlete who had dated a normal amount in high school. And with the time he spent in locker rooms, he had heard all the boastful talk about how often and how manfully all the other guys performed. Only a few, like Ivan, didn't join in the locker-room brag; but Ivan suspected that the difference between the talkers and the quiet ones wasn't experience, it was honesty. If these clowns had really treated the girls they dated the way they claimed, why did women not fall over themselves clamoring for more of the miraculous pleasure that these love gods supposedly provided?

Not that *nobody* was getting any in high school. But the statistics in those social-science surveys were such hoke. If those "scientific" results came from teenage boys telling the truth about their sex lives, the scientists should be doing horoscopes or reading palms—they were more reliable. Or so Ivan had said to Ruth once, and Ruth laughingly agreed. She was a virgin, too, and didn't know any girls who admitted to anything else. There were girls with reputations as mattresses and guys whose reputations as cocksmen Ivan believed, but they were a lowlife fringe that didn't touch Ivan's life.

All this he had concluded years before; but there was one complication. About half the time, he didn't believe it. About half the time, he looked at the people around him and thought, They all know the secret, they've all done it. Any girl I marry will have slept with enough men to have some serious expectations, and I won't know what I'm doing. I'll fumble around, I'll give her no pleasure at all, she'll hate sex with me and within days she'll have an annulment going, if not a lawsuit for infliction of emotional distress. Or assault and battery.

So it didn't help one bit that every single person in Taina above the age of six seemed to know all about sex and have inflated ideas about exactly what Ivan's sexual prowess would be like. The crude comments about how he was going to keep the princess turning on the spit longer than a suckling pig gave him a new appreciation for the Jewish ban on pork. And the children who asked if they could come play in the tent that his erection would make of the bedcovers left him speechless.

It's all jokes, he told himself. It's a celebration of life. It's a holdover from pagan fertility rites.

One thing was sure, though. If somebody talked like this coming out of a wedding in upstate New York, they'd better be drunk or they'd never get another invitation anywhere in their lives.

Through it all, Katerina seemed not to hear a thing. At first Ivan thought she was as embarrassed as he was. But of course that could not be so—she must have attended other weddings in Taina. For all he knew, as a child she had invented some of the ribald jokes now being retold at top volume along the path to the king's house. Her grim silence had another cause entirely, he was sure. For to her, marrying him was a vile duty forced on her by the needs of her country.

And to him, she was a woman far more magnificent than he would ever have selected for himself.

A thought which made him feel utterly disloyal to Ruth, as if he hadn't already. Ruth was a pleasant, attractive young woman, but Katerina was heartbreakingly beautiful, translucent with inner glory. Men like Ivan didn't imagine for a moment that they were worthy of approaching such a woman. In fact, the only men who tried to date such women were the arrogant assholes who thought every woman wanted them to drop trou and let the poor bitch have a glimpse of Dr. Love. Even if Ivan hadn't known his script from the fairy tales, he certainly would have known that the only way he could ever kiss such a woman was in her sleep.

At long last—and yet far too soon—they reached Katerina's flower-strewn room and waited while the charivari continued for another few minutes. Ivan even submitted to letting the teenage boys strip off his outer clothing and throw it out the window to the amusement of those who hadn't been able to fit inside the house.

There *were* limits. No one laid a hand on Katerina. Indeed, she was surrounded by women primping her and whispering to her and glancing pointedly at Ivan from time to time, as if to make last-minute assessments of just how badly he was going to treat her and how to keep herself from screaming her way out of the room. He could imagine them saying, "Just lie there and endure it. It's the burden of a woman."

Then the rest were gone. The door closed.

The singing and hand-clapping continued outside their window. The people were waiting. Ivan had vague memories of some culture or other in which the people would expect to be shown bloodstained sheets. But surely that wasn't ninth-century Russia, was it?

He just wasn't getting into the spirit of this. Standing there in his linen tunic, he was keenly aware of how unready he was for any kind of sexual performance. He was so utterly unaroused that for the first time in his life, he actually wondered: Am I gay? After all, I did wear women's clothing.

She looked at him, her face hard-set. Still beautiful, of course. But grim.

"Ivan," she said. "Come closer so I can talk softly."

Stiffly he walked toward her. To his horror, the very act of approaching her changed everything. Instantly he became aroused, a fact which his simple linen tunic did nothing to disguise. She glanced down and then looked away—in disgust?

"I'm sorry," he apologized feebly, wondering what he was apologizing for. When he wasn't aroused, he had felt the need to apologize for that, too.

She put her hand up to silence him.

Her voice was soft. "There's a plot to kill you as soon as our marriage is consummated."

It was amazing how fast his poor libido went slack again.

"We aren't sure who," she said. "Sergei overheard the plotters and told Father Lukas, and he warned me, and I've been wracking my brain trying to think of what we can do about it."

The obvious answer, he saw at once, was never to consummate this marriage. He offered the suggestion.

She rolled her eyes. "Oh, excellent plan. Then the Widow gets her way, *and* everybody is convinced you really do belong in women's garb."

"All right, then, we hop on the bed and do the deed and then I go out and have them stand in line for the privilege of killing me. It will end the suspense."

"All the way up here from the wedding," she said—ignoring him as if he hadn't spoken—"I've been thinking, and I finally reached a conclusion."

He thought she meant she had reached a solution to the problem. But it was nothing so helpful.

"My father has condoned this. The druzhina would not do this unless they believed they were doing his will. And that means I don't dare ask for his help in getting you away."

"Getting me away?" asked Ivan.

"If you and I don't consummate this marriage, you can't stay here. Don't you see? If they've decided to kill you after we're married, but before we know I'm with child, it means they've decided to defy the witch's curse. They have just as much reason to get you out of the way if you *don't* become my husband. I have to get you back to your own world."

"Oh, *now* you decide it's time."

Her eyes burned through him. "I didn't choose you. I've done my best to help you. I know you've done your best as well, but it wasn't enough, was it? We've both failed, and now my people are going to pay the price of our failure. There's no reason for you to go down with the rest of us. You didn't know what you were setting in motion when you woke me. You thought you were saving a woman trapped by a bear. You don't deserve to die for it, even if you aren't the stuff that kings are made of."

Ivan had never felt more worthless in his life. But he was going home.

Sergei was glad he had rushed straight to Ivan's room after the wedding and tucked the parchments under his robe. Thank heaven that Ivan had finally started rolling them up to store them. He was leaving the room when Father Lukas arrived with King Matfei. "Ivan won't be needing this room now, so you're welcome to use it until a new church can be built."

"You're very kind," said Father Lukas. "Sergei, there you are. Where is that book of Gospels? It's the only treasure left to me."

Sergei felt a pang of guilt over the lie that was causing the priest such grief. But compared to the rage Father Lukas would feel if he knew the truth—that Sergei had written all over the parchments and that he and Ivan had both lied—it seemed preferable to go to hell for these sins later.

Whom would Sergei ever be able to confess these sins to? There was no hope for him, none at all. And now Ivan would be killed and . . .

"Sergei? Are you deaf?"

"Father Lukas, the book of Gospels is on the table. I have to go outside."

"No, come in with me and help me arrange the room for the two of us to share."

"Father, it's already arranged for two."

King Matfei became irritated. "Sergei, your master told you to—"

Sergei almost obeyed; but the idea of keeping the manuscripts tucked inside his robe while trying to serve Father Lukas was intolerable. Something would happen to reveal the secret. He could not do it. Besides, Father Lukas was not his master.

"Your Majesty," said Sergei, "I did not know that I, who was born a free man, had become a slave."

The king's face flushed with embarrassment. "I did not mean that you were his . . ."

"My master is Jesus Christ our Lord," said Sergei. "And in the infinite wisdom of God, I find that I am desperate to get outside to void my bowels."

Father Lukas waved him out. "By all means, go, go."

Sergei rushed away.

Outside, he looked around. Where could he possibly hide the manuscripts? He thought of hurrying home to his mother's house, but no, his mother, the poor trusting soul, had apparently befriended Baba Yaga unawares. She could hardly be relied on to keep such a secret as this—she'd confess it first thing to Father Lukas himself.

Is there time to bury it?

There was no place where Sergei had any privacy, no place where he could conceal something and hope that it would remain undisturbed. Should he leave the parchments under a rock in the woods and hope they would still be there when he had a chance to get back to them? He might as well have really put the parchments in the fire as to leave them exposed to the elements like that.

This was all Ivan's fault, thinking of this mad project in the first place. Now Sergei was going to go to hell for another man's sin.

Be honest, he told himself. You thought it was crazy but you went along with it. And once you started writing, you warmed to it right enough. It's not for Ivan's sake anymore that you want to keep these parchments safe. It's because you love the way you wrote the stories on them.

Could there be a clearer case of loving your own sins?

Still, Ivan started it. Sergei might have no place to call his own, but Ivan was the husband of the princess. Let him deal with it.

Sergei headed back inside the king's house. In the corridor, he could hear the voices of Father Lukas and the king; they were still inside Ivan's old room. If they came out, Sergei would be right back where he started.

The revelers were still chanting and singing and laughing outside the house, but there was no one in the corridor. If Sergei knocked loudly enough to be heard over the noise outside the window, Father Lukas and the king would also hear, and would no doubt come out into the corridor to see who was knocking.

Sergei had no choice. He reached down, pulled the latch of the door, and slipped inside the bridal chamber, closing the door silently after himself. He was careful to keep his eyes to the wall as he fumbled inside his robe to pull out the parchments.

He had half-expected a screech from the startled bride or an exclamation from Ivan, but there was not a sound. Then he heard a chuckle from Katerina.

"Look what God has sent us," she said.

"You can turn around," said Ivan.

There stood the princess, fully clothed. And Ivan, in his linen tunic. Nobody naked, thank God. They were standing side by side, looking at him, the princess with amusement, Ivan with consternation.

"Sorry to interrupt," said Sergei. He held out the parchments.

Ivan strode to him, took them. "This isn't the moment I would have chosen."

"I didn't choose the moment," said Sergei. "The king has given Father Lukas the room you were using. Since you won't need it now."

"What sort of conspiracy is this?" asked the princess. "I thought these parchments burned."

Ivan unrolled them and showed her the back of one. He knew that she was literate; she had studied for her baptism far more rigorously than he had. In the ninth century it was not yet shocking for a woman to read—it was shocking for *anyone* to read.

She scanned Sergei's writing quickly, just a few sentences. "The story of I-Know-Not-What? Why would you write this down?" Then she shook her head. "It was for *this* that you wanted parchment, Ivan?"

"These stories have all been changed in my time. No one understands how old they are, and how they used to be."

"But they're just stories." Katerina shook her head. "Never mind. I have no hope of understanding you. I feel sorry for the trouble you'll get Sergei in, when this comes out."

"Why would it come out?" asked Ivan, looking her in the eye.

"I see," she said. "All right, I'll keep these in my room. The secret won't come out."

"Thank you," said Sergei. He laid his hand upon the latch, ready to leave again. But Katerina's voice stopped him.

"Not so fast," she said. "I need something from you in return."

"What?" asked Sergei. "Anything."

"I need you to go fetch Father Lukas. Tell him that I wish him to come into this room, just him and you, to shrive us both again and to pray for us that we will conceive at once, and a boy child."

"But you were already shriven in the—"

"Tell him in these words," said Katerina. "Say that *I* say that since the fire in the church prevented me from completing my confession, I would like him to come and do it now. And then the rest, about the prayer. And Ivan wants you to come with him, Sergei. Do it."

Sergei nodded, glancing at Ivan, who only raised his eyebrows, as if to say he had no idea what was going on, but don't question the motives of women. Since to Sergei women were all an unplumbable mystery, most especially Katerina, whose beauty made it impossible for men to think around her, he had no intention of trying to understand anything except what his errand was supposed to be.

When Sergei returned to the room that was now Father Lukas's, the king was still there.

"Took you long enough," said the king.

"I was thinking that he returned rather quickly," said Father Lukas.

"As I passed along the corridor," said Sergei, keeping his eyes down, hoping that the appearance of humility would mask his second calculated lie of the day, "the door to the bridal chamber opened, and the princess said, 'Go to Father Lukas, and tell him that since the fire in the church prevented him from hearing my confession this morning, I would like him to come now, and bring you with him, and shrive both me and my husband, and bless us that we will conceive a boychild from our first union."

It took all his self-discipline, but Sergei did not look up to see how Father Lukas took this message. For Father Lukas would know at once that it was a lie. What mattered was, would he think it was Katerina's lie or Sergei's?

"Your Majesty," said Father Lukas, "let me go and ease your daughter's troubled heart. The burden of responsibility weighs on her, and perhaps with God's help that burden can be eased on this day that should be happy for a woman."

"Go, go," said the king, "though it sounds like pious nonsense to me. You already blessed her during the wedding, didn't you? And why would you need Sergei?"

"I believe," said Sergei softly, "that it was Ivan who wanted to see me. Perhaps he, too, has an errand for me."

"It just seems strange to me," said the king, "that a bridegroom should ask for a young man to visit him in the bridal chamber, especially the young man with whom he has been sharing a room."

"You must be careful about giving voice to such thoughts," said Father Lukas. "What to you sounds like idle wondering will sound to another like an accusation."

"Who would hear?" said the king.

"Anyone standing in the corridor would hear words spoken in this room," said Father Lukas. "Just as anyone in this room would hear words spoken in the corridor."

For a moment, Sergei was afraid that Father Lukas meant to tell the king what he had overheard just that morning in this very room. But to his relief, Father Lukas merely bade the king good-bye for the moment and then glided from the room, Sergei bobbing along behind him in his wake.

Father Lukas slipped into the room and, as Sergei closed the door, looked at Katerina with annoyance and amusement. "Interesting, to use a lie to send me a message. We finished your confession."

"The message you understood was true. I needed you to come here, and needed you to have a reasonable excuse for doing it."

"Why does a princess need an old priest in her bridal chamber?" Father Lukas looked at Ivan. "Or is it you who needs help? Surely you don't expect me to give you lessons on this subject."

"I need to get Ivan out of here and safely away from the house."

"Because the marriage has been consummated? Or because it has not?"

"Let's leave everyone wondering about that," said Katerina.

"What's your plan?"

"Have Sergei and Ivan trade clothes. Ivan leaves limping, his face hooded, following close behind you. Who will look at him?"

"And then what?"

"Sergei and I wait for a little while. You bring back more of his proper clothing for Sergei to wear. While Ivan runs away, Sergei and I emerge, asking what happened to Ivan, he disappeared suddenly."

Father Lukas frowned. "Which is only slightly true."

"They have to believe the Pretender spirited him away, or they'll start to search too soon."

"And you consent to this?" Father Lukas asked Ivan. "Running away on your wedding night?"

"It seems more prudent than bloodshed," said Ivan.

"We have to hurry," said Katerina. "You can be sure several people have cast spells to see if I am still a virgin. The longer we take, the more impatient the plotters will become."

Father Lukas turned to Sergei. "Does that robe come off, or weren't you listening?"

Sergei doffed his robe at once. He and Ivan exchanged a glance:

What if Father Lukas had ordered this while Sergei still had the parchments tucked under the robe?

Ivan pulled it on over his head. Then he put up the hood.

"Thank you, Father," said Katerina.

"I don't like lying."

"To save a life, is it a sin?" she asked.

"Perhaps just a venial one."

Ivan turned to Katerina. "I can't get over the bridge without you there."

"I'll get there as soon as I can. You simply have to hide till then."

"I'm not sure I know the way."

"Follow the trail of broken branches you left behind you as you came through."

Ivan shook his head. "I'm no hunter, I don't know how to follow signs like that."

She seemed to make an effort to be patient. "Can you figure out where west is?"

"As long as the sun's up."

"And uphill, do you know that one?"

Ivan glared at her.

"I wasn't being nasty," she said. "You don't always understand every word I say, I just wanted to make sure you knew. I have to be able to find you out there."

"You have to find me, and they mustn't find me, and it's the same trail."

She reached up and pulled three or four strands of her hair out of her head. "Tie these around your wrist," she said. "I'll find you."

Ivan couldn't do it one-handed. Sergei helped him.

"Now go," said Katerina. "We have to play the scene out before dark."

Ivan took a few steps, trying to get Sergei's limp right.

"No, no," said Sergei. "You look like you're *trying* to limp. I try *not* to limp."

Ivan tried again. It wasn't good, but it was better.

"Come on," said Father Lukas. "I'll give you something heavy to carry, and that will explain the change in your gait."

Father Lukas led the way out of the room. Ivan followed close behind. Limping, his foot twisted.

Sergei rushed to the door and latched it behind him. There he stood in his tattered linen undergarment, so full of holes it was like wearing a fishing net. Katerina was not looking at him, which meant she *had* looked at him and now was looking away so as not to cause him shame.

"Thank you for keeping the secret of the parchments," he said to her.

"A lot of secrets are being kept tonight," she said softly.

"I don't belong in this room."

"Neither of us does. But sometimes we're put in a place and we have to do our best."

Sergei appreciated her modesty, but knew that even if she believed it, her statement wasn't true. "You'd be a princess no matter where you were."

"We'll soon see," said Katerina.

"What do you mean?"

"Nothing," she said. "Don't be afraid of me. I've seen men bathing, I have no particular fear of seeing through the holes in your tunic."

"I'm not afraid, I just . . . I'm not the one who should be here."

"Oh, now I understand you. Well, Ivan didn't belong here either. Just bad luck, him finding me."

"Not luck, I don't think," said Sergei. "He's your husband now."

"An oath, but it can be annulled if it isn't acted on."

"I think," said Sergei, "that he's a better man than you believe he is."

"I believe he's a very good man," said Katerina. "Not a king, though."

"A bird can't pull a plow."

"I needed God to send me a plowhorse. I tried to make do with what he sent instead. I failed."

"Maybe God's message is that you don't need plowing." Then Sergei realized the double meaning of what he said. "Not to say he's the plow and you're the—I mean, I—"

"I understood you," she said.

There was a soft knock on the door. Sergei opened it. A hand thrust another robe through the door. Sergei took it, then closed the door again. He pulled a priestly robe over his head. It had fresh burn holes on the back. Of course—Father Lukas couldn't continue wearing a damaged garment.

"Imagine," said Katerina. "A Slavic priest."

"I do imagine it," said Sergei. "But it will not be me."

"Why not?"

"Never me."

"And I say, why not?"

Sergei laughed bitterly. "How convincing will I be, talking about how Jesus healed all the sick and the crippled? What more proof does anyone need that I'm not a man of faith?"

"Jesus isn't here."

"Jesus is everywhere. And as he often said, 'Your faith has made you whole.' "

"So don't be a priest," said Katerina. "But if you aren't that, what are you?"

"Is that how priestly vocation comes?" asked Sergei. "Because my foot was born twisted, I must be God's chosen servant?"

"We are all called to be servants of God in whatever way we can. Perhaps I can serve him as a princess. Perhaps you as a priest."

"Do you think I served God when I wrote down those old stories?"

Katerina shrugged. "That's beyond my judging."

"I'll tell you what I think. I think God made all men, including the people who told these stories. So these things are the creations of God. Or the creations of his creations, but it amounts to the same thing. And if God created the people who would make up these stories and tell them, then by saving them I'm also honoring God."

"God made the murderers and adulterers, too."

"I think these stories are good. I think they teach us to love goodness."

"Or to wish for the power to do great deeds," she answered. "But we've given them time enough. We need to give the alarm."

Sergei winced. "You do all the talking, would you?"

"Yes," she said. "I'm good at talking, I suppose." Then, without warning, she gave a shriek.

They could hear the crowd outside the window fall silent, then set to murmuring. Who screeched? Was it the princess? Is he hurting her?

Katerina rushed to the window, flung open the shutters. "Did he come out here? Did you see him pass?"

"Who?" asked the people.

"My husband! We were new-shriven, Father Lukas left, Ivan and I were talking, and suddenly he wasn't there!"

The people took only a moment to digest the tale before they reached the only conclusion that made sense. "The Widow took him! Another curse! Another spell!"

Katerina burst into tears. "Am I never to be free of the witch's plots?"

Even as she wept, however, she was scanning the crowd, watching to see who reacted. A couple of druzhinniks started walking briskly around the crowd, heading for what? Some rendezvous. If only she could see more clearly at such a distance. Who was it? Which of the king's knights? She would know who the plotters were by seeing who began first to search for Ivan.

"Were you bedded?" asked an elderly peasant woman.

Katerina bowed her head. "We had the blessing of the priest. How could I guess the devil could reach us through that wall of glory?"

From the walk, Katerina recognized one of them. Dimitri. A part of her said, No, not Dimitri, not the hero, the man who should be king. Another part of her said, Of course Dimitri. Who else? If he was in the plot, then it was his plot. Even if he didn't begin it, once in he would lead it. Ivan's danger was worse than she had feared. For in the back of her mind, she had counted on Dimitri being on the king's side.

Unless by plotting to kill Ivan he *was* on the king's side. Or thought he was.

Katerina began crying harder, but pretending less. She reached out and drew the shutter closed. The moment the crowd could no longer see her, her tears stopped. "I have to get out of here now, with no one following me."

"Good luck," said Sergei. "Dressed like that, you can hide just about as easily as you can stuff a rainbow into a pot."

"Almost I wish I could wear your clothes."

"*Men's* clothing?"

"It wouldn't work," said Katerina. "There's only one priest in Taina, and there's no way I can pass for Father Lukas."

"So what will you do?"

"Ask you to turn your back, while I change into something less becoming."

Sergei complied, trying not to imagine what the rustling sounds he was hearing might mean, or what the sight of her might be at any given moment. Katerina was not and never could be for him; there was no point in thinking thoughts that would excite desires that could never be satisfied. It would only make his life taste more bitter, to dwell on the sweetness that could not be his.

"Thank you," she said. "We can go now."

Sergei turned and saw her in her simplest dress, the one she wore when she helped with the harvest. Every year she bound sheaves with the best of them, her fingers as deft as any woman's at tying them off, and Sergei had often seen this dress covered in straw and dust. No matter. She was as beautiful in this simple clothing as she ever was in the more royal finery.

She opened the door for him.

"But it's my place to open the latch for you, princess," he said.

"I'm on my way to help my lord escape from this land," she said. "What do I care about courtesy?"

Sergei followed her out the door. "Then the marriage," he said softly. "It's real, despite all?"

"I'll have no other," she said. "My word is given."

At that moment, they heard a tumult outside. Shouting. Much running.

"I think perhaps I heard someone shout your husband's name," said Sergei.

Katerina stopped, crossed herself. "Holy Mother, make me fleet of foot," she said. Then, hiking up her skirts, she scampered down the corridor, into the great room, and out the door.

Ivan thought everything was going so well. Father Lukas might be humorless and rigid about religion, but when it came to politics, he knew how to be flexible. Why was Ivan surprised? There was a reason why Christianity thrived in the barbarian kingdoms of Europe, and this was it: The missionary priests knew how to make themselves useful, how to put royalty into their debt. Katerina wanted to save the life of this preposterous husband she acquired through witchcraft? Very well, Father Lukas would do his part.

They headed westward through the village, toward the gap in the woods where Katerina had first shown him the village. A few children ran along, chattering to the priest, calling out to him. Many people waved a greeting. But one little girl, snot-lipped and covered with dirt, paid no attention to Father Lukas. She came right up to Ivan, tugged at his robe, tagged along beside him.

"What's wrong with your foot?" she demanded.

Ivan did not want to speak. He didn't want anybody hearing that his voice was not Sergei's. Ivan's accent wasn't bad—but it wasn't native, either, not in proto-Slavonic.

"I said, what's wrong with your foot!"

Father Lukas came to his rescue. "His foot has been twisted from birth."

"*Sergei's* foot is twisted, but this one's just pretending!" cried the little girl at top volume.

"That *is* Sergei. Now hush and go away."

"That's not Sergei," said the little girl. "Sergei always calls me dewdrop and warns the fairies not to switch me for a changeling."

Ivan cursed silently. There was no way he could have prepared himself for this.

"He did not speak to you because he has taken a vow of silence," said Father Lukas.

Ivan welcomed the lie. Everyone was probably going to hell, now—who was left who hadn't lied today?—but it was decent of Father Lukas to do it.

"He did not!" said the girl. She began running around, shouting at any villager who might listen. "The new man is wearing Sergei's clothes! The new man is wearing Sergei's clothes!"

People began paying attention. People weren't the problem, though. It was the knights of the druzhina they were trying to avoid. Ivan had not seen any along the way, though with his head in a hood and his face downcast, it's not as though he had much of a view.

Father Lukas quickened his pace. Ivan could hear adults now, asking questions. "*Is* it Katerina's husband? Is it the new man? What's he doing? Where's he going?" Some even called out to Father Lukas. "Who's that with you, Father Lukas?" In answer, Father Lukas walked even more quickly.

And then, abruptly, he stopped. Ivan bumped into him.

Father Lukas's voice was so soft that it took a moment for Ivan to realize he was speaking. "Now would be a good time to run."

"What?" asked Ivan.

Father Lukas's answer was much louder this time. "Cast off the hood, hitch up the skirts, and run, you fool!"

Ivan cast off the hood and saw Dimitri and two other druzhinniks jogging toward him, weapons in hand.

"It *is* the interloper!" said one of them.

"Running away!"

"Deserting King Matfei and Princess Katerina."

Ivan recognized this as an attempt to justify in advance the unfortunate necessity of killing the traitorous Ivan. He started to run for the woods, but his legs got caught up in the skirts and he fell on his face in the grass. He might have got right up, but Father Lukas was trying to help him by gripping his robe and pulling in the wrong direction. Ivan couldn't get purchase with his hands to push himself up, and Lukas hadn't the strength to stand him up by main strength.

Finally, with the pounding of the knights' feet almost upon them,

Ivan simply raised his arms straight above his head and slipped out of the robe, the linen undergarment and all. Once again, he was as naked as the day he arrived there. Only this time he didn't give a damn about that. At least he was leathershod—he'd be able to run much better this time without every pebble or twig slicing at the bottoms of his feet.

"Look at the coward!" said one man.

"Father Lukas has plucked his feathers—now to get him on the spit for roasting!" cried Dimitri.

But their good cheer evaporated quickly when they realized that Ivan was twice as fast as any of them, laden as they were with weapons, and untrained for speed. He reached the woods long before they were even close. Good thing none of them has a bow, he thought.

An arrow twanged into the trunk of a tree ten feet from his head.

All right, so they had a bowman. Just not a good one.

Ivan dodged among the trees, taking care to put as many trunks as possible between himself and his pursuers.

"He won't get far in the woods!" shouted Dimitri. "Where are the dogs!"

The tumult continued, and Ivan heard some crashing in the underbrush far behind him, but he couldn't make out any more words.

Maybe the king would call off the search before it got too far, Ivan thought as the branches again whipped and sliced his skin. He couldn't go full speed in the woods. Worse yet, he had no idea where he was going. Katerina had not led him on a straight path coming here, and everything looked different in this direction, anyway. It was uphill, too—but Ivan was used to that on his daily runs back in Tantalus. In the future, to train for this, he'd have to run naked with two assistants alongside, whipping him with wands and switches every few seconds. He wondered if there was any chance of making that an Olympic event.

Katerina came outside the house to find the village in an uproar, everybody running toward the west, calling out that Katerina's husband was running away. Katerina did not join the general pursuit. Instead, she took a circuitous route among the houses, entering the woods well to the south of where Ivan had gone in.

Sergei watched her go, unable to keep up, and not particularly interested in trying. It was all out of his hands.

Still, he was curious, so he limped along the grassy main street until he came upon Father Lukas, who was grumpily coming the other way. "Foolish business anyway," he said. "That snot-faced little girl you call 'dewdrop' caught on that it wasn't you in the robe and wouldn't shut up about it."

"Dewdrop?" said Sergei. "Dewdrop is dead. She died when I was only nine years old."

Father Lukas glared at him for a moment; then the expression gave away to something else. Fear? Not Father Lukas, surely.

"Never mind," said Sergei. "We know the Widow uses us like sheep, shearing us or skinning us at her pleasure."

"A girl about this tall?" asked Father Lukas, still trying to make sense of things.

"Yes, yes," said Sergei. "But it wasn't her. There's been no resurrection, Father Lukas. It was the Widow, as I said."

"Making us see a little girl?"

"Why not? She showed herself as an old woman before she burned down the church this morning," said Sergei. "She wants this Ivan dead, and she's going to keep trying till he's filleted and roasted."

"Not those stories of her eating her captives again," said Father Lukas.

"They say she does."

"Who says?" said Father Lukas. "Who is it who saw her eating, but she didn't eat *them*?" He held out the robe and undergarment Ivan had been wearing. "Now you can have these back."

"What's Ivan wearing?" asked Sergei.

"What Adam wore in the garden," said Father Lukas. "What Noah wore when he was drunk in his tent after the flood. What David wore when he danced in triumph in the streets after his victory."

"Naked come we into the world," said Sergei, getting into the spirit of things, "and naked we go out of it."

"Well," said Father Lukas, "naked except for boots."

Sergei took the clothing. "The robe is mine, all right," he said. "But the linen is his."

"He's running at full speed through the woods," said Father Lukas. "You're welcome to follow him and return it." With that, Father Lukas passed him and headed back toward the king's house.

Father Lukas had been joking, but Sergei liked the idea better the more he thought of it. But there was no point in following Ivan—he'd be running, and dodging all pursuers. The princess, however, would be dodging no one—if a druzhinnik met her in the woods they'd do her no harm, and she was still under the protection of the spells that had counteracted Baba Yaga's curse in the first place, so she had nothing to fear from that source, either.

Sergei left the street and wandered among the houses till he found the place where Katerina had gone into the woods. It was a plain enough path; she had not departed from it. Nor was she moving all that quickly. When she stopped at the rendezvous place, Sergei wouldn't be all that far behind her.

It was near dark, and though the moon was almost full, not that much light penetrated to the lower reaches of the forest. Ivan was hopelessly lost, but it had been a couple of hours since he last heard dogs barking or men calling out to each other. So he was safe enough. Unless Baba Yaga sent the bear back for a second try. Or he fell off a cliff in the darkness. Or he sprained his ankle and died of exposure trying to crawl back to civilization.

Civilization? Yes, that's what Taina was, by contemporary standards. Men with swords who had no qualms about killing a man and expected to have no punishment for it—it was civilization in the same sense that some drug dealer's turf was civilized. What was the difference between Dimitri and some thug with an Uzi?

Not fair. Dimitri lived in a different time. If he were in the U.S. in 1992 and wanted Ivan out of the way, he'd hire a lawyer and sue. Had he been in Kiev in 1970, he'd have whispered a hint to the KGB. He wielded a sword here in Taina because that's what men used to settle quarrels.

Why am I giving the man who wants to kill me the benefit of the doubt? Screw him. Let *him* break his ankle and fall off a cliff and get eaten by a bear. Let *him* marry the princess and become the king. Come to think of it, that's probably what Dimitri had in mind. He'd make the better husband. It should have been him all along. If I died right now it would be better for everybody.

The hell it would. It would be worse for *me*, and selfish as it might be, I want to live. I even want to go home.

The path, such as it was, went straight, but Ivan turned to the left and slid down a rather steep slope. Why did I do that? he wondered. Why did I choose that way? It came to him that for the past hour, he had been following, not the line of least resistance, as he had before, but a fairly straight line toward . . .

Toward Katerina. The hairs tied around his wrist. She was calling him. He should have known that she'd anticipate his lack of skill in the woods.

It wasn't long after that before he followed his "intuition" into a wide, moon-washed clearing, perfectly round, with a pit in the middle of it, and a pedestal rising in the middle of the pit. Katerina was waiting for him in the moonlight.

Ivan looked around to see if anyone else was there.

"No one," she said. "The place is hidden from anyone but us, because the bridges are ours. Even the Widow can't see, though she put me here, and her bear to guard me. If she couldn't see here, who else would ever find me?"

Ivan hardly listened. He was trying not to be shy of his nakedness. Then he laughed at the impulse. He had nothing to hide from her now. Not only had she seen him before, she was now his wife.

He had almost reached her when he saw movement behind her, at the edge of the woods. "If this place is hidden," he said, "who's that?"

She turned, startled, afraid. "Come out!" she said. "Show yourself!"

A shadow emerged from the wood, moving with a strange, rolling gait. When it reached the moonlight, it turned into Sergei.

Ivan called out in greeting, but Katerina was annoyed. "How did you find this place?"

"I followed you," he said.

Ivan laughed. "So much for this place being hidden."

"It *is*. Sergei must have a right to be here."

Ivan shrugged. "I don't know how these things work."

"I'll be gone soon enough," said Sergei. "I only brought these for Ivan." He held out the wool robe and linen tunic Ivan had been wearing.

"But that's *your* robe," Ivan said.

"I'm not naked."

"Trade me, at least," said Ivan. "Your own proper robe for you, and I'll wear the one that Father Lukas burned holes in today." He pulled the tunic on over his head. The cloth snagged on the rough and broken skin of his chest and thighs, and his wounds stung as the linen brushed them. But it was good to be dressed again. "Thank you, Sergei," he said.

In the meantime, Sergei had doffed Father Lukas's castoff clothing, and Ivan pulled it on. It smelled of smoke. Burnt wool—a nasty odor. Wool and fire and something else, too. Horsehair. Was there horsehair woven into the robe?

No, of course not. Father Lukas wears a hair shirt. The private penance of those who feared they were not humble enough. Ivan rather liked the fact that at least Father Lukas knew his own primary sin and was trying to deal with it.

Sergei wriggled inside his own clothes, clearly pleased to have them back.

The comedy was over. Everybody was going to be back where they belonged. Ivan had no idea what he would tell people back in America about this. Or even what he'd tell Cousin Marek. I went for a run in the woods, and I got lost for a few weeks, and here I am . . .

A few weeks? Eleven hundred years had passed while Katerina lay on that pedestal, and yet it had taken only a few months in Taina. If that proportion held true, even the weeks he had spent here could be a century or more. His family might be gone, the world might be so changed that he'd be unable to function in it . . .

Get a grip. Don't borrow trouble. The pedestal is one thing, a magic place. The rules of time might be identical, or time might flow in unpredictable ways. There was nothing he could do about it.

Katerina took him by the hand. At once he could see the bridge to the pedestal—her bridge. She led him across. Sergei stood, watching them, mesmerized.

"How do you do it?" he said. "Walking through the air?"

"There's a bridge," said Ivan. "But only Katerina can see it. Katerina and whomever she holds by the hand."

"Where will you go?" asked Sergei.

"Home," said Ivan. "I'll go home, and Katerina will return to you, and—"

"I'll do no such thing," she said.

They reached the pedestal. She did not let go of his hand.

"What do you mean?" asked Ivan.

"I'm coming with you," she said.

"You can't do that."

"Why can't I? Hold my hand and lead me across your bridge."

"But your people need you."

"If I stay, then I'm a bride abandoned by her husband with the marriage unconsummated. The Pretender will be down our throats in a few days. But if I go with you, then I'm a bride off on a journey with her new husband. Let the old hag wonder whether or when the marriage becomes complete."

"I can't hear you!" Sergei called. "Are you talking about leaving us, princess?"

"I'm traveling with my husband, to visit his parents," said Katerina.

"What will I tell the others?"

"Tell them that. It's no secret. Tell everyone."

"What about this place? Can I show them this place?"

"No," said Katerina. "Tell them it's enchanted and you can't find it again without me to guide you."

"But I could find it quite easily," he said.

"I have no doubt you could," said Katerina. "But if you *tell* them it's enchanted, they'll believe you and won't press you to say more."

"You mean . . . *lie?*"

Katerina burst out laughing. So did Ivan. Sergei smiled shyly. They had liked his joke.

"You've been a good friend to me," said Ivan.

"And you to me," said Sergei. "But what will happen to the parchments? Where did you hide them, princess?"

"In my room. In the rag chest, where no man would touch it."

Sergei didn't like thinking about what women used those rags for.

"But as soon as you can," Katerina said, "you must get them and bring them here. To this enchanted place."

Sergei winced at the thought of actually rummaging through her intimate things. But there was a hopeful meaning to the assignment as well.

"So you will come back. Won't you?" Sergei asked.

"Yes," said Katerina. "If I can."

"And you, Ivan?"

"What for?" asked Ivan. "I'm no good at living here."

Sergei couldn't argue with him. Neither could Katerina.

"All the same," said Sergei. "I hope you do come back."

"Maybe," said Ivan. "Maybe long enough to find out where those manuscripts will be hidden. So I can discover them in my own land."

It still made no sense to Sergei. He shook his head and watched as Ivan walked to the edge of the pedestal and seemed to step off into nothing.

Ivan disappeared. All at once, the moment he set foot on the invisible bridge, he was gone. And a moment later, as the princess followed him, she was gone, too.

Sergei stood there for a few moments, gazing at the place where they had been. This was serious magic here. Not like the spells and curses that were commonplace in the village, and which didn't work half the time anyway. To make two people disappear in the moonlight—it made Sergei wonder. If I had magic power like this, it wouldn't matter that I have a crippled foot. And for a moment he imagined himself standing before Baba Yaga, the two of them on a great stone between two mighty armies, facing each other, five feet apart. She would raise her hand and cast a spell at him, chanting unspeakable words, and he would laugh, wave off her pathetic powers, and utter a single word of power. No, not a word, even. He would trace the shape of a rune in the air, and she would turn into a goose and rise honking into the air, terrified, confused, filled with a sudden inexplicable longing to fly south forever . . .

Just a dream, and a foolish one at that. Sergei was God's servant now, with no powers of his own, only the power to obey. But for a few moments he had been part of great events. Grand adventures. None of the boys who had grown up with him, with their two equal feet, their smooth walk, their level stance, none of them had been trusted to stand here with the princess and her husband. None of them had been given the task of writing down all the old stories, so they could live on in another time and place.

The future will be full of men like Ivan. Someday, a thousand years from now, that's what Ivan said. A world where men can live by reading and writing, by talking and thinking. A world where a man like me could be something other than a slops boy for a foreign priest.

He turned and walked away from the pit, back along the path he had taken. The night was chilly, and he was tired. When he got back there would be questions. There would be no concealing his own involvement in the escape—Ivan had been wearing his clothes, and now Sergei was returning with those same clothes on his back. But Dimitri would not lift a hand against him. There was no honor in hitting a cripple. And Sergei was not his own man. What could he do but obey? There would be no blame for him. And some would think him something of a hero, in his own small way. He was the one that Ivan and Katerina had trusted to see them fly away into another world.

BABA YAGA

She came home in a foul temper. Bear had expected it, so he knew to be away for the first few hours. When he finally figured it was safe—the howling had stopped, the birds were flying normally, and the wolves weren't whimpering anymore—he shambled back into the castle and on into his wife's fine warm house, which was all the warmer now, since she had broken up a considerable amount of furniture and thrown it on the fire.

"That's very wasteful," he said.

"Shut up."

"You were an old woman today and started a fire, and you were a little girl and started a manhunt in the forest, and it all came to nothing."

"She's gone!" cried Baba Yaga. "Out of my power! What did those bitches do to my curse? They left a bridge to his world. They left a bridge behind, and she crossed over!"

"So what will you do? She's gone. What's stopping you now from having Taina?"

"She's not dead, that's what's stopping me. She's not dead and everyone knows she's not dead. They'll go off and make a baby where I can't reach them, and come home with an heir, and then if I attack the whole Kievan league will come down on me and *you* will betray me and it's not fair!"

Baba Yaga always said that it wasn't fair, but to Bear it looked like things had worked out pretty evenly. Nobody had what they wanted. Baba Yaga didn't have Taina, but neither did Katerina. Equality of suffering—what could be more fair than that?

"Well, they can't get away from me that easily," said Baba Yaga.

"Oh?"

"I'll follow them. I'll go into wherever the hell he came from, and I'll tear it apart till I find them."

"Be careful," said Bear. "You don't know what wizards might be waiting for you there."

"If he's a sample of what they've got in that world, then I have nothing to fear."

"If you can get there."

"If those meddling do-gooders can make a pathway to his world, so can I. It will take a little research, but I'll find my way. Besides, I know her scent. I can follow her anywhere. Through time and space, wherever she is—I have the taste of her in my mouth. I'll eat the little bitch for breakfast."

Bear yawned. He had heard all this before.

"I will! Don't think I won't!"

"Whatever," said Bear. "Unfortunately, I'll no doubt be here when you get back."

"It won't take me long," she muttered. "I'll figure out where they went, I'll find a way to get there, and I'll have her back here in a week. Then you can feast on womanflesh! How's that, my beautiful Bear?"

"Fish are better. But I never interfere with my wife in the kitchen."

"Very funny," said Baba Yaga. "As if I cooked."

"As if I would ever trust anything you gave me to eat," said Bear.

"Sometimes you do," she said.

"You always poison me, though."

"If I poisoned you, you'd never know it, because you'd be dead."

"Just a little poison. Every damn time, it's some new potion or powder. I never know if it's going to be dysentery or a headache or impotence or priapism."

"You sound as if I did nothing but abuse you."

"What else?" said the Bear. "You think I don't know why you haven't killed me? Why I'm still around for you to do these things to? Making me run around that pit for a thousand years, for instance! Losing an eye, for instance!"

"*He* did that. I'll serve *him* for your supper, too."

"The only reason you didn't kill me long ago is because you can't."

"It's because I love you. And my enchantment of you isn't all bad. You like having the power of speech well enough."

"Gods don't need to speak. They only need to desire, and they have it."

"You wish."

"You've harnessed me and you're using my power somehow and I can't even hate you for it, because whenever I think of how much rage I ought to feel, my whole being is suffused with warmth and passion and lust for your miserable wizened old body."

"You should be a poet, the way you bandy words of love."

"I just thought you'd be interested to know that I've figured it all out."

"It took you long enough, but you *are* a bear, after all."

"I think I've figured it out before, and then you give me something to make me forget."

"Memory is so fickle," said Baba Yaga. "Just keep loving me, my pet."

"Oh, I do," said Bear. "With all my bitter heart, I love you."

"And you promise that you'll miss me when I'm gone to that place where Ivan and Katerina are hiding from me?"

"I'll smell your scent on the bedclothes and go mad from missing you."

"Give me a kiss then. And come to bed with me. You notice I didn't burn the bed. So you see I do love you."

Bear shook his great head back and forth. "Bed's not burnt, no."

"Then let's burn it now. A bonfire of passion. Many a woman has had her triumphs under the bedclothes, but I . . . I have tamed a bear! I have slept with Winter and I have made him warm!"

Bear growled a little, but he did as he was bidden.

10

OLD GODS

here is always a symmetry in magical things, a balance, so Katerina well knew what to expect when she stepped off the invisible bridge into the land of Ivan's birth. Nothing could be carried across the bridge; only what you already had would be restored to you. So yes, of course, the fire-holed priestly robe disappeared from Ivan's body and was replaced by the clothing he had been wearing on that fateful day when he fought his way to the place of her enchantment and kissed her awake. And yes, she felt the cool breeze of evening all over her body, for her own clothing had vanished, to be replaced by nothing, for she had never been in this place and had no vestment here.

The shame of it made her breathless for a moment. True, Ivan was her husband; but since he did not love her and would never come to her as husband now, she felt no stirring of anticipation to soften the shock of being exposed before a man. A woman's nakedness was a precious thing, to be protected until it was given as a gift to her husband. Or, in this case, to her people, for was it not for their sake that she had done all these things? Made a vow to this stranger, and crossed this bridge, and now exposed herself to any eye?

Ivan laughed.

In that moment she hated him, that he would laugh at her.

"Oh, you're angry?" he said.

She did not like the taunting tone of his voice, and turned her back on him.

"I wasn't laughing at you," said Ivan, "I was laughing at fate. The—" He searched for a word. "—malice of fate."

No, she was not going to hide from him, as if *she* had cause for shame. She turned to face him, though she could not stop herself from covering her breasts with her arms. "I'm naked and you're laughing," she said.

"I'm not laughing now," he said. "But it's childish of you to be angry at me. You laughed at *my* nakedness."

"I did not," she said. Though the moment she said it, she could not remember if she had or not. But why shouldn't she? "You're a man. Men are naked whenever they want."

"Not in my world," said Ivan. "In my world, it's women who are more often naked. But I'm sorry that I laughed."

He began unfastening his shirt. What, did he think she'd feel better if he joined her in nakedness? Or did he think this was a good moment to consummate their marriage vows?

Neither. He shrugged the shirt off his shoulders, pulled the sleeves over his wrists, and then offered the thing to her.

"And what would I do with this?"

"Wear it," he said.

Was he insane? Had he learned nothing? "I'm a Christian woman," she said. "What you suggest is too wicked to imagine."

He rolled his eyes, as if she were an annoying child. "In your world, you were right, and I was wrong to wear women's clothing. It was better to be naked."

"Then why are you offering me this?"

"Because this isn't your world. And here, it's no sin for a woman to wear men's clothing. In fact, it's done all the time, and it means nothing. Christian women do it and no one thinks ill of them. A woman puts on her husband's shirt and we think it's charming. That it shows love and intimacy between them."

She was horrified to think that Christianity had come to such a pass. "And does the husband put on his wife's dress?"

He looked embarrassed. "Well, actually, no. I mean, some do, but we think of that as . . . strange."

"The world may be insane, but I am not," she said. She turned her back on him again. "Wherever we're going, let's go. The day is late, and I'll be cold if I spend the night in the forest."

"Katerina," he said. His tone of voice was one she hadn't heard from him before. Angry. No, masterful.

"What?" she said.

"Look at me," he said.

She turned to face him, letting her own anger show. "What is this? Are you claiming the right of a husband? Or do you forget that even as your wife, I'm the princess of Taina?"

"I'm forgetting nothing. I'm claiming nothing." But his tone did not become meek again. "You're the one forgetting something. This is not your world. There is no Taina here, and no princesses. Only a naked woman and a man with clothing on. And in *this* world, people will suspect only two possible explanations. One is that he has raped her. The other is that she's a whore."

The insult was unbearable. Without even thinking, she slapped him.

"Oh, good," he said, not even seeming to register the sting of the slap, though his cheek turned red. "So you've decided to make them think I've raped you. What will happen, of course, is that I'll be taken to . . . I'll be taken away and punished. And since you don't speak the language here, and can't prove who you are, and if they do understand you you'll have these wild stories about being an enchanted princess, I can bet you'll be put in a . . . pen for crazy people. And that's the end of the story."

She had no idea what he was talking about. A pen for crazy people? A man taken away for rape? Either he married the woman or was killed for it by the woman's family.

She hadn't really thought of it before—though she should have, she saw that now. His bizarre behavior when he arrived in Taina wasn't a private madness of his own. He came from a mad world, and by crossing the bridge, she had entered into madness. The rules were different here; that's why he came to Taina with strange expectations.

But how much did a Christian woman have to compromise just because she was in a strange place? Her first instinct was: Compromise nothing. God's law is not changed, just because a woman travels from one place to another. It is still a shame for a woman to be naked, still a worse shame for her to put a man's clothing upon her.

And yet . . . if he told the truth, what then? She was not a whore; should she behave in a way that made people think that she was? That was a kind of lying, wasn't it? And he had not raped her—indeed, he *could* not rape her, for the vows had been said, and it was his right to use her body as he saw fit. So he was the opposite of a rapist, he was a kind husband who had not forced his reluctant wife, and he even now respected her decency by not eyeing her naked body even though it was on plain display for him. Instead, he was offering her a way to cover herself.

"Adam and Eve covered themselves with leaves," said Ivan.

"That would keep us warm for a night," she said. "But we couldn't walk far."

"They covered themselves to hide their nakedness," said Ivan. "They covered themselves with whatever they had available. Here is a piece of cloth with sleeves for your arms and a way to fasten it closed across your body. It may once have been used as clothing by another person, but that person renounces it. It is not his clothing. It is not clothing at all. Here . . . it's garbage." He dropped the shirt on the ground. "Look!" he said. "A piece of cloth! I wonder what it could be? Look, Katerina, maybe you could use it as a kind of gown."

Was he mocking her with this childish pretense? "Do you think I'm so stupid as to be deceived?"

His face flashed again with anger, but he controlled it, kept his voice calm and measured. "Listen, Katerina. To me, the idea of walking naked into your village was the most shameful, humiliating thing I could imagine. You could not have found a better way of debasing me, in my own eyes. But you told me that this is how it *had* to be done, in your world, and I obeyed, no matter how hard it was for me. I trusted you."

"This is how the devil talks," she said coldly. "I didn't tell you that you couldn't wear my hoose 'in my world,' I said a decent man wouldn't even try to wear a hoose at all!"

"In *your world*," he said again, insisting, his voice angrier. "In *my* world, a decent man would not let his wife—no, *any* woman that he respected—stand naked before others. It would be the most shameful thing you could do to me—again. *Again,* because you're always right and nobody else knows anything, *again* you are determined to shame me."

The vehemence of his tone shook her. "Do you, as my husband, command me to defile myself by wearing this shirt?"

He seemed to despair at this. "In my world a man doesn't command his wife, he persuades her. If he can."

"Then why are you raising your voice to me, if not to command?"

"I obeyed *you,* when you told me what to do in your world," he said. His voice was soft now, but no less intense.

"Of course you did. I'm the princess of Taina."

"In my world, princesses can stamp their pretty little feet and issue commands to their heart's content, but the only people who obey them are their paid servants. Common people like me pay no attention at all."

These words frightened her even more than his immoral claims about women wearing men's clothing. "Is the world turned upside down, then?"

"At least in our world we don't have witches threatening to take over a kingdom unless the princess marries a complete stranger who fights a bear and jumps a moat and kisses her awake."

She didn't understand how a world could even exist where people had no respect for authority, where women wore men's clothing and husbands did not command their wives. And she was cold. The sun was behind the trees now, and in the shade the breeze began to have teeth to it.

She bent over and picked up the shirt. She tried not to weep, but could not contain the tears of shame that came to her eyes. She put it on like a hoose. The sleeves hung longer than her arms. She did not know how to fasten the big heavy buttons, and couldn't keep the sleeves from falling over her fingers as she tried.

He came to her then and buttoned the shirt, his hands awkward between her breasts, at her belly; but he was gentle, and he seemed genuinely sorry for her tears. He tried once to wipe them away with his hand, but by reflex she shied away from him. He withdrew his hand at once, as if she had slapped him again.

"It's all right," she said. "You can touch me. It's your right."

"It's my right," he said, "to touch a woman who loves me and trusts me and gives herself to me freely, and not just because of some ancient witch's curse or her duty to her country."

She could not help thinking: This is not the way Dimitri would have acted, if he were my husband. She honored Ivan for the difference.

He fastened the last button, his hands brushing against her groin, but only incidentally, without any intimate intent; but that very detachment on his part, that lack of interest, made his touch all the more disturbing. She shuddered.

"Sorry," he murmured. "I've never dressed a woman before."

When he stood up, he was blushing. Now she saw that it wasn't weakness in him, to be so sensitive to shame. It was kindness. He cared about her, about how she was feeling. Just as he had cared for Lybed. Just as he had tried his best to do his duty and become a soldier for her sake. Katerina tried to imagine a druzhinnik blushing for any reason. The only time their faces turned red was when they were full of drink, or when they had worked themselves into a sweat on the practice field.

Ivan began to roll up her sleeves. He did this more deftly than he had done the buttoning. Soon her hands were free.

"If you had done this first," she said, "I could have—"

"I know," he said. "But I didn't think of it till after. Let's just add it to the long list of stupid mistakes I've made."

The job done, he stepped away from her. He looked at her face for a moment, but what he saw there must have displeased him, for he turned his back and walked to the edge of the pit and looked down.

What had he seen in her face? All she felt was fear, uncertainty. She was wearing a shameful thing and trying not to act ashamed. Was that what made him turn away?

She could see that Ivan was trying to be a good man. He was not a devil, nor a servant of Satan. She had seen his actions long enough to know that he was almost priestlike in his gentleness. He had never used a sword. He was peaceable as a lamb. Wasn't that more Christian than to be a druzhinnik, spending his days preparing to kill other men?

How could she, a Christian, have failed to see such Christlike attributes in this stranger? Jesus said to judge not, lest ye be judged. How unjustly have I judged him, again and again?

"Ivan," she said softly.

He did not turn to face her. "What," he said, his voice dispirited.

She had to know if he really was the man of peace she had just imagined him to be. "When you fought the bear—had you ever fought an enemy before?"

He did not answer.

She asked again. "Was it the first time you ever used a weapon, when you flung that stone and put out the bear's eye?"

He turned on her, and to her shock there were tears on his cheeks. He made no effort to brush them away, and he sounded, not sad, but angry when he answered her. "You're right," he said, "I'm a contemptible weakling, I'm not strong and brave like the men in your father's druzhina, you're right to despise me."

She would have interrupted him, told him that her question had not implied criticism of him; but he gave her no chance to speak.

"I never fought an enemy," he said. "I never held a weapon in my hands, and I never intended to, and I *still* never intend to, now that I'm not in Taina anymore. And if, for some reason, I ever did have to take up a weapon and use it against an enemy, there is one thing I can promise: I would *not* be doing it to impress you with how manly I am, because I don't give a rat's ass what you think of me."

She had never heard anyone curse by referring to the anus of a rat before. It was a loathsome thought, and her face showed her disgust.

"Whatever you may think of *me*," he said, "and however you may hate wearing that shirt, I know where there's a warm house and a clean bed, and plenty of food and water, so I'd suggest you follow me. *Princess.*"

And to think that for a moment there, I was actually imagining him to be a little bit like Jesus.

But he knew the way to the house and the fire, to the food and the drink. And he was her husband, and she knew her duty. He had dressed her in rags of shame, and now she would come and bear her shame among his people. She stepped toward him. He turned his back on her and strode off into the woods. She followed him. Only now and then did he glance back to make sure she was with him. She always was.

Katerina's nakedness might be somewhat covered, but her appearance would certainly excite comment if she were seen. Besides, her feet were bare, and the road, so smooth to the tires of a car or the soles of Ivan's American running shoes, would be rough to feet more accustomed to meadows or the leafmeal forest floor. So they stayed in the woods, within sight of the road, except where they had to cross a stream or avoid a steep hill.

Katerina said nothing—never asked for help, and her breath never grew labored—so he had to glance back to be sure she was still with him. Only now, when her body was covered, did he allow himself to think of the sight of her body, of the electric moments when his hand brushed against her. My wife, he thought. By right, the woman whose body I should know, the woman who should know me. Each glance at her, dressed loosely in his shirt, the cloth sliding across her skin as she moved, filled his imagination and fed his desire for her.

It also fed the bitterness in his heart. Of course she was being unfair to him. What difference did that make? In games of love there is no umpire to call foul. By twentieth-century standards he wasn't a bad guy, but Katerina had no way of knowing that. He could see her beauty and wit and nobility, while easily forgiving the flaws that came from her culture; but she could see only his flaws and forgave nothing, and that was that.

He had no business loving her in the first place. It was Ruth he was engaged to, Ruth he should have married. How was he going to explain this to Ruth? *Something came up when I was vacationing in the ninth century, and I married this girl who hates me. In 1992 we'll celebrate our eleven-hundred-and-second anniversary. Oh, and she doesn't speak any language now spoken on earth, and I had to become a Christian to marry her, and . . . you understand, don't you, Ruth?*

The marriage hadn't been consummated. It could still be annulled, couldn't it?

Of course it couldn't. Baba Yaga still threatened Taina, and was held at bay only by the fact that Ivan was married to Katerina.

Only now, walking alongside this modern road, Taina already seemed less real. How could something he did now in the twentieth century have any effect on the distant past?

He glanced back again. She was still behind him. Still beautiful. Still the woman whom he had come to admire and love. Without him, whom would she speak to? Where would she go? The only merciful thing would be to annul the marriage and take her back to the pedestal and leave her where he found her. *You cross your bridge, baby, and I'll cross mine. Status quo ante. Have a nice life.*

Only it wouldn't be a nice life, if she went back to Taina without a husband.

I'm stuck.

He heard a truck engine, the indescribable rattling noises that can only be produced by Soviet-made vehicles. It was coming up the road toward them, the wrong direction for him to ask for a lift.

He glanced back again and, for the first time since he had known her, saw Katerina frozen with fear.

"She's coming for us," said Katerina.

"What?"

"The Pretender," she said.

"She can't make a noise like that. It's only a . . . truck." He had no choice but to use the modern Russian word, *gruzovik;* there was no proto-Slavonic equivalent.

His use of a strange word didn't help much, but his utter lack of apprehension did seem to have a calming affect. He took her shoulder and led her off into the brush by the side of the road. By the time the truck came along, they were invisible to the driver. Ivan kept his arm around Katerina, and she stayed close to him. It was sweet to have her body beside his, to feel her—well, technically, his—shirt pressed against his bare chest. He wondered fleetingly if Dimitri would stand so calmly in the face of the hideous monster now coming up the road. But that was a cheap thought, and he despised himself for thinking it. He was not brave to face the coming of the truck. He knew there was no danger. But a druzhinnik showed courage in the face of enemies that Ivan could never dream of fighting off.

When the truck rattled by, she put an arm around his waist and retreated deeper into the crook of his arm. Let there be a hundred such trucks, he thought.

"You saw the man inside," he said. "It's like a wagon, but instead of horses or oxen to pull it, there's a . . . fire inside. An oven. Not for cooking. An oven that makes the wagon roll."

"It was rolling uphill, and nothing pulled," she said. "Why did you lie to me?"

"Lie? When did I lie?"

"You said there was no magic in your world."

"This isn't magic. This is . . . a tool. Like a scythe or a basket. A tool for doing work. The truck carries the man and whatever load he needs to bear. Just like a wagon. Only faster, and bigger loads, and the truck doesn't need to rest as often as a horse."

She put her free hand to her face, the fingers touching her forehead. Not covering her eyes, really. Just . . . hiding.

"It's gone now," he said. "There's nothing to fear."

She shook her head. "I'm ashamed," she said.

"Of what?"

"You were so foolish in our world," she said. "But now I see that I'm a fool in yours."

Well. This is progress. "Not a fool," he answered. "I learned as quickly as I could, and you'll do the same."

"I know of no spell to make a wagon move by itself. It would take the Widow herself to do such a thing."

"The Widow wouldn't want to make a truck like *that*," he said, even though he knew she wouldn't understand the joke.

"Gruzovik," she said, using the Russian word he had used for the truck.

"That's good," he said. "A new word."

"How many new words are there?" she asked.

"A lot," he answered.

"A hundred?"

Let's see, he thought. Toilet, vaccine, magazine, movie, television, bank, automatic teller machine—a triple threat!—hamburger, ice cream, pizza, shampoo, tampon . . . No, it was not his job to explain *that* to her.

Whose job was it, then? What woman who spoke proto-Slavonic would be able to instruct her on how to unwrap it and insert it and . . .

If *he* had to explain it, she was going to learn about sanitary napkins. It's not like she was going to wear a bikini anytime soon.

What am I doing? What am I in for?

She stirred under his arm. "We should go on before it gets dark," she said.

"Yes, of course," he replied. "I'm sorry, I . . . I don't know how to begin teaching you the new words. I'm not even sure I should try, because if you go home with me to my family's house, most people don't speak Russian."

She snorted at the mention of the Scandinavian Rus'.

"I mean the language of the word *gruzovik*. They speak another language there, and a gruzovik is called 'truck.' "

"Truck," she said. She could not shape the English word very well.

"Never mind," he said. "Plenty of time."

But as they continued to walk toward Cousin Marek's house, he began to realize how impossible everything was going to be. He couldn't take her to America for the simple reason that she had no passport and no way to get one. There were no birth certificates in the ninth century, and it wouldn't matter if there were, no one would believe the date on it anyway. She did not exist, in fact. And the moment she opened her mouth, she would be branded as foreign, from some unidentifiable Slavic country, definitely in Ukraine illegally. However people in Taina might have regarded him with suspicion, they didn't assume he was a criminal because he talked strangely and arrived naked. It helped that it was the daughter of the head of state who led him into the village, of course, but . . . modern life was complicated.

If she couldn't go to America, neither could he stay here. His visa was not forever.

His visa.

How long had he been in Taina? Weeks, anyway. But when Katerina was asleep on that pedestal, a few months in Taina were eleven hundred years on this side of the chasm. Had he just pulled a Rip van Winkle stunt? Gone for a walk in the woods, and when he came back, twenty years had passed? A hundred?

No way could a Soviet-made gruzovik still be running after twenty years, let alone a hundred.

But even if he had disappeared for only the weeks that he was aware of having lived through, it must have caused terrible consternation here. Cousin Marek would have become alarmed by nightfall, and the next day there would have been a search. By now the search would be over, everyone convinced that he was dead somewhere in the forest. Mother and Father must be grieving, and Ruth. Would Ruth grieve? Of course she would, what a thing to doubt!

I have to explain. Gone for weeks, and when I come back, I have a girl with me who happens to be wearing nothing but my shirt.

Don't borrow trouble, he told himself. We have no choice but to go to Cousin Marek's house, and once we're there, with clothing, food, shelter, we'll figure out what to do next.

The sun was setting red behind them when they made the last turn and Cousin Marek's farm spread out before them like a Grant Wood painting. Ivan stopped for a moment, drinking in the familiar view. It had not been twenty years, that was certain, for nothing was changed.

"Taina," whispered Katerina.

She misses her home, thought Ivan.

"What have they done to Taina?"

"Taina is another time and place," he started to explain.

Then he looked again, as if with her eyes, and realized what had never crossed his mind until now: Cousin Marek's farm was on exactly the site of the village of Taina. His house was on the same spot as King Matfei's house.

In fact, estimating the positions of the two houses, Ivan realized that he had slept in about the same place in both. How could that happen? Mere coincidence? No one in Taina could have known where he slept in Cousin Marek's house. And yet they led him to the very spot.

It could not be. Impossible. And even if it was true, it was meaningless.

Ivan looked around for the high ground where the fort had been, with the practice field where he had been trained—or was it tortured?—by Dimitri. No building stood there now; it was a stand of trees, newish growth with lots of underbrush. But amid the clutter, were the outlines of the walls still there?

"Taina is gone," she said. "We failed. My people are destroyed." She was weeping.

"No, no," he said, pulling her to him and comforting her like a child, letting her cry against his chest. "Eleven centuries have passed. Cities rise and fall, and villages come and go, but it doesn't mean that the Pretender defeated your father, I promise you. If we went back and crossed the bridges, we'd see that nothing was changed. When I went to Taina, all of this disappeared and was replaced by your village. But it was still here when I crossed the bridge. Do you understand?"

She nodded, pulled away from him. "You understand these things," she said. "But to see the land with my father's house gone, replaced by this great castle."

"It's not a castle, it's just a house. We build taller houses in our time. Warmer ones, too. Let's go inside."

"This is your house?"

"My cousin's house. But Marek and Sophia have always made me as welcome as if I had been born here."

"Where is the village?"

"A long way from here, if you're walking. But not far by gruzovik."

"The servants live there?" She pointed.

"No, they keep birds there." Chicken wasn't part of the regular diet in Taina, and Ivan had never learned the word, if they even had one. "Like geese, only they don't roam free."

"To keep them safe from the foxes?"

"Yes," said Ivan. It occurred to him that the new henhouse Marek had shown him so proudly stood exactly where the church had been until it burned down yesterday.

No, it wasn't yesterday, it was this morning. His wedding morning. All of this in a single day? No wonder he was tired and hungry.

They came to the door and Ivan knocked.

The door was flung open so immediately that Ivan was momentarily frightened. Had Marek been watching at the window?

No, it was Sophia. "Vanya's back!" she called over her shoulder. Then she turned back to face Ivan, radiant with joy at seeing him. She opened her arms and was about to embrace him when she saw Katerina.

"What's this? What are you wearing? You must be freezing! And Itzak, you foolish boy, where is your—oh, she's wearing it. What was she wearing *before* she was wearing your—never mind, come in, get warm, get warm, time for stories in the kitchen, are you hungry? I have a big soup, I made plenty of borscht today, as if I knew you were coming, and cold, come in, don't dawdle."

Laughing, relieved at the welcome, Ivan ushered Katerina into the house. How much of Sophia's torrent of words did Katerina understand?

She stayed close to him, her arm around him, as she looked around her at the wonders of the house.

He tried to see the room through her eyes. Dimly lighted by the setting sun through the windows, it was a mass of shadowy shapes, hummocky furniture, and vaguely reflective frames on the walls. A fireplace. A rug on the wooden floor. How did that feel on her bare feet, the varnished wood? Or maybe she was merely looking for the fire that was keeping this room so warm.

They came into the kitchen, and Katerina blinked against the brightness of the electric light.

"You keep a fire on the air," she said in awe.

Sophia stopped cold. "What accent is *that*?" she asked. "I can't place it."

"It's not an accent," said Ivan. "It's another language . . . you understood her?"

Sophia ignored his question. "It's not a fire, child, it's an electric light," she said to Katerina.

The word made no sense to the princess. She reached up toward the dangling light.

"Don't touch it," said Ivan. "It can burn your hand."

"But it's not a fire," said Katerina. "It's like a single drop of water, alive with light, and larger than any water droplet ever was."

Ivan could not resist impressing her further. He reached for the light switch, toggled it off. The room went almost fully dark, for the kitchen window faced east, the direction of darkness in the evening.

"Turn it on, foolish boy," said Sophia.

Ivan obeyed.

Katerina turned to him, her eyes full of wonder and consternation. "Why did you not do this in Taina, if you had this power?"

"I told you," said Ivan, "it's not *my* power. It's a tool." He showed her the switch, made her touch it, then turn the light off and on again.

"So the magic is here on the wall, for anyone to use," she said. "Who ever heard of witches sharing their power so readily?"

Ivan might have tried to explain more, though he was acutely aware of Sophia watching them, her eyes sharp with curiosity; but the conversation was interrupted by the arrival of Cousin Marek, freshly bathed after the day's work. "Vanya, you young fool, do you know how worried Sophia and I have been these three days since you went off in the woods and didn't come home?"

So it was only three days that he was gone?

He might have pondered more about the differing flow of time between Taina and the modern world, but he was distracted by Katerina. For upon seeing Cousin Marek's face, she sank to her knees and hid her face in her hands. "What's wrong?" Ivan asked her.

"You have brought me to the land of the gods," she said. "Are you a god yourself?"

"Gods?" asked Ivan. "What do you mean?"

"Does Jesus live here, too," she asked, "or is there another land where Christ and Mary live?"

"This is my cousin Marek," Ivan said. "He has a big voice and a big heart, and he's strong as an ox, but that doesn't make a god of him."

She looked at him as if he were an idiot. "You are his cousin? Why didn't you tell me?"

Ivan looked from Marek to Sophia. "She's saying that she thinks Cousin Marek is a god. I have no idea why she—"

But neither Marek nor Sophia was looking at Ivan or listening to his explanation. Instead they were looking at each other, with a very serious look on their faces. Without letting her gaze leave her husband's face, Sophia said, "Where did you find this girl, Vanya?"

"Lying asleep on a stone in the woods," Ivan said, not sure whether this was a good moment to tell the whole story.

"What's your name, child?" Cousin Marek asked Katerina. It took a moment for Ivan to realize that he was speaking to her in fluent, unaccented proto-Slavonic.

"Katerina," she said. "Daughter of King Matfei of Taina."

"Taina," said Marek. His face grew wistful. "I loved that place. But I stayed away too long." He took a step toward Katerina, reached out a hand to her. She took it, let him raise her up. "Matfei had a daughter. I saw her last when she was two years old, clinging to her father's leg when she met me. But she let go of him, and did me a courtesy such as the one you offer now, and I raised her up like this."

"I was the little girl," said Katerina. "I remember. My earliest memory, the sight of you. When you reached out to me, I stopped being afraid."

"Of course," said Marek. "I didn't want you to be afraid of me. I'm no enemy to such a one as you, Princess."

Ivan could hardly grasp what they were saying. "You've met each other? You knew her as a child?" Ivan laughed. "She was a child a thousand years ago, Cousin Marek."

At his words, Marek again looked at Sophia; one of them was asking something with a look, and the other answering, but Ivan had no idea what the question was, or who was questioning.

It was Katerina who answered him, after his words hung un-answered through a long silence. "Ivan, is it possible that you don't know?"

"Know what?"

"You call him Cousin Marek," she said, "but in Taina every child knows his name." She turned to face Marek. "Mikola Mozhaiski," she said. "You said you were my father's friend. Where were you when he needed you? And now you live where his house used to be, and he is gone, and the whole village, and only I am here." She burst into tears.

Ivan moved to comfort her, but Sophia was nearer and quicker. So Ivan watched as Cousin Marek strode to Sophia and also put his arms around the weeping girl. Ivan saw that, and yet he also saw quite another thing: He saw Mikola Mozhaiski, protector of sailors, ancient but unforgotten god, enfold the enchanted princess of Taina in his arms. It was the stuff of great legends; it was a charming farmhouse scene.

One thing was obvious: When Ivan told Katerina that there was no magic in his world, he had no idea what he was talking about.

Esther had never been much for reading, especially in English, a language which could not be spelled correctly even if you managed to remember that when you see *R* it means *P* and not Я, *P* means П, *B* means 6, *C* sometimes means *K*, and never mind about *Y* and *H* and *N*. Hopeless. But she had to do something to pass the time. Piotr didn't want her to interrupt him; he didn't take it seriously, her worry about Vanya. "If something was wrong, you think Cousin Marek wouldn't call us?"

She had no answer for that. Cousin Marek should have called. The fact that he hadn't meant that he thought everything was all right. Certainly Esther knew that Vanya was alive, wherever he was. She would bide her time.

But how was time supposed to be bided, when every moment was filled with urgency for which there was no action? So she opened books and magazines. She looked at the faces in *People* and didn't rec-ognize anybody, even though she had known all the faces only last week. It was as if all the time she had been in America was a mistake. If she had stayed in Kiev, then Vanya would not have been without her, she might have been able to follow him into this place, whatever it was.

Can't think about that. Close *American Heritage* and open *Na-tional Geographic*. More pictures of people who mean nothing to her.

Find a book on the shelf. One in Cyrillic this time. The letters string across the page like kites, bobbing here and there in random patterns. Very pretty. Close the book, find another. Hebrew. Dots like measles surrounding the letters. Nothing held her.

She got up and went outside, touched the basin where it sat on its pedestal, already covered with the dander of the sky—dust, a feather, tiny twigs, several leaves, and dead insects, enough to portend a massacre if she were doing omens, which she was definitely not, there was nothing to read in this thing. She tipped the bowl to spill a little, then picked it up and dashed the fouled water onto the lawn. Then she put the basin back onto its pedestal and looked down into the blackness. A few insect bodies clung to the inner surface; one was alive, beginning to dry out, moving a frail wing. She thought of crushing it to vent her fury. Instead she blew lightly, drying it faster. In moments, it began to crawl along the basin. Then it flew, or rather staggered, into the air. Some bird would eat the sluggish thing before too long. It had survived the basin only to die in the air. There was no tragedy in that, only cliché. Each day every man and woman and child on earth either died or didn't, and if they didn't, then they'd die another day.

Yet it made all the difference to her, if it was her husband or her child. For that moment's flight out of the basin, she would give her life.

Or take someone else's. That, too, in case anyone cared. If once she got Vanya safely home again, then whatever enchanter wanted him would have to reckon with her. After leaving Kiev, she had thought never to use the wardings and curses that she learned from Baba Tila, for now there was no danger, no more KGB, no more gulag, no more fear of someone getting rousted in the night.

The trouble was, what Baba Tila taught her was for use against those with no such powers of their own. The old lady had said that Esther had a talent for it, that there must be some Hebrew magic of her own that she was adding to the spells. But would that be enough, if she had to have it out with an enemy who knew as much as Baba Tila, or more?

If only she knew who her enemy was.

O God of Israel, wilt thou not suffer a witch's son to live? I've never called on Satan, or spoken to the dead like the cursed witch of Endor. I've sought to use this power for the good of good people, and if it's a sin, then let the sin be upon my head, but not my child, not my son.

Can't think like this. There's no point in praying. I long since chose another road, consigned myself to Sheol, there's no looking back from that, Baba Tila was plain about it, you can have what your grandmother had, but only if you choose what your grandmother chose.

Esther picked up the basin and started back to the house.

Then gasped and dropped the basin, caring not a bit if it chipped or broke, for she had felt him step back into the world, just as she had felt him go; as, before, she had lost the sense of him and felt desolation in its place, so now she felt the desolation leave her like a toothache suddenly cured. The world was right again. Vanya was in it.

Didst thou, O God, save him?

She hesitated before bending over to pick up the basin. If God did it, would he then see it as a repudiation of his gift, if she tried to save a tool of her witchery?

It might as easily be that God cares not at all whether I do spells or not, that the rabbis are all wrong about it, and . . .

And it might also be that God had nothing to do with it, that it was just the moment that it would have happened anyway, whether she prayed or not.

Indeed, over the past three days, when might it have happened that would not have been within an hour of a prayer?

She reached down; the sore place in her back pained her, but she felt no fresh pull of muscle, there was no new stab of pain. Her fingers went under the basin rim, for it had fallen facedown; when she pulled it up, torn grass came with it. Small deaths, for one life saved.

If I offend thee, O God, forgive me, but I know not whether it was thy hand that brought him back, or not, and if not, I can't take the chance of giving up what small powers I have to protect my family. If thou wouldst have me cease this work, then speak, or show me by some simple sign, and I'll obey, and trust in thee, O God of Israel.

She waited. She looked around her, searching for something that might have been sent from God to speak to her. She listened in her own mind, for the still small voice that Elijah heard. But all was silent, except for that sweet presence of Vanya in her heart.

Cousin Marek tried to be gentle in answering Katerina's questions, and when he grew impatient, Sophia shushed him, calmed him down. Finally the princess seemed to see that Mikola Mozhaiski was not omnipotent, like the Christians claimed their God to be, nor omniscient either, and he was away on business. In one of his testier moments, he snapped, "It wasn't my job to look out for Taina, you know, it was your father's. And yours!" But that set Katerina to crying again, and Sophia gave Cousin Marek such a look as would freeze the heart of a mortal man.

Ivan watched and listened, waiting with his own set of questions, but also ready for sleep. It had been a long day, full of surprise but also of disappointment. He had thought Katerina would need him in the modern world, but no, she comes straight to a place where everyone speaks proto-Slavonic better than Ivan. Well, maybe this would let Ivan off the hook. Now that Mikola Mozhaiski was in the picture, Ivan was free to move on. Deus ex machina. The god had just popped out of the sky—the second-story bedroom, actually—and he'd take care of the damsel in distress. Ivan's whole purpose had been nothing more than to bring Katerina here. That was done. He was ready to sleep.

No sooner thought of than done. He woke to Sophia shaking his shoulder. "Wake up so you can sleep in your bed," she said to him. "Poor boy, so many centuries, all in a few days."

Sleepily he asked her, as he might have in a dream, "Are you a goddess?"

"Oh my no," she said. "Immortal by association."

It sounded like a dream answer, too. But then she tousled his hair and he decided he was awake after all. Katerina and Cousin Marek were gone. Well, of course. Maybe they already went back to Taina. Ivan was too tired to care. He walked up the stairs to his room and barely remembered to take his shoes and pants off before sliding under the covers.

My wedding night, he thought. You lucky bridegroom, you. Got away from the people who wanted you dead, didn't you? Greedy to wish for more.

In the morning, though, waking at first light of dawn, he had a different attitude. He'd been jerked around by fate, and every decent impulse had led him into ever deeper trouble. Now the game had finally moved to the part of the field where the referees were standing around having coffee. Time to get them back on the job. Put Baba Yaga in her place, get this marriage annulled, send Katerina back home, and let me get on the plane to America. I've got a dissertation to write, parents who miss me, and a wedding—a real one this time, with a bride who doesn't think I'm a geek.

When he came downstairs, Katerina was learning the workings of a modern stove—well, what passed for one in rural Ukraine. She was wearing an old dress of Sophia's—a very old one, apparently, because, though it fit her loosely, it wasn't as voluminous as it ought to be. Sophia greeted Ivan with a cheery smile, but Katerina didn't look up.

True, she was involved with the complicated business of cooking, which was pretty unfamiliar to her even without the modern conveniences. But to Ivan, it was just one more reminder that she was no wife of his, and never would be.

"Where's Cousin Marek?" asked Ivan.

Thoughtlessly, he had spoken in modern Ukrainian, but the question wasn't hard to grasp for Katerina, and before Sophia could answer, she laughed rather nastily and said, "You still call him that?"

Ivan didn't want a fight with her, though he thought it might have been more appropriate if she had remembered just a little of how she clung to him yesterday as the truck passed by.

"Don't be annoyed, Vanya," said Sophia—could she read his mind? "The princess is angry with my husband, not with you."

"What good does it do to be angry with an immortal?" asked Katerina.

"None at all," said Sophia cheerfully. "But there's no accounting for tempers. I'm surprised you slept through all the shouting last night, Vanya."

"Nobody was shouting at me, I figure, so I didn't care," said Ivan. "Still don't."

"Well, you will," said Sophia.

"No he won't," said Katerina. "He never cared about anything. Long ago he wished he had never fought the bear and kissed me awake."

Well, that was true enough. Though there had also been moments where he was glad of it, too. No need to mention that right now, however.

"That business with the bear," said Sophia. "We always wondered how that happened, and we weren't about to ask."

"What happened?"

"How Bear lost his eye, of course. Never would have imagined it was our little Vanya."

"That bear is still around?"

"He's not laying for you, if that's what you're wondering. He stays well to the north and east of here these last few centuries. It's Moscow where he has his den, where the winter still is his. But he mostly lies low. Came out to give a hard blow to Napoleon, and again to stop Hitler. Armies wake him up, but otherwise, he doesn't much care about the doings of human beings."

"So her bear is still alive," said Ivan. "Does that mean she is, too?"

"Thank you for not saying her name in this house," said Sophia.

"And I have no idea where the old bat might be. Not a trace of her in many a year. But my husband has some idea that she might have followed you here. That's why he's out looking over the land."

"Did he do that when I disappeared?" asked Ivan.

"He knew where you were going—into the enchanted place where he couldn't see."

Ivan snorted. "Are all the immortals around here half-blind?"

Sophia looked at him sharply. Katerina seemed not to breathe.

"Oh, I see, now that I know who he really is, I can't tease."

Sophia laughed. "Marek sees as well as ever. But into a strange place like that, no one sees."

"Except me."

"You *walked* in there."

"So what stops *him*?"

"He can't, that's all. He walks straight toward it, then finds he's walked past it, and his path was straight, but still it bent."

Ivan shook his head. "And yet I walked in as easy as could be."

"You walked in because wherever you ran, it was always nearby," said Sophia. "It was calling to you."

"*It,*" echoed Ivan. "What is the *it* that was calling me?"

"The place."

"Someone made the place. Or made it what it is. Didn't they?"

Katerina spoke up. "Maybe no one made the place, Ivan. It follows no plan. The enemy cursed me to die; my aunts cast spells to leave me somewhere short of death, and set rules by which I could be saved again, but where the place was, they couldn't choose and didn't know."

"And the Widow, she didn't choose, either?"

"Maybe she did," said Sophia. "But she didn't make the place. She only used it."

"So who made the chasm? Who built the bridges?"

"The chasm is how the Widow's curse expressed itself," said Sophia. "Bear ended up trapped in it, because it was by his power that her original curse of killing was made. By her plan, Bear was supposed to appear and tear Katerina cruelly apart. But instead he went round and round under the leaves. Katerina and Marek and I talked this out this morning, before you were awake."

"I see I wasn't important enough to include," said Ivan, unable to keep a nasty edge out of his voice.

"What did *you* know about it?" asked Katerina. Perhaps she meant no insult by it, but all he heard was scorn.

"We're including you *now*," said Sophia, soothingly.

"Look, I've never had any power," said Ivan, "so I don't even want to know. Cousin Marek can fix things now, have it out with the old witch. Then Katerina can have the marriage annulled and go back and marry somebody appropriate. And I can go home and marry Ruthie."

It was Katerina's turn to recoil as if slapped. "You repudiate me?"

"We aren't really married," said Ivan. "You never wanted me, and I'm engaged to someone else, so it'll all work out nicely for everyone."

Katerina looked to Sophia, but the older woman simply looked away. She was not going to be part of this.

So Katerina looked at Ivan. For a long time she looked, till he squirmed like a first-grader caught in a lie. "There is no divorce in Christ," she finally said.

"There's no marriage until I've bedded you," he answered, using a harsh proto-Slavonic term for it.

"Aren't we the polite one," said Sophia.

"Did I use too crude a word?" asked Ivan. "It's the one used by the men out in the practice field."

"It's not the word," said Sophia, "it's the heartlessness of what you said."

"Heartless?" said Ivan. "My supposed wife has never felt anything but contempt for me. How tender am I supposed to feel in return? My supposed father-in-law plotted to kill me. Exactly how seriously should I take their religion?"

"He didn't plot," said Katerina.

"You said yourself that Dimitri would never have attempted my murder if he didn't have your father's consent."

"If he didn't *think* he had my father's—"

"Don't hurt each other any more, children," said Sophia.

"How could I hurt her?" said Ivan. "She'd have to love me before I could do that. All I am to her or anybody in Taina is either a tool or an obstacle. I was the tool that woke her from her enchantment and got her home safely. Of course, I can't claim credit for that, either, since you tell me I was forced into it."

"Led up to it." Then Sophia switched to modern Ukrainian. "Don't you love her? This beauty, this bright and powerful woman?"

"She understands Ukrainian well enough," said Ivan, "so this won't let us have a private conversation in front of her."

True enough, Katerina was blushing at Sophia's praise—or perhaps at the bluntness of her question.

"What does it matter what language I speak, then?" said Sophia. "Everybody understands everything, and nobody understands anything."

"I think it's all very clear," said Ivan.

"So do I," said Katerina. She looked Ivan in the eye. "I release you now. We'll get the annulment. You were already betrothed to another woman, so you could not enter into the vow."

"He wasn't engaged to anyone," said Sophia. "He married you a thousand years before he ever met Ruthie."

"It's his own life that he'll be judged by, and, in his life, before he said he'd marry me, he said he'd marry her." Katerina looked at Ivan scornfully. "Not much of a king you'd make after all, to be so easily forsworn."

"It was agree to marry you or get killed by a bear," said Ivan.

"I'd rather die than break an oath."

"That always seems to be my choice," said Ivan, "but where would you be if I had chosen *your* way?"

"Still enchanted," she said, "waiting for a man of honor."

"Stop it!" shouted Sophia. "Enough, you two! These are terrible things that you'll be a long time wishing you could unsay."

She was right. Ivan already wished it. When he offered to annul the marriage, he realized now, he had been half-hoping that she'd refuse, that she'd insist that she wanted to be his wife. That she loved him, or might love him, or wanted to love him. Instead, he had provoked this outburst, in which she had exposed the full measure of her contempt for him. Because of his engagement to Ruthie, Katerina didn't even regard herself as sworn to him now. So his last hope with her was gone—if there had ever been a hope.

"What a shame you didn't let Dimitri kill me," said Ivan. "Having me alive is inconvenient to everyone. Me not least." He got up and left the table. No one said anything to call him back.

Katerina was so angry she could hardly eat, though the food was good and she didn't wish to offend Sophia.

Sophia, for her part, ate with gusto, while smiling in amusement at Katerina's lack of appetite. "He really makes you angry, doesn't he."

"I hate a man whose oath is worthless."

"Men and women these days break off engagements whenever they want. No one thinks of it as oath breaking."

"And you approve of this?"

"Approve or not, that's the world in which Ivan and his Ruthie agreed to marry. Either one of them is free to break the engagement, without cause. So you can give up this nonsense about despising him for breaking his engagement with her."

"So was his engagement to me just as worthless?"

"He married you, didn't he?"

"And annulled it the first chance he had."

"He offered to annul it, *if* that's what you wanted."

"When did he give *me* any choice? When a man says he wants to annul—"

"You have to understand, Katerina, customs have changed. A woman in this world is as free to make choices as a man is. So maybe when he offered to annul the marriage, he thought he was giving you what *you* wanted."

"Why would I want to be shamed in such a way?"

Sophia sighed. "Katerina, are you *trying* to be slow of understanding?"

Katerina flushed with anger, but she contained it. Sophia was the wife of a god.

"Vanya—your Ivan—is a good man," said Sophia. "And he was a good boy, when he first came here. I don't know why he was drawn to you, when even my husband couldn't enter your prison in the woods. Was it someone's plan? I don't think so. I think that the spell that bound you could only be opened by one who was . . . extraordinary in some way."

Since Katerina had already thought of this, she was a little resentful at the reminder. "You think I haven't tried to think of something praiseworthy about him?"

"Oh, and you're going to tell me now that you haven't ever seen anything to honor in this man?"

Katerina shook her head. "I won't tell you that. He seemed to be trying, back in Taina, to be a decent man. My father said that Ivan seemed to have a king's heart. But the moment he crossed the bridge into this place, he began acting foully. Making me wear his shirt!"

"He was correct and you were wrong."

Katerina was stunned. "You! Does the wife of Mikola—"

"No names, no names," said Sophia. "Call him Marek, now, please, as all do in this place."

"Does the wife of such a man as Marek think that it's right for a woman to wear a man's clothing?"

"No one would have mistaken you for a man. Men generally wear pants with their shirts."

"It's not about being mistaken, it's about—"

"About being decent," said Sophia. "And I tell you that decency changes from year to year, from land to land, and you have to learn the customs of the place you're in. Vanya did things for your sake that felt shameful to him—and you, for his sake, did things that were shameful to you. I think that's a good beginning to your marriage."

"Shame?"

"Bending."

"It's hardly a beginning to our marriage, is it, when he's about to annul it?"

"Do you want him to? Is there a man back in Taina that you love?"

Katerina wasn't sure what she meant. "Whom would I have loved? It was not for me to choose." She thought of Dimitri. She certainly didn't love him, nor he her.

"There you have it," said Sophia. "In Vanya's world, young people marry for their own reasons—usually for love, or desire that they think is love. The parents barely get a chance to give advice. Vanya's mother thought his engagement to Ruth was deeply wrong, but he hardly listened to her."

"So everyone marries like peasants? A wink and a nod and a hop over the broom?"

"Vanya keeps looking for a sign that you love him."

Katerina was completely flustered by this. "How would I love him? I barely know him."

"Nonsense," said Sophia. "You've had ample opportunity to see the kind of man he is. But all you ever show him is your disapproval."

"Because I disapprove of what he does!"

"Yes, you're honest enough, child. But he has, quite logically, come to the conclusion that you find him loathsome and, being a decent man, he has offered you your freedom from your marriage vow, so you don't have to be married to someone you find so distasteful."

"What does any of that matter? I married him to save my kingdom. My kingdom still needs saving."

"He thinks my husband can save it. So with that reason gone . . ."

It was a strange way of looking at the situation. Katerina tried to understand. "So he would give up the right to be my father's heir, because he thinks it would make me . . ."

"Happy? Yes."

Katerina tried to digest this thought. In all her life, she had never been aware of a man doing something solely because it would make a woman happy. Well, not true; she knew several henpecked peasants who watched every word they said, so as to avoid getting a tongue-lashing or worse from a shrewish wife. But such men were despised, and . . . and Ivan was nothing like them. "Why does he care whether I'm happy?"

"That's a very good question," said Sophia. "And it's one you need to answer, because he's been trying to make you happy for quite a while. From what you told me this morning, he walked naked through the woods, getting whipped by branches, because he wanted to make you happy."

Her memory of this event now looked different to her. She thought of the shrewish peasant wives and realized that this might well be the reason Ivan had complied with her. Having betrothed himself to her, he found himself subject to a woman who spoke scornfully and he meekly bowed to her will.

She was not such a woman. He was not such a man. "I don't understand it," she said. "I thought he had simply come to see what was right and wrong, and chose the right."

"Maybe that was it," said Sophia, but amusement still played around the corners of her lips. Katerina would have probed more, for the conversation was teaching her to see events in a new way, and she felt herself to be on the verge of acquiring a bit of wisdom, but at that moment the door opened and Mikola Mozhaiski—no, *Marek*—strode into the room, the floor booming like a drum under his bold steps.

"I'm hungry," he announced as he came into the kitchen. "What, is Vanya still asleep?"

"He isn't hungry," said Sophia dryly.

Apparently some communication passed between them without words, for now Katerina saw the same half-hidden smile lurking on Marek's face. Sophia laid a plate before him, and piled it with bread and lard, cheese and fruit. He ate with such gusto that the food seemed to melt from the plate like fog. Marek saw the wonder on her face and misunderstood her thoughts. "Of course I eat. I'm immortal, but my body still wants food. I wouldn't die if I never ate—but I'd get very, very hungry."

"What did you find on your search?" asked Sophia.

"She's here," said Marek simply.

Katerina felt her heart begin to race. "She followed us!"

"She didn't come through in the same place," he said. "If she had, I wouldn't have seen her spoor. But there was a trace of stink in the rocky hills south of the road, overlooking that Armenian fellow's farm."

"The Arkanians," said Sophia. "And his father bought the farm before he was born. You act as if he were a recent immigrant."

"I just don't bother learning the family name till they've been here for a few centuries." Marek grinned.

"You seem cheerful enough, with *her* here."

"She didn't bring Bear with her," said Marek, "or much of his power, if any. There was no scent of him at all."

"Without him, she could never have made such a crossing," said Sophia. "So she *does* have his power."

"Not ready to hand," Marek insisted. "I know what I'm talking about. She left footprints, that's what I mean."

Everyone knew that Baba Yaga did not leave footprints on the ground or reflections in water. Katerina was astonished. "Is she weak, then? Is this our chance to kill her?"

"Don't even think of that," said Marek. "Even at a quarter of her normal strength, she's more than a match for any weapon in this world or yours. No, you must avoid her."

"I meant *you* could stop her . . . permanently."

Marek shook his head. "Don't you understand? That's not how my powers run. Sailors call on me because I have an affinity for wind and rain. Snow in the north. Sometimes a little lightning. Drought, if I'm angry enough, though it takes constant vigilance to maintain a good long one, and I rarely have the temper for it. I'm not much for war. And assassination is out of my league entirely. That's a matter for Petun, and those who put their trust in *him* are usually sorry, I can promise that. He's not good at clean killings. There are always some unintended targets that fall whenever he tries to bring down an enemy."

Katerina sank back in her chair. "So Ivan doesn't get his wish," she said.

"What wish?" asked Marek, looking from Katerina to Sophia and back again.

Sophia finally answered. "Vanya offered to annul the marriage as soon as you finish off the old bat."

"Why would he do something as stupid as that?" asked Marek.

Katerina felt a moment's triumph.

Then Marek rolled his eyes knowingly. "Being noble, wasn't he. You know he cares for the girl."

"Everyone knows it but him," said Sophia. "And the girl, of course."

Marek thought that Ivan cared for her? He seemed to say it as if it mattered, too. But why would it? Did even an immortal change to fit the world he lived in? She had always thought that one of the attributes of the immortals was their changelessness. Didn't Father Lukas say that God was the same yesterday, today, and tomorrow? Was there anything that she had believed in before that was still true now?

"What should we do?" asked Katerina. "Go back to Taina?"

"Oh, what a clever idea, you lure the most dangerous woman I've ever heard of into this world, and then you want to go right back and leave her here for other people to deal with. People who are singularly ill-equipped, I might add. *You* have your bits of spells, I assume, even if your mother didn't live long enough to teach you. But there are precious few here like Vanya's mother, seeking out the old lore and putting it into practice. What every woman used to know, hardly any even imagine in these benighted times. No, she'd create havoc here."

"How am I to prevent that?"

"I don't know if you can. She knows this land too well. Your best hope is for her to lose you here, and then give up and go home without finding you."

"Can we hide here?" asked Katerina.

"If I stayed in the house with you, yes. If I left all my lands unwatched-over, yes, you could stay. But I think it's better if you go somewhere else entirely. To a land where she doesn't speak the language, where she'll constantly be getting into trouble with the authorities." Marek grinned. "I'd love to see her come up against an American assault force. I wonder if they'd beat her as easily as they beat the vast military of Grenada."

Katerina had no idea what he was talking about, but Sophia chuckled. "Don't have much use for America, do you?"

"Arrogant newcomers who think they're smarter than everybody just because they can make a machine that washes dishes."

"In other words, no one there remembers your name."

Marek's temper flashed across his face. But he calmed himself. Katerina wondered what would happen to Sophia if Marek ever grew uncontrollably angry at her. But then she dismissed the thought— Marek wasn't the kind of man to lose control.

Man? How did she know what kind of man a god might be?

"This America you speak of—this is Ivan's birthplace?"

"No, no, he first went there when he was a child. But his parents live there. It's his home now."

"And we'll be safe there?"

"How should I know?" said Marek. "Safer than here, though, I imagine."

At that moment Ivan spoke up from the doorway leading to the stairs. "Safer, but I can't get her out of the country without a passport."

Katerina had no idea what a passport was, nor was she wondering. What occupied her mind was a different question: When did Ivan come back down the stairs? For that matter, had she ever heard him go *up* the stairs? Had he stood outside the kitchen door, listening to her entire conversation with Sophia? Monstrous thought!

"Passport," said Marek dismissively. "I'll have one of those drawn up, of course."

"You can't fight the witch, but you can conjure a passport?" asked Ivan.

"I won't conjure anything. I have a few friends left in this world. I can get her a legitimate legal passport. And an American entry visa— false ones are expensive on the black market, but we can probably get you a real one, since you're Ivan's wife. We'll get a certificate drawn up for that, too."

"You're taking me with you?" she asked Ivan.

"I took an oath, didn't I?" said Ivan. "That I'd protect you, right? I'm not a fighter, but I'm famous for running away."

His tone was so bitter and ironic that she ordinarily would have thought he was furious at her, that he hated her. But thinking of what Sophia had said, Katerina heard something different now. His ironic nastiness was because he thought that *she* scorned *him*.

Well, he *wasn't* a fighter. She couldn't help that, could she?

And she didn't scorn him. She needed him. Taina needed him. And if it took pretending to love him, as Sophia had suggested, then she'd try to act as if she did. Nobody could expect more of her than that.

"Whither thou goest, I will go," she said, quoting a passage she had learned from the Book of Ruth—an unfortunate name indeed, she realized as she spoke. "Where thou lodgest, I will lodge. Thy people shall be my people, and thy God . . ."

Her voice trailed off. He seemed not to recognize the words.

"Your family aren't Christian, are they?" she asked.

"If you refer to the Christian habit of plotting to murder their in-laws, then no, they don't qualify as Christian."

"Vanya," said Sophia sharply.

He did not apologize, though he did wither under her stare.

And why should he apologize, thought Katerina. His complaint was not unjustified.

"I'll follow you to your parents' home," said Katerina. "As you followed me to mine."

"Naked?" asked Ivan.

"Young man!" cried Sophia.

But Katerina only laughed. "I thought you told me I didn't have that option."

"I'll take you," said Ivan. "It's up to you whether I introduce you as a friend of mine, or as my wife."

"As you choose," said Katerina.

"That's not my decision," said Ivan.

"Yes it is," said Katerina.

"No it isn't," he said in a firmer voice. "If you are only calling yourself my wife out of duty to Taina, then I don't want to make such a claim. My parents will see at once how you feel about me, or, more to the point, how you *don't* feel about me. It will worry my mother. So you can only come as my wife if you promise to pretend to my parents that you think I'm a good catch."

"A good what?" asked Katerina.

"A good husband," he explained. "That you think you did well to choose to be my wife. If you can't pretend to believe that, then it's better to introduce you as nothing more than a friend of mine."

"Coward," said Sophia softly.

"Taina still needs us married, as much as ever," said Katerina. Beyond that, she did not know what to say, or even what he wanted her to say.

Ivan searched her face—for what, she didn't know. Nor did he find what he was looking for. She knew this because of the way he sagged a little, then nodded. "All right then. I'll tell them you're my wife. Let them believe what they believe."

I hurt him again, thought Katerina. I meant to pretend to love him, but in the moment I simply told the truth, which is my habit. And I don't know that I want to change that habit. You can tell a lie now and then, but what happens to you when you try to live your whole life inside a lie?

Still, he had chosen to keep her, even though he clearly wasn't all that happy about it. Could Sophia be right? Did he truly care for her? Or was he agreeing to stay married solely out of duty?

More to the point, Katerina wondered, am I?

BABA YAGA

Long ago she had found this still pool in the darkness of the cave, deep in a subterranean chamber. By torchlight she had come here from time to time, to draw upon the majesty of the place. But she had never used the water to travel, for until now there was nowhere she wanted to go that she could not reach more easily another way.

The surface of the water was absolutely still. That was important; unfortunately, it meant that she could not douse the torch in the water, for then she could not see when the surface became still again. She tried stubbing it out in the dirt, but that did nothing; she beat it on the ground, but it only burned more hotly. Finally, she smothered it with her own skirts, singeing them badly but what did she care? People would see her as she chose to be seen.

In the darkness, she was momentarily disoriented. She had to find the water by the smell of it, and by feeling forward with one dainty foot until she was near the brink. Then, in a loud voice, she proclaimed the words of the spell that would turn this vast empty mirror into a gateway. She could not see, but she could feel the surface trembling with her voice—that was the only disturbance that could be permitted here.

Last of all she proclaimed the name of the princess, which had been stated so openly at her baptism, so that all comers knew the name by which the gods knew her. Fool. She could never hide from Baba Yaga once her name was known.

The name still echoed in the chamber as Baba Yaga leaned forward, toppling off the brink like a cup off a table. The spell worked:

She never touched water. Instead, the surface carried her like strong hands into the place she asked for.

She found herself lying on something hard and rough.

A loud, roaring, rattling sound was getting louder and louder. What could it be?

She raised her head from the ground, opening her eyes into the twilight.

A new noise at once was added, something screeching, metal on metal. She rose to her feet, looking for the source of the noise.

A big, awkward-looking house made all of tin sat on four black feet, like a crippled animal, in the middle of the hard surface where she had been lying. The surface itself was of miraculous smoothness, as if someone had scythed the earth itself. Then she realized—this was a road, like the ones the Romans built, only wider and less finished on the top. And this house must be capable of movement.

A man leaned out the window of the house, shouting at her in some barbarous dialect. She only caught a few words of what he said, and didn't care. She waved him to silence.

It didn't work. He didn't even pause.

Terror thrilled through her. Had she taken herself to a place where her powers didn't work?

She tried a much stronger spell of silence, murmuring the words and making the signs behind her back—no need to anger him, if she turned out to be utterly powerless.

This spell should have silenced him for weeks; instead, it merely calmed him down. He mumbled a little more—unthinkable that he should have a voice at all!—and then, without so much as making a single pass through the air or dusting his house with powder, he caused it to move forward, moving around her and passing her, leaving her behind in a cloud of dust.

She couldn't be sure it was her spell that calmed him down or simply that he had run out of wrath. This was an urgent question that had to be settled right away.

She sniffed the air, turning in all directions. Her sense of power was weakened, but it was not gone. She caught faint traces of the princess—she had walked near this very road, and not long ago—but her smell was all but lost in another one that left her stunned. Mikola Mozhaiski! After all her pains to cast spells to make him neglect his beloved land of Taina and his friends there, she had ended up coming to the very place that was now the center of his power. No wonder her powers were so sharply suppressed here! And no wonder that awful boy had caused her so many problems—he came from Mikola Mozhaiski, and when he led the princess out of this world, of course he brought her back to his master.

Well, there are more gods in this world. She had the power of Bear, didn't she? And Bear was more than a match for Mozhaiski.

Except that the source of her power was far off, and she had to draw on it across time and space, while Mozhaiski was powerful here, in the present moment.

She sniffed the air more deeply. Yes, masked by the heavy scent of Mozhaiski's benign, summery air, there was still a trace of winter in the air. Bear was still in this world.

She raised her hand to summon him, but then caught herself in time: In this world, Bear was not necessarily under her spell. The Bear whose power she controlled was the Bear of another time and place; here he might well be free, or under the power of a great wizard with whom she dared not do battle in her weakened state.

Tread softly, she told herself. Plenty of time to watch and wait, see how the land lies here, find out who makes the magic of tin houses on rolling feet. Not Mozhaiski—this was not the sort of thing he did, generally confining himself to meddlesome rescues of sailors and gifts of rain to farmers' fields. No, a greater wizardry was at work in the world, or some god only just now coming into his own.

Let the princess lead her through this world. Baba Yaga could afford to wait. Though she was bound not to lay hands on the princess directly, that boy was still with her. She'd find some way to kill him through some other hand, or at least rend them apart, breaking the spell.

She thought back to yesterday's burning of the church. Such a fine idea! She raised no hand against the princess, but rather simply ignited the dried wood of that ugly magicless sanctuary for the untalented devotees of a distant and disinterested god. Of course the princess got out—whether because of a spell or simply because she was a clever and lucky woman, Baba Yaga could not guess. But even if the church-burning failed to kill the girl and solve Baba Yaga's problems all in one blow, the thing had been worth doing for its own sake.

She'd find other ways in this world; there would be other tools to use. Even if her powers were weaker here, even if there were strong rivals that she dared not provoke, she'd make do, she'd find a way to win.

Or if she couldn't, or if her life was in danger, she'd simply cover herself with the cloth she had soaked with the oil from Bear's fur, speak a single word, and all that was encompassed by the cloth would be carried back home in a moment. If that included the princess or her lackey ur-husband, or both, so much the better. For them to come back to Baba Yaga's house under her power would be sweet indeed.

11

AIRPORTS

 f Ivan had doubted Cousin Marek's magical power, he would have been convinced by this: A genuine passport and visa for Katerina, in her name, and only a day after telephoning a friend in the new passport office in Kiev.

"The independent government of Ukraine is only a few months old, and already you have connections?"

"My connections are older than the government," said Marek.

Katerina looked through the pages of the book. "So much paper, and almost nothing written in it. And these letters—" She pointed to a word in the Roman alphabet. "—I don't know some of them."

"The letters Kirill gave to your language," said Ivan, "are not the only letters in the world."

"And you know all the letters?" she asked.

"All the letters in that book," he said.

"But there aren't very many here," as if his achievement were not so remarkable after all. Was she teasing him, or scorning him? How could he hope to tell?

"I know two alphabets," said Ivan. "The one that's used here, in the land of my birth—the one Kirill invented. And the one that's used in America, where my family lives."

"And which of these lands do you call your own?" asked Cousin Marek. "I'm curious, is all."

"I'm at home in both places," said Ivan. "But more a stranger here, I think, than there. Maybe I'm foreign in every land."

Marek chuckled. "Aren't we all."

Katerina was studying her own passport photo. "This seems a remarkably faithful likeness of the woman," she said. "Who is she, and why is her portrait in this book?"

It took Ivan a moment to realize she wasn't joking. But then, how would she recognize herself? The shining metal of a sword was the only mirror in King Matfei's court, and before modern times no one in Russia had much use for mirrors, since they believed a spirit from another world could leap from a mirror to possess them or attack. She had probably seen her own face in a pool—rippling, distorted, with fish darting between her eyes.

"The portrait is of you," said Ivan.

"When did the painter spy on me?" she said.

"It's not painted," said Ivan. "The man yesterday, who made the light flash—"

"That's what that spell was for? To take my picture from me?"

"Not a spell, a *tool*, like the light switch and the running water in the kitchen."

"You keep insisting on this, but isn't it time you explained to me why spells aren't also tools?"

Ivan shook his head. "You are being obstinate," he said. "You know the difference perfectly well yourself. You've handled a scythe—it cuts because the blade shears the stalks of grain. But a spell has no such contact between one thing and another."

"Then you've proved my point," she said. She walked to the light switch and turned it on and off. "There—what connection did my action have with that light? And this portrait—the light flashed, but nothing touched me."

"The light touched you."

She laughed. "And when I wave my hands in the air to cast a spell, there's no doubt a wind, too."

Ivan despaired. "Why do you have to argue with me? You're not stupid. This is my world, not yours, and if I tell you that magic is different from tools and the difference matters, then you should spend your time trying to understand the difference, not arguing with me."

She seemed about to answer with another argument, but then stopped herself. "The difference really is important?"

"Yes."

"Then explain it to me, and I'll try to understand."

The result was a painful hour of explaining electricity and wires and circuits, along with a vague explanation of cameras. And by the end, Ivan wasn't altogether sure that she understood anything. Except the one most important thing: That she not use magic in this world, not in front of other people, nor even speak of it.

"They don't believe in it?" she said. "Even though it works?"

"It takes talent and training to use magic," said Cousin Marek, who had listened to Ivan's explanations without helping once. "While any fool can use a machine."

"Any fool who can afford to buy one," said Ivan.

"And any fool who can afford to hire a wizard has magical power at his command, too," said Cousin Marek. "And now who's arguing for the sake of argument?"

The next day, the tickets arrived for Katerina's flight, and Ivan changed his reservations so they could sit together. "You can conjure money out of thin air?" Ivan asked Cousin Marek.

"Of course not," he answered.

"Then what magic did you use to buy her ticket?"

"American Express," said Marek.

"An immortal carries American Express?"

"Not *my* American Express," said Marek. "What use would I have for such a thing? When I want to travel, I walk. No, the card belongs to a friend. Your family are not the only folk to leave this land and go across the sea. And not all who leave this place forget their Cousin Marek."

For the first time, Ivan realized that this might have happened before. "Did you help us get our visas to leave the Soviet Union, back when Mother and Father and I lived here with you?"

"I tried."

"Then why did it take all those months?"

"I didn't have such good connections in Moscow," said Marek. "And I wasn't all that eager for you to leave."

With passport and ticket, and a decent selection of clothes that more or less fit her, Katerina was ready to go. Ivan was not, for when he returned to America he would have to face Ruthie and Father and Mother and somehow explain Katerina to them all. But there were no more reasons for delay, and many reasons to move quickly, not least of which was that Baba Yaga was still hovering nearby, plotting who-knew-what nastiness.

They bade good-bye to Sophia and rode with Cousin Marek to the train station. Ivan noticed that Katerina showed no fear of climbing inside Marek's truck. Perhaps that was because her trust in Mikola Mozhaiski overrode any fear. Or perhaps she had believed him when he told her it was simply a tool. Though, given the number of people who died each year in auto accidents, it might have been wiser for Ivan to warn her not to get into any kind of car.

When they got to the train station, Katerina immediately grasped the idea of many cars being pulled along a track by a single engine. "The locomotive is the ox," she said, "and it pulls these houses like sledges across snow." Close enough, thought Ivan.

Cousin Marek walked the length of the train. Only when he was assured that Baba Yaga wasn't aboard did he let Ivan and Katerina get on. "Be alert," he said to them both. "Watch for her, and don't let her talk to you. She can persuade the sun it's a pudding."

"She can't outrun a train, can she?" said Ivan. "Or outfly a jet? So we're safe."

Marek scowled at him. "Don't wear the hide until the bear is dead," he said.

"How will we know her if we see her?" said Katerina. "We might have seen her yesterday, but she can seem to be whatever she pleases."

"Look at her eyes," said Marek, "and you'll know. She can't change those, not without being blind."

"Look at the eyes and see what?" asked Ivan.

"The enemy."

Ivan had long since learned that when Cousin Marek didn't want to give a straight answer, he went in circles, and they were circling now. Rather the way Ivan had led the bear around the chasm till it gave up.

As the train pulled out of the station, Ivan felt a thrill of fear. Cousin Marek was no longer with them—as he said, why leave a trail fifty feet wide for the old hag to follow—and now it was up to him, Ivan the nonfighter, Ivan the scholar with his nose in a book, to keep Katerina safe and guide her through this dangerous world.

What if she gets airsick and throws up on the plane? Did Sophia explain to her about how to deal with her period here, or is Mother going to have to explain that in America? What if there's some disease she isn't immune to? He thought of *War of the Worlds*, when the alien invader is felled by the common cold.

Katerina was hardly the alien invader, and as for Baba Yaga, he knew better than to count on some microbe-ex-machina to save them from her. For all he knew, the witch had gotten on the train at the first stop, making Marek's check of the train useless. How far did her powers of illusion go, anyway? Could she be on board disguised as a suitcase? How did he know what was possible? The world that only a few days ago had seemed, if not safe, then at least comprehensible, was now fraught with new dangers and possibilities. It made everything new again. New and frightening, the way America was when Ivan first arrived, and everything he said and did seemed foolish, not only to the other children in school, but to himself. Add to this Katerina's insistence on making her own decisions, whether she understood all the consequences or not, and Ivan knew he'd get very little rest, on the train, in the air, or at home.

Katerina tried her best to remain as calm and brave as Ivan had when he came to Taina. She would not be shamed in front of him by showing cowardice. Now she understood how baffling and frightening it was to be in a strange place where the old rules no longer applied and no one knew how to value her. In Mikola Mozhaiski's house, she hadn't really grasped it yet, for she was among people whose language she understood; indeed, it was Ivan who still sounded like the accented stranger. But now in the cacophony of the station and the train, where everything was unexpected and she only understood one word in fifty, she was nauseated with fear. She found herself wanting to cling to Ivan's arm and beg him to come back to Taina with her. Better the known danger than the unknown! But she couldn't ask that, for in Taina it was *his* life that was in danger, while here, as far as she knew, neither of them was threatened. Her fear was foolish. Ivan would protect her, and if he couldn't, she might be able to help herself with a little magic. And if that didn't work, well, her life was in the hands of God, wasn't it? If he wanted her dead here, then nothing could save her; if he wanted her to live, then nothing could harm her.

The airport was a nightmare, though Ivan assured her that all was normal and safe. The customs official who looked at her with no respect whatsoever, as if she were a peasant with an unpleasant stink, and then rattled off a stream of the strange language that they spoke here—she barely kept herself from bursting into tears. Then Ivan interposed himself between her and the official, said a few words, showed the little book, and the man's demeanor softened. She was just about to smile at him when he suddenly picked up something heavy and slammed it down on a pad of wet blue cloth and then on her blank book, staining it and making a brutal pounding noise. She jumped back and screeched inadvertently before regaining her composure. The official laughed in her face, the swine. She felt humiliated, though Ivan simply hurried her along and spoke soothingly to her that this was a common thing, he should have warned her, he was so sorry, they always stamp the passport.

She wondered how many things in her kingdom might have

surprised or frightened him, and she had never thought to warn him or prepare him for anything. Instead she had scorned him for not already knowing what any child knew. But now she knew a bit of wisdom: Whoever travels to a new land is always a child.

She thought back to when Mikola Mozhaiski woke up the gruzovik and made it go forward, controlling it effortlessly with a wheel in his hands and with devices he pushed with his feet. She had imagined herself trying to control this moving house. Impossible. Yet hadn't she expected Ivan to pick up a sword and know how to use it instantly? She wanted to tell him she was sorry for not understanding what he was going through. But as she was about to do it, she wondered whether he really had felt the same fear as she. After all, he had traveled from land to land before, and even learned a new language, so he was used to new experiences. She didn't remember him showing fear in any obvious way, either, except reluctance to do certain things. So to say anything about fear right now would merely be a confession of her own.

As the airplane lumbered over the runway and then rose into the air, she wanted to scream in terror—and in delight, both at once. She was flying! She wanted to look out the window; but when she did, it made her want to throw up, to see the ground fall away like that, everything becoming small. And when the airplane made a sharp turn in the air soon after takeoff, she did throw up.

Oh, the unspeakable humiliation of it! Ivan was there at once with a little bag in case she vomited more, but it was too late, wasn't it? Her blouse was smeared with vomit, and even after the attendant led her to the bathroom and helped her rinse that part of the blouse, the smell lingered on the cloth *and* she had a cold wet spot that was quite uncomfortable. She had thought that the bra Sophia had bought for her in the village could not possibly be any more uncomfortable, but now she knew better. She could be cold, wet, humiliated, and smell like vomit.

When she got back to her seat, she looked out the window to hide her face from Ivan. By now the airplane was so high that all she could see was clouds below her, and she pretended it was only snow, and this was a huge sleigh gliding along, occasionally hitting an inexplicable bump—no doubt a bird or a particularly thick cloud. I don't want to be here, she thought. I want to go home, where I'm not humiliated every moment, where I can speak and be spoken to, where people know that I'm Princess Katerina and treat me with respect instead of contempt or pity.

Mustn't think this way, she told herself. Keep control. No crying.

Then she felt Ivan's hand gently but firmly take hold of hers, and he leaned close to her and whispered in her ear, "You're doing very well, and many people get sick in airplanes, so don't be ashamed of it." Then he kissed her cheek the way her father might have, when she was a little girl, and it was too much for her. She burst into tears. Or rather, burst out with a single sob, and then wept in silence, turning her face toward him, hiding her tears against his chest as he held her. Oh, if only it were my father here with me! she cried silently, but then rebuked herself. This is what a husband should do for his wife, and he is doing it. A wife should not wish that she were still with her father. That was undutiful and childish.

And yet she did wish it, as she made his shirt almost as wet as her own. Did a man forget his mother just because he had a wife? She should hope not. So why would it be wrong for a woman to remember her father, even if she had a husband?

The flight went on for hours and hours, broken only by a landing in Vienna, where they stayed on the plane. It was miserable, trying to sleep sitting upright, but at least the chairs were the softest she had ever sat in, and the clever little pillow was unbelievably soft and yet held its shape much better than feather pillows. And when she and Ivan were both awake, he tried to teach her to read the modern Russian printed in a magazine. When it was written down, it was easier for her to see how it was related to the language she spoke, and to find patterns in the differences. She was feeling pretty good about it, until he reminded her that in America very few people spoke this language, either.

"But my mother and father do, and that's what counts at first, that you be able to talk with them. My father speaks your language, too, after a fashion, and my mother will do her best. You'll see. They're gracious people."

"So that's how you learned," she said softly.

If he heard her, he said nothing. She hoped, at least a little, that he hadn't heard, because it would shame her to be kind, if he despised her kindness. Then it would feel like surrender. But she also hoped, perhaps a little more, that he *had* heard, for they were also words of apology. She regretted her arrogance and criticism, how she had hurt his feelings in her own world and when they first arrived in his. Everything he told her had turned out to be true. For instance, many women dressed just like the men. In fact they all dressed in clothing that she found appalling at first, but was now getting used to. The shoes were amazing, shaped differently for the right and left feet, and even at that, Ivan and Sophia both assured her that they'd find her shoes that fit much better once they got to America, where there was no shortage of shoes the way there were in Ukraine that year.

The officials in the airport in America were even ruder than the ones in Kiev had been, barking orders and shouting in a jumpy, harsh-sounding language that was offensive to hear. To her relief, when Ivan spoke the same language back to them it was not as jumpy and strident, and his calm voice seemed to calm them down as well. More stamping—this time she didn't flinch—and Ivan had to open his bags for them to look through what he brought with him, but soon they were out of the lines and into a crush of people holding up signs in the strange alphabet and calling out to people and hugging them. For a moment she feared that someone would grab her and hug her, too, but then realized they were hugging people they already knew. And here, she knew no one.

But Ivan knew someone. A man and two women.

"God hates me," said Ivan softly in her language. "I told my mother on the phone *not* to bring Ruthie."

"Your betrothed," murmured Katerina.

Ivan said nothing to that.

Katerina sized up the younger of the women—her confident bearing, her easy grace as she embraced Ivan and then embraced Katerina—and realized that what seemed so familiar about her was that Ruthie felt herself to be a princess as surely as Katerina did. She murmured this to Ivan, who smiled and translated her remark, or some version of it, for the others. Ruthie blushed and smiled, then leaned over and kissed Katerina's cheek.

"I've told them," Ivan murmured, "that the language you speak is an obscure dialect from the Carpathians. And that you're a friend I brought with me. I'll tell them the truth very quickly, but not here in the airport, because it would be wrong to embarrass Ruthie in a public place like this."

Katerina noticed that Ivan's father was listening as best he could to what they were saying. His eyes narrowed, and he began looking back and forth between her and Ivan. But Ivan's mother only embraced her and said something softly in her ear—so softly that she couldn't hear the words, though she'd probably not have been able to understand them even if she'd heard.

"What did your mother say?"

Ivan asked his mother, and, blushing, she whispered the same words to him. He turned red, but then leaned down to translate for Katerina. "Mother says that you are the woman she always hoped I would marry."

Katerina smiled at Mother, even as she murmured back to him, "I thought you didn't tell them we're married."

"I didn't," said Ivan. "My mother is simply a little strange."

"Or very wise," said Katerina.

"That's what *she* thinks," said Ivan. Then he translated some version of their conversation and the others laughed and nodded. She had no idea what Ivan told them that she'd said, but she nodded and smiled right back at them. Language wasn't going to be a problem after all, because apparently it didn't matter what she said—Ivan would turn it into the right thing when he interpreted.

Katerina looked away from Ivan's mother and saw that Ruthie was staring at her with cold rage in her eyes. There would be no need to tell her that her engagement with Ivan was off. Obviously, she already knew.

If only Mikola had learned to read and write back when it was a new idea. Instead he had only picked it up during the past fifty years, when literacy became universal in the Soviet Union and you had to be able to read signs and newspapers in order to function in society. Even then he still thought of it as something of a fad, until now, when he realized that his shortsightedness might cost him dearly.

Back in the old days the stories inscribed in the priests' books seemed trivial and distant to him. He had his own life, his own duties, his own powers. Why learn to read about their god, who ministered to another people in a faraway land, when he had his own business to attend to?

Only once in those early days of literacy did it occur to him that he might learn to read and write. He was telling his wife at that time— Hilda? Bruna?—the story of the time when Bear first wandered across the Urals, thinking that whatever land he came to would be his alone. Bear was wilder then, ignorant, barbarian—but dangerous, volatile, full of powers that Mikola had never faced before. He had to be inventive, combine spells and incantations, devise clever invisible fences across time. He laughingly told his wife about the time he inadvertently put every bear in the forest to sleep for three days before he figured out how to make his new spell more selective. And his wife asked him—Hilda, definitely, the one who ran off with Loki when the Norsemen first started raiding down the rivers—Hilda asked him what he did to make all the bears sleep. And Mikola couldn't remember.

He had sat there thinking, and then took a walk and thought some more, and still he could not remember. Only late that night, lying awake in his bed, did he remember the simple and obvious mistake that had put the bears to sleep. He almost woke Hilda right then, to tell her, but she was tired and he didn't like annoying her because she had the most amazing temper. And as he lay there listening to her snore he realized that remembering that old spell wasn't what mattered. The important discovery was the fact that Mikola Mozhaiski was capable of forgetting a spell. He hadn't known that could happen.

I should write them all down, he thought as he lay awake that night. I should get some priest to teach me to write, and then I could record all my spells so I don't have to try to remember them. Commands to the waves and the wind, those I remember because I use them so often. The flow of the great sky river, that I could direct in my sleep. But the commands to each plant to wake up in the spring, I barely remember those, because they generally do it well enough without my help. And the spells to control insects in their flight, and the song to calm the birds—how did those go? He definitely should learn this new alphabet and all the words so he could write it all down and never have to worry about remembering.

But then he thought some more, and decided that it was a bad idea, for two reasons: What if he came to rely on the book, and then lost it? He'd be worse off than now. And—even more dire—what if someone stole the book and used the spells against him? Better to keep his memory sharp, so he would never need a book that might empower an enemy. That was when he began his long custom of rehearsing every spell he knew at least once a year.

He kept it up, too, for several centuries, until his people grew so rational that he had no more rivals, no enemies disrupting the right order with their local spells. Witchcraft and wizardry had so effectively been denied that his own powers began to weaken, for there were few who contributed to his strength by invoking his name. He could cast all the old spells, of course, but it cost him more, wore him out, and he stopped doing any spells but the essential ones, and began to look out for less and less of the old lands, until most of his effort was spent caring for this area that was sometimes Poland, sometimes Russia, sometimes Ukraine and Belarus, even bits of Slovakia. Names could change, armies could pass by, but they concerned him little. He steered them around his little godhold, or made sure they passed lightly over the land and interfered little with the people. Beyond that, he simply tended to the weather.

Until now. Until Baba Yaga brought her stink into the land. And now he had no book to remind him of the spells of combat, techniques he hadn't used since the early days, when his people first separated from the main tribe in the hills of Iran and woke a new god to be their protector. He still had vague memories of childhood, of an idyllic life playing on the slopes of a mountain, the animals all talking to him, the plants making a constant music to which he often sang along. And then they woke him, called him by a name that he knew at once was his own, though it had never been spoken before. It filled him with vigor and he leapt down from the mountain as eager as any adolescent boy, ready to take on all comers. Oh, he fought his battles then, putting others in their place—or getting put down himself, from time to time. Zeus especially loved to torment him, until Mikola finally learned all the weathers of the sky and matched him bolt for bolt.

The time of battles was over, though, long since. Even that arrogant sex fiend Zeus had retired from public life, though he still had a sort of fame that kept wakening him from his lazy philandering and henpecked domesticity—but to no purpose. It was just the sound of his name being murmured in a thousand classrooms; it had no strength in it. Mikola looked at Zeus these days and saw his own future, when his people had at last forgotten him. But until then, he was still guardian. And now a great danger had come into the land, and he could hardly remember how to aim lightning. If only, if only I had written it down.

So he struggled to remember as he trailed after Baba Yaga, following the odor of her passage through the land, cleaning up after her, casting little spells to make people forget her visit, removing the vile little curses she always left on any house that let her in or gave her anything to eat or a place to sleep. It took a great deal of ingenuity on his part, because she was so maliciously clever, laying traps for him, so that when he released one curse, a worse one would slip into place, unless he took precautions in advance.

Most important, he kept renewing the spell that kept Bear and Baba Yaga from finding each other. They both smelled each other, but whenever Baba Yaga thought of seeking him out, or Bear stirred in his somnolence, Mikola filled the air between them with so much of the forgetful haze of summer that they'd become distracted and think of something else, with only a feeling of fitfulness and ennui to remind them of their forgotten desire.

Mikola was no fool. He recognized that Baba Yaga was following the children's trail toward Kiev, even though she must have thought the twisting and turning of her path would deceive him. But he knew what she did not—that in Kiev, their trail took to the air and soared at thirty-five thousand feet across Europe and the Atlantic, heights and distances that would be utterly incomprehensible to a woman who, powerful as she might be, was still only a mortal who had never followed the flow of the great sky river around the world. She might make it to the airport and see the great planes lumber into the sky and figure out that Vanya and Katerina had flown off in one of them. But that wouldn't tell her where they went, and it wouldn't help her follow them. She would stand there, baffled, helpless, and gradually realize that they were out of her grasp.

Mikola imagined her going into one of her tantrums. The authorities wouldn't stand for it, of course. He could imagine the antiterrorist police surrounding her as she madly screamed and sprayed fiery spells through the airport, finally getting a good shot and taking her out just as in those American movies that had taught police all over the world how to walk with the swagger that made them ridiculous and frightening, both at once. Baba Yaga would see the silliness; not knowing the accuracy and range of rifles with scopes, she would not have sense enough to fear them, too. The bloom of a bullet in her head, spraying blood and brains in a fan-shaped pattern on the airport floor—the mere thought of it brought back feelings that Mikola had not let himself feel in years. He could smell battle. And even though he would not strike the blow himself, it made him feel no less triumphant to know that Baba Yaga would never survive in a world where he had managed to preserve a niche for himself and his beloved Sophia.

The whole drive to the airport had been awkward. Ruth just didn't have that much to say to Ivan's parents. During Ivan's long absence in Russia, Ruth had tried to keep in close contact with her future in-laws, and at first it seemed to work, but as the months went by, she got more and more of a sense that they entertained her only out of a sense of duty. In fact, Ivan's father was always distracted—nice, almost too nice, for a few minutes, then anxious to get back to his work. Back to his books. How terrible, for the husband to work at home. Much better the way her parents were—leave the job at the office, come home and really be home. Of course, Ivan would probably expect to live like his father, since they were both pursuing the same career. And that would be fine, Ruth would learn to live with it, that distraction, that there-but-not-there coolness. Besides, unlike Mrs. Smetski, Ruth would have a job. A career of her own.

Mrs. Smetski. *She* was the problem. Ruth suspected from the start that Mrs. Smetski thought that Ivan could have found a better girl to marry. She wasn't distracted like Professor Smetski. On the contrary, she focused completely, almost smotheringly, on Ruth. But there was this sense of amusement in everything she said. A sense of irony. *I know something you don't know.*

Ruth had tried to point it out to Ivan, but he never saw it. "That's just Mom," he'd say. "She's always having an out-of-body experience. Looking down on everything from the ceiling. Never part of it. It's nothing to do with you."

But Ruth knew better. A woman knows these things—though of course she didn't say that to Ivan, he got quite testy when Ruth asserted her female power, as if her womanliness threatened him. Of course, he tried to sound like a doctrinaire feminist about it. "Either the only differences between men and women are cultural, or they're innate," Ivan would say. "So if you go for the women's intuition thing, then you have to take that whole package, pedestal and all. And if you want equality, then you have to give up that idea that women have secret ways of knowing."

As if.

But, for the sake of harmony, she allowed his threatened male ego to have its protected space, and didn't push the point. She simply knew, that's all, that Mrs. Smetski disdained her for some reason.

And during the months while Ivan was gone, it became more obvious. Ivan's dad had work to do; Mrs. Smetski had no such excuse. She would wander out of a room sometimes when Ruth was talking. And it wasn't an accident, either. Because when she came back in, she'd resume the conversation with a bland, "You were saying, Ruthie?" in that thickly accented English.

To her, I don't exist. Ruthie could reach no other conclusion.

Come home, Ivan, before your parents make me have second thoughts.

Well, the time had finally come. Of course Mrs. Smetski had hinted that maybe Ruthie should drive her own car, but Professor Smetski put the kibosh on that immediately. "We have to go together, it would be cruel to make Vanya choose between his parents and his bride-to-be. You know he would choose the bride, and then wouldn't we feel foolish!"

"I just thought it might be crowded on the ride home," said Mrs. Smetski.

Crowded? It wasn't as though their car was tiny. Like so many Russians, the Smetskis luxuriated in the American sense of scale. A big old Crown Victoria was their choice—cheap, for a big car; or was it big for a cheap one? Plenty of room.

Too much room. Professor Smetski tried to get Mrs. Smetski to sit in back with Ruth on the way there, "to keep her company," but Mrs. Smetski just laughed and said, "You know I get sick in the back seat," and that was that. And when Ruth tried to engage them in conversation, Professor Smetski was the only one who seemed to be paying attention, and not very much at that. Mrs. Smetski just looked at the scenery. Trees were trees. Ruth knew that Mrs. Smetski was looking at them just so she didn't have to talk to Ruth.

Ivan, we have to have a talk. Your parents don't like me, or at least your mother doesn't, and that's a problem. Then he would kiss her and reassure her that it would never be a problem, Mom likes you just fine, yadda yadda.

Maybe the whole thing was a mistake. Maybe Mrs. Smetski was right. Ivan was charming, smart, fascinating with his sultry foreignness, that fragility hidden within the muscular, lithe runner's body, the sensitive eyes in a sculpted face. But charm, intelligence, and good looks, did they add up to love? As Ruth's own mother kept saying, What kind of boy is it asks a girl to marry him, then he runs off to Russia for long enough to get a girl pregnant and watch it be born before he comes home to his fiancée?

She didn't even want to think about that. Ivan wasn't that kind of boy, damn his shyness. It was so embarrassing to tell the girls at college that no, they hadn't slept together, Ivan believed in waiting—the whooping and laughing! "He's gay," they all said at once, and when she assured them that she had ample reason to believe that he was not, they treated her like she was in love with a cripple. "Did he have a childhood injury?" one of them asked, and then it became a joke. Ruth's fiancé's tragic childhood injury. They kept thinking up some new malady to explain his lack of sexual drive. "He has elephantiasis of the testicles"—that was a favorite—"his balls weigh thirty pounds each." Or "he was just one of those kids who slides down every banister, even the ones with those cruel little spikes every few feet." Or "his parents left him alone with the cat and without a diaper, and you know how cats are when they find something to play with."

The thing is, some of their joking was genuinely funny. Ruth felt disloyal to laugh at such crude talk about her future husband's private parts, but wasn't it his own fault? She had done everything but strip naked and hide in his bed, and he just laughed and kissed her and said, "Plenty of time for that when we're married."

Here's a news flash, Ivan. The reason I wanted to sleep with you was not because I thought we were going to run out of time later!

But it was also kind of sweet. After all the boys who had tried to get into her pants from the time she was eleven, or at least so it seemed in retrospect, Ivan was an entirely different creature.

No, he couldn't be gay. *Damn* them for making her wonder.

If Mrs. Smetski had only been willing to talk, Ruth wouldn't have been thinking about all these negatives. About how Ivan's letters grew rarer and rarer as the months went by. How he wrote romantically at first, but more perfunctorily later. You'd think he'd be getting hornier, wouldn't you? Unless he found somebody else.

Somebody Russian. Somebody from his childhood. Some woman who'd set her cap for him the moment he arrived, since he represented a ticket to the States. Long walks along the river—there was a river in Kiev, wasn't there?—talking in his beloved Russian, discussing Dostoyevsky or Tolstoy or—who was that poet? Eugene Onegin? No, that was the name of the poem. Pushcart? Pushpin?

Pushkin!

Or maybe he was just into his research and there was no woman. This was Ivan, after all. Not the ordinary man. She wouldn't have fallen in love with him if he were the kind of man who couldn't keep his word to the woman he loved. Not that he'd actually given his word. Ruth could imagine *that* conversation. "No getting laid in Ukraine, my love." "Oh, really? That would bother you? All right, my pet." "No kissing either." "But in Russia, we kiss for greeting!" "No tongue." "Definitely no tongue. Thank you for providing me with moral guidelines for traveling fiancés! You think of everything!"

"Good flying weather," said Professor Smetski as they got out of the car at the airport.

"A clear day," said Ruth.

"I mean, no wind," said the professor. "Safer for landing."

"The USAir terminal is this way," said Mrs. Smetski. Then she took off, and Ruth and Professor Smetski had to make their way as best they could.

So there they stood, making small talk—smaller even than usual—watching the gate to see him the moment he appeared. Like a contest—I caught first glimpse of him, so I love him more! And then he appears, bearded, suntanned—definitely a scholarly look! Oh, he was hard at the books, wasn't he!—and he was helping a woman up the ramp, wasn't he? How nice.

Only she didn't leave him when they reached the door. In fact, his arm was around her waist, guiding her along. She was . . . she was *with* him.

Ruth felt sick. The woman was Russian, but not in that exaggerated wide-faced almost-Mongolian way that gave you a pretty good idea what the Golden Horde was doing all those years they ruled the steppe. She wasn't Nordic, either. Something else. But one thing was certain: Definitely not Jewish. Not that Ruthie was politically incorrect, of course; it was her duty to pretend that you couldn't tell a Russian Jew just by looking. But in this case, you could certainly tell that she was *not* a Jew. In fact, if she had been born to a Jewish mother, this girl would constitute proof of adultery.

Someone he met. That's all. Some scholarly woman who was coming to America anyway and he accompanied her because . . . because . . . her English wasn't good!

Surely he wouldn't bring her home, though, as a guest. Well, what if he did? This stranger wasn't Ivan's fiancée, Ruth was—and Ruth would make sure that Ivan had very little time to lounge around home with this shiksa princess. If the girl wanted to speak Russian, Ivan's parents would be *excellent* company for her. While Ruth would make sure that she was Ivan's constant companion.

They came closer, and there was something in the way that Ivan looked. A shiftiness. He saw Ruth, smiled at her sheepishly, but then he looked down, looked away. Looked at his mother and father. Anywhere but at the girl. Pretending that he didn't know she was there. But still, his arm around her waist. Ushering, sheltering, protecting. That is not her place, you bastard. You let somebody else into my place.

Don't get angry. You don't know yet.

Yes you do.

Katerina? Oh, what a pleasure, says Professor Smetski.

And back comes a string of Russian.

Only it isn't Russian, is it? Or if it is, it's some weird accent, anyway, because Professor Smetski asks her to repeat what she said, and when he answers her it's with a different tone from the way he usually speaks. And his eyes are wide and he's absolutely *fascinated* with her language.

But Mrs. Smetski, *she's* completely wacked out. Smiling. Like a kid who won the prize. Doesn't try to talk to the shiksa, but just *loves* her. Hug hug, kiss kiss kiss, hug again. Can't take her eyes off this goyishe princess.

And princess is right. The way the girl holds herself. As if the space around her for about six blocks belongs to her. As if Ivan belongs to her. And not like a man, either, but like a . . . servant. She thinks she *owns* him. Like Nancy Reagan, that's what she looks like, beaming because this man is hers. Defiant, arrogant.

And all the time Ruth was thinking this, Ivan was talking. "I met her near Cousin Marek's place. She wanted to visit in America, but she never studied English, so I volunteered."

Ruth wanted to scream at him, "That's a lie, you moron! She's obviously more than some neighbor girl you're doing a favor for! Tell the truth, tell it right away, and have done with it!"

Instead, Ruth went hug hug, kiss kiss kiss, and hug again. "What a lovely girl," she said. "Are you Ivan's niece?"

Ivan laughed awkwardly and translated.

Only when the translation was complete did Katerina's full attention turn to Ruth. And the look on her face—what *was* that look?

Pity.

She thinks she's got him. She thinks she's already won, and she's feeling sorry for me.

Well, save your little pity-eyes for somebody who gives up easily. Maybe Ivan got all gooey-eyed over you there in Kiev, but I can hold my own, thanks a lot. I can definitely outdress you, you poor thing. Where did you get those clothes? Hand-me-downs from some farmer's daughter?

"I must take her shopping," said Ruth to Ivan. "Please tell her— we must spend an afternoon together at the mall."

"Oh, definitely not," said Mrs. Smetski, intervening before Ivan could even translate. "You and Vanya will be together all the time. I find American clothings for Katerina."

If Mrs. Smetski had ever looked at me the way she's looking at this shiksa, I would never have had a moment's worry.

And then it dawned on her. Mrs. Smetski *always* wanted a shiksa for her boy. For her Russian boy. She was one of those self-hating, anti-Semitic Jews! Hadn't Ivan told her that it was entirely his father's idea to become serious Jews and emigrate from Russia on a visa to Israel? Mrs. Smetski never wanted Ivan to become serious about his Jewish identity. She wanted him to marry a nice Russian girl, and . . . he-e-e-e-ere's Katerina!

They were speaking Russian together, all of them, as if Ruth did not exist, as if courtesy were an old legend that no one believed in anymore.

Ruth felt a momentary twinge of despair. I've already lost. They've formed a closed group now. Ivan's already got his protective-male thing going with her, and his father is fascinated by every word she says, and Mrs. Smetski is absolutely in *love* with her. Mrs. Smetski looks so smug. As if she had defeated me. And maybe she has. Definitely she has. I'm gone. If only I had my own car and could just get out of here and drive home by myself and . . .

Mrs. Smetski already knew. That's why she wanted separate cars. She *knew* that the Crown Victoria would be way too crowded on the trip home because she knew this shiksa was getting off the plane. Ivan must have told them. But no one bothered to tell *me*.

Ruth couldn't let this deception go unchallenged. "So, when did you call your parents and tell them Katerina was coming?"

They all looked at her like she was crazy. "He didn't call," said Professor Smetski.

"*I* didn't even know I was bringing her till the last minute," said Ivan.

He certainly didn't seem to be lying.

Only Mrs. Smetski said nothing. Because she knew. Somehow, even without a phone call, *she* knew. And, dear sweet compassionate loving gracious woman that she was, she had tried to spare Ruth's feelings by giving her an escape route so she wouldn't have to suffer the long ride home from the airport trapped in the back seat with Ivan and his . . .

On impulse—on damnable, uncontrollable impulse—Ruth asked him point-blank. "So, are you and Katerina engaged already, or are you waiting to make it formal until you've had a chance to get rid of me?"

The embarrassment on all their faces. How inconvenient of her, to lay it on the line like this. To demand that they face up to what was obvious to all of them. Oh, is this making you uncomfortable? You poor dears.

"Ruthie, don't be silly," Professor Smetski was saying, "Vanya is just helping her on the—"

Ivan held up his hand to stop his father. "I don't know, Ruth, I don't know how you—I wanted to have a chance to talk to you alone, I didn't want it to be right here, but . . ."

Ruth's heart sank. She wanted to cry, in shame, in grief. "You *are* engaged?"

Ivan shook his head.

Ruth knew a moment of hope. Still a chance.

"We're married," said Ivan.

It struck her like a blow. Married. The door, not just closing, but closed, locked, slammed in her face. Married!

"How . . . sudden," she said.

She turned her back on them then. They would not see the tears that leapt into her eyes.

She felt his hand on her shoulder. She shrugged it off.

"I'm sorry I didn't write," he was saying. "Or call. I know it's hard to believe, but I really couldn't. And it wasn't as sudden as it seems, either, it . . . Ruth, you have to believe me, I didn't want it to be this way."

"If you didn't want it to be this way," she said, controlling her voice almost perfectly, "then it wouldn't *be* this way, would it? Or are you seriously telling me the two of you *had* to get married?" Ruth turned around and pointedly scanned Katerina's body, as if the pregnancy might already be visible.

"We haven't even slept together," Ivan protested.

"No, of course not," said Ruth scornfully. "Not *you*. If your wife ever has children, it'll be a virgin birth. That's why you needed a shiksa, isn't it? That's their specialty."

"Ruthie," said Professor Smetski, "this is as much a shock to us as it is to you, completely unexpected, but let's try to stay calm, it's a long ride home, and—"

"No, Professor Smetski, I don't think we'll be riding home together. I have a roommate who lives here in Syracuse. It was lovely to meet you, Katerina. Just a word of advice. Don't let Ivan out of your sight."

Of course the girl didn't understand a word Ruth said, but she wasn't a fool, this Ukrainian princess, and her eyes were full of tears. Remorse? Pity? Keep your crocodile tears, darling. If he wants *you*, then I don't want *him*. The man I loved wouldn't have gotten married without bothering to break off his previous engagement. So whatever you've got there with his arm attached to your back, it's not a man I ever knew or ever wanted. Somebody else, somebody faithless. I deserve better. So save your tears for yourself.

Bitch.

Without another word, Ruth turned and walked away. Out of the terminal. The payphones were all inside, but she wanted a clean break. Exit scenes had to be managed. No lingering where they could see you, see how you cry when you finally get Emilia on the phone and tell her, Bring your hot yellow roadster out to the airport, Nancy Drew, because your friend Ruthie needs a long ride with a strong breeze on her face to dry these silly damn tears.

Baba Yaga

Baba Yaga was astonished and delighted with these houses-that-fly. Long lodges like the halls of great lords, into which a hundred people crowded themselves, and then they scooted along the ground on their skinny chicken legs until they rose like geese into the sky, trailing smoke behind them from their sideways chimneys.

She knew at once that the princess and her unmanly husband had gone into one of these flying houses and traveled to a faraway place.

Why? To escape Baba Yaga, of course. There are no trails in the sky, no scent of Katerina's magic left behind. And they'd go a long way, too, to a land where Bear had no power, so Baba Yaga would be weaker yet. They thought that would stop her from following them.

It was always pleasant when an intended victim imagined himself to be safe; that added zest to her life, for it meant that the surprise would be all the more delicious. But for such a person really to *be* safe, that was unbearable, that sat in her belly like bad meat, churning, aching. They were not going to get away just because they had friends with such powerful magic that they could make houses fly.

Inside the airport, though, everything was confusing. Everybody seemed to know where they were going, which line to stand in. Lines meant nothing to her, of course, but when she tried to go past one particularly long line, a burly man stopped her, quite forcefully. Baba Yaga was appearing as an old woman at the time, so he wasn't rough with her, just kept explaining to her, talking more and more slowly, but none of it made sense. The people in the line had brought gifts, apparently, which they placed into the gaping mouth of a large box. The box engulfed it, and the people passed through a gate, and then they got their gift *back* on the other side. This made no sense at all. She had no gift, but without one, she apparently couldn't get through, even though people got their gifts *back*.

So Baba Yaga put on Shadow, the charm that made her unnoticeable. It wore her down to wear it—it took strength from *her*, apparently, with Bear so far away—but she used it only long enough to take away a woman's bag. A light one. She carried it to the box, put it in. The porch of the box moved, drew it inside. Then they let her pass through the gate.

Only it made a loud noise as she passed through it. They indicated she should step back and walk through again. Again the noise. They asked her questions she didn't understand. They took her by the arm and led her to a place where someone began to wave a wand around her. She had no idea what spell they were casting on her, but she had no intention of finding out. She drew out Shadow, put it on, and they didn't notice when she moved away. They shuffled around a little, looking vague and distracted. She walked off and left them wondering why they thought they were wanding somebody at the security gate, when no one could remember seeing anybody set off the alarm.

Exhausting as it was, she kept the shadow charm around her neck past the other gates. There was no important magic at any of them. She didn't know how the floor in front of the box moved, and she didn't know why the loud sound came when she walked through; but if it was magic, it wasn't much, because a simple charm like Shadow fooled them all. It shouldn't have. It was for common people, not for wizards, it would never work with wizards. But apparently wizards were in short supply in this place.

Finally she came to the place where she could see the houses-that-fly through large windows, magnificent clear windows without leading. How could such windows be sustained without magic? And yet she detected no trace of a spell on them. A lot of old prayers had been whispered here at the windows, and especially near the doorways that led down to the houses-that-fly, but that was god business, humble petitioners, obedient servants, nothing to do with the way that Baba Yaga used power.

She walked through an open doorway and made her way to the

entrance of the house. She touched the wall of it. Hard, like the blade of a sword. Cold and smooth. She loved the feel of it. But where was the flying spell? She could smell strange things in the air, but recognized none of it. She slipped through the entrance and found row on row of chairs, all facing the same way. Soft chairs, like thrones, and she sat in an empty one.

She watched the people around her and learned how to lower the table, how to fasten a belt around her—what for, she couldn't imagine, but they all seemed to take it seriously. Finally the only people moving around were the servants in livery and one middle-aged man. The man held a piece of paper in his hand, and the servants kept looking at it. They moved up and down the rows of seats, looking down at the paper, then up at letters written above the seats, checking, checking. Checking what?

Finally she realized: Every seat in this house was full. Every person in here had a paper, and the writing on the paper told where they were supposed to sit. She was in the seat that this man was assigned to, but because she wore Shadow, they kept overlooking the place where she was. Therefore they couldn't find his seat. And until they found his seat, they were not going to let the house rise into the sky.

The ingeniousness of the system intrigued her. The wizard who created all this magic used ordinary people without a speck of power, and yet they had managed to stymie Baba Yaga herself, simply because they were so stupid that they would fuss around, go back and forth, talk and argue, but the plane would not rise into the sky until they found this man's seat. If Baba Yaga took off her charm, they would know she was in his chair, and they would try to get her to leave because she didn't have the paper she needed. She might kill a few of them for daring to refuse her—but she knew that the wizard who designed this system would have foreseen the possibility, and the house simply would not fly.

Well, have your cursed chair, you poor stupid fools. I'll stand.

She got up and moved away from the chair.

At once the servants found the seat and the man settled into it. Baba Yaga had left an itch in the upholstery—it would get through his clothes after an hour or so. And it would keep working on everyone who ever sat in the chair. It was one of her favorite curselets.

She was standing near one of the servants when she took a black-handled whip from the wall and spoke to it, as if invoking a god. Only, her voice was repeated throughout the house. Baba Yaga couldn't understand much of what she said. Only a few words, like *Kiev* and *to* and . . .

To. The woman was telling the people what the destination of the house was. Only then did Baba Yaga realize that of course the houses didn't all fly to the same place. Certain houses went to certain places, and everyone knew where except her—no doubt because the information was written on those nasty little papers, which she couldn't read, or it was said aloud in a language that she couldn't speak.

The door to the house-that-flies was closed, and she couldn't open it.

The house began to move; it almost knocked her down when it started.

If she was taken away from here, she didn't know how she'd find her way back. And since she didn't know where Katerina and Ivan had gone, there would be no hope of finding them without this as her starting place. She had failed.

She almost took out that little cloth and draped it over her head. But it made her too . . . not frightened—she wasn't *frightened*—too *ashamed* at the very thought of giving up, going back home empty-handed, blocked by a wizard who used cattle like these as his servants. She would not do it.

She pulled off Shadow and began to weep loudly, shifting her appearance so she looked like a frightened, confused country woman she had robbed out in the farm country a few days ago. Not knowing the language hampered her, but she hoped they'd just assume she was old and senile.

Oh, these servants were in fine form, running around, searching for her seat. Only there were no seats, she had no ticket, she heard them babble at her and comprehended nothing, and finally the house-that-flies stopped while the servants talked to men from a little room in front, who looked at Baba Yaga in exasperation and spoke in savage whispers to the women before they finally went back into their room and made the house glide back to the doorway.

They opened it, they ushered her outside, they left.

So the houses were controlled in that little room in front—that was good to know. And you really did have to have a paper with those letters on it so that there'd be a seat for you. And you had to know where you were going, or you'd end up somewhere else.

That was why Baba Yaga lingered in the airport for several days, watching. She tried to use Shadow only sparingly as she ate the over-salted, oversweetened food that nobody noticed her stealing. She learned to use the toilets and began to imitate their obsessive hand-washing. She rifled through luggage until she found clothing that fit her and would allow her to blend in with the locals when she wasn't wearing Shadow.

Most important, however, she learned about tickets and money and credit cards. She accosted an employee and put him under a brief spell of talkativeness. She made him talk slowly and repeat things until she thought she understood what he was talking about. Money was no longer made of gold, she discovered, it was just magical numbers that were stored in tiny houses with a single large window called *computers*, and credit cards were the charms that commanded a distant servant to send these magical numbers through thin wires to other computers, and then, behold! You got a piece of paper with magic words on it that would compel the people in the flying houses to give you a seat and carry you with them to your destination.

Now that she knew credit cards were valuable, Baba Yaga began to collect as many of them as she could. She would slip Shadow on over her head, walk right up to people as they were paying for their tickets, and take the cards out of their hands. Soon she had dozens of them.

But what good would they do her, when she didn't know where Katerina and her consort had gone? Not till she got one of the ticket sellers to explain the computer screen to her did she finally get it. This was not all the work of a single wizard. Each of the different lords-of-the-air had his own livery, so his servants could be identified by the colors of their uniforms. And each lord had a different realm, so certain liveries would take you only to certain places. Also, they kept records of everyone who flew in their houses. Since Baba Yaga knew more or less when Katerina and Ivan had flown away, it wasn't hard—just time-consuming—to find out which lord-of-the-air had transported them, and where they had gone. It was a simple matter after that to get a ticket to carry her to the same destination.

Conveniently enough, Ivan's address was even listed in the computer. Baba Yaga had the ticket seller write it down for her. Everyone was so helpful. She paid using the prettiest credit card, and then left it with the ticket seller as a gift. Along with a minor curse—a bladder infection and diarrhea—just because she *was* Baba Yaga, and certain things were expected. Then, familiar now with all the airport routines, she bypassed every one of them without incident, got on the house-that-flies, and sat down in a seat, clutching in her hands the tickets that would take her first to Berlin, then to New York Kennedy, and then to

Syracuse. From there she would somehow get transportation—a train, perhaps?—to Tantalus. The place where Ivan and Katerina had gone.

The gods and wizards of this world were no match for Baba Yaga, even in her weakened state. She got the better of every opponent. And every ally, too, for that matter. Even death. Someday she'd find a way around that, too. If feebleminded old gods like Mikola Mozhaiski could do it, so could she.

12
CHARMS

here was no way to explain it all to Father in an orderly way, Ivan realized that at once. No matter what he said, Father was going to pepper him with questions, while the whole picture was salted by Father's utter unbelief.

Mother was a marvel, though, merely nodding from time to time and otherwise holding hands with Katerina and smiling at her at odd moments. The conversation was half in proto-Slavonic and half in Ukrainian, but everyone seemed to understand everything. Except that Father understood nothing.

Ivan hadn't even meant to try to explain anything about the century that Katerina came from, but Father simply knew too much about the language. "There is no way that a pocket of pure proto-Slavonic could survive all these centuries," Father declared as a conversation-opener, almost as soon as they were in the car together. "A language in isolation is conservative, yes, but not *that* conservative. Even the Basque language is not the same as it was five hundred years ago. So the real question is, is your bride here the result of some weird Soviet language experiment or is this an elaborate practical joke that turned out not to be funny?" That much was in English, but Ivan immediately shifted the conversation to a combination of languages that he figured Katerina and Mother could both understand.

"What does the soviet have to do with language?" asked Katerina.

"There was a government in your country for the past seventy years or so that did strange and terrible things," Ivan explained.

"How isolated *is* her community?" Father demanded. "They didn't *notice* the Soviet government?"

With that, there was really no choice. Ivan had to start talking about getting drawn back into the ninth century and thinking he was going to live there forever, so he married Katerina there but then he came back and brought her with him. Father leapt to the conclusion that this was some weird sci-fi gimmick—"An alien abduction through time?"—until Mother patted his arm and said, "Think of it as magic, dear. Think of it as . . . finding Sleeping Beauty and wakening her with a kiss."

Father gave a sharp, derisive laugh at that.

"Father," Ivan said patiently, "don't think of it 'as if' I found Sleeping Beauty and woke her up. Katerina *is* Sleeping Beauty. The child cursed by an evil witch. By *the* evil witch, the Widow." He caught himself. To Father, he had to speak her name. He wasn't in Taina now. "Baba Yaga. And her aunts, in an effort to save her from the curse of death, ended up getting her stranded, asleep in the middle of a moat that was patrolled by a giant bear. For about eleven hundred years."

"My how time flies," said Father dryly.

Katerina looked strangely at Ivan.

"What?" he asked her.

"Are you known as such a liar here, that your father doesn't believe you?" Then she winked.

Father didn't see the wink. "Liar? Vanya's no liar. What I'm worried about is his sanity." Only for *sanity* he had to use the modern Russian word and Katerina didn't get it. To Ivan's surprise, Mother came up with some halting proto-Slavonic.

"My husband thinks Vanya is crazy," she explained.

"You speak proto-Slavonic?" Ivan asked.

Mother shrugged. "I'm deaf? I can't hear you two tossing this language back and forth all the time?" But there was more to it than that, Ivan knew. What he and Father had spoken was Old Church Slavonic, the formal written language of the Church. What Mother had spoken was the oral language—with a slightly different accent from that of Taina, perhaps, but nothing she could have picked up from Father and Ivan's conversations.

He would have pursued the matter, but Father was back with more questions, and by the time they pulled into their driveway in Tantalus, Father knew what he needed to know . . . and maybe almost partly believed a small fraction of it. Father stalked off and went to his office, though what answers he hoped to find there Ivan didn't know, while Mother ushered Katerina into the kitchen and Ivan carried in their bags.

For Katerina, her second modern kitchen was perhaps more interesting than the first, not because it was so different from Sophia's, but because she now realized that everyone had these items in the whole world, and not just the wives of the gods. But then, as Ivan watched them together, laughing over the awkwardness of their language, he began to realize that there was a level of communication that he hadn't appreciated before, a level below language—or was it above?—in which two people recognize each other and leap to correct intuitions about what the other means and wants and feels. Do all women have this? Ivan wondered. And then thought: No. Mother never had this with Ruthie.

In Sophia's kitchen, Katerina had not even attempted to be helpful, as if she felt that the level of magic was beyond her. But in Mother's kitchen, Katerina, unasked, immediately set to work helping. In a way this didn't surprise Ivan at all—in Taina there had been no sense of princesses as fragile creatures who had to be waited on hand and foot. He had heard much about what a deft hand Katerina had at the harvest, able to tie off a sheaf of wheat faster than anybody, with fingers so agile that, as the saying was, "She could sew without a needle." Pampered princesses came much later in history, at least in Russia. What surprised him was not her willingness to work, then, but rather her instinctive grasp of what Mother needed her to do. She seemed to understand loading and unloading the dishwasher immediately, even though no one had explained to her what the dishwasher was or what it did. She seemed to know what tool Mother wanted and, most amazing of all, *where* it was in the kitchen. This was something that Ivan had never grasped. He had grown up helping his mother from time to time in the kitchen, certainly with the dishes, but he always had to ask where the more obscure tools went.

Finally, when Katerina went straight to a drawer and found the weird little grabbing tool that Mother used to pull the stems out of strawberries, Ivan had to flat-out ask, "How did you know?"

They looked at him like he was crazy.

"She told me," said Katerina.

"She was talking about how the field-grown strawberries were finally coming ripe, so it wasn't all greenhouse berries. She never once said what she needed or where it was."

Mother and Katerina looked at each other in puzzlement.

"Yes I did," said Mother finally. "You just weren't listening."

"On the contrary," said Ivan. "I was listening very closely, because I was amazed at how much proto-Slavonic you have already fallen into using, and I was amazed at how much modern Ukrainian Katerina was understanding. I could repeat your conversation to you word for word, if you wanted."

Mother looked at him in helpless bafflement. "But I could have sworn I said . . . I needed a . . ." And as she spoke, her hands moved exactly as they would have had she been grasping the tool and using it on a berry. Now Ivan remembered that she *had* made that gesture, and saw what he had not noticed before, that Katerina's hands imitated it. So what was passing was mechanical knowledge, not language, and Katerina apparently recognized the tool when she saw it, because her hands already knew how to use it. Not only that, but she had got such a feel for the kitchen already that she knew where in the kitchen Mother would have put such a tool.

Ivan tried to express this to them, but now language did fail them all, language and, perhaps, philosophy, since neither Mother nor Katerina had the male obsessiveness with mechanical cause—the mechanisms by which things worked in the natural world. What they cared for was intentional cause, motivation, *purpose*. When they wanted to know how to do something, it was because they intended to do it and needed to know. While Ivan wanted to know how things worked precisely because he couldn't do them himself and he felt a need to understand everything around him. In both cases, it was a matter of trying to be in control of the surrounding world. For Ivan, the question came up immediately: Was this thing between Mother and Katerina something all women could do? Or only these two women? While to them, all that mattered was that they were in the kitchen together, and they liked and understood each other despite the language barrier, and the mechanism, as long as it worked, was unimportant.

So Ivan stopped intruding, taking part in the conversation only when he was needed as an interpreter. He continued to watch, however, and gradually realized that Katerina and Mother had something else in common, something that he had never noticed in all the years he had spent in Mother's kitchen.

Mother used magic.

Why hadn't he recognized it in the kitchen just outside King Matfei's house? The tiny bowl of salt and crust of bread near the cookfire—in Taina, he assumed it was an offering to a god that was not officially worshiped in that newly Christian land. But Mother also had these things on the stove. When Ivan was young and asked her why she never used the salt from the tiny bowl, she explained that it was "to take moisture out of the air." Later, Ivan realized that it was an old superstition that Mother had learned from her mother and on back, from time immemorial. Only when he got to Taina did he learn that these old gods were real, and that the salt and bread were not offerings at all, but charms—that is, they weren't there for some god to figuratively eat, but rather because they had been enchanted with power to drive off misfortunes. They were magical in themselves.

So when Katerina, the first time she approached the stove, dried her finger on her skirt and touched the salt and the bread, Ivan realized that this was no obeisance to a long-forgotten god, but rather a way to bring herself within the enchanted protection of the kitchen. And Katerina, who had a sense of these things, did not for a moment act as if the bread and salt might have been improperly magicked up—on the contrary, Katerina acted right at home in Mother's kitchen. No protections needed, because the place was already protected.

Ivan looked around. The string of garlic hanging in the pantry—again, a folk remedy, Ivan had thought, but now remembered the magical properties of garlic in folklore. He could no longer assume that anything was a "mere" superstition, and it occurred to him that keeping rats, roaches, and other vermin out of the pantry by the use of lightly enchanted garlic was certainly healthier than putting a No-Pest Strip in there to leak indiscriminate poison into the air.

Just how enchanted was the house he grew up in? And did Mother know that the rituals she followed really worked?

Of course she knew.

Ivan had grown up knowing his father's work, loving it, learning it, following in his footsteps. But he had been surrounded by another sort of lore entirely, just as ancient—no, more so, for instead of studying ancient things from a modern point of view, Mother actually *did* the ancient things, keeping alive that long unbroken tradition—and he had remained oblivious to it.

Still, he said nothing about it there in the kitchen. If they didn't discuss it with men—and Mother had certainly never discussed it with Ivan, or Father either, Ivan was quite sure—then there was no reason to plague them with questions they wouldn't answer.

Though back in Taina, men were not kept in ignorance of magic. In Taina, they knew perfectly well what the women were doing, and they did their own magic, what with the enchantments of the swordsmith at

252 ORSON SCOTT CARD

the forge and the farmer at the plow, the mushroom-gatherer and the hunter in the forest. So it wasn't men per se, it was rational men, men of science and scholarship, men like Father. And like me.

Father was grumpy—no, downright surly—when he came downstairs for supper. Uncharacteristically, he said little during the beginning of the meal, though his eyes burned a little when Katerina crossed herself and muttered a short Christian prayer before setting fork to food. Ivan tried to ignore his father's ill temper, preferring to watch the way Katerina learned the customs of the table, different here from Cousin Marek's. From the imperious traveler she had been upon crossing the bridge, contemptuous of strange customs, Katerina had in a few days changed herself amazingly, becoming downright adaptable, perhaps even welcoming of change. She fumbled now and then, but with a charming manner, and when Ivan did notice his father it was because his father was noticing Katerina and giving her grudging respect.

Or was that it? For after the meal, when Katerina and Mother were clearing away—Ivan would have helped, but both women insisted that this time he let them work together—Father leaned back in his chair and, a cynical little smile at his lips, said, "She certainly is picking up modern customs *quickly*, isn't she?"

The implication was clear—that Katerina was only pretending not to be a modern woman.

"How stupid do you think people of the ninth century were, and how difficult and complicated do you think our customs are?" asked Ivan.

"Don't get sarcastic with me," said Father. "You're asking me to believe in a pretty far-fetched story, when Occam's razor demands a much simpler explanation."

"Believe me, Father, if there were a simpler explanation, Occam and I would both be happy."

"You believe what you want to believe," said Father. "I must believe the evidence."

Ivan could hardly believe what he was hearing. Switching into English—his natural language for savage intellectual argument—he leaned in and said, "How often in my life have you known me to get sucked into some confidence game? Have I claimed to see UFOs? Did I join the Communist Party? Where exactly did I earn this reputation as an unskeptical believer of whatever bullshit comes down the pike? And you, Father, when did you become the supreme rationalist, the impartial judge of evidence you haven't even *seen*? It seems to me that *I'm* the eyewitness, and *you're* the one making judgments based solely on your preexisting *faith*."

"Faith in a rational universe, yes."

"No, Father. You don't have faith in a rational universe. This is a universe where nothing can move faster than the utterly arbitrary speed of 186,000 miles per second, where feathers and rocks fall at the same speed in a vacuum, where a measurable but unexplainable force called gravity binds people to planets and planets to stars, and where a butterfly's wing in China might cause a hurricane in the Caribbean. But you have faith in all this incomprehensible mumbo-jumbo which you don't *begin* to understand, solely because the priests of the established church of the intellectuals have declared these to be immutable laws and you, being a faithful supplicant at their altar, don't even think to question them."

"You sound like a convert to a new religion yourself," said Father dryly.

"Maybe I am. Or maybe I'm the guy who crawled out of the cave, and you're still back inside it, trying to understand the universe by studying shadows on the wall. Well, Father, I've seen things that can only be explained by magic. Now, I guess I'm really still a closet materialist, because I believe these things all have rational explanations, using principles of nature that are not yet known to us. But what I can't do is close my eyes and pretend that the things that have happened to me will go away if I just say 'Einstein' five times fast."

"I was invoking Occam, you'll remember," said Father.

That was enough of a touch of humor to defuse the situation a little. "Look, Father, I can't argue with you, I can't persuade you, because you weren't there. All I can tell you is this: No language can survive without a community of speakers. As you said yourself, the proto-Slavonic that Katerina speaks is far too pure and ancient to come from an isolated pocket in the mountains somewhere. Occam's razor demands only one answer: She actually is from the ninth century."

"No, Vanya, it demands a completely different one—she's an Eliza Doolittle. She's been trained to speak proto-Slavonic, fluently."

"No!" Ivan slapped the table in frustration. "Listen to yourself! Listen to *her*. You of all people know that language is the one thing that can't be faked. She knows too many words that we don't know. She has an accent that neither of us could have guessed at—the vowels are shaped right, but not exactly as predicted, and the nasals are already fading sooner than we thought. A modern scholar would have taught her using the assumptions of modern scholarship. The nasals would be pure. The palatals more pronounced."

"Unless he realized that these vowels should be different—"

"Father!" said Ivan. "You sound like . . . like one of those bone-heads who thinks the Trilateral Commission is controlling every nation to fulfil some nefarious plan! What conceivable motive could anyone have for putting on such a fraud? What great wealth and power await the plotters who are able to train a young woman to fake proto-Slavonic as her native language? You know every scholar in the field, personally—which of them did it? Whose creature is she?"

Father shook his head. "I don't know. I just can't—you're not a liar, Vanya, so I have to assume you're being fooled yourself. But I watched her all during dinner, and I . . . I liked her, but I thought, of course I like her, they chose her because she's likeable, if you want to run a con game you choose somebody that people will like and trust, and . . . but you're right, who is the 'they' I'm assuming? It makes no sense at all. But . . . even if—Sleeping Beauty, I thought it was a French fairy tale—but even if it happened, why you? Why us?"

"Why not us?" asked Ivan. "It has to be somebody."

"And why now? No, I know your answer—why not now?"

Ivan laughed. "There, that'll put the last nail in Occam's coffin."

"You can cut yourself when you use somebody else's old razor, anyway," said Father. "For the time being, then, will I have to pretend to live in this fantastic universe you've conjured up?"

Impulsively, Ivan took his father's hand. They hadn't held hands much—like good Russians, they greeted with a kiss, and the last time Ivan could remember clasping his father's hand in anything but a handshake was when he was little, and Father helped him cross streets in Kiev. But the hand felt familiar to him all the same. Some memories don't fade, some physical memories are forever. The feel of your father's hand; the sound of your mother's voice. Only, Father's hand was smaller now. No, Ivan's was larger, but to him, it was his father who had shrunk, who no longer had the power of the giant, of the god, to enfold him and keep him safe. If anything, it was Ivan who was the guide now, the one helping the other to cross the perilous, unfamiliar street. "Father, Mother knew about this. Not the whole thing, but she told me when I got engaged to Ruthie that I shouldn't, that it was wrong. Like an old story out of Jewish folklore, she told me that I was already bound by oath to someone else, and it would be an offense to God for me to marry another. I thought she was completely wacked out, but . . . she was right. I had already married Katerina eleven hundred years before."

"Her intuitions," said Father. "When I first claimed the right of a Jew to immigrate to Israel, she told me No, I mustn't do it, you had things yet to learn in Ukraine. And then after we went to Cousin Marek's house, she stopped being agitated. She was perfectly happy to go when we left. Now that you've told me the story, I do see a pattern. You had seen Sleeping Beauty. That's all that was needed. Having seen her, you'd go back." Father sighed deeply. "She couldn't explain it to me. I'd never have believed her. I'm only pretending to believe it now."

But he was not pretending, not now. He had recognized that it was the only story that made sense of things. "So did Mother know everything all along?" asked Ivan.

"No, no," said Father. "If she had known what it was you needed to do, she would have told me, even if I didn't believe it. It wasn't even her idea to go stay with Cousin Marek. No, she just had a feeling. So . . . I didn't take it seriously. A feeling! What's a feeling? But now. If what you say is real, then who's the fool?"

"No fools," said Ivan. "Except those who think they understand the world. *Those* are the fools, don't you think?"

Father shrugged. "Fools, but when they build rocket ships, they mostly fly, and when they drill for oil, it mostly comes up."

"Those are the engineers doing those things, Father. It's the professors who are the fools."

"It's a good thing you smiled when you said that," said Father, "or I'd take it personally."

"I want to *be* a professor, remember?"

"Oh?" said Father. "I thought you were going to be prince consort of the magical kingdom of Taina."

"Prince consort in exile," said Ivan. "And as long as we live in America, I need an American job. I've got a dissertation to write this summer. Believe it or not, I really did my research, before any of this happened, and now I've got to . . ."

"Got to what?"

Ivan shook his head, laughing bitterly. "I haven't thought about my dissertation till this moment, not even when I toted the papers across the Atlantic. How can I write it now? I've met Saint Kirill's clerk. I've seen documents written in Kirill's own hand. I *know* exactly how the letters were formed. I know exactly how the language was spoken and how the priests transformed it in writing it down."

"Oh Lord," said Father, realizing.

"Before I kissed Katerina, I was all set to write a valid scholarly paper. Now if I write it, I either have to pretend to complete ignorance, or—well, there's no other choice. I can't very well write the truth and then cite, as my source, 'personal experience among the proto-Slavonic speakers of the kingdom of Taina, a realm that left behind no written records whatsoever and does not rate a mention in any history.' " Then Ivan told Father about Sergei, and the records he had the young cleric write in the margins and on the back of Saint Kirill's manuscript. "But I wasn't expecting to leave as suddenly as I did," said Ivan. "So there's no chance of the documents surviving. I don't even know how to prepare them so they *might* have a chance. They have to survive with their provenance attached. If they make their way to some library in Constantinople, for instance, no one will believe they're genuine. Someone's bound to ascribe the annotations to some anonymous clerk in the fourteenth century or whatever. Or some nationalistic fraud. I mean, if the parchments survive at all, they'll make a splash—but someone else will find them and interpret them all wrong. *I* have to find them, and in such a way that I can publish about them and affirm that they are exactly what they purport to be—documents written by Kirill himself and then added to by Sergei with his accounting of contemporary history and folklore."

"You speak as if you expect to go back to Taina."

"I do," said Ivan. "Because coming here was temporary. Katerina won't be happy until she saves her people. Coming here didn't do that. Coming here only saved *me*."

It was Father's turn to take Ivan's hand now. "I have to ask you, son. I see you being protective toward her, but you don't look as though—forgive me, but you don't seem to be easy with each other. You married because of a kiss and a promise made with a bear looming over you, right? But does she *love* you?"

Ivan laughed. "Now, *that's* the question, isn't it? No, she doesn't. I think she likes me a little better now that she's passed through the experience of changing worlds. I mean, she has a little less contempt for me. But love? That's not even part of why people marry each other, not princesses, anyway."

"Your mother and I, in some ways we're still strangers to each other, I think all married people are. But we fit together, we know each other as well as two strangers can." Father smiled ruefully. "I love her, Vanya, and she loves me. We're devoted. We don't make a great show of it, but we are."

"I know."

"You deserve that, son. I had my doubts about Ruthie—she

seemed a little too assertive of how she adored you, too *public* about it for it to be real—forgive me, I didn't say anything because you loved her—but this one makes Ruthie look like the queen of wifeliness. I don't like the thought of you being married to a woman who always thinks she married down."

"That's a problem, isn't it?" said Ivan. "But the truth is, she did."

"No," said Father. "No, that's not true. There is no woman alive who, marrying you, would be marrying down."

The words came to Ivan too suddenly, too unexpectedly. "I thought—that's a thing Mother would say."

"Yes," said Father. "Mothers say things like that more than fathers do."

"I'm proud that you feel that way about me," said Ivan. "But that doesn't mean that I believe you're right in such an assessment."

"I know," said Father. "That's what breaks my heart. That you would believe that this woman did you a favor to marry you."

"Well, as far as that goes, I think Katerina and I agree that neither of us did the other much of a favor with this particular match-up."

Father nodded. "Life," he said, with that resigned bitterness that only Russians can put into the word. Though Russian Jews manage somehow to slip a little bit of pride into it. Life is vile, but at least I'm one of the *chosen* victims.

"Why didn't you teach me to use a sword when I was little?" asked Ivan.

"None of the other professors' children were learning it," said Father. "But think a moment—at least I gave you Old Church Slavonic. You understood her when she spoke."

Ivan grinned and saluted his father.

Katerina had been terrified from the beginning of the journey, though she subdued it, tried to contain it, even deny it. Not until she got into the car with Ivan's mother and father did the fear begin to fade, though at that point she did not understand why. This was nothing like the gruzovik—it moved at a terrifying speed, weaving in and out among other fast-moving vehicles, while Ivan's father barely seemed to be paying attention to his driving. And yet she was not afraid. She felt protected.

Only when she entered Ivan's home did she realize why. The house really was protected, as she now realized the car had been. An old wasps' nest hung in the eave over the entrance of the house—

Katerina knew at once that there were others above every other door, and all the windows would have a daub of menstrual blood on the frames.

There was music playing as they entered the house, coming from nowhere and everywhere, but it did not frighten her, for she saw charms of harmony and understood that a very deft and subtle witch had put this house under guard. No hate would last here, and no hypocrisy, while any enemy who entered here would leave in confusion. Katerina had made no great study of magic—the aunts, if they were still alive, had never strayed from their distant homes, what with Baba Yaga sworn to kill them because of their thwarting of her curse on Katerina—and so who was there to teach her the deepest arts? She learned what was available to learn. Enough to recognize the touch of a master in the subtle work. For the charms were concealed, embedded into objects that seemed to be mere decorations when they couldn't be disguised as natural stains or, like the wasps' nests, the work of innocent creatures.

The little porcelain on the mantel was an invocation of Bear, though, and that worried Katerina, considering that Bear was rumored to be under Baba Yaga's sway. Still, gods were gods, and whoever protected this house was no fool. Bear would not be invoked if Bear were an enemy in this time and place.

In the kitchen, she found herself so in harmony with Ivan's mother that they hardly needed to talk; yet when Ivan pointed it out, his mother seemed unaware of how they had been communing beyond the level of speech. Interesting. Was this kind witch unaware of the great power she had? In my time, thought Katerina, you would have been enough to worry Baba Yaga. Of course, that would have guaranteed your death, so it's just as well you didn't live then.

Only when supper was over and Ivan stayed in the dining room with his father was Katerina able to ask Mother—for so she already thought of her—just how widely known magic was. "Ivan seemed to know nothing of it," said Katerina. "And yet . . . he lived in this house."

Mother smiled and looked shyly down at the dishwater in the sink—for the pots did not go in the machine, since the dishwasher could not preserve the charms that made the food in the pots always wholesome and flavorful. "Most are like Vanya," she said, trying to use old words whenever she knew them. "Most know nothing. I had a teacher."

"A teacher, yes. But talent also."

Mother didn't know the word that Katerina used.

"You have it in you," Katerina explained. "Not just learned. It's in you."

Mother shook her head. "I'm nothing special. But we lived in a hard place, in a hard time. I was born at the end of the war, but my mother told me how it was. Terrible things happened. My father and older brothers died when the Germans came through. Reported and taken off as Jews. Only my mother and my sister survived by hiding. Like this."

Mother pulled the bib of her old-fashioned apron up over her face. At once she became unnoticeable. Katerina found it disconcerting. She knew Mother was there, that in fact she was perfectly visible standing by the sink. Yet Katerina had no choice but to look elsewhere, and it was very hard to force herself to continue thinking of Mother, to not allow herself to forget whom she was talking to, and what they were talking about. Then Mother was there again, the apron restored to its place. "I was in my mother's womb at the time," said Mother. "My father's last gift to her. But she taught me. That sometimes the old ways are the only way to stop new evils. So I learned. She died too soon to teach me all, and she didn't know that much, anyway. But before she died, she introduced me to Baba Tila, in Kiev."

I had a Tetka Tila once, Katerina remembered. One of the aunts who modified Baba Yaga's curse. But Tetka Tila lived farthest away of all, and never visited after I was little. She saved my life, but taught me nothing.

"She was very old," Mother was saying, "but even a powerful old witch like her couldn't live forever. I was her last pupil." Mother sighed. "Everyone dies so soon."

"You keep it secret?"

"The Church, the Christians—they killed witches. Rarely the real witches, you understand. Just old women who foolishly muttered something, or people that had enemies who charged witchcraft just to get rid of them. The real witches could hide from their vindictiveness. But it wasn't good, the way people hated the very idea of witches. So we kept it to ourselves. I speak as if I were one of them. Not much of one. Do you even understand me? Baba Tila taught me the old language, but it's been so long, and I've forgotten so much."

"I understand everything," said Katerina. "Or almost."

"Now they don't even believe witches ever existed. That makes it easier. They don't look for us. There *are* foolish women who call themselves witches and prance around naked—they think it has something to do with talking to the devil! Or some nature religion. They have no idea. They embarrass me." Mother laughed. "But then, at least they wouldn't fear us. My husband . . . if he knew . . . your coming here, it threatens to reveal the truth to him."

"I'll keep still," said Katerina.

Mother shook her head. "Too late. Vanya knows, and Vanya will tell his father, meaning no harm."

"Can't you ask him not to?"

"Vanya has no talent for lying or even for concealing the truth. We'll see what Piotr does about it. It's time he knew."

They talked more, about what Mother knew about Ivan as he was growing up. "Only that he was important, for some reason. All mothers think that about their children, though, don't they? Fathers too. Piotr always knew Vanya was something special. Not that he was an easy child. All this running. He wanted to be an athlete. Piotr wanted him to be a scholar. I just wanted him to be good."

"You all got your wish." And Katerina thought: A strong knight. A wise mind. A pure heart.

Mother patted Katerina's hand and smiled. "Oh, yes, praise my child and you know that *we'll* be friends."

"I tell only what I know," said Katerina. "He *is* good. I depend on that. It's my hope."

"I was so afraid when he left this world," said Mother. "I didn't know he had found you. I only knew he was gone. But then I saw that he was alive, and so I didn't worry. Whatever need drew him to you—and it has been calling to him, I've heard it, since he was little— whatever need that was, I knew that he would be man enough for it, in the end."

Katerina loved this woman with her simple manner and her deep wisdom, loved her like the mother she barely remembered. Piotr also seemed a good man, though he was so full of his own doubts that Katerina could hardly talk to him. And for the first time in her life, inside this protected house, knowing that Baba Yaga was thousands of miles away, Katerina felt utterly safe and at peace.

She was, in fact, happy. It was not an unfamiliar feeling—she had been happy many times. Standing with her father after a hard day at the harvest, watching the people dance despite their weariness. Delighting in the children, dancing at a wedding, there was often joy in her life. But it was always joy in others, the happiness of a princess glad that her people are happy. Or sometimes it was the momentary peace of confession, of communion, knowing that the God of love had forgiven her and would welcome her to him when her life ended, even if Baba Yaga had found some terrible way to overmaster her beforehand—peace was also a familiar feeling. But here in this house it simply . . . well, it did not end. She would be happy and at peace one moment, and then, the next moment, she would still be happy, still be at peace. She wanted to cry. When Mother showed her to her own room, not one to be shared with Ivan, and offered it to her, she did cry. "No," she said. "I want to share your son's room."

"He already told me," said Mother. "That you would be more comfortable apart from him."

Katerina shook her head. "No, you don't understand. In this house I am comfortable everywhere."

"Then let me say it another way. He would be more comfortable apart from *you*."

The two women looked at each other a moment, and then burst into laughter, though for Katerina the laughter was tinged with despair. "All right then," said Katerina. "My own room for now. But I do mean to be a true wife to your son. However we began, I do mean for it to end well."

Mother touched a finger to Katerina's lips. "I know that," she said. "There isn't much time in this world, but there is always enough time, if you know how to use it."

Katerina shook her head. "Not enough time for everything," she said. "Not enough time with my mother."

Ivan's mother reached out and embraced her. "Your mother surrounds you every moment," she said. "I know, because I feel her love for you in my own arms, around you now."

Katerina was weeping as Mother gently closed the door behind her, leaving her alone in the room. And that, too, was joy, for there are tears of joy, and tears of peace as well.

Ruth cried bitterly about the broken engagement, and her mother made sure that within hours every Jew in Tantalus knew that Ivan Smetski had broken his vow to Ruthie in order to marry a shiksa, and the first Ruthie heard about it was at the airport, seeing the girl hanging on Ivan like a goiter. Everyone was properly horrified, which helped Ruth's parents feel better. But not Ruth.

Nor did talking to her friends at school and listening to their almost triumphant response. What do you expect of men? Women as property, men as walking cauldrons of hormones, yadda yadda, she had heard it all before and wasn't particularly glad to have provided the occasion for more triumphant feminism. What she wanted from them was sympathy—because she still felt, or at least feared, that Ivan was a good man and she had lost a prize. But if he was a good man, how could he leave me? So he must not be a good man. But if he isn't good, then why does it hurt so much to lose him? Is it just my pride that's wounded?

Maybe. But she still knew, deep in her heart, that this was not true, either. Because if Ivan came back to her, even now, she would go to him. She wouldn't *trust* him, but she would take him back. Because she really did love him. And love doesn't disappear just because of the vile unworthiness of the loved one.

She had always thought Ivan was the kind of man who kept a promise.

Time, that's what was supposed to heal this kind of injury. Plus keeping busy so the time would pass. A flurry of shopping; but when she got home she didn't even bother taking things out of the sacks and boxes. A book, another book, another. All dog-eared at page ten or twenty, all stacked beside her bed. She even typed up her résumé in the vain thought that it was time for her to get out in the real world and earn a living. When she typed, "Last position: Fiancée. Reason for leaving: Replaced by shiksa," she knew it wasn't going to happen.

"Do what I do," her mother said. Which is how Ruth ended up at the beauty parlor getting her nails done and her hair cut, dyed, and permed at the same time—which was going to be terrible on her hair and her allergies, but she'd come out of it looking like a new woman.

"You're so beautiful," said the old woman next to her. "I can't think why you'd want to change that gorgeous long hair."

It was actually a marginally creepy thing to say, especially because of the way the woman looked at her—are there ninety-year-old lesbians who cruise the beauty parlors?—but Ruth was polite. "A change is as good as a rest."

"So what was it, a man or a job?"

"What?"

"This angry self-destructive action," said the old lady. "This obliteration of your self. Either you lost a job or you lost a man."

"Forgive me," said Ruth, "but . . . have we met?"

"We're meeting now," said the old woman. "You need more than a bob-and-dye, sweetie. Get him back."

"You mean get *him*? Or get *back* at him?"

"Whatever."

The woman's eyes were dancing with delight.

And then, abruptly, there was only a wasp sitting on the chair beside her. It walked around the fake leather for a few minutes, then flew out the door.

I'm losing my mind, thought Ruth.

She worried for a little while about a woman who turned into a wasp—or a wasp into a woman, whichever. And then she worried about depression so deep it led to hallucinations, and whether Prozac was really as good as people said it was.

And then she thought about what the woman said. Get him back. Get him back. And for the life of her she couldn't decide what she herself wanted. Revenge or reconciliation?

She walked along the street, looking for her car. Where had she parked? That's another sign I'm losing my mind, she thought. Lately I don't remember things like where I parked or whether I had breakfast. Just since he dumped me. The bastard. That bitch.

Sitting on the sidewalk, leaning against the wall opposite her car, was a homeless woman. No, she was dirty and all, but she wasn't begging. She was selling. A little cloth was spread out before her, with weird little bags and corked vials and tiny jars stopped up with clay. Ruth stopped and looked at her wares.

The gypsy reached behind her and took out a small piece of paper. On it were written the words *Get him back*.

This was too weird. Especially because a moment later, the words on the paper changed into nothing but meaningless squiggles. The paper said nothing at all, or at least it wasn't an alphabet she had ever seen before. She must have hallucinated the words she read.

The gypsy held up a tiny bag and pointed to Ruth with her other hand.

"I don't want it," said Ruth.

The gypsy woman smiled. She had no teeth.

"This will make him love me?"

The gypsy woman thought for a moment, as if translating laboriously. Then she shook her head, set down the bag, and picked up a little clay-stopped jar.

"*This* one, then?" asked Ruth. "And he'll forget the bitch and love me?"

The gypsy nodded, grinning.

"How much?" I can't believe I'm asking. I can't believe I'm going to buy it.

But there she was, pulling her wallet out of her purse. "Hmm? How much?"

The gypsy just kept smiling.

Ruth pulled out a five. The gypsy didn't seem to respond at all. A ten? No. A twenty.

What's happening to me?

The gypsy took the twenty. She looked dubious. Then she beamed at Ruth. She wasn't *completely* toothless. She had a couple of blackened molars.

"How do I use it?" asked Ruth. "I mean, do I wear it? Eat it? Drink it? Serve it to him?"

At this last phrase, the gypsy nodded vigorously.

"Right, like he and I are going to have a picnic," said Ruth. She felt cheated. But how stupid did she have to be, anyway? She was buying a love potion from a gypsy street vendor. All because a stranger in a beauty shop had told her to get him back? Ivan has driven me insane. Do I even *want* him to love me?

She was getting into her car, but at this thought she impulsively got back out. The gypsy woman cocked her head and looked quizzically at her.

Ruth pointed to the bag that the gypsy had first offered. "What does that do?"

The gypsy started scratching herself and cackling with laughter. Ruth wasn't sure whether this meant that Ivan would itch, that someone would tickle him, or that he would turn into a monkey, but in any event, it sounded promising.

Besides, nothing said she had to give it to Ivan. It might be more useful to give it to the shiksa bitch.

Again, she had to know—bake it into cookies? Dash it in his face?

The gypsy pantomimed eating.

"Just like the other one," said Ruth.

The gypsy nodded.

"The bag gets even, the jar gets him to love me."

The gypsy held out her hand. Ruth gave her another twenty. The gypsy shook her head. Ruth added another twenty. The gypsy tucked it down into her bosom, then gathered up the cloth, tied the top into a knot, and got up and walked away.

That's it? I'm the only customer of the day?

Or maybe when she gets sixty bucks from one sucker, she can go buy enough wine to stay drunk for a week.

I'm not going to use these. When would I have a chance? And considering I don't even know what I want. Maybe I should give him both. Or better yet, make both of them fall in love with me. Then it would be *my* turn to jilt him for the same woman! Now *that* would be ironic.

Maybe what I should have bought is a gun.

The moment she thought of it, it felt like poison in her mind. A gun! For him? For her? For me? What's happening to me? I don't want anybody dead. I just want my life to go on.

She dropped the little jar and the little sack into the trashbox she kept on the floor of her car. Sixty bucks down the drain, but that's cheaper than buying a new dress that I don't even take out of the bag when I get it home.

BABA YAGA

She was exhausted. If magic had been hard before, it was almost impossible now, so far from Bear's land. Baba Yaga hadn't realized how dependent she was on his power till she tried to do magic without it.

But nothing was going to stop her. She was days behind Ivan and Katerina, but it was easy enough to find them. The house was protected, though, and Baba Yaga was too weak to get through all the magic. It infuriated her to be stopped by a witch that ordinarily she could blow away with a puff of air. But she had to deal with the world the way she found it. Ivan and Katerina were inside the house. Baba Yaga was able to probe just enough to be certain that the marriage was not complete yet. But almost instantaneously, the curtains were flung open and there in the window stood a middle-aged woman, staring right at her.

I'm not supposed to be noticeable, thought Baba Yaga. And yet she knew where to look.

So maybe it would have taken more than a puff of air, she thought.

She turned away from the house, wondering what to do next.

Listen, that's what she'd do. She might not be able to work magic on anyone in that house without being noticed and blocked, but that witch couldn't prevent her from doing magic on herself.

It took hours to put it all together, and she had to make do with substitute herbs, but it worked well enough, a spell of hearing. After she had chewed the mixture into paste and then swallowed it, she sat in the darkness under a tree and began to focus the sounds as they rushed in upon her. People eating, doing dishes, cooking, arguing, listening to machines that talked. House after house. Baba Yaga tuned them out, turned them into nothing in her own mind. Until at last there was only the sound from one house left.

By the time the spell wore off, a couple of hours later, Baba Yaga knew only that there was a woman named Ruth to whom Ivan had been betrothed.

A jilted woman, thought Baba Yaga. I can use her.

Not knowing where she lived, Baba Yaga again had to use magic to find her. It took two days, searching for rage and pain. There was plenty of it to be found—what angry people these are!—but finally, after casting her net rather widely, she detected Ruth driving along the freeway. So quickly everyone moved! But now that she had Ruth's soul imprinted in her heart, Baba Yaga would always be able to find her.

Not speaking the language, Baba Yaga had to do the wasp trick, guiding the little pricker into the beauty parlor and then causing Ruth herself to imagine the woman and the words and the language to draw out of Ruth's turmoil of feelings about Ivan the ones that Baba Yaga figured would be most useful to her: The desire to have him back, and the desire to destroy him.

Then, on the sidewalk, Baba Yaga appeared in person, because this time it couldn't be hallucination, the potions had to be real. Sixty dollars? Baba Yaga wanted to laugh at the money. But she knew she had to take it, or Ruth wouldn't believe the potions had any value.

Whichever one she chooses will suit me fine, thought Baba Yaga.

The next morning, Ruth woke up to find all her hair lying on her pillow. The mirror confirmed it: She was bald as an egg. She screamed. She wept. She resolved that she was going to *get back at Ivan*, because somehow this crowning misery had to be his fault, too. She wouldn't have had a perm and a dye on the same day if it hadn't been for him!

Out in the woods, where Baba Yaga was catching insects and killing them for the magic they held in their tiny bodies, Baba Yaga sensed Ruth's rage and horror. This time the curse wasn't just a bit of extra fun. Within hours, Ruth would fish the potions out of the trash in her car. For in Ruth's mind, her baldness was also, however indirectly, Ivan's and Katerina's fault, and someone was going to pay, one way or another.

13

PICNIC

van saw his bags in the corner of his room. He hadn't unpacked, not even a toothbrush, since Mother had a new one waiting for him in the bathroom when he got home, and there were plenty of clean clothes. But the dirty ones in the suitcases needed washing. He wasn't even sure why he had been reluctant to unpack upon arriving. This *was* his home; and yet he felt as if he were only here in transit. He was married now; that meant he could never be more than a visitor in his parents' home.

He tossed the bags on the bed and opened them, pulling out the tightly rolled clothes. He couldn't remember now which were dirty and which were clean—Mother would insist on washing them all anyway, and this time he'd give in and let her. Into the laundry basket went the clothing.

Onto his desk went the books, the papers, the notes. His dissertation. His future? Not likely. It would be too hard, to devote a year or more to writing as if he were still as ignorant as any ordinary scholar. It was bad enough that dissertations all had to be written in the miserably pedantic language of scholarship; to have it be false as well would be unbearable. Did it even matter? He had to go back to Taina with Katerina, and if he lived he would be king there, at least in name. As a career choice, it was generally regarded as ranking somewhere above professor. Not to him, though, having no inclination for it.

I belong in neither world now—each has spoiled me for the other.

The bags were empty. On impulse he lifted each one and shook it. A slip of paper floated down and slid under the bed.

He fell to his knees, suddenly filled with urgency. He knew at once what this paper was. It was the note that had been left in Baba Tila's window. He was home now, and Mother had been Baba Tila's pupil. Now he understood what she had been learning. Maybe the note would mean something to her.

But Mother was as baffled as he had been. She and Katerina both looked at it; Mother held it up to the window, passed it over a flame, even laid it gently on a bowl of water, to see if some other message became visible. Nothing. It continued to say, simply, "Deliver this message."

"And you found it in Baba Tila's window?" Mother asked again.

"Between the stones, where she left notes for you before."

"I wasn't her only student."

Ivan shrugged. "It's not as if there weren't several years for someone else to find it."

"It's simple enough," said Katerina.

They looked at her, waiting for the explanation.

"I mean, the message is not for you, or you'd understand it."

"Then I should put it back," said Ivan.

"No," said Katerina. "It *was* for you to *find*. It says to you the thing that *you* must do."

"Deliver it—but to whom?"

Katerina shrugged. "Not to me."

"It can't be anybody in your world—I can't carry anything there."

"Mikola—" Katerina caught herself. "I mean, might it not be for Cousin Marek?"

"I should have thought of it, but it was in my bags, and I hardly opened them. A lot happened between finding this note and returning to Marek and Sophia's."

"It's not for him," said Mother firmly. "Baba Tila had no need of messengers or papers to send messages to the Farmer of the Wind."

"They were . . . connected?" asked Ivan.

Baba Tila knew Mikola Mozhaiski. Katerina could not help but wonder if Baba Tila and her Tetka Tila—but no, her aunt was not one of the immortals. More likely the name was handed down over the centuries, like the old language. *Her* language.

"Nothing so marvelous," said Mother. "They used pigeons. Baba Tila loved them." She grew thoughtful. "I wonder what happened to them all after she died."

"Maybe she took them with her," said Ivan.

Mother glared at him. "Don't mock what you don't understand."

"I wasn't mocking."

"The thing is," said Mother, "she probably did. There was a part of her in the birds. They watched things for her, or rather she watched things through them. When she died, it would have left them suddenly empty, or partly empty, and I imagine they died at once. Or soon after."

"How sad," said Katerina. "But how wonderful, to know the flight of birds."

"So we still don't know who it's for."

"You will," said Mother. "Keep it with you."

"*On* me?" Ivan didn't like that. For some reason it made him nervous, to think of keeping it in his pocket.

"Only if you want to," said Mother. "Near you is good enough. When you find the person you should give it to, you'll know, and then you should be able to get it quickly."

Until I get to Taina, Ivan thought. Then it won't be within reach at all. And somehow I can't imagine that telling the recipient about the message would be at all the same as handing him the actual note.

"I hope I didn't ruin it by letting it float on the water," said Mother.

"It was the flame that worried me," said Ivan.

"Sillies," said Katerina. "If it was made well, neither flame nor water could harm it. And if it was made badly, then it isn't a message of power and it hardly matters."

But all this talk about the message filled Ivan with other ideas. "Isn't there *some* way we can take things across the bridges, Mother?"

"I should know?" she asked.

Katerina shook her head.

"What if I swallowed something," said Ivan. "Then it would be inside me."

"Don't try it," said Mother. "The rules about such things can be very strict, and it might be dangerous to you if you had anything but food in your body. *Any* opening of your body."

"These are honest spells," said Katerina. "Made to counteract a deceiver. They work *against* a deceiver. You see? The Wicked Widow can't use the bridge because she's made of lies, filled with them, covered with them. You don't want to see what would happen if you tried to cross as a sneak or a liar."

Ivan chuckled. "Then we should provide a service, and give certificates to politicians who can cross the bridges."

The Ukrainian word for *politician* baffled Katerina, and neither Mother nor Ivan wanted to try to explain it.

"You can take only what's in your head," said Katerina. "And in your heart."

"What's in my head is nothing but confusion. And Russian literature."

It dawned on Mother and Ivan at the same time. "Why not learn what you need to know in order to make things there?" said Mother, and Ivan was already nodding.

"Learn what?" said Katerina.

"There are weapons," said Ivan. "Bombs. I think I already have a good idea how to make Molotov cocktails—if we distilled alcohol . . ."

"Oh, excellent," said Mother. "Introduce vodka to Russia centuries ahead of time."

"I can't very well use gasoline."

"What are you talking about?" said Katerina. "I don't know these words."

"Modern things," said Ivan. "Weapons. Whatever we can learn how to make *here*, so we can teach the people how to make them and use them *there*."

"What weapons?" said Katerina. "You don't have swords—I've seen no one carrying them—and as for magic, most people have no idea."

"Oh, Katerina, you haven't seen weapons till you've seen what our civilization produces. Weapons that could destroy the whole world—though of course no one uses *those*. And weapons of disease—but we can't use those, because it would kill far more innocent people and might not reach the enemy at all. We need more sharply-aimed weapons, right, Mother? Iron technology isn't at a point where we can make cannon, I don't think, not in the ninth century. Though they did cast early guns in bronze. That's worth a thought. What is gunpowder? I remember it has something to do with saltpeter . . . that's nitrate of something, isn't it? What about dynamite?"

"You're asking *me*?" said Mother.

Ivan laughed. "Oh, I know where to find it out. There've got to be wacko places on the Internet. If the government sees what I'm doing, they'll assume I'm a terrorist."

"Everything depends on what's available back then. Katerina has to help you with that," said Mother. "She'll know what can and can't be made there in her own village."

Katerina nodded. She prided herself on having a clear understanding of the work of every man and woman in Taina. She might not be able to do all the jobs—smiths and plowmen needed more strength and bulk than she would ever have—but at least she knew what they could do, and what they needed in order to be able to do it.

"And transportation," said Ivan. "We can't make cars, but maybe we can—what, I don't know, improve the cart?" He laughed. "Faster carts, that'll strike terror into Baba Yaga's heart."

Mother brought her hand down hard on Ivan's head.

"Ouch! What!"

"You said her name."

"We're not in Taina now," said Ivan, rubbing his head.

"It gives her the power to push past the protections of the house," said Mother.

"She's on the other side of the world, Mother."

"No," said Mother. "She's here."

Katerina at once grew alarmed. "Here? In this city?"

"A few days ago. Someone probed at the house. I felt it—no, I *smelled* her. Foul. Like . . . never mind what it was like. I went to the window. I couldn't see her—she had a glamour around her—but I could see where she was. Just across the street. Watching."

"Why didn't you say anything?" said Ivan.

"Because the house was sufficient to stop her. She's weaker here. I think she was angry to find that she couldn't get through our defenses."

"She knows where we are," said Katerina. "Oh, God help us now."

"Amen," said Mother. "But it doesn't change anything. You still have to learn whatever's worth learning, and you still have to go back."

"But with her at our tail," said Ivan.

"I've been thinking about ways to send her home," said Mother.

Katerina shook her head vigorously. "Don't think of it," she said. "You're very talented, but weak as she might be, you're no match for her."

"I think I might be, here on my own ground," said Mother.

"Don't try it, I warn you," said Katerina. "The very act of confronting her, that's pride, don't you see? It gives her power over you, because she rules through pride. You need to stay meek. It's the protection of Christ. The meekness of the obedient followers of Jesus, that protects us from the she-wolf."

"I'm not a Christian," said Mother.

"But you have never acted in pride before, have you? Never challenged a rival, have you?"

"No," said Mother. "I've never needed to."

"You don't need to now, either," said Katerina. "You must believe me. I don't know as much as you about these things, but I know more than you about the Widow. If you face her, challenge her, she has you then."

Mother shuddered. "Well, then," she said. "Well, then."

"Don't tell me you were looking forward to it," said Ivan.

"No, no, no," said Mother. "The opposite. And I'm relieved to think I don't have to. And frightened to think how close I came to trying it when I faced her there through the glass of our window. I came *this* close."

There was a greater sense of urgency now. No more time for desultory talks with Father and Mother, for pleasant household chores with Katerina and Mother, for explorations of language with Katerina and Father. Now Ivan spent his days at the computer terminal in his bedroom, linked to the university computer system and through it to the rest of the Internet. He wrote thirty emails to various people he knew, and began to get answers: How gunpowder was made, how to make a match, where deposits of the necessary minerals were known to have been located in the Carpathian foothills, or how they could be extracted from plants or what substitutes might do almost as well. Constantly he quizzed Katerina about materials, though most of the discussion was always spent trying to find language to describe exactly what he was trying to find out about. Father even got into the fray, querying his own network of friends.

They didn't stray from the house, Ivan and Katerina. Mother and Father were safe enough, Mother decided—though she insisted that Father wear a charm, which just about killed him from shame; but he went along. Ivan and Katerina, though, walked only around the back yard—which was large enough at first, but seemed to grow smaller as they spent day after day unable to leave it. The only consolation for Ivan was this: If he had to be trapped on a desert island, at least he had Katerina for company.

Partly it was the project they were working on. As he made his first batch of gunpowder—which nearly blew his hand off—she began to gain new respect for him; but he also gained respect for her, as she insisted on learning how to do everything herself, as well. "What if one of us is killed?" she said. "Does she then win the victory?" And then she made him take her hands and guide her through the process of grinding the material to powder. He was terrified of killing her with a mistake, but she joked all through it, teased him about how protective he was. He was close to her hour after hour, the smell of her, the touch of her breath on the hairs of his arms or on his ears as she leaned over his shoulder to watch. He thought sometimes he might go insane with desire for her; but he could not think of a way to change what lay between them, and though he thought she liked him well enough now, he still didn't know if their friendship was yet the thing a marriage should be made of.

Do you love me? he wanted to ask her, to demand of her. But, fearing the answer would be a wan "I'm sorry, Ivan," he did not speak.

She learned to throw practice Molotov cocktails, she learned to make and strike matches. They made a still in a Sears storage shed Father bought for that purpose, grumbling all the time about how it would look in the papers, "Professor arrested for making vodka in back-yard shed."

They decided they would test everything on the Fourth of July. "Nobody will mind a few explosions and fires that day," Father said, and he was obviously right. They'd find out then what their gunpowder could do. Minute quantities, for they didn't want to blow anything up, just to see if it would explode at all. Firecrackers, really. And a few Molotov cocktails thrown at a pile of logs, so they would be doing nothing more than igniting a celebratory bonfire. Afterward they'd roast sausages over the coals like good Americans. Well, not quite— they could never bring themselves to eat those clammy, nasty wieners Americans used as their hot dogs. Good, hearty Polish and Russian and Italian sausages, that's what they'd eat, and on a hearty bread, not those squishy spongy confections designed so that you didn't need teeth to eat them.

And then Ivan got the phone call from Ruthie.

"No one sees you anymore, Ivan. Are you hiding? Is the honeymoon still so engaging?"

Was she being bitter and nasty? Or cheerful and friendly? Hard to know. "She's learning the language," said Ivan. Which was true enough—though the language she was learning at the moment was modern Russian. As with so many Russian schoolchildren for generations, it was Pushkin who was her teacher, as they read to each other before going to bed. The stanzas of Tatyana's dream had disturbed her greatly—the girl being chased through the snow by a bear. Ivan wondered, then and now, how close Pushkin's vision had been to what Katerina herself went through, before she was enchanted in that magic place. He wondered also how Pushkin could have known. What influence did the bear still have in the world, at the time when Pushkin wrote?

Ruthie's voice brought him back to the present. "I'd like to take you on a picnic for the Fourth."

"A picnic?" It sounded bizarre. But if you looked at it another way, it was rather sweet, too. "That would be nice, but—"

"The three of us, of course. I still think of you as a friend, Ivan. Can't I? Is that wrong?"

"Not wrong, no, of course not. I wish we could, but we need to stay home, kind of a family thing—"

"No, no, I understand. I'm not part of the family, and she is, and that's that. I really am fine with it, Ivan. I don't pretend I understand what happened—maybe that's part of why I want to spend a little time with the two of you."

"She doesn't really speak much English yet," said Ivan.

"You can translate. What if we do it the day before? The third. Ivan, don't turn me away empty-handed."

No way were he and Katerina going to leave the safety of Mother's protected house. And yet it seemed churlish to turn down this over-ture of reconciliation. "The third, all right, but why don't you come over here? I know Mother and Father would like to see you again."

A moment's hesitation on the other end of the phone. "But you have to let me bring the food," she finally said.

"Mother won't hear of it," said Ivan.

"Then who's inviting whom? It's my picnic, Ivan. Even if we have it in your back yard."

Why did he have such a creepy feeling about this? I should tell her no, Ivan thought. This is wrong, this is a mistake. It's dangerous.

But he couldn't think *why* it was dangerous. And he had wronged her. He owed her a debt of guilt. If she wanted to mend fences, how could he let some vague, unnameable fear stand between them now?

Truth to tell, there was another reason he didn't want to have this picnic: In the weeks since returning to America, since seeing her at the airport, Ivan had come to realize that he didn't really miss Ruthie. That in fact he probably had never loved her. Now that he could compare his feelings toward Ruthie with his feelings toward Katerina, he knew there was no comparison. He hadn't been ready for marriage at all. It would have been a struggle to make it work with Ruthie. They would have bored each other so quickly.

And if he was completely honest with himself, he had to admit she had bored him already, before he left for Kiev. He was glad to leave her behind, he realized that now. He didn't miss her. He had never really loved her.

And *that* made him feel so guilty that it overrode any other consideration. "Your food, my house, noon. This is sweet of you, Ruthie."

"Don't patronize me, Ivan. I'm still not sure that I don't want to put the potato salad over your head. And maybe rub it in a little."

The breath of honesty came as a relief to him. "Whatever you think is right," said Ivan. "I won't protest that I don't deserve it. But not Katerina, please. She didn't know about you when she said yes to me."

"Oh. Well, you really are a two-faced son-of-a-bitch," said Ruthie cheerfully.

"There it is," said Ivan. "But at least I saved you from being married to one."

Ruthie laughed lightly. "I'll come by at noon on the third."

"We'll be here with bells on," said Ivan. Only after they hung up did he feel a twinge of embarrassment at his own phoniness. Be there with bells on? What B movie from the thirties did he get *that* line from? There wasn't an honest moment in that whole conversation, except when she talked about shampooing him with potato salad.

I don't want her here. There'll be a scene. Someone will cry. Someone will swear. No one will enjoy the food. If I had any spine at all, I'd have said no.

But what's done is done.

Yes, Esther was afraid for her son, for her new daughter-in-law, for the whole family. Yes, she worried about how her husband feared and hated the magic that had intruded into his life, and how he resented her for having known it all along. The power and malice she had sensed in Baba Yaga, that was the most terrifying of all. And yet all these fears did not diminish her joy, for this was the moment she had lived for. All those years ago, learning from Baba Tila, she had thought these charms and potions, spells and curses were to protect her family from the KGB or from some future pogrom. But now she saw that her whole life had been directed toward this moment, when she could protect the future queen and king of Taina from the most dangerous witch in history. And, more than her own pride, she was joyful because she saw her son growing into his manhood now. He, too, had been directed in his life—all that running, jumping, hurling of shot and discus and javelin, it seemed so foolish to Piotr and to Esther both; yet because of it he was able to get past the Bear and kiss the sleeping beauty. He and his father had learned to be as fluent in Old Church Slavonic as any two people alive, which proved to be vital for Vanya.

But who was doing all this directing? Was it a god? More to the point, was it God? And if the latter, was he helping them because they were Jews? Or helping Taina because it was a Christian kingdom? Or simply shaping the world to be able to put an end to Baba Yaga's great evil?

Or was there a fate greater than all gods, that could not bear a truly great malice, and had to bend reality, including a backward passage through time, until that malice could be put to rest?

There were no answers to such questions, of course. And in truth, Esther was not interested in them past the asking. Enough for her that whatever had chosen her and her son, they had so far been up to the challenge. It had worried her, watching Vanya grow up, that while he sometimes worried her and did not always choose wisely— look at Ruthie—he was nevertheless good, in some hidden place in his heart where the deepest choices are made. Any rule of life that he truly believed in, he obeyed; any course of action that he thought was right, he pursued. Resentfully, sometimes, but he did his duty.

Perhaps that's how the great ones are chosen, she thought. No outward sign of genius. Vanya was clever enough in school, an apt scholar, a good athlete. But no one would have picked him as the one to stand against a terrible enemy. No one would have expected him to be a hero.

Even now, Esther could see that neither Vanya nor Katerina expected him to be the one to stand against the witch. He was going to help train the knights and villagers with new weapons, but it was Katerina who was princess, Katerina who was bound around with the enchantments her aunts had created for her. And they might be right. It might be Katerina who faced the witch and beat her, perhaps in battle, perhaps simply by surviving and having babies. Endurance, after all, was a kind of victory; a kind of heroism, too.

And that would be good enough for Esther, too. Let them live. Let them love each other. Let them have babies that grow to adulthood, not just one but many of them. Even if they live in another time, another world, where I never see them, where I'm only a story to them, a name without a face, so be it, if my son and his bride can live. That is joy—joy in the midst of grief, perhaps, and loneliness, but joy and triumph all the same.

Katerina came to her in the night. She was restless—worrying about seeing Ruthie again, she said. But that wasn't all, Esther knew. And sure enough, Katerina soon led her down to the shelf in the garage where she had put the basin in which the still water had shown her Vanya's face.

"A black bowl?" asked Katerina.

"It showed me Vanya when he was with you," said Esther.

"I've heard of it, but never seen it."

"You can only look at one you love deeply," said Esther. "It isn't always satisfying."

"There's more to it than that," said Katerina. "If it's large enough, a black pool, you can see a place and then leap into the water and go there. I think that's how the Widow followed us."

"Then let me say that all my dear old Baba Tila taught me was to look."

"Let's look, then," said Katerina. "My father. Who knows how many days or months have passed for him? Time does not flow the same there as it does here."

So they got out the basin and filled it, set it out in the yard, leveled it, and waited together on this hot still summer evening for it to become truly still. To do it, they had to charm away the mosquitoes, but Katerina was deft at it, making the hand motions with a style and confidence that Esther had never thought of, having been taught by an old woman with shaking hands. At last, well after midnight, the water was still.

"May I see what you see?" asked Esther. It was a presumption, but Katerina smiled and nodded.

Silently they approached the basin, standing on opposite sides of it, their clothing tucked back behind them so that no bit of cloth, no thread, not even a strand of hair could fall onto the water. Katerina lowered her face over the water first, scarcely breathing; Esther then leaned over, remaining always higher than Katerina and therefore farther from the water, so it would be Katerina's will that controlled the vision.

It took only moments, and the face of a middle-aged man appeared. No doubt King Matfei, asleep, looking peaceful. But then, to Esther's surprise, Katerina made some unfamiliar movements with her hands above the water, and the vision zoomed back to show the whole scene around her father. He was lying on a bed, yes, and he was asleep; but he was also bound hand and foot, and two knights stood guard in the room.

Katerina made the vision zoom in so that it showed only her father's face. Then, placing her hand near her mouth to stop the breath of speech from stirring the waters, Katerina said his name softly. Once. Twice. A third time.

His eyes opened.

"Do not speak," said Katerina. "Do not wake the guards. Look upward to tell me yes. Look downward to tell me no. Are you a prisoner, as it seems?"

His eyes rolled upward.

"Soldiers of the Widow?"

A downward look. No.

"Another enemy?"

No.

"Our own people?"

Hesitation. Then a yes.

"Oh, Father. Dimitri? Because Ivan and I fled?"

Yes.

"*She* has done it, Father, you know that. Dimitri was a true man— he must have been deceived."

No response at all.

"You're right, it doesn't matter why. A man can't be deceived unless he wants to believe the lie. But Father, we *are* coming home. Soon. We've learned things. I've seen marvels—but now is not the time. Be content that we will return, and Dimitri will be taken out of his place and you will be restored to the throne."

No.

"No? Why not?"

He rolled his eyes.

"I know, you can't tell me why. But you *are* the king. You *must* be king."

No. No.

"Then who, Father? Dimitri?"

No.

"Ivan?"

Yes.

"Ivan isn't ready."

Yes.

"Neither am I, to rule through him."

Yes. No. Yes. Her statement had been ambiguous, and so he couldn't answer clearly.

"You think I *am* ready?"

Yes. There it was.

"When we come back we'll discuss it. After you're free. But you *are* our war leader."

No. No. No. And a tear came to one eye.

"You can't lead us in war?"

No. Yes. No. Again, the question could not be answered as she asked it. If he agreed, should he say, Yes, your statement is true, or No, I can't lead in war?

"Have you been injured, Father?"

Yes.

"A physical injury?"

Yes.

"He *hurt* you?"

Yes.

"I'll kill him," said Katerina simply.

Yes.

"Your arms? Your legs?"

No. And no.

"How can I know your injury?"

He opened his mouth.

It took a moment to realize what they were not seeing. He had no tongue.

Katerina gasped, stepped back, began to sob quietly into her hands. Esther also backed away from the basin and carefully walked around it, then enfolded her daughter-in-law in her arms.

"She couldn't kill him, she couldn't even get Dimitri to kill him," whispered Katerina. "But she made it impossible for him to lead in battle. She made it impossible for him to be king."

"It wasn't a wound," said Esther. "Did you see that? It was *Molchaniye*. Stillness. *She* gave the traitor—Dimitri, yes?—she gave him the potion to carry the spell inside your father's body. The most powerful I've seen, to shrink the tongue like that. But it must be maintained by the power of the witch who invokes it."

"Is this comfort to me?" asked Katerina. "The Widow will never release him from it."

"No, she won't. As long as she lives."

"She will long be alive after my father and I have rotted away in our graves. She's already more than a hundred years old, and her magic has the power to give her many centuries more."

"But in my time she has long been dead," said Esther. "No one knows how, but she was destroyed or she weakened and died, one or the other, but there was no trace of her until she followed you here."

"I refuse to believe in false hopes," said Katerina. "Even if you came back with us, no one could stand against her and break her power."

"She *can* be killed," said Esther.

"How?"

"I don't know how. But Baba Tila said that no protection is perfect. There's always a way through."

Katerina raised her head and looked Esther in the eye. "Then there's a way through the protections on this house, yes?"

"Of course. I don't know what it is, but that's why I'm so vigilant."

Katerina pulled away from her, returned to her father.

"Ivan's mother is a witch," she said. "A good one. Not as strong as the Widow, but strong enough to withstand her here."

Matfei looked alarmed.

"Yes, she's here. That's why her armies haven't followed up on Taina's weakness, with you imprisoned and silenced as you are. Father, be patient. I *will* come back. You *will* be freed. And we *will* get this curse taken from you."

He closed his eyes.

"That's right, Father. Sleep. And pay no attention to what I will whisper now to the men who guard you."

He opened his eyes only long enough to wink at her. Then he closed them again.

She zoomed the vision back. Now the guards were visible.

"Shame on you," she whispered. "Shame on you."

Both men at once grew alert.

"Did you hear that?" one of them murmured.

"Hear what?" the other one lied.

"Dimitri made you do it," she said. "Dimitri is in the service of the Vile Widow. She comes to him by night and tells him what to do. She gave him the spell that keeps King Matfei silent. He is the servant of the enemy. But you are the servants of Christ."

Both men crossed themselves.

"I am Katerina, and I will return. I will have my husband, Ivan, with me, and he will teach you the wizardry of his strange and powerful land. All those who stand with Dimitri will be destroyed. All those who stand with me will live, and we will free our land from the shadow of the Widow. You have heard me. As loyal men, true Christians and sons of God, you will keep faith with the oath you made to my father. Prepare the others as well. Let no man move against Dimitri before I come, but let no man stand beside him when I do."

"Yes, Princess," they murmured. "I promise, Katerina."

"And let no further harm come to my father. Mercy will be remembered."

At once one of the men moved to Matfei's side and unfastened the bands that held his wrists together. The other quickly set to work on his ankles.

"Now I see you are true friends of the king, and true Christians. I watch you sometimes, from afar; Jesus watches you always, from inside your heart." She took a deep breath. "Look up, into the air above you, and see the face of her whom you will follow."

At once Esther stepped back, uncertain of what Katerina was going to do. She had never heard of such a thing.

Katerina spat into her hands, rubbed her hands together, then smeared the saliva on her face, rubbing, rubbing. Then, before it could dry, she lowered her face to the water and gently pressed through the surface tension. Esther leaned in, looked over her shoulder. The water shimmered, but the vision held long enough for Esther to see how the soldiers looked up and saw the face of their princess.

Then Katerina lifted her dripping face from the basin. The water spilled and sloshed. There was no more vision in it. Katerina raised her skirts to her face, wiped away the water and the spit. And then wept again into her skirts.

"It's a monstrous enemy you're fighting," said Esther, putting an arm around her daughter-in-law's trembling back. "But you're luckier than she is, for *she* has to face *you*, and I have never seen anyone so fierce."

Katerina only wept louder, and buried her face in her mother-in-law's shoulder.

Ivan stood in the front yard, waiting for Ruthie to arrive. The twelve-year-old boy across the street was fumbling with the string on a new kite. Not the most mechanically gifted of children, Ivan concluded. But there was a good breeze this morning, so it wouldn't be as oppressively hot out in the back yard as it had been yesterday. The forecast was thunderstorms late in the afternoon, and then clear again—hot and muggy, in fact—for the Fourth. Today, though, there was a breeze, and that called for a kite.

Katerina has never seen a kite, Ivan realized. They were a Chinese invention and they didn't come to Europe until . . . well, until later. Before Benjamin Franklin, but after Baba Yaga. So much for my future as a historian.

The boy across the street—what was his name? Terrel Sprewel. Never Terry, just Terrel, even though the name Terrel was clearly invented as a back-formation to allow the nickname Terry without saddling the kid with a really geeky name like Terence. Though you might as well tape a kick-me sign on your baby as to give him a name that was not only weird but rhymed.

Terrel used to try to follow Ivan, back when Ivan was in middle school and he ran through the neighborhood instead of around the lake. Back when it was still faintly ridiculous in the neighbors' eyes that a Jewish kid should be jogging. Terrel was a toddler then, and Ivan had to stop and make him go back. What's he doing in the front yard without a parent watching him, anyway? Once he had to take Terrel to the front door, the kid was so persistent, and his mom acted as if Ivan had somehow committed a crime by suggesting that she ought to prevent the child from following Ivan on his five-mile run. Maybe she thought I should take him along. Maybe she *wished*. That would be sad, to grow up with a mother who kind of hoped you'd run away.

Maybe you'd end up all by yourself, trying to get a string tied onto a kite so it has some hope of flying.

Ivan's impulse was to cross the street and lend a hand, show the kid how it was done.

Then he remembered—it wasn't safe for him to cross the street by himself. Who's the toddler now?

The string was tied. It wasn't in exactly the right place, but it would probably do. Terrel carried the kite to the end of the block before he started his run. Ivan wondered why he would do that. Why not start running from his own front yard? The answer was obvious, though. Terrel wanted to get the kite flying just as he reached his yard, so he could stand there in front of the windows with the kite in the air where his parents could look out and see him. Maybe they were better parents than Ivan thought. Maybe they would be looking. But he thought not. They never watched. Terrel was always alone. No applause. And yet it still mattered to the kid. He was still hungry to have his mom or dad tell him he did OK, or even watch him without a word, just to have their eyes see that he could get a kite up into the air.

Ivan practically willed it up. Run faster, he thought. Let out more string as you go. Let it catch. Rise up! Faster now! Good, it's working. It's caught! Let the string bleed out now, a little more.

He wasn't doing it. He was keeping the kite on too short a tether. It was going to fall.

"Let out more string!" Ivan called.

Terrel didn't even look over. He just obeyed. The string spun out; the kite staggered a moment, but the breeze caught it, carried it up. Terrel stood there, letting out a little more. A little more. Only when the kite was definitely up there, quite high, did Terrel look over at Ivan and grin.

It wasn't his parents he wanted to have watch him. It was me.

"Good job!" cried Ivan. "First try."

Terrel held up the string in his hand, offering Ivan the control of the kite. Ivan waved it back. "You're the kite-flyer, Terrel. It's all yours!" Then Ivan pointedly turned to look up into the sky, watching the kite, so Terrel wouldn't try to insist.

I can't go to your side of the street, Terrel, or the witch will get me.

The gusty wind was making the kite dance. Ivan wondered what it would be like, to be up there himself, in a hang glider, for instance, and catch one of those downdrafts. Drop like a stone for fifty feet, then recover and soar again.

Hang glider. That's something they could build in Taina, definitely. It wouldn't be paper, but Matfei had some silk, it had been part of his wife's dowry. Light dry wood for the frame—if Ivan learned enough about the aerodynamics of it, surely he could build at least one. That might be useful, to get someone inside Baba Yaga's fortress.

Someone alone and unarmed—how useful would that be? Because there was no way that someone carrying a heavy sword and buckler would be able to fly in a hang glider.

Oh, well. Never mind.

The front door opened. Terrel's mother came out onto the porch with a woman from up the street. For a moment Ivan thought, with some relief, that his assessment was wrong, that Terrel had indeed earned some applause for getting the kite into the air. But the women ignored the boy, continuing an animated conversation.

A small hairy dog charged out of the front door, dodged between the women on the porch, and ran straight for Terrel. With his eyes on the kite, stepping forward and backward as he kept the kiteline taut, Terrel was completely unaware of the dog until it was bashing into his legs, tripping him up. Terrel lost his balance for a moment, and in the effort to keep from falling, he stepped on the dog. Not too hard, but enough to send the dog yipping and yelping toward Terrel's mom.

Now she noticed him. "What are you doing! Are you trying to kill him? You think a *kite* is more important than a *living creature*? You make me *sick* sometimes, Terrel, the way you step on everybody and everything around you!"

It was an astonishing display of temper. The neighbor lady was as appalled by it as Ivan was. But Terrel took it all in stride; he assumed a submissive pose, looking at the ground, no longer watching the kite. Apparently he knew—probably had learned it very young—that this was the only pose that turned away wrath. Ivan noticed, however, that behind his back he kept a firm grip on the kitestring and was surreptitiously trying to keep it taut.

Terrel's mother was holding the dog now, speaking comfortingly to it, but with snide barbs at Terrel. "Did the mean boy kick you and step on you?" And then she turned her full attention back to her son. "Let go of that kite right now. You heard me! Let it go this instant! You will learn that living creatures are more important than *toys*." She poured so much scorn into the last word that Ivan wanted to smack her.

He knew he should keep his mouth shut, but it really was unbearable. He spoke in a loud voice, so he could be heard across the street. "Mrs. Sprewel, I was watching the whole thing, and Terrel could *not* have avoided what happened. The dog tripped him up before he even knew it was there."

Mrs. Sprewel glared at him like a bug in the frosting. "Thank you for your observation," she said. "I'm sure that makes poor Edwin feel *much* better." It took a moment to realize that Edwin was the dog.

Ivan tried to soften the whole thing by turning it away from the issue of dog-stomping. "Terrel did a great job of getting the kite up there on his first try—a gusty day like this, it wasn't easy."

"Excuse me, but I don't recall inviting you into this conversation," said Mrs. Sprewel. Behind her, the neighbor woman rolled her eyes.

Ruthie's car pulled up in front of the house.

Momentarily ignoring Ruthie's arrival, Ivan smiled and waved cheerily at Mrs. Sprewel. "You're quite right, Mrs. Sprewel. But I did wonder why your dog wasn't penned up or on a leash, as the law in Tantalus requires."

"He's on our property!" Mrs. Sprewel said, outraged but now on the defensive, which was all Ivan had hoped for.

"The dog wasn't on your property when it tripped your son and nearly killed him," said Ivan. "You really should watch that dog. It's a menace!" Then, with a wave but without another glance, he turned to Ruthie and greeted her with a smile as she got out of the car. Ruthie, unaware of the contretemps with the neighbors, gave him a friendly hug and a sisterly peck on the cheek.

Only after she pulled away from him and headed for the back of the car did he realize how deftly she had manipulated the greeting. Old habit had made him hold her just a little too tightly and a little too long. And perhaps she broke away a little more quickly than would have been normal, even for a perfunctory social greeting. He could almost hear the thought in her head: Take *that*, lover boy.

He also noticed that she was wearing a wig. How odd. Had she gone Hasidic all of a sudden? Not likely. No doubt just having a bad hair day.

Ruthie opened the trunk. Ivan stepped into the road just long enough to get the picnic hamper out, then carried it around the house into the back yard. Behind him, the dog barked. But Mrs. Sprewel wasn't yelling at Terrel anymore, and the kite was still up.

Ruth saw the wasp land on Ivan's back as he bent over the trunk to pick up the hamper. She didn't say anything to Ivan. Instead she silently invoked the wasp: Sting the bastard! Thinks he can hold me like old times, thinks he still has the *right* to pull me close enough to mash my breasts up against his chest and hold me there—well, that's a right I give to those who deserve it.

The wasp didn't sting him. But it didn't fly away, either. As Ruth followed him around the house, she could see the wasp crawling along his shirt. Plenty of time. Besides, if the wasp didn't sting him, she had the brownies. Plenty of itch and sting in *those*, if she chose to serve them to him. Not all the brownies, of course. Just two of them on which she placed the itching powder from the gypsy's bag, then put icing over them. She probably wouldn't serve those to Ivan and his bride. She had much greater hopes for the one big piece of chicken breast that she injected with the thin clear fluid from the gypsy's jar. Let Ivan eat that while Katerina was in the house on some made-up little errand and see whether he wanted to be married to the shiksa after that.

I can't believe I'm even taking these things seriously, thought Ruth. This is magic, witchcraft, superstition.

But why shouldn't it work? Witchcraft was simply an alternate way of viewing the universe, every bit as valid as science. Folkways were often wiser and more in harmony with the earth than the hard-edged metallic thinking of the engineers. Ivan used to laugh at her when she said things like that, and once he asked her if she believed that principle applied to recipes and directions. "Don't you expect directions to have a one-to-one correspondence with the highway system?" But that was just patriarchal thinking. Anything women said or thought had to be put down by men. She hadn't realized that Ivan was such a patriarchalist until after he betrayed her, but love is blind.

"Can I ask you one question?" she said as she followed him around the side of the house.

"Sure," said Ivan.

"Did you marry her as Ivan Smetski or Itzak Shlomo?"

"What?"

"Was it a Christian wedding or a Jewish one?"

He didn't answer. Which meant it was a Christian wedding. He betrayed everybody, from God to all the Jews who died in the Holocaust, and right on down to Ruth. And he didn't care. Because he was in love.

Well, what happens if you fall back in love with me? Do you switch religions again? How many times does this make? What are you, God's little tennis match, back and forth, back and forth? Double fault this time, *Itzak*.

"Why do you care?" asked Ivan.

For a moment she wondered what he was asking about. Then she realized he was finally answering her question from before. "Every time a Jew dies, all other Jews should mourn," she said.

He stopped abruptly and turned around. Standing there holding the heavy picnic hamper, he looked her in the eye and said, "If this is a sample of what this picnic's about, let's get this stuff back in your trunk and you can go on home."

"No, I'm—I'm sorry, Ivan, no, I'm not going to snipe at you. I was just remembering what my grandmother always said."

"My parents don't think I'm dead because I married her."

"I'm sure they don't," said Ruth. "Nor do I. I'm here, aren't I?"

"*Why* are you here?"

"For lunch," said Ruth. "And to try to make sense of my own life. I suddenly find myself at loose ends. I not only lost a fiancé, I also lost a very close friend. I'd like to see if I can have the friend back."

"Not like before," said Ivan. "I'm part of something else now."

"I know, Ivan. But what if *she* likes me, too? Then maybe I can be friends with the two of you."

He regarded her for a moment.

What, you think you have polygraph eyes? You can tell if I'm lying just by looking at me?

"You're a class act, Ruth," said Ivan.

"Also, the lunch is good. But simple. I was going to get really fancy, but I didn't dare serve caviar to a Russian."

He laughed, turned around, and continued around the outside of the house.

Katerina had no idea what to make of Ivan's exaggerated sense of courtesy. Yes, he had broken his betrothal to this woman, but that was all the more reason to avoid her. Ivan insisted that there was nothing to fear except, perhaps, an emotional scene, and they could avoid that just by being generous and natural and patient in their conversation.

Katerina had much more specific fears, mostly involving poisons in the food and drink. To her, it was an immediate danger sign that Ruthie had insisted on providing all the food herself. She found it incomprehensible that Ivan thought this was a laughable idea. Had they never heard of poison here?

Esther had reassured her. "All our food comes from outside the house," Esther explained, "so I have many charms and spells against it here. And not just poisons, but against potions and powders and whatnot. Vigilance is always good, but I don't think you'll take any harm from what you can eat. Or at least you won't be able to eat what would do you harm."

She showed Katerina what charms she used, and at Katerina's insistence provided Ivan and Katerina with additional charms that they wore around their necks—not that either of them told Ivan what his charm was for. "There's a general spell to protect you by sensing if someone at the table knows that some of the food is poisoned," Esther explained, "and there are charms that should make it impossible to eat anything that is not what it's supposed to be. But I'm no match for the knowledge of the Wicked Widow, so keep your own watch."

With those protections and warnings, Katerina felt barely reassured enough to go ahead with the picnic. And she had to admit to herself that part of the reason she dreaded the event was because, after all, this was the woman that Ivan had chosen for himself *without* an angry bear looming over him.

Ruthie was gracious enough—no sniping remarks, or at least nothing that made Ivan hesitate in his translation. But it was obvious that Ruthie loved the fact that the conversation was in English, and that much of it moved so rapidly that Ivan could only translate the gist of what was said, and then only after the fact. Katerina was being systematically excluded. But that was to be expected. As long as Katerina didn't let it get her angry enough to leave, she was fine.

Ruthie set out the chicken on their plates and then handed several jars to Ivan to open. Katerina reached for one—her grip was as good as Ivan's, or better, as they both knew—but Ruthie babbled something in English to Ivan, who turned to Katerina and, with only the faintest hint of a smile to let her know that he was aware of how Ruthie was manipulating them, he translated: "She forgot the salt. She wants you to go get it from the kitchen."

Esther felt it as a chill creeping up her back. She shuddered. Something had just come into her protected realm. But not a person. She wasn't sure what it could be.

She looked out the window into the back yard, where Vanya was having his incomprehensible picnic with Ruthie and Katerina. It reminded her of those old pictures of Roosevelt, Churchill, and Stalin. Except none of them was wearing such an obvious wig as Ruthie. What kind of fashion statement was she trying to make? Or was it just a terrible haircut or dye job that she had to cover up for a few weeks?

Esther watched them setting up the picnic—laying out a couple of blankets on the grass, setting out plates and glasses, pulling food out of the hamper Ruthie had brought.

Things Ruthie brought. There were charms to protect from the food, but was it possible she carried some living thing with her? What if Baba Yaga found out about Ruthie? If she did, she would try to use her.

What Esther sensed was an intruder. Smaller than a human being, but with some fragment of human spirit within it. An observer. An agent.

A familiar.

How? She had charms and spells enough to keep any familiar from gaining entry by itself. It would have to be carried in, close to the body of a human being who had trusted access. But it would also have to be a creature of high enough function to be useful to the witch who controlled it. A flea or louse would hardly be useful, however appropriate such a creature would be as Baba Yaga's familiar.

She could not ignore this. She had to find the familiar and eliminate the threat. She rinsed her hands at the sink.

The back door opened. Katerina came inside.

Esther looked at her in shock. "You left them alone together?"

"She 'forgot' the salt," said Katerina. "Which suggests that she has a love potion."

Esther rolled her eyes. "She couldn't get him into bed with her before he married you, so now she wants to do it with a potion."

"They . . . never?" asked Katerina.

"He's a strange boy," said Esther. "I thought you knew."

By now Katerina had the salt. "Well, time for a little seasoning."

"Watch for a familiar," said Esther.

Katerina turned, looking much more serious now. "What kind?"

"Small," said Esther. "Brought in by someone who is not an enemy."

Ivan raised his eyebrows at Ruthie. "Well, she's gone now. What did you want to say?"

Ruthie looked flustered. "Ivan, I could have said whatever secrets I might have over the phone. I'm sorry you're so suspicious. I simply forgot the salt."

"Sorry," said Ivan. "Here are the jars, all duly opened."

Father came over from the shed, where he had been putting away the lawn mower and hedge trimmer. "How are you doing? Where's Katerina?"

"She's inside getting the salt," said Ivan. "And we're having fun. I'm glad Ruthie invited us to do this."

Piotr smiled cheerfully at them and headed for the house.

"Ivan, would you taste the chicken and tell me if it's all right?" asked Ruthie. "I made them myself from my mother's recipe, and they don't look exactly the same as hers."

"They look the same to me," said Ivan. "Which means it should be great." Ruthie's mother was locally famous for her chicken, and not just among the Jews. Ivan reached down and picked up the large piece of chicken breast that she had put on his plate.

It slipped out of his fingers before he could get it to his mouth.

"I'm glad that didn't happen with the pickle jar," said Ivan, picking the chicken up from the blanket. "Maybe tiny blanket fibers will be just the thing to make it taste Kentucky-fried."

Piotr came in from the back yard just as Katerina and Esther reached the door. Katerina ducked outside with the salt in hand. Piotr and Esther paused a moment at the threshold.

"Nobody's killed anybody yet," said Piotr, joking.

"That's what I'm going outside to change," said Esther, only partly joking.

"Don't do any killing that the police will ask about later," said Piotr, not joking at all now.

"Nothing that talks."

As Esther came through the door onto the patio in back, Katerina was standing a few yards away from Vanya and Ruthie, watching. It was a sight to see: Ivan picking up a chicken breast and then fumbling it, dropping it on his lap, on the blanket, on the grass. He got up, his face red with embarrassment, to pick it up off the lawn, apologizing to Ruthie as he did.

To Esther it was obvious, as it would be to Katerina, that there was something wrong with the chicken and the charms were working. So much for Ruthie's benign intent.

Then Esther heard a dog barking. No, yipping. It was coming around the side of the house. Could this be the familiar she was looking for?

It was the annoying hairball that Mrs. Sprewel doted on. Normally it didn't wander around loose, and Esther's suspicions were fully aroused. She moved to intervene, but she wasn't quick enough. The dog took a flying leap at Vanya. Esther screamed—but the sound was barely out of her mouth when the dog, instead of going for Vanya's jugular, snatched the chicken breast out of his hands and took off with it around the corner of the house.

It wasn't Baba Yaga that had brought the dog, it was the charm. Vanya was so insistent on eating the damn chicken that the charm had been forced to draw someone or something else to take the chicken away from him. So much for Ruthie's love potion, if that's what it was.

And from Ruthie's face, it was indeed a cataclysmic failure. But she controlled herself, and managed a smile. "I guess that means the chicken *is* good enough to eat," said Ruthie.

"I'll bet that piece was particularly fine," said Esther.

Ruthie smiled at her, but there was rage barely concealed behind the grin. "I suppose I did save the best for Ivan," she said. "But it turned out to be the dog's piece."

Vanya was, of course, oblivious to this barely disguised jab, but Esther heard it, and she knew that Ruthie had a great deal of malice in her. She *has* been influenced by Baba Yaga, thought Esther. Ruthie had faults, but malice wasn't one of them. Still, people surprise you.

Katerina murmured to Esther in proto-Slavonic, "That dog is going to be mounting every cat and squirrel in the neighborhood."

The dog had not come alone. Terrel Sprewel was standing there holding a kite in his hands. "Sorry about the dog," he said. "I guess he followed me over here and smelled the chicken."

"No problem," said Vanya. "Dogs are dogs. Next time you step on him, though, make it count."

Terrel laughed—it must be some in-joke, Esther thought, since she had no idea what Vanya was talking about.

Ruthie's hands were stroking the lid of a Tupperware tray. Whatever was in there, Esther was reasonably sure, was Ruthie's backup plan. Cookies or brownies laced with laxative?

Terrel was battling on, embarrassed. "I just wondered if, you know, after the picnic or whatever, you wanted to take a turn with the kite."

"Good idea," said Vanya. "My wife, Katerina, I don't know if she's ever flown a kite." He turned to her and asked in proto-Slavonic.

But Katerina wasn't looking at the kite at all. "The dog," she said.

Ruthie opened the Tupperware container. Brownies.

Vanya looked where Katerina was looking. So did Terrel. Vanya was halfway there before Esther saw. The dog was lying by the fence, its legs trembling, its back as tightly bent as a bow.

Vanya picked up the dog. In his arms it shuddered and died.

Terrel approached Vanya in awe. "What was in that chicken?" he asked.

Everyone turned to look at Ruthie. She was standing now, looking in horror at the dog. "It can't be the chicken," she said.

And Esther believed her. Ruthie had been acting as if the chicken had a love potion in it. If she had known it was lethal, Esther doubted she would have sent Katerina away.

"Oh, Ivan," said Ruthie. "You were that close to eating it. You have to believe me, I didn't know."

"I believe you," said Vanya. But he turned away from her, and toward Katerina, taking her hand. It had the effect of closing a door in Ruthie's face.

In proto-Slavonic, Katerina said to Vanya, "I can't wait to eat the rest of the meal."

But Esther was watching Ruthie, who had dumped the Tupperware tray of brownies onto the lawn and was grinding them into the grass with her feet. She saw Esther looking at her. Tears were streaming down her face. "If I were any damn good as a cook maybe he would have married *me*," said Ruthie. "But I never thought this shit would really hurt anybody."

"It's all those additives," said Esther dryly.

Ruthie gathered up the rest of the food and put it back in the hamper. "I'm going home," said Ruthie. "I'm sorry about the dog. I— I'm sorry about everything."

"Bye, Ruthie," said Vanya. "Thanks for lunch."

In halting English, Katerina echoed him. "Bye, Rut'ie."

Clutching her hamper to her, Ruthie staggered around the side of the house. Somehow her wig had become askew on her head. It suited the moment.

Esther walked over to where Ruthie had ground the brownies into the lawn. The brownies themselves might be biodegradable, but Esther wondered what the poison would do to the grass. Not to mention the insects that lived in the lawn.

Well, she'd find out soon enough. A wasp landed on the mess of brownies and was crawling all over it. In fact, it looked for all the world as though it were deliberately smearing it on its abdomen.

On its stinger.

The wasp rose into the air and headed straight toward Vanya.

"The wasp!" shouted Esther, realizing at once that she had found Baba Yaga's familiar.

Vanya turned around just as the wasp reached him. It was going for his throat. Whatever the poison was, apparently Baba Yaga knew it was potent enough that just the little bit carried on the wasp's stinger would be enough. And there was no way Esther could get there in time to stop it. The question then was how quickly the poison would act. The dog had died in only a couple of minutes.

Piotr's voice came from right beside her. She hadn't heard him come back out. "Vanya, close your eyes!" A stream of liquid spurted fifteen feet from Piotr's hand, catching the wasp as it reached Vanya's neck. Vanya was splashed with the stuff and there was definitely some of it in his eyes, but all Esther cared about at the moment was the wasp. It crawled feebly for a second on the neck of Vanya's T-shirt. Then it dropped dead into the grass without stinging him.

"Got the little bastard," said Piotr. He was holding a can of Raid Wasp & Hornet Killer.

"My eyes!" shouted Vanya.

Piotr was already reading the directions on the can. In Old Church Slavonic he called out, "Wash his eyes with water, and keep on washing them!"

Esther turned on the hose as Piotr got the business end pointed at Vanya's eyes. Not too strong, just enough to bathe the eyes, not sandblast them. Katerina fussed over him, helpless because she didn't understand the magic that Piotr had sprayed from the can.

Terrel looked at them in awe. "Man, you guys are really quick with wasps." He picked up dead Edwin, whose little corpse had fallen when Vanya grabbed at his eyes. "I better get home with the dog," he said.

"No!" said Vanya.

"Wait a minute, Terrel," said Esther, in her heavily accented English.

In proto-Slavonic, Vanya explained. "If he takes the dog home dead, they're going to find the poison and then we have to explain how Ruthie was trying to kill me and got the dog by mistake. I don't think we want to testify at Ruthie's trial."

Esther moved immediately to examine the corpse Terrel was holding. She closed her eyes, passed her hands over the animal, and then stroked its belly while inhaling deeply. Sniffing.

In Ukrainian she said, "She didn't use any kind of detectable poison. It was a spell carried on a potion. There'll be nothing that a chemist would recognize."

"How did you do that?" asked Katerina. "How did you test it without tasting it?"

Esther was ready to explain, but then Terrel, increasingly frustrated with all the unintelligible language, interrupted. "I got to get home with this."

Vanya answered him in English. "You've got to know—it wasn't poison that got him. Nothing that any vet is going to find if there's an autopsy."

"They do autopsies on dogs? Cool."

"They do when people think the dog must have been poisoned. But I'm telling you that there won't be any poison to find. So why mention anything beyond finding the dog dead?"

Terrel's face was impassive as he answered. "You mean I don't get to tell Mom how he twitched his little legs while he was croaking?"

"You shouldn't take the dog back, anyway, Terrel," said Vanya. Water was still trickling into his open eyes, carrying away the Raid. "Let me do it. Or my father. We'll just say we found it dead in our yard. You shouldn't be involved."

"No way," said Terrel. "*I* get to hand little Edwin to her." He sounded very firm about it. A little frantic, even.

"Whatever," said Vanya. "It's your life."

"No," said Piotr. "It's his life, but he is not going to take the dog to his mother. Give it to me." He handed the hose to Esther, to continue bathing Vanya's eyes. He strode to Terrel and took the dog out of his arms. "Esther and I have watched what you endure, ever since your family moved into the neighborhood. Because your mother loves the dog more than you, you *think* you want the revenge of giving her the dead body. But what you really want is for your mother to love you. Therefore she must *not* have the memory of this dog's body in your outstretched arms. Do you understand me? You must be a mile from here, flying your kite, when she gets this dog that we found dead in our yard."

Terrel thought about this for a moment. "Whatever," he said.

"So you should go now," said Piotr.

But Terrel wasn't done. "What about the kite, Ivan? You want to take it up?"

"Later. Tomorrow. You going to be in town for the Fourth?"

"You kidding? We never go anywhere."

"Tomorrow, then. You get it up and bring it over here, we can fly it from our yard."

"If he's not blind," added Piotr.

Terrel seemed excited. "Any chance of that?"

"Don't get too thrilled about the idea," said Vanya dryly. "Blind people are only interesting for the first ten minutes."

"He's joking," said Esther.

"So was I," said Terrel. "I better go now. And, uh . . . thanks." He took the kite and trotted out of the yard.

When he was gone, they were silent for a few moments, until Piotr set down the dog's corpse. Then he sighed. "Well, that's one less yipping pest."

"That dog died for me," said Vanya. "Speak no ill of him."

"He was talking about Terrel," said Esther. "And it wasn't a nice thing to say."

"Maybe I was talking about Ruthie," said Piotr.

"Oh," said Esther.

"I think my eyes are OK now," said Vanya. "Hose down those brownies. Dilute them into the lawn."

"It's going to be a bad day for the earthworms," said Piotr.

"Was it the Bitch Widow who put her up to it?" Vanya asked in proto-Slavonic.

"I think she lied to Ruthie about what the potions would do. The chicken was obviously supposed to be a love potion."

"What about the wasp?" asked Vanya.

"The Widow's familiar," said Esther.

"So is she dead now?"

"The wasp is. But the Widow is still ruining perfectly good air by breathing it."

Piotr brandished the can. "Your magic may be good for some things, but it was Johnson and I who stopped the wasp."

Esther hugged him. "Even though you don't understand all that we do, Piotr, you stood beside us when it counted."

"I feel like I just won a joust," said Piotr.

"Good lance work," said Ivan.

"I can't believe she found a way in," said Katerina.

"There's always a way in," said Esther. "Always."

"I hope so," said Vanya. "Because somehow we've got to return the favor and get past *her* defenses."

"You'll do it, too," said Esther. "But the picnic strategy is out."

They laughed. Nervously.

BABA YAGA

That afternoon in Tantalus the fire department was called out seven times, and not one of the fires was a false alarm. No one died, but five houses, a gas station, and a barn were lost. Every one of the fires was obviously arson, even without the presence of detectable accelerants, because they started in such impossible places. But no one saw anything suspicious before or after the fires, and after this one night of rage, the arsonist never struck again in Tantalus.

14

FIREWORKS

aterina could hardly bring herself to eat supper that night. Not that she wasn't hungry—she was. But they had come so close to dying. The food here was already strange. None of it looked like anything. Everything was flavored with something else, so nothing tasted like itself. She hadn't really had much appetite since she left Sophia's house. And now Baba Yaga had found a way to get curses past the perfect protection of Ivan's mother's house.

Using Ruthie wouldn't be tried again. But Baba Yaga would find someone else. That boy, for instance. He was seething with resentments. Right now he seemed to like Ivan and his parents, but that could change, if Baba Yaga enticed him the right way, or fooled him about what he was doing, the way Ruthie was deceived. Or it might be Piotr himself, or Mother; every day they left the house to work, to shop, to run errands. Who knew what they might bring back with them? What familiar? What curse concealed in papers in Piotr's briefcase? Or in the grocery bags that Ivan helped Mother bring in from the car?

It was just a matter of time.

What was this food? Mother said it was potatoes, sliced thin, with a cheese sauce. But nothing looked or tasted like cheese, and she had no idea what potatoes were. Everything felt strange in her mouth.

She ate it anyway, chewing methodically. When one is at war with Baba Yaga, it's good to do it on a full stomach. You never know when the crisis might come, and you have to be at full strength.

298

But what strength did they have? All these tasks that Ivan had been working on, the gunpowder, the alcohol, the bombs, the Molotov cocktails—what good would such mechanical things do against magic? Yet Mother had such faith in them that Katerina went along.

And . . . there was the killing of the wasp today. That stream of liquid, and the wasp went down and died. A creature sustained as a familiar was very hard to kill. So maybe there was something to it after all . . .

He could have died. A bite of that piece of chicken, and he would have twitched himself to death within a few minutes. Not really my husband yet, but the only one I'll ever have. No child in me yet to inherit.

The time for waiting is over. Leaving the marriage half-done was supposed to keep Baba Yaga from attacking Taina. But it only provoked her all the more to attack Katerina and Ivan. And without Katerina, Taina was lost.

"You don't like it?" asked Mother.

It took Katerina a moment to realize what she was asking. Oh, yes. The potatoes. Or no—Mother had just offered her another platter. Of something. Stuff. It looked like strange turds on the platter, from some large, possibly sick animal.

"Salmon cakes," said Mother. "I make them myself, but not too spicy this time, I notice you don't like them spicy."

Katerina had learned the Ukrainian word *spicy* very quickly, after her first taste of jalapeños. Piotr and Ivan only laughed at her as she panicked, looking for water, something to stop the burning in her mouth. They made her eat bread, which worked much better than the water. "I forgot," said Ivan. "I forgot how hard it is to get used to the American way of cooking."

"Not as hard as the Jewish way of cooking," said Piotr.

Ivan rolled his eyes. "Kosher is good, too. Just different."

"Everything carried to extremes. The rabbi who made Jews keep two kitchens—I hope God has a special place in hell for him. What an absurdly elaborate effort, just to make sure you never accidentally boil a baby goat in its mother's milk!"

"I never made you eat kosher," Mother reminded him mildly.

"So we slip now and then," said Piotr. "For company."

Ivan laughed. "I think Katerina would have preferred kosher."

That was back when she first came here. Now she was more used to the flavors, and some were good—cinnamon, nutmeg—though Ivan loathed nutmeg and wouldn't eat anything in which it was detectable.

Still, each new food was an unpleasant adventure. Couldn't they just leave meat in its natural form now and then? Couldn't bread look like bread, a fish like a fish?

"What's troubling you?" asked Piotr. "It's not the spiciness of the food."

"No, it's just . . . it's time to go back."

Piotr nodded, but his eyes teared up. It seemed to surprise him, how the emotion came so quickly to the surface. "Sorry," he said, dabbing at his eyes. "What a baby! But everything is so strange where you come from, this business of witches. Today I faced the worst thing in the world—to see your child die. I keep seeing him out there, like Edwin, limp, cold, empty. I held the dog and I thought, it was supposed to be Vanya. I gave the body to Mrs. Sprewell, and she burst into tears, sobbing, and I thought, that would have been me, grieving. How do I know I'll ever see you again, Vanya, once you leave?"

"You don't," said Ivan. "But here we're easy targets. The Maginot Line."

Katerina had no idea what he was talking about. But Piotr understood. "I know," he said, "it's right to go. And with Katerina's father in trouble—no, you have to go."

"What I don't understand," said Mother, "is why we can't go, too."

Everyone looked at her in surprise. Piotr immediately thought it was a good idea. Ivan seemed to have doubts, but was slow to answer. It fell to Katerina.

"You're not trained for war," said Katerina. "You're very good—but when the Widow is at her full strength, you're no match for her."

"And you are?"

"I'm the princess," said Katerina. "The hearts of the people are gathered in me. When a king has the love of the people, then whatever he does has the power of the people in it. My spells will have that. I've learned from you, Mother, and that's good. But in Taina, when I cast the same spell, it will have many times the strength than if you were to cast it. Do you understand me?"

Mother nodded, closing her eyes. "I understand, but I can't believe I wouldn't be useful."

"You would be useful to her," said Katerina. "She would use her power to overwhelm you, and then rule you."

"She could never turn me."

"She turned Dimitri," said Katerina.

"Dimitri wanted to be turned," said Ivan.

Katerina shook her head. "No. She lied to him."

"Dimitri wanted to be king," said Ivan. "She can only use the desires already in a man's heart."

"When did you become a scholar of magic?" asked Katerina hotly.

Ivan raised his eyebrows. "I've read every damn thing ever written about the folklore of magic."

"But you didn't believe in it," said Katerina.

"I do now."

"And you've never done it."

"No," said Ivan. "And you've never led an army into battle. And I had never fought a bear before. But go ahead, you're probably right, except if the Widow can force people to want what they never wanted, then who is safe? Whom can you trust?"

His argument was compelling. Baba Yaga hadn't turned many people, and Katerina was sure it wasn't from lack of trying. She could fool poor simple folk, like Sergei's mother, but only in fairly innocuous ways—she could get the old woman to spread false gossip by lying to her. But she couldn't have made her kill. She could get information out of people, but she couldn't make them betray their neighbors. Dimitri did what he did because it was already in his heart to do it.

And nothing was certain in life.

"I have to trust everyone," said Katerina, "and yet there's no one I can really be sure of."

"You can be sure of me," said Ivan.

She looked at him, searching his face. I've known you so little time. The others I knew all my life. The others are my own people. You are a stranger, from a strange time and place. I know what they can do, what they will do. I have no idea of what you are or what is in your hands and heart and mind.

And yet when you tell me I can be sure of you, I *am* sure.

It is myself I can't trust. Because I know that my trust in you, Ivan, my husband, my stranger, is not the result of reason and experience. I trust you because I've come to know you, and coming to know you, I've learned to love you. I've fallen in love with your boldness, your humility, your innocence, your kindness, your willingness. I know that you will stand by me as best you can. But you don't know what my husband needs to know. You can't do what my husband needs to do. I can trust your heart, your king's heart, but your mind doesn't know what it needs to know, your hands don't have in them the skill they need to have.

I had no choice but to marry you. But little by little I have come to long for you to include me within the circle of your arms, of your mind, of your pure love. To embrace me, to give me the babies I was born to have, to help me raise them. And I don't care which world we raise them in, yours or mine or some other that we haven't seen yet. I'm sure of you, Ivan. I want you as my husband.

But as my king? How could I trust you to be king?

Ivan looked at her face and saw . . . compassion.

It couldn't be clearer. "You can be sure of me," he had said. He hadn't meant it as some kind of declaration. He was only saying what should be obvious to everyone—what his parents already knew about him. She was supposed to laugh and say, Yes, of course, I know that.

Instead, her only answer was this silence, this pity.

They say that love conquers all. They say that because they're idiots. Love can't conquer anything. Love can't make a scholar into a warrior. Loving her can't make her love me.

Now his parents could see how it was between them. They could see that their son offered his life to this woman, and, poor thing, she had no idea what to do with it. The gift was worthless to her.

So he laughed. "Well, there you go." He held up his hands. "Soft. Dimitri told me I had a woman's hands. But the women of Taina, their hands are callused. From sewing, weaving, from endless spinning. What I have are the hands of a princess." He reached out to her, took her hands between his. "And you," he said, "you have the heart of a warrior." He leaned over and kissed her cheek. Like a brother. Like a friend.

Katerina looked down at the table. She certainly wasn't helping to smooth over this embarrassing moment.

"Father," said Ivan, "I hope you have enough room on some credit card to charge two tickets to Kiev." He turned to his mother. "Only two, Mom. Sorry." And then to Katerina. "I'll see if we can fly day after tomorrow. After we've tested the fireworks. Or the first flight we can get after that."

"Thank you," said Katerina.

"Yes, well, it's about time you got home. Though I must say you've done a better job of fitting in here than I did there."

She looked upset. But her words were mild. "I had someone helping me. You didn't."

"Yes, well, you happened to come to the one family in the world where everybody speaks at least a little ancient Slavonic. You'd think someone had planned all this." He got up from the table. "I'll see you all in the morning."

Ivan went to his room. To his empty room. It was good to have a place where nobody else had a right to go. What had he been thinking of, wanting to marry Ruthie—wanting to marry at all? He wasn't afraid of solitude. No scholar could afford to be.

He lay down fully dressed on his bed, not meaning to fall asleep yet. He just needed to think. About what, he wasn't sure.

So instead he thought about nothing. About things in the room. About the athletic trophies in a box in the closet. How much of his life was that? The shelves of books—so much time reading. Neither of them amounted to anything. He ran. He lost or he won. No one remembered a week later. And the books he read—what did that amount to? University people were always so proud of being readers instead of television watchers, but what was the difference, really? It was a one-way transmission. I read, but it made no difference to the writer. He never knew. And when I'm dead, what will it matter the books I read? My memory is where the book ends up, just like the TV show, and when I'm dead, that memory is gone from the world.

Like running the hurdles. Work so hard, jump over every one, fast, high enough but no higher, because you can't afford to hang in the air. And then, when the race is over, you're dripping with sweat, either they beat you or you beat them . . . and then a couple of guys come out and move the hurdles out of the way. Turns out they were nothing. All that work to jump over them, but now they're gone.

What will it matter, then, if I was happy or . . . whatever? After I'm dead, my parents will miss me, sure, but then someday they'll die, and then who'll remember me? Nobody. And that's fine. Because it doesn't matter. Baba Yaga will win or she'll lose. A thousand years later, nobody will believe she ever existed. And Taina will be completely forgotten. So what does it matter that some stranger loved the princess of Taina but never had her love in return?

He reached over and switched on the CD player. He had a Bruce Cockburn album in it. So Cockburn talks about how he's thinking about Turkish drummers, only it doesn't take long because he doesn't know much about Turkish drummers. A pounding in his head. Unshed tears. Bloated like the dead. This was not the best song to be listening to.

He let it keep playing.

When he woke up it was dark and silent. Night outside. He needed to pee, hadn't gone before he went to bed. He hated sleeping in his clothes. His pants always got twisted around and his clothes didn't fit right after sleeping in them. He pulled down his pants and Jockeys in one movement, then pried each shoe off with the other foot while he was unbuttoning his shirt. By the time he pulled his stocking feet out of his pant legs, his shirt was off. He peeled off his socks, then felt around in the dark for his bathrobe and drew it closed around his body as he opened the door.

The hall was dark, too. He stood in the hall, listening. How late was it? He didn't look at the clock. He heard his father snoring softly in his room. But just the one snore, not the duet, his mother and father snoring together.

He padded toward the bathroom. Then walked past it and stood outside the door to Katerina's room. Listening for her breath. Some sound.

But there was nothing there for him. And he really had to pee.

In the bathroom he had to turn the light on so he wouldn't miss. It blinded him. And then, when he was done, he turned it off and he was blind again. Can't win. He thought of getting Raid in his eyes. He thought of the wasp. What if the wasp had stung him? Got the potion into him, the curse. He would have had a bad five minutes there, but by now it would be over. He wouldn't have this dull ache in his heart, the sharp yearning in his throat, the words trying to escape.

"You can be sure of me." What an ass.

He opened the door and then remembered to close his bathrobe. He stepped out into the hall. Still just Father's snoring.

Maybe Mother was up. Downstairs somewhere.

He walked softly down the stairs not wanting to waken anybody. The lower floor was dark, too. So Mom wasn't up.

Or maybe she was in the back yard.

He walked to the kitchen door, opened it, stepped barefoot out onto the patio. The concrete felt cold on his feet. There was a breeze. It was the third of July, or maybe early on the Fourth. Shouldn't be this cool. Breeze off the lake.

He walked out onto the grass. It was damp on his feet. Away from the house, the breeze was stronger. It moved his hair. He opened his robe, to let the breeze move across his whole body. After a moment, he shrugged off the robe. Eyes closed, he stood there wondering why it felt so good to have the wind touch your whole body at once. And if it felt so good, why did people wear clothes all the time so they could never feel it?

He remembered standing there naked at the edge of the chasm, desperate to cover himself. What a fool. Naked is how you first feel the air, coming out of the womb. That's what it feels like—being born.

A rowboat was moving on the lake. Some predawn fisherman getting a head start on the Fourth of July crowds. In the moonlight it felt like he could see forever. But not a car moving. No fireworks, either—no late-night revelers getting a head start on the Fourth. Just silence. He imagined he could hear the dipping of the oars into the water, the tinkling of the drops falling from the oars when they rose again.

Then a bird began squawking in a nearby tree. Another picked up the tune. Not squawking, really. Just the normal twitter to announce the coming of day. But it was so loud, after the silence.

Time to go in. Go back to bed. Not that he was likely to get any sleep. He'd probably already had eight hours.

He turned around and picked up his robe, but as he was bending over to get it, he thought he saw a motion from the storage shed. Scooping up the robe, he looked sharply. Someone was standing by the door. His first thought was: The witch has found her way past Mother's protections. His second thought was: It's Mother, and she's seen me standing out here naked as a baby.

Then she stepped from the shadow. It was Katerina.

She just stood there. Not a word. Not a smile. Just looking at him.

She'd seen him naked often enough. He stopped holding the robe in front of him and, facing her, pulled it on, then drew it closed, tied it. She watched, but showed no expression.

Whatever conversation might happen at this time of night, out here in the back yard, Ivan didn't want to work that hard. If she wasn't going to insist on some kind of empty chat, he certainly wouldn't. He walked across the grass and the patio, then went back into the house without looking at her again.

He went back into his room and this time looked at the clock. Three-thirty. Too early to be up. He turned the CD player on softly. Skipped ahead a few tracks. "Birmingham Shadows." Maybe the loneliest song anybody ever wrote. "Wearing the role of the young upstart." He smiled at that—he heard it as wearing the *robe*. "You show a little— I let something show, too." Cockburn always sounded so jaded. And hurt. On a night like this Ivan should be listening to something else. The Pointer Sisters' greatest hits or something. "Fire," yeah, that was the song. That old Springsteen chestnut. Or better yet: "He's So Shy."

Still, he didn't change the music. He took off the robe and pulled down the sheets, but he didn't slide his feet under the covers, he lay there on top, spread like a deerskin, feeling about as dry and empty as that. He thought of Katerina's face. Thought of her sweet, beautiful body. Thought of her voice, the way she gestured when she talked.

Thought of her in Taina, surrounded by the love of the people, knowing everyone, having a hand in every task, every frolic. Thought of her here, so afraid at first, so uncertain, but taking it all in stride, mastering it. The way she took to Mother, the way she enjoyed Father, answered his questions patiently. He thought of reaching out and touching her cheek and having her smile and lean into his hand, and then turn her face and kiss the palm, kiss his fingers.

"If I fall down and die without saying good-bye, I give you this, you'll have lost a friend." Cockburn was cutting too close to the heart. "It's now or not at all." Could that be true?

He tried not to move. Kept his hands still, though they wanted to move, they knew the way. Then finally he did move, his whole body. He got up from the bed and walked to the door and opened it.

And there she stood, leaning against the opposite wall, watching the door of his room as he had stood watching hers. He was startled for a moment, but then he realized that he had been expecting her. That this was the reason he had to get up. Not because of some lonely depressed song. But because the princess was standing at the door, waiting for it to open.

"Ivan," she whispered. "All I could think of was . . . how close I came to losing you."

Not close enough, he thought bitterly.

And then: How could you lose me, when you've never had me, never wanted me?

But he said nothing. She wanted to talk, but he didn't. He didn't want her in his room tonight, not to have her sit there talking through plans and worries the way she had so many nights since they got here. So he didn't invite her in. And she didn't ask.

After the silence stretched on interminably, he stepped back. She didn't move. He turned his back on her and walked to the bed. He left the door open behind him. He lay down on it, facing away from the door.

He heard the door close.

"Some men rob whole countries dry," sang Cockburn. Yeah, some women, too.

A sound. The bed moved. He felt a thrill run through him. He was not alone in the room. She had closed the door, but from the inside.

He rolled onto his back, and there she was, as naked as he was, lying on her side, leaning on her elbow. He reached out a hand, touched her cheek. She leaned into his hand. Then turned her face, kissed his palm.

He wanted to ask her: Was this a political decision? Did you decide it was time to consummate the marriage as a declaration of war on Baba Yaga? Or was it pity? That compassionate look on your face at dinner, when you couldn't accept the pathetic token this shabby knight offered you?

But he kept his suspicions to himself. As long as no one said anything, he could pretend that it was love. That she felt about him as he felt about her. That the best thing that happened in his life was the day he came to the clearing in the woods and saw the shape of a woman under the leaves, a princess lying there asleep, enchanted, waiting for him to grow up so he could waken her with a kiss.

With this kiss. This gentle, leisurely kiss. No bear leaning over us. No curse to be removed. Just this man and the woman he loved, who also loved him. Or so he could believe, tonight on the cool sheets, in the dark, her lips brushing his, the scent of her in his head like music, drowning out all other songs.

Katerina woke just before dawn, as she always did. She saw Ivan sprawled in the bed beside her—a huge bed, large enough for a family. The faint light from the window made a meandering ribbon of reflection along the crest of his body. She wanted to touch him, touch the light on him. But she didn't want to waken him, for she was certain that when he woke, the magic of the night would end. He would speak; being Ivan, he would apologize. For something—she had no idea now what it would be.

The women had warned her, in the days before her wedding. Most of them spoke of the casual brutality of men, like dogs that mount bitches, boars on sows. It will hurt, they warned her, when he forces his way in the first time. But it's over soon—he'll finish quickly.

Many of them also had private advice, which they dared not let others hear because it confessed too much about their own lives. One who took her aside warned her not to cry out in pain—some men will think it should always be like that, they'll come back for more of your pain instead of for your love. Several told her to pretend that she enjoyed it, because a good man has to believe he's pleasing his wife. If you don't make him welcome, he'll find someone else who will. Others told her to be grateful when he found someone else, because then he'd only bother her when it was time to make babies.

Another told her that Ivan looked like the type who would be weak in bed, who wouldn't have the strength in him to finish. You have to coax him, she said. You have to entice him. Though how that was done, the woman wouldn't say.

And then there were the few who laughed at all warnings. One of them said, "You'll love it. He'll never be enough for you, though, this weakling who can't lift a sword. Better take a lover or two on the side. What he doesn't know won't hurt him, and there's no reason for a woman to be without the only pleasure God gives us."

All this advice—and it had told her nothing. She put it all out of her mind. Whatever it was, women managed to endure it or there'd be no children in the world. So, after listening to all the women, after watching the animals from childhood on, she could only experience for herself, when Ivan showed her, what this man did with this woman in his bed.

None of their advice applied to Ivan.

He was so gentle, whispering to her, asking her sometimes, "Is that good? Does that please you?" and other times, "You are so beautiful." Here, he would whisper, this curve, this hollow, this crest, I can't believe that I am the man who can touch this loveliness, that you're giving this to me. Unfamiliar feelings swept over her, strange changes in her body, trembling in places where she had never trembled, new tensions, new longings. He was so slow, she grew impatient. "Now," she whispered, pressing herself to him, but he answered, "Soon, not yet, soon."

"How do you know?" she asked. "You've never done this either."

"I've read books," he said, laughing softly. "I studied hard for this."

She didn't believe him at first—no one could *write* about this, it was far too private—and so she began to think maybe this was a kind of magic, too, that he was casting spells on her body, that he was in control of what she felt, making her body do things it had never done, could never have done before she came to his bed.

And then he told her that she *was* ready, and he was right. As the women had warned her, there was pain, but it was not as awful as they said, and even though it took the edge off the pleasure, it did not dull the love that swept through her. She clung to him, would not let him go when he finished, and he laughed again and held her, stroked her, as she also caressed him. Until he fell asleep. Until she also slept.

Now, remembering it in the morning, she wondered: Why did I wait? He had this gift for me all along.

But she knew the answer. She could not have received the gift until she loved him, and she could not have come to love him without seeing him first in his own world, his own family—in a place where he was a man held in respect, and not a despised stranger. His was a gift with no one fit to receive it, until now.

He stirred. Maybe he felt her gaze on him; maybe it was the change in her breathing; maybe it was a dream of her that woke him. He turned his head and saw her and searched her face. For what? It reminded her of yesterday, that awful time at the dinner table, when she waited too long to answer, when her silence shamed him in front of his parents. She would not wait today, with his gaze upon her. Instead she slid toward him, kissed him.

"I was afraid," he whispered to her.

"Of what?"

"That in the morning you'd regret what you gave to me last night."

"What did I give you, that you didn't give me ten times over?"

He held her close. "What was it that we did last night?"

"Don't you remember?"

"I didn't know even at the time. Was it a man and a woman, drawn together, body to body? Was it a princess wanting to make the baby that will carry on the dynasty? Was it a strategy, to strike the next blow against the Widow? Was it the fear of death, which came so close yesterday?"

It devastated her to know what he thought of her. That he did not understand at all.

"I've hurt you," he whispered. "I'm sorry, I didn't mean to. All of those are good reasons, don't you see? Because no matter what *you* meant by it, what you have is a husband, a father for your children, as long as I'm alive. I love you, Katerina, whether you love me or not, whether you even want me or not."

She pulled him close, partly because she could see how it hurt him not to be sure of her, partly so he couldn't see her tears.

But he felt them. "No, I've made you cry, I'm sorry, I shouldn't have spoken, I'm spoiling it and all I wanted was to—"

"Hush," she said. As mothers said it to their babies, who still whimpered even after they had been given the breast to suckle on. Hush, you already have what you yearn for, so be quiet and take it and be glad. "Would it disappoint you so much, Ivan, if you were wrong, and last night meant only that a wife came to her husband, and gave herself to him for love alone?"

"I hate to be wrong," he murmured. "But I can live with it."

*   *   *

Esther felt the change in the house from the break of day. Even if she hadn't caught a glimpse of Katerina in Vanya's bathrobe, going from his room to the bathroom, she would have known. For the emotional wall that had so thickened the hall between their rooms was gone. The air was clear; the light danced brightly on the walls.

At breakfast Vanya and Katerina were giddy and pensive by turns. Inexplicable silences, and then laughter at anything that could remotely pass for wit. Halfway through the meal, Piotr, always dense about such things, actually sensed the change. "Is something going on that I don't know about?" Which caused another burst of laughter from the young lovers. Esther caught his eye and shook her head a little. Don't ask. I'll tell you later. And because they had been married so long, he understood. Later, when the children were out in the back yard readying the Molotov cocktails, Esther was able to satisfy Piotr's curiosity. "It's love, you old fool," she said. "Don't you remember?"

"I was never so silly about it. And besides, they've been married since before they got here."

Esther kissed him. "They've been sleeping in separate rooms, Piotr."

"Well, some people do."

"But last night they slept in the *same* room."

It finally dawned on him. "You mean—they *haven't* been sleeping together?"

"The marriage wasn't consummated until last night. And, judging from the spring in Katerina's step, this morning as well."

"Esther," Piotr said sternly. "You shouldn't be thinking that way about your own son."

"What, I'm supposed to think he found a better way to make babies?"

Piotr sighed. "So they're going to be honeymooning all day?"

"That and blowing things up. Which isn't a bad combination. You're supposed to have fireworks."

"I thought it was violins. I thought the fireworks were last night at dinner."

"Last night was two people who were fed up with not being fully committed to each other. Vanya declared his commitment to her, and she didn't answer. But I imagine she gave her answer a few hours later. Perhaps it was after Katerina and I went out in the back yard to make a few spells that she didn't know, that she might need. We were in the shed when Vanya came out in his bathrobe. I decided I wasn't needed there anymore, so I went back in the house and left them alone. Apparently she had brains enough to stay out there with him."

Piotr looked at her suspiciously. "So now I'm not supposed to think you cast some spell on them? To help them get past their . . . shyness, or whatever it was?"

"I don't do love potions," said Esther. "Those are never about love, they're about coercion. And besides, they already loved each other, they were just too stupid to know it."

"But you didn't do *nothing*," said Piotr.

"I cast a spell of Truth on the house," said Esther. "It's very simple, really. It makes people willing to act according to what they believe. To say what's in their hearts, regardless of shame. It doesn't change what they feel, what they want. It just helps . . . loosen them up."

"You needed magic for that? Wine has been around for centuries. *In vino veritas.*"

Esther laughed. "The amount of wine that it would have taken to get Vanya to forget his pride and speak his heart—well, let's just say that it might not have helped him later, when they finally understood each other."

"I married a Pandarus," said Piotr.

"I don't manipulate people, Piotr. I just help them achieve their good desires."

"Not Pandarus, then. The tooth fairy?"

She kissed him, then slapped him playfully. "Let's go out and blow things up, shall we?"

After the coolness of the night, the day was already turning muggy. They got out the Molotov cocktails and the gunpowder crackers. Ivan let his father throw the first cocktail, lighting the fuse and heaving it at the piled-up logs. It worked much better than they expected—or wanted. Burning alcohol splattered all over the logs, yes, but also onto the weeds five yards beyond. They had to turn the hose on all the little fires to put them out, and for a few moments they were afraid the whole thing would get out of hand. They didn't relish explaining to the police why they had a dozen Molotov cocktails—not the traditional fireworks for the Fourth. And when they tried the first of the crackers, it was even more disastrous. For one thing, the fuse, made out of homespun string, burned about ten times faster than they expected—Ivan barely got it out of his hand before it blew up. And then it exploded with more force than they imagined possible for such a small amount of gunpowder. Logs that were still burning from the Molotov cocktail were thrown thirty feet across the yard; one of them hit Piotr in the chest, knocking him down, though fortunately it didn't catch him on fire. And the window over the sink in the kitchen broke—when the bomblet boomed, the glass collapsed in shards all over the sink inside and the patio outside.

It was an insane five minutes, running around after burning logs, picking them up with garden tools and carrying them back to the bonfire. Checking Piotr for serious injuries—nothing broken, though, just a bruise. Cleaning up glass inside and out and then discovering that all the glaziers in town had taken the Fourth as a holiday. They spent hours then, reducing the charges in the firecrackers and pouring out alcohol from the cocktails.

And all the while, they had to keep answering the phone, telling neighbors that they had bought inferior fireworks and nobody was injured and no, they wouldn't be setting off any more like that. Then Terrel came over with his kite and sadly reported that there wasn't a breath of wind today. "The only way to fly a kite is to take it out in a convertible," he said.

But Ivan wanted to show Katerina what a kite was anyway, so he and Terrel took turns a couple of times, running up and down the yard, trailing the kite behind them. Ivan tried to explain to her that when there was a wind, it rose even higher, and you didn't have to keep running. Finally, after Terrel went home, Ivan explained to his parents and Katerina what he had in mind. "A book on hang gliding. If we can make a hang glider out of materials there in Taina, it gives us a way to fly over the walls."

Katerina kept her doubts to herself—if big metal buildings could fly without even flapping their wings, then maybe a man could fly by wearing a kite. Though it was hard to believe even the kite could fly, considering that it kept crashing to the ground whenever they stopped running. Add the weight of a man with a sword and buckler, and . . . well, what did she know?

As for the Molotov cocktails and the firecrackers—those were impressive. She had heard of Greek fire, but had never seen it. And as for the firecracker, it made her ears ring for hours afterward, and she knew that these things had the power to terrify an enemy—especially one that was only motivated by fear. Like Baba Yaga's army.

Only after dark, when the fireworks began over the lake, did they dare to try again. The little bombs made a lot less noise, with their reduced charges—but they were able to time the fuses better. Ivan and Katerina also became rather adept at throwing the cocktails. "You're learning this much faster than I learned the sword," said Ivan.

"You couldn't even lift the sword at first," said Katerina. "It takes practice. This is easy."

Piotr laughed at that. "That's how we got so many people involved in waging war—it used to be a skilled profession, but now it's within the grasp of unskilled labor."

The bonfire was too hot to enjoy on a muggy summer night like this. But they burned some marshmallows and made Polish-sausage hot dogs and ate them as far from the fire as they could get, right under the cardboard covering the kitchen window. "I think," said Ivan, "that the experiment is definitely a success. Everything works. And we know that if we had really wanted to, we could have blown up the house."

"Almost did anyway," said Esther.

"And the best news of all," said Ivan. "Tomorrow we fly."

"No," said Esther. "That isn't good news." Then she burst into tears and fled into the house, Piotr following close behind her.

"My mother worries about us," said Ivan.

"So do I," said Katerina.

They walked out beyond the fire and watched the fireworks bursting in the air over the lake. The boom of each explosion was carried over the water—it was deafening. Katerina covered her ears for a little while, but it didn't help, and she finally gave up and enjoyed the show. "Can you do *that* in Taina?" she asked.

"Theoretically, yes," said Ivan. "But people get killed sometimes setting off those rockets—I don't want to run the risk of having our weapons do more damage to us than to them."

"I can imagine the Hag working herself to death trying to duplicate those lights in the sky."

"But not running from them."

"She isn't much for running away," said Katerina. "She doesn't give up."

"Yes, well, you aren't a quitter either," said Ivan. "Nor am I."

"Maybe these firecrackers can make her army run away. Maybe the Molotov cocktails will burn out her fortress. Maybe the spells I've learned will get me face to face with her—"

"Get *us* face to face."

"I'm the one who has to match her, spell for spell. I'm the one who has the power of my people inside me. Their love for me. It gives me great strength."

"So you'll win. No one could possibly love *her*."

"Cousin Marek tried to explain it to us, Ivan. She isn't relying on the power that comes from her own people. It's the power of a god she's got under her control—the love of the people for *him*."

"The bear."

"Bear. The savage cold of winter. All the people have respect for *him*. Not just the people of one kingdom. Many kingdoms, Ivan. And he's a god by nature. Even if she can only use a fraction of his power, it's more than my people can give to me."

"Why does he let her?"

"Why do you think he has a choice? Spells of binding, that's what she does best. That's how she got her first husband to marry her. How she got the people of her kingdom to accept the idea of widow-right instead of electing a new king when her first husband died without an heir."

"But she can't coerce people against their will," said Ivan.

"It's not that simple," said Katerina. "She can find desires inside you that you didn't even know you had."

"Well, thanks," said Ivan. "For a little while there, I had some hope."

"There *is* hope, Ivan."

"Oh? You didn't mention any just now."

"You didn't find me just by chance, Ivan. Some force, some fate, wanted you to find me, brought us together, brought you to Taina, brought me here. Whatever that power is, if it wants us to win, then we'll have the victory."

"So why are we working so hard?"

"Why did you have to hit the Bear with a stone? Why didn't you just fly over the moat?"

Ivan shook his head. "I can't put my trust in some unidentified fate that's pushing us around. It wasn't fate that brought me back to you. It was my own desire."

"Yes," said Katerina. "And your goodness, and your purity. The very reasons you were chosen."

"And now?" said Ivan. "Are we weaker because we're not so pure?"

She shook her head. "It doesn't work that way. We're married, so our coupling isn't impure. In fact, it strengthens us. Makes each of us as strong as if we contained both souls within us. And . . . if we've made a baby, if I have a child inside me when I face her, then I have a power she's never had. Well, she's conceived babies, the people say, but the children were always born monsters who died at once, and now her husband isn't the kind who's likely to give her a baby."

"You never know, with gods," said Ivan. "There are tales of swans and bulls."

"If we've made a child," said Katerina, "there will be magic in it. Power."

He was silent for a while.

She understood the silence. "No, Ivan. That's not why I came to you last night."

He pretended that wasn't what he was thinking. "It would be all right if you did."

"No," said Katerina. "It would not be all right. A child shouldn't be conceived as a strategy in war. What do you think of me?"

He took her in his arms and kissed her, long and hard. "That's what I think of you."

"Is that what you call thinking?" Then she kissed him back, even harder.

"So," he said, when he could breathe again. "Even though we'd never do it as a strategic move in war, would you like to try again? Just in case we don't already have a baby started?"

"And miss the rest of the fireworks?" she said.

He grinned and dutifully turned back to look at the fireworks. A big one went off, red, white, and blue.

"All right," she said. "I'm done now."

"See one rocket go off, you've seen them all," said Ivan.

She almost dragged him back to the house. Piotr and Esther had to come out later to put the bonfire out. They didn't mind. They knew their son had finally moved on beyond them. Even if he made it back from Taina somehow, he would never again live as a child in this house. It was just the two of them now. But they were comfortable with each other. The prospect of sharing the rest of their lives held no dread for them. And the things they did dread—losing their only child, for instance—they did not need to talk about, at least not now, for every word and movement between them carried their history and their future, like background movement, shaping each moment even when they weren't aware of it.

BABA YAGA

She might not be able to get past their defenses, but she could still listen to their conversations, and so she knew they had a ticket scheduled for the next day's flight. Within a couple of hours she was at the airport, and a helpful clerk stayed late to arrange her own reservation on the same flight, though afterward he had a terrible time trying to explain to his wife why he was so late getting home from work, having no memory of the time he spent with Baba Yaga.

She spent the rest of the night at the airport, preparing the spells and charms for the next day's work. Ivan and Katerina were going back to Taina, yes, but on her terms, not theirs. Baba Yaga would not come home empty-handed. She'd get the princess because she had the scholar—for now that Ruthie had uttered his true name in front of her familiar, he would not be able to resist her when she put a binding on that name.

Not only that, but she was determined to bring back one of the huge flying houses that moved on chicken legs. All the kings of the earth would bow down to her when she had a castle that carried her wherever she wanted to go, even into the heart of their kingdoms.

15

HIJACKING

 van and Katerina didn't pack much for the return trip. Katerina had quite a lot of American clothes now, but she wasn't going to be wearing them long. They knew they had to get back to the bridge as soon as possible. Once they left the protection of Mother's house, Baba Yaga could make a run at them anywhere. Yet there was no way to avoid the exposure. As Mother put it, "She found out that you were in America. She got here somehow. She found out about Ruthie and got to *her*. We're not going to keep many secrets from her. All you can do is try to move fast enough that she can't get ahead of you and lay traps."

So they made the reservation and paid for first-class seats even though it cost ten thousand dollars—because those were the only seats they could find on the fifth of July. Ivan was cautious to please even his mother: He wrote a note on a napkin explaining to Katerina and his parents that they would fly out of Rochester instead of Syracuse even though it was an hour farther away. Then he soaked the note in water and ran it down the garbage disposal. Then he made the reservation over the Internet so no one ever said "Rochester" out loud. With any luck, Baba Yaga would never realize that they didn't have to depart from the same airport they arrived at.

Mother and Father drove them, and on the way, Mother sat in the back with Katerina, explaining the charms and talismans, spells and wards she had prepared. "I can't take any of these across the bridge," said Katerina.

"I know," Mother replied, "but I'd like you to live to *reach* the bridge."

She had made two of almost everything, so each was wearing one. The most important was the one she called Aware.

"I thought of making Suspicion for you both, but that just makes you jumpy and it would weaken your trust in each other. Also, she can nullify it if she has a strong enough Friend charm. So this is best. It's not very specific, but that's good, because we never know what she's going to throw at you."

Katerina held the little woven mat to her forehead and closed her eyes. "This is very strong," she said. "Very clever."

"Put it on," said Mother.

They hung the strings around their necks, letting the charms fall inside their clothing. "I hope I'm not allergic to any of the materials," said Ivan.

"I practice hypoallergenic magic," said Mother—in English, because she had no clue how to say it in proto-Slavonic. Of course, that only meant that Ivan had to spend a few frustrating minutes explaining the whole concept of allergies to Katerina so she wouldn't feel left out of the joke.

The last charm was one for Katerina alone. "I know this one," she said.

"It's called Little One," said Mother.

"Do I need it?" asked Katerina.

"Are you sure that you don't?" asked Mother.

Katerina put it on.

"What?" asked Ivan. "What is it and why don't I have one?"

Katerina laughed. "Is there a chance that you're pregnant?"

"You tell *me*," said Ivan. "I don't know which rules apply anymore."

"Magic has never improved on *that*," said Katerina.

"Nor on the method of conception," said Father. "Though I think we can safely say that science has done a better job of reducing the hazards of bearing children than magic ever did."

"Though science presents its own set of hazards," said Mother. It was an old argument between them, and it was settled this time with a wink and a grin.

Everything went smoothly at the airport. They weren't as familiar with Rochester, only using its airport occasionally to meet visitors who couldn't easily connect through Syracuse. So Ivan wasn't sure he'd recognize if Baba Yaga had altered anything. He was wearing Aware, but it didn't make him feel any sharper-witted than usual. Maybe that meant nothing unusual had happened; maybe it meant he was always so alert that magic couldn't improve on his normal abilities; or maybe it meant Baba Yaga was smarter than Mother. Ivan preferred to think that Baba Yaga was off in Syracuse, watching for them.

They checked in, but then waited in another gate area until their plane had been mostly boarded. Then they kissed and hugged and the women cried a little and Father held on to Ivan a little more than usual. They all knew this might be the last time they ever saw each other. They knew that if Ivan and Katerina got back to Taina and died there, the only hint of it would be when Mother failed to find Ivan's image in the blackwater bowl.

Ivan watched everything, even glancing into the pilots' cabin for a moment, though he had no clue how he'd know if anything were wrong. What did he expect to see, Baba Yaga herself, sitting in the pilot's seat and cackling madly, "I'll get you, my pretty, and your little dog, too!" Come to think of it, she *had* gotten the little dog, even if it wasn't theirs.

They flew from Rochester to Kennedy without a hitch. Not even the turbulence that had marred the transatlantic flight before. Katerina already knew the rules about seatbelts and when to stow luggage. "You're getting to be an old hand at this," he said.

"I hope I get to use the skill many times in the future," she replied.

Ivan thought about this for a moment. "You mean you want to come back?"

"Don't you think our children should know your parents as well as they know mine?"

"If they can," said Ivan. "I didn't know you'd want to."

"Not like this," said Katerina. "Not watching out for the Widow all the time. But yes, they should fly through the air."

Kennedy was its normal nightmarish self, probably the worst airport Ivan ever flew through. It wasn't as bad leaving as it was arriving, which is rather like saying tuberculosis doesn't kill you as fast as pneumonia. There was the normal chaos and tumult at the gate, and the six-mile walk down tubes and ramps before they got to the airplanes, which apparently parked in Sag Harbor. Through it all, Ivan and Katerina watched everyone and everything that happened; but Ivan knew that it was primarily his responsibility, since he was the more experienced flyer and would be more likely to know if something was wrong.

The maddening thing was that they had no idea what they were looking for. Baba Yaga herself? She could look like anybody, or make herself unnoticeable. Some sabotage to the plane? As if either of them could tell! A passenger or crew member under Baba Yaga's spell? Maybe they could detect that. Or maybe not. They certainly hadn't guessed about Ruthie, and Ivan knew her well. He did notice that she was acting strange—in retrospect, the picnic was an absurd idea even if nothing had been booby-trapped. But Ivan had made allowances for her because he felt guilty. With strangers, guilt wouldn't be clouding the issue.

Ivan had thought first class was nice on the plane from Rochester— roomy seats, a better variety of snacks. As they settled into their places on the international flight, everything was so cushy Ivan began to wonder if the flight attendant planned to sing them to sleep. There were bags for their shoes, a toothbrush and toothpaste, and all kinds of completely useless amenities, including strange aromatherapy soaps and lotions. Katerina looked at them with suspicion, but after opening each one she pronounced them safe. "Except that they all smell as bad as a skunk," she said. Apparently perfume would be a tough sell in Taina.

"Look," said Ivan. "You push a button, and a thing comes out for you to rest your feet on."

Katerina loved it. But then she grew serious. "Look at us," she said. "How alert are we being now?"

"She's still in Tantalus or Syracuse," said Ivan. "We've lost her."

"No," said Katerina. "It's not that easy. Not with her." She unfastened her seatbelt and started to sidle past him to the aisle.

"Where are you going?" asked Ivan.

"To walk through the plane," she said. "To see if I notice anything."

"I'll come with you."

"No," she said. "One of us stays here to guard our place. So she can't leave a curse for us here."

"Then I'll walk the plane," said Ivan. "I'm more likely to notice if something is wrong."

She agreed. Ivan got up and walked back into coach. People were still boarding, but the crowd was thinner—most people were in their seats. At the back, Ivan scanned the lavatories. He even thought of lifting the toilet lids, and then laughed at himself for such an absurd idea—and then had to go in and lift every last one of them, because once he had thought of it, he had to do it, in case it was Aware that had caused him to pick up on some subliminal clue. Naturally, the toilets were normal—stained with blue fluid, in rooms so tiny that you had to be a ballet dancer to turn around. There was nothing wrong with them that hadn't started at the design phase.

"Is something wrong?" asked the flight attendant behind him.

"No," said Ivan. He came out of the bathroom.

"It's a good time to take your seat, sir," she said.

He was a little embarrassed, but now it felt all the more urgent to him that he check every toilet. Yet he had already checked every one of them, hadn't he?

On impulse, he asked the flight attendant, "How many lavatories are there back here?"

"Just here in the back?" she asked. "Six."

"That's funny," said Ivan. "I only counted five."

"You only need one at a time, anyway," she said with a smile.

"Really? Six?"

Humoring him, she pointed to them all in turn. "One, two, three, four, five. See?"

"OK," he said. It was clear she had no idea what she had just said.

He needed to get her out of the way. "Do I have time to use one?" he asked.

"If you're quick." She smiled her official smile—the one that said "You're an idiot but I'm paid to be nice to you"—and went back up the aisle, helping people settle in.

Ivan thought about what had just happened. Or tried to. His brain was a muddle, suddenly. She *had* said there were six bathrooms, hadn't she? He tried to count them. He placed a hand on each door and said the number. And he got to six, all right. But had he counted one of them twice? Had he touched every door?

And then he realized. It didn't matter where the missing bathroom was, or even if there was a bathroom missing. The flight attendant had said six and then counted five. He himself was confused about what was before his eyes. Maybe it was just nerves or carelessness. But maybe it wasn't. And Ivan wasn't taking any chances.

He walked briskly to the front of the plane. The flight attendant was about to close the door. "Wait," he said to her. "We're getting off."

"What? Why?" she demanded.

"It doesn't matter," he said. "We've decided not to go."

"You're going to delay the whole flight," she said. "We can't take off until we've found your luggage underneath and removed it."

"It doesn't matter. We're getting off."

He took a step toward first class to get Katerina, but out of the corner of his eye he saw the flight attendant resume closing the door. He whirled around. "If you close that door I'll sue the airline and you for kidnapping!"

"What are you talking about?" she said.

"I asked you not to close the door."

"I have to close the door. We can't take off unless we close the door."

Another flight attendant came up to him. "Sir, please take your seat now."

"I'm not flying on this plane! I'm getting off! I told her not to close the door, I have to get my wife. She doesn't speak English. We're not taking this flight."

"Of course, sir. Even though that will be an inconvenience to everyone else, since we have to wait while your luggage is unloaded, and—"

"The other flight attendant already explained that," said Ivan.

"Honestly," the first one said, "he never said a word about it to me."

To Ivan, the confusion, the forgetfulness—they were proof that he was absolutely right. There was magic on this plane, and he was not going to be in it when it took off. He couldn't walk away from the door of the plane or they would forget that he was leaving and close it—and he knew that once it closed, they would cite FAA regulations or some such nonsense and refuse to open it again. Yet he also was quite sure that if he sent one of them to get Katerina, she'd forget what she was doing before she got to Katerina's seat, or screw it up in some other way.

So he called out. Not Katerina's name, because there was a chance Baba Yaga, who was almost certainly hiding in a bathroom stall, could hear him. So he called, "Ruthie!" And again. And a third time, until finally Katerina turned around. He beckoned to her. She unfastened her seatbelt and came toward him. "Bring your things," he said, when she was close enough to hear a whisper. "Hurry."

She rushed back to their places, pulled everything out from under the seats, and came back. The whole time, Ivan had to keep saying, "My wife is coming, she's getting our things, please be patient, don't close the door." As long as he kept talking, they remembered that he was leaving. If he left a pause, they forgot everything and he had to start all over.

Only when they were physically off the plane, standing at the entrance, did the flight attendants finally recover their short-term memory. Now they were quite cold to him and Katerina. But despite all the folderol, the baggage compartment hadn't even been closed yet, and it took only a couple of minutes for one of the baggage handlers to return with the two small suitcases they had checked. Bags in hand, Ivan and Katerina hurried back along the ramp and the tunnel just far enough for the flight attendants to stop glaring at them and get back to business. There the two of them waited until the door of the plane closed. Then they quickly made their way back to the gate, where the clerk at the desk demanded an explanation of why they had changed their minds about the flight.

"I'm superstitious," Ivan finally said. "This didn't feel like a lucky plane to me."

"You realize that a report will be filed on this," said the clerk.

"I'm counting on it," said Ivan. "And now, would you be kind enough to book us on the next flight?"

"How will I know if it's lucky?" he said sarcastically.

"I'll tell you before takeoff," said Ivan.

Only then did Katerina get to ask him what it was that made him get off the plane. He tried to describe what happened at the lavatories, and to his relief, she agreed with him immediately. "You were right. It might not have been her, but if it was, that's just how you would feel. Confused."

"The frightening thing is how close I came to not even noticing it."

"You're not supposed to notice it. That's what the Widow's spells are all about."

"So was it Mother's Aware charm that did it?"

Katerina smiled. "Remember telling me about vaccinations? Well, when you don't get the disease, do you know whether it was the vaccination that saved you, or just that you never happened to catch it?"

Ivan grinned. "And to think you never even went to college."

When the tickets were changed to a flight two days later—the next day's flight was full—Ivan was faced with the problem of what to do in New York for two days. Not that he would mind holing up in a hotel with Katerina—in fact, that was his preferred solution—but he didn't have the money for it. So he did what every self-respecting young husband would have done in such a situation. He phoned his parents.

They told him to call back in fifteen minutes to find out where to pick up the money they were wiring. He and Katerina browsed around the shops. That's where they were when they began to notice airline personnel scurrying around quite urgently, and a buzz of conversation, knots of people jabbering about something. It was probably just Aware still working on him, Ivan thought. Until the clerk from the gate pointed out Ivan and Katerina to a couple of security guards, who approached quickly with their hands on their guns, ready to draw. "Ivan Smetski and Katerina Taina?" asked the one.

"Is there a problem here?" asked Ivan.

"We need to talk to the two of you," said the security guard. "Separately."

"Good luck," said Ivan. "My wife doesn't speak English."

"We'll get an interpreter."

"No you won't," said Ivan. "Because she speaks an obscure dialect of Russian, and I guarantee you that the only person in New York City who speaks it, besides her, is me."

It took an hour for them to believe him, and another half hour of intense questioning about why they left the plane. Katerina tried to ask him what was going on, but they were quick to stop any crosstalk between them. "You will *only* interpret what we ask and what she answers," the interrogator insisted.

Finally they explained why they were so intensely interested in Ivan and Katerina. The airplane that they had left just before takeoff lost radio contact over the ocean. It also disappeared from radar. A massive search was under way, and no debris had yet been found, but they were acting under the assumption that the plane had gone down. And the two people who got off in a rush at the last second were obviously the ones they were most anxious to talk to.

It solved the question of what they would do with their time in New York, at least for the first day. Once Ivan realized what was happening, he called his father, who contacted friends who arranged for a very high-powered attorney to be in attendance for the rest of the questioning. Ivan scarcely had a chance to learn the man's name, because once he was there, the questioning was pretty much over. Ivan and Katerina had both made their statements, Ivan faithfully translating all of Katerina's recollections, even when they differed from his in some detail or other. He figured that it was more plausible if they weren't completely in unison than if they were suspiciously identical. And since their checked bags had been removed from the plane, it was hard to see how they could have caused whatever the problem was.

And that was the clincher, as far as their attorney was concerned.

"You don't even know what happened to the airplane, and here you are questioning these two honeymooners as if you had some evidence linking them to a bomb. You not only don't have a link, you don't even have a bomb."

As they were leaving the interview room for the last time, one of the men who had been fairly quiet until now stopped Ivan at the door. "Please," he said. "I know you didn't cause it. But you've got to admit, you're the luckiest person on that airplane. Why did you get off? What triggered it? It could help us to know what happened to the plane."

"Honestly," said Ivan, "it was just a feeling I had. Muddled. Confused. A sense that something was there that shouldn't be. If I had actually seen something, don't you think I would have warned the crew?"

All of which was true. And anything more he might have told the man, he wouldn't have believed anyway, so what was the point of that? There was a ninth-century witch in one of the bathrooms with a spell of unnoticeability on her, but I trumped it with my mother's charm of awareness.

Yeah, right.

Ivan was just glad that they couldn't make him take a lie-detector test, because he was sure he would have failed that miserably.

They got the money from Western Union, which made Ivan feel guilty, because his parents weren't exactly wealthy. Ivan didn't take Katerina into Manhattan. Instead they found a place farther out on Long Island. Not easy to do, since it was the height of the beach season. But if you stay far enough inland, the motels empty out a little.

They didn't stay in their room the whole time, though. Katerina needed the outdoors, and so did Ivan—he'd spent these past weeks cooped up in house or yard, unable to run every day for the first time in years. They felt safe from Baba Yaga, and so they went out, Ivan to run, Katerina to walk and enjoy the good weather. She tried to run alongside him at first, but she didn't see the pleasure in it. For her, fitness came naturally, from work, not from play.

In the park there were more kites, and Ivan remembered that he had wanted to learn how to make a hang glider. He found a couple of books on hang gliding in a store and figured he could read them during the rest of the trip.

At night, Ivan and Katerina speculated on what Baba Yaga had done to the plane. Ivan explained about how terrorists blew up planes sometimes, which made Katerina sick at heart to hear about it. "Like

Attila the Hun," she said—for Attila was still the bugbear of tales to frighten children, in those centuries before the Mongols came. "Slaughtering everyone. Laying waste to everything."

"The Widow wouldn't do that?"

"Why would she? What would it accomplish? We weren't on the plane."

"Did she *know* we weren't on the plane?" asked Ivan.

"*She* was on the plane. She didn't blow it up."

"Then what happened to it?"

Katerina shrugged. "Maybe she took it home with her."

"Took it home? Passengers and all? What did she do, put it in a sack and sling it over her shoulder?"

"I don't know."

"We can't even take our clothes with us from one world to the other. She can take a 747?"

Katerina smiled thinly. "What the Widow wants, the Widow takes."

The next morning, the seventh of July, Ivan looked for the small carry-on bag that he had filled with reading material for the trip, along with a couple of gifts for Marek and Sophia. He wanted to add the hang-gliding books to the bag. But he couldn't find it anywhere.

Only then did he realize that Katerina had only gathered up their belongings from under the seats in front of theirs. She probably hadn't even seen him put that bag in the overhead compartment. And he had forgotten completely that it existed until this very moment.

For one horrible instant he wondered if Baba Yaga had somehow put a bomb in that bag, so that Ivan really had carried it onto the plane. But no, Katerina was right, it couldn't have been an explosion. The bag was just an oversight.

An oversight? "Katerina," he said, "shouldn't Aware have told me that I was leaving that bag on the plane?"

"Yes," she said, looking as worried as he felt. "But I *didn't* notice you put it in the overhead, or if I did I forgot—that shouldn't have happened, either."

"And I didn't remember it for two days. Just as well—if I'd thought of it while they were questioning us and blurted something out about leaving one little bag on the plane, they would never have let us go."

Katerina slipped Aware off and looked at it. "This has to be the charm that let you notice the Pretender was there, or at least notice that you were being kept from noticing. So why didn't it make us aware that we were leaving the bag?"

"It makes no sense for the Widow to let us go, but keep our bag," said Ivan.

"Maybe it does," said Katerina. "Tell me everything that was in the bag."

He sat down and methodically wrote down everything. Nothing offered the slightest clue as to what Baba Yaga might have wanted with the bag, until Ivan remembered one last item. "I put that message from Baba Tila in there, too," he said. "Along with the gifts for Marek and Sophia. Because I wanted to ask them about it."

Katerina thought about that for a few minutes. "So, whatever that message meant, the Pretender just took it to Taina."

"How did she even know I had it?" asked Ivan.

"Who says she did know?" said Katerina. "We still don't know who the message is for, or who it's from. It might have nothing to do with her. But if it's supposed to be delivered to somebody in Taina, putting it on a plane that the Widow took back with her is the only way it could ever be delivered. Since you and I certainly couldn't have taken it with us."

"So we're back to your theory that some fate is helping us."

"It makes me wonder if maybe we should have *stayed* on the plane."

"No," said Ivan. "Absolutely not. The Widow doesn't control the bridge. That's why we have to get to Taina that way. On the airplane, even if she took us there, we'd arrive as her prisoners."

"Yes, you're right," said Katerina.

"That bag I left on the plane, that message—I just hope it *was* some kindly fate helping us. Because if it wasn't, then the likeliest outcome is that my boneheaded blunder might cost us dearly somewhere along the line."

"*Your* blunder? Give me my share of the credit."

They went to the airport early. Some of the same clerks were on duty, watching Ivan and Katerina very carefully, but treating them with more politeness than usual, which, at Kennedy, isn't a hard standard to surpass. Ivan and Katerina were, for their part, just as careful as before, but this time there was no sign of danger, before and after they boarded the plane.

It began to look as though Katerina might be right, that Baba Yaga had disappeared right along with that first plane, back to the ninth century. Which meant that maybe they wouldn't have to worry again until they crossed the bridge.

They were so relaxed, they even slept on the flight. And when they finally got to Cousin Marek's house, exhausted from travel and from too much alertness, he confirmed it for them. "She's no longer in this world. But when she left, she didn't leave alone."

"So she took the passengers with her?" asked Ivan.

"They're all back there, where she is," said Marek. "Poor things."

"What can we do? How can we bring them back?"

"Two ways," said Marek. "First, you persuade old Yaga to send them back."

"All right, we'll do that," said Ivan.

Katerina looked at him as if he were insane.

"I was joking."

"What's the other way?" Katerina asked Cousin Marek.

"Break her power," said Marek.

"Bring me the broomstick of the Witch of the West," said Ivan.

"What?"

"A movie. *The Wizard of Oz.* The only way to break her power is to kill her, isn't it?"

Marek shrugged. "That would certainly work. But I can't tell you that it's the only way."

"Do you know of another?"

"I'm only a god, Vanya, not an expert."

With Baba Yaga no longer gunning for them, they didn't have quite the same urgency to get back. Whatever mischief she was doing in Taina, time flowed differently there from here, and so hurrying made no sense, if something could be gained by lingering.

And something could, Ivan hoped. Together Cousin Marek and Ivan and a couple of other farmers from the area worked on making a hang glider out of available wood—some seasoned lumber for the most rigid heart of the frame, but the rest springier, newer wood, thin wands of it. And tightly woven fabric—cotton for now, but rough linen would have to do, when they got to Taina. Unless they could find silk. Katerina remembered that she had once seen a length of imported silk. If it was still there, not cut up into too many smaller pieces, they might be able to use it.

They had sense enough not to make the test flights by jumping off cliffs, and after several tries, they were able to make a glider that worked. Katerina insisted on learning to fly it, too, and while neither of them became brilliant at it, they also didn't die, which was how you graduated from a do-it-yourself hang-gliding school, Ivan figured.

They knew all that they could think of that might be useful. They had done all they could think of to prepare and practice and plan. There was nothing but fear to hold them any longer, and so they decided, as one, that it was time to cross the bridge, this time as rulers of Taina, first to drive the usurpers out of power, and then to strike the blow that would set them free of Baba Yaga once and for all.

Or they'd die trying.

BABA YAGA

It was not until the house-that-flies was in the air that Baba Yaga ventured out of the bathroom to walk the aisles. She had had a shaky moment when the boy stood right outside the door of the restroom where she was hiding. The spells that his mother had prepared for him were powerful, and she could feel how the Aware spell struggled against her Oblivious. When he went away, though, she was sure he hadn't seen her. She only wished she could understand what they were saying.

Seats 2-A and 2-B. Empty.

Were they simply out of their seats? In the bathroom? Visiting the cockpit?

No and no. They had left the plane. They were nowhere on it.

Baba Yaga was filled with helpless rage. All of last night's work had been for nothing. She was sure Ivan had said they had their reservation, and yet their names were nowhere in the computers. Only when she redoubled the spell of helpfulness on the stupid weary ticket agent did he come up with the bright idea that maybe they had flown from a different airport.

Baba Yaga finally found their reservation—but not till they had already taken off from Rochester. As it was, she had to scramble to catch a Syracuse flight that would get her to Kennedy before they embarked on the transatlantic leg of their journey. She was angry that they had tricked her—not just that they had succeeded, but that they had dared to try—but they hadn't eluded her for long. It was the big transatlantic plane that she wanted, anyway.

Now to find that they had gotten off the flight was almost unbearable. She screamed and ranted all the way up and down the plane, spewing nauseating, annoying little curses between screeches. Nobody noticed her, of course, and all the spell-casting left her exhausted. She could barely sustain Shadow by the time she was done. But it didn't matter. In a few minutes she and the plane would be back in her own world—the world where Bear could replenish her strength whenever she needed. And casting the spell to bring it all home would be easy enough. She had the cloth already prepared, hadn't she? And sooner or later, Ivan and Katerina would return to Taina. It would have been nice to destroy them in Ivan's world, but in the end, destroying them in Taina would have the added benefit of demoralizing the entire population of Taina. It was really better this way. They had escaped one trap, but inevitably they would walk into another, sooner rather than later. And in Taina, there'd be no more interference from the mousy little witch Ivan called Mother.

When the seatbelt light went dark and people started moving around again, Baba Yaga began following one of the flight attendants around, filling her with wordless curiosity, along with images of the pilot as the man with the answers. And when the flight attendant finally went to the cockpit, Baba Yaga didn't have to understand English to know what was being said, for she was feeding the girl questions below the level of language.

"What is the head of the plane?" asked the flight attendant.

The pilot looked at her as if she were insane.

Baba Yaga cast Understanding on him, which in her weakened state didn't confer actual comprehension, but did make him listen attentively, setting aside biases and expectations that would have interfered. In the end, the pilot told her, "The thing that leads the plane is me, and the tool I use to do it is this." He pointed to the thing that looked something like a car steering wheel.

At once the flight attendant relaxed, then looked confused. "What am I doing up here? Did you want something?"

"No," said the pilot, laughing. "We didn't want anything."

"Then you shouldn't have called me," she said. She rushed out of the cockpit, embarrassed.

The pilot only had time to say "I think somebody's been hitting the bottle" before Baba Yaga, unnoticeable as ever, leaned over his shoulder and draped a small cloth over the control that he had indicated. Baba Yaga herself might be weak here, but the cloth had been given its power at a time when she had her full strength. It would do its work. The plane and everything in it would follow where the cloth took them.

Home.

One moment they were flying over the Atlantic, still not quite out of the sight of land. The next moment, they were in the air over the deep forest of western Rus'. The panic in the cockpit lasted only until Baba Yaga cast off Shadow and revealed herself. For in the transition from one world to the other, the power of Bear had flooded back into her. She felt like a girl again; all the weariness was gone. And now it was a simple matter to impose Understanding on the pilot, the crew, and all the passengers—not just openness, but real comprehension of every word she spoke, though not one of them spoke her language.

"I have brought you here. Take me to my kingdom!"

They seemed reluctant at first. Not until the copilot and several flight attendants were vomiting or dancing around insanely did the pilot really understand the kind of power he was dealing with. And the pilot didn't actually get cooperative until she had given him a crippling rectal itch, which he had no choice but to scratch at savagely, until finally he persuaded Baba Yaga that yes, he would take her wherever she wanted to go, and no, he would not make any more foolish demands about taking them back to Kennedy at once.

This was the primeval forest of Mother Russia. They circled around for many hours in search of a stretch of flat, treeless ground where a 747 could land. Finally the coming darkness of night forced a decision—a meadow that wasn't really long enough or level enough, but it was their only chance. Baba Yaga helped with the landing, making it smoother than they had any right to expect, and then stopping it quite abruptly before they ran into the forest edge. She was in her strength again, her powers filling her, her spells as potent as ever, and she rather enjoyed the pain and panic and injuries suffered by the passengers because of the sudden stop. What she cared about was keeping the flying house from being damaged by a collision. The people were here only because they happened to be in the airplane when she took it. Though the sound of shrieking and weeping was music to her ears.

As the sounds of pain and panic died down, Baba Yaga seized the microphone and, with the help of a vigorous new spell of Understanding, she announced to the entire plane, "You have reached your final destination."

After the meaning of her announcement had a chance to sink in, the crying and screaming started up again in earnest.

16

RESTORATION

very morning Sergei arose at dawn and walked to the door of his hut to see if Ivan and the princess had returned. Every day, all he saw was the chasm, the empty pedestal, and no future at all for him and poor Father Lukas.

Who could have guessed that within days of Princess Katerina's departure, Dimitri would revolt? And who could have guessed that the moment he had power, Dimitri would declare Christianity to be a false religion and forbid its teaching in all of Taina? Father Lukas was all for becoming a martyr, and tried to persuade Sergei to do the same, but in the end it was Sergei who carried the day by asking which Christ would rather have, two dead clerics or two living missionaries who might someday restore Christianity in this benighted place?

Ever since then, they had been living in the one place Sergei knew that no man of Taina had ever succeeded in finding, at least not when the princess was lying here in enchanted slumber. Of course he was not so foolish as to tell Father Lukas of the significance of the place, just as he did not tell Father Lukas of the precious parchments hidden in a sack inside a box under a stone just inside the woods. To the priest, this was a place of penance and prayer. To Sergei, it was a rendezvous. Katerina and Ivan would come back, and when that happened, Dimitri's support would melt away. It was only with the princess gone that the people despaired and listened to his claim that they needed a strong warrior to save them from Baba Yaga. When Katerina returned, the people would flock to her again; indeed, they

were already deeply ashamed of having followed Dimitri, especially after he used some hideous magic to strike old King Matfei dumb, and
longed for—prayed for—her safe return.

So disgusted were they with Dimitri's strutting and boasting and
bossing and bullying that they even prayed for Ivan to come with her,
for they realized now that having a king meant more than leadership in
battle. King Matfei's hand had rested lightly upon them. Dimitri's hand
was not so deft.

And yet even he was better than Baba Yaga. So they did not revolt, not yet. And when Sergei crept back to the village to hear news
and gossip, he heard more and more resignation in the voices of those
he spoke to. They were still faithful Christians, they assured him. But
how could they shrug off Dimitri's kingship when Baba Yaga might return at any time?

For even those who did not believe in Katerina's return had no
doubt of Baba Yaga's. That's the way of the world: The princess can
disappear, but the witch is forever.

So it was that the two clerics dwelt in the hut that Sergei built, living on whatever herbs and berries, roots and mushrooms Sergei could
find in the forest. Neither of them was much of a cook, either, so the
only seasoning that made the food palatable was starvation. They both
grew thinner; Father Lukas lost the rest of his hair; and Sergei had
dreams of naked women coming to him in the night, so that he hardly
slept at all, what with Father Lukas shaking him and demanding that he
stop having dreams of pleasure at a time like this. It was hard for Sergei
to figure out how hell might be worse.

This morning, like so many others, Sergei staggered out of the
hut at first light, looked to see if by any chance Katerina and Ivan were
back, then walked over to the edge of the chasm, lifted his robe, and
relieved himself of the night's urine. That's what he was doing when
Ivan and Katerina suddenly appeared out of nowhere, stepping onto
the pedestal from an invisible bridge.

"Sergei," said Ivan.

Startled, Sergei dropped his robe, which meant he peed all over
the inside of it. Inadvertently he cursed, and then forgot all about it,
because they were back. Even before they crossed over another invisible bridge to the side Sergei was standing on, he was shouting to them
the story of all that had happened. The tumult brought Father Lukas
out of his hut, and to Sergei's surprise the priest looked happy—no,
ecstatic. He almost danced he was so happy. It almost made Sergei
wish he had told Father Lukas of Katerina's promise to return—it

would have given him hope. But it also would have given Father Lukas something more to berate Sergei about. As if Sergei needed Father Lukas to tell him that if only he had told the truth to King Matfei about where Katerina and Ivan had gone, Dimitri might not have been able to win support and take over.

What Father Lukas didn't understand was that if Sergei had told, Dimitri would have been standing here with a sword when Ivan and Katerina arrived, and Ivan's head would have rolled into the chasm within moments.

For half an hour they all talked—or rather, Sergei and Father Lukas talked while Katerina and Ivan listened, saying little, but looking more sorrowful and more grimly determined as each tale unfolded. Finally, Katerina turned to Ivan and said, "You see? Maybe it's Christ who has been helping us all along, for unless we defeat the Pretender, Christianity is lost in this part of the world."

"Baba Yaga isn't the problem of the moment," said Father Lukas. "There's plenty of time to drive out the servants of the devil from other kingdoms, once we rid ourselves of the devil in our midst."

"Dimitri," Sergei explained.

"Poor man," said Ivan.

"You pity him?" said Katerina. "After what he did to my father?"

"And you would be wise to pity him, too," said Ivan. "He isn't the first person that the Widow has deceived into acting in a way that he never would have on his own."

"He shriveled my father's tongue in his mouth," said Katerina.

"Did he know the spell would do that?" said Ivan. "Or was he like Ruthie, who never knew what she was doing?"

Clearly Ivan and Katerina had had experiences of their own since leaving Taina. But this discussion was leading nowhere. "The story is that the Pretender returned yesterday, with more magic than ever," said Sergei.

"Only yesterday?" asked Katerina. "That's good."

"Good?"

"She left the land where Ivan's family lives more than a week ago. We were afraid she would strike before we could get back."

"They say she has a huge new house that walks around on chicken legs. It's as white as snow and as hard as a sword's blade. So they say," said Sergei.

"Gossip spreads fast," said Ivan.

"She wanted everyone to know," said Katerina. "She probably spread the stories herself."

"The question is," said Ivan, "will we have time to prepare before she attacks?"

"Who knows?" said Katerina. "All we can do is work as quickly as we can and hope that it's enough time."

"But that's all the more reason to be merciful to Dimitri," said Ivan. "We don't have time to deal with putting down a revolt. Pardon him, forgive all who followed him, and then concentrate on finding the materials we need."

"If only we could have made them there and brought them with us," said Katerina.

"In what pockets?" asked Ivan. The two of them laughed ruefully.

Sergei was surprised at how many words the two of them used that he had never heard before. What happened to them while they were gone? Whatever it was, one thing was plain: They liked each other now. No, they loved each other. Sergei could see it in the way Katerina looked at Ivan, in the way Ivan oriented himself around her at every moment. It was as if she was now included within his protective circle—though a look at Ivan's arms showed that he hadn't acquired the muscles of a swordsman.

"You're wearing that robe I burned on your wedding day," said Father Lukas. "I thought Brother Sergei had it last."

"Well, nobody wants *this* robe," said Sergei, hoping that joking about his peed-on clothing would distract Father Lukas from the nastiness that Sergei could see coming.

It didn't work. Father Lukas simply ignored him. "It seems that Sergei kept *secrets* from me."

"If he did," said Katerina, "it was at my command, Father Lukas."

"You have no authority over a scribe's truthfulness to his priest," said Father Lukas mildly.

Ivan made as if to answer then, but Katerina raised a hand, just slightly, and Ivan immediately fell silent, deferring to her. "Father Lukas, when a subject gives obedience to his sovereign, yet in doing so commits no sin, does he have anything to confess?"

"The sin was in not telling me," said Father Lukas, growing grumpier.

"Then perhaps you don't wish to have me rule as a Christian sovereign in Taina," said Katerina. "For I could never rule if I thought my subjects owed obedience to the priest before me."

"Sergei is a cleric," said Father Lukas.

"Tell me now," said Katerina. "Are clerics subject to my rule or not? If not, then I won't bother trying to restore Christianity to Taina.

It would be a seditious influence, for everyone who took holy orders would believe himself to owe no further obedience to the king."

Father Lukas realized the dilemma he had placed himself in.

"Either priests are subject to kings in whatever land you visit, or you are not, and if you are not, then God and his angels had better help you, for no mortal force can do it."

"I beg your forgiveness, Princess," said Father Lukas. "I spoke in the midst of annoyance at having been kept in the dark. Of course Sergei acted properly in obeying you."

Katerina said nothing, merely waited. He had apparently left something out.

In a few moments he figured out what it was. "And I, of course. I am also your good subject while I dwell in Taina."

Katerina immediately smiled and took his hands. "Ah, my dear confessor, it will be the great joy of my life to be the instrument of the Lord in restoring the gospel of Jesus Christ to its rightful primacy in the land God has given my family to rule."

Sergei had never seen Father Lukas openly humbled before. It was refreshing. It filled Sergei with optimism for the future. Katerina did know how to rule. If both her husband and Father Lukas deferred to her, then there was hope that Dimitri and Baba Yaga might also someday bow.

Baba Yaga? I'm a fool, thought Sergei.

And yet, was God not more powerful than kings or wizards? And was it not embedded somewhere in natural law that goodness must ultimately prevail over evil? If not, then natural law was poorly planned, in Sergei's opinion. A second-rate creation. If even he, a poor fool of a scribe, could imagine a better universe, then any Creator who was worth worshiping must be able to do as well. Therefore, God must have so ordained this world, and that gave hope to the righteous no matter how bleak their cause.

If, in fact, we are the righteous.

But Sergei quickly put *that* doubt out of his mind. Between the people of Taina, with all their sins and pride and weakness and fear, and Baba Yaga, there was no question about which was on God's side.

"May I ask," said Sergei to Katerina, "what we are to call you now? With your father muted by the Pretender's spell, who will be the king that leads us into war?"

"My father is still the king," said Katerina. "He may have lost his speech, but he can read and write, and so can I, and so can Ivan. We will learn his will and obey him."

"But in battle, who will lead?"

Katerina did not so much as glance at Ivan. "Whoever is most fit to fulfil my father's will."

Yes, she was already queen, for she had mastered the art of answering honestly without answering at all.

When Ivan saw Sergei there waiting for them, he was just as glad that he and Katerina had clothes on both sides of the bridge now. Let someone else be humiliated—Ivan had had his fill of it. He was coming back now to the place he had fled to save his life, a place where he was despised, resented, or pitied, but not respected. And somehow he had to lead these people in creating new technologies, learning to use them, and then deploying them in battle.

At least this time he'd have Katerina solidly on his side. It was such a relief, not to be alone. He hoped she felt the same, that having him beside her was a strength, and not a burden. There was no point in asking her—she would say he was a help to her, and would even mean it. Whether it was true would be revealed by events.

Baba Yaga knew they were back, but they weren't in Taina yet, not in the village, and Ivan and Katerina had already planned that they would not return until they had some of their new weapons ready. Otherwise, they would have to face Dimitri with nothing but Katerina's will and the people's love for her. Both were strong—but Dimitri would claim to be the only one who could stand against Baba Yaga, and fear of the witch might well prevail over love for Katerina. Especially with Ivan standing beside Katerina, reminding everyone of his weakness. No, they had to have something more.

Now they had Sergei and Father Lukas to help them, at least by tending fires and keeping watch over pots. Instead of searching for saltpeter first, Ivan began by constructing a distillery. There were items Sergei had to sneak into town to obtain, and some that he had to ask the smith to make for him, but the smith served the king and only obeyed Dimitri out of fear for his family—he was glad to help, especially when Sergei, following instructions, let slip the news that Katerina and Ivan were back.

"Where?" asked the smith.

"In the forest, biding their time," said Sergei. "Dimitri's days are numbered. Those who are wise would do well to prepare to follow Katerina when she returns."

The smith had his doubts, though. Until Sergei laughed. "Do you think Dimitri's sword will stand against the Widow's curses? Already he has been deceived by the witch and doesn't even know it. No, it takes a woman of power to stand against the wicked one."

There it was, the seed planted. When Sergei reported on the conversation, Ivan and Katerina were well satisfied. Word would spread. Many people would stop believing that Dimitri was their only hope. How could a soldier stand against a witch?

Running a still wasn't easy, but Father Lukas took to it naturally, even after he realized that the result would be an extremely potent beverage. The problem was supplying the still with fermentable foodstuffs. After a couple of days, Katerina authorized Sergei to bring a couple of teenage boys from the village, enlisting them as the first of her own druzhina, though their labor was pilfering grain sacks and toting them miles through the forest, rather than swordplay. "Whatever my people need, I do," she said, "and my druzhina will not be too good to do the same." They knew that she spoke the truth, and so they obeyed her and felt noble for doing it—as they should.

And in the process, they began to get to know Ivan. He made it a point never to command anyone, but always to ask; nor did he teach imperiously, but rather couched everything in phrases like, "The way I was taught . . ." or "I think it might work better if . . ." And then he got along with the young men, never pretending to be one of them, but enjoying their humor and refusing to become impatient with their playfulness.

So when it was time to pour alcohol into brittle pots and put in the fuses, the young men already liked Ivan. He showed them how to light the fuses and then throw the pots into the chasm. They were impressed, of course. But Ivan pointed out that they wouldn't be throwing them at rocks. "Imagine the old hag's knights receiving a dose of this."

The boys' eyes widened. And for the first time they realized that with weapons like these, boys might bring down mounted warriors. "We *are* her druzhina," said one of them. "I'd like to use this on Dimitri," said another.

"No," Ivan said. "Dimitri is one of our own."

"Not after what he did to King Matfei."

"Nevertheless, these weapons don't replace swords. We need his strength on our side."

Grudgingly they agreed. And then began to practice throwing stones of about the same weight as the Molotov cocktails, working on improving their aim.

Ivan had done a good job of learning the location of historically known mineral deposits in the area, and it took very little fumbling to get what he needed for gunpowder. Now that they had seen the Molotov cocktails, they took Ivan seriously when he warned them to handle the gunpowder carefully. Soon they were loading serious quantities of gunpowder into little bronze canisters with fuses. The smith couldn't spare any iron, for Dimitri would have noticed if it went missing, but bronze grenades would do well enough, Ivan figured. What mattered was shrapnel, to turn them from cherry bombs into legitimate weapons.

Since the fuse material was different, they had to practice to get the timing right. Soon, though, the boys were learning to throw grenades as well as cocktails, though they only practiced with tiny charges of gunpowder that went off with no more than a pop, and didn't damage the canisters. To everyone's surprise, Sergei emerged as one of the better throwers, and on some days the best.

"Time to return to Taina," Katerina announced, when their supply was adequate. "We must all return together, so let's close down the still." When the fires were out, they hid the unused gunpowder and the materials used to make it, then shouldered their bags of cocktails and grenades and made their way along Sergei's path through the woods.

Sergei had been careful never to follow the same route twice, so he couldn't easily be followed, but the boys had not been so careful. Clearly the only reason they had not been found was that some of the enchantment lingered, protecting their hiding place by the chasm. Now there would be no protection. And Ivan knew that Dimitri, having tasted power, would not surrender it easily. Especially if he feared that he would be punished for his treason. Katerina was still not fully persuaded that Dimitri should be pardoned, if he gave his word. "He has no honor now," she insisted. "His word will mean nothing, to him or to the people or to me."

"Maybe you're right," said Ivan. "But if he's a good man, then he'll take this opportunity to begin to restore his honor. And if he's not, then no one can say you didn't give him every chance."

"Every chance to do what? To stab us in the back?"

"Yes," said Ivan. "But we take that risk with anyone we trust."

"I don't trust Dimitri."

"Then do as you will," said Ivan. He could say that because he knew that she was still considering what he said. If she decided otherwise, he would never criticize her; if she agreed with him, it would be because she had come to believe he was right, and not because she wanted to please Ivan. She was the one whom the people followed,

Ivan knew. It was not his place to tell her how to do her work. It was the career she was born for and trained for. He was a novice. And yet, novice or not, she listened to his counsel, which was all he could ask for, when it came to leading the kingdom.

At the edge of the wood, they contemplated stopping and waiting till morning, but Katerina decided against it. "The Widow knows we're here. She's probably warned him already. So we must go on."

Ivan remembered well the first time he came with her into Taina. The people cheered her then, and only looked at Ivan with mild curiosity, as a naked stranger tagging along with their beloved Katerina. Now it was different. They were uncertain, and while a few people waved to her and called out her name, and all came out of their huts to watch, there was no cheering.

This was not good, and while Katerina could not ask for cheering, Ivan could. To the boys nearest him, he said, "Go into the crowd and raise a cheer for the princess, and then come back." They understood at once—public relations is one of the inborn human skills—and within moments there were loud cries and cheers and clapping of hands for the princess. All it took was for a few to raise their voices, and then the others took courage and joined in.

Now it was a triumphal march through the village to the king's house. But Dimitri was not there to greet them—nor was King Matfei. The house was empty.

"They're at the fortress," said Katerina. "It's a good sign. Dimitri didn't have confidence that the people would stay with him."

Katerina and Ivan led the way, Father Lukas after them, and the young druzhinniks close behind. Sergei could not keep up, but he had given the match—a lanternlike container alight with slow-burning fuel—to one of the boys, so they'd be able to light their fuses, if the need arose.

Dimitri met them standing at the gate, with King Matfei held between two strong men. Other soldiers waited inside the gate of the fort.

"I have come," Katerina said, "to report to the king my father and receive his instructions."

Dimitri shook his head. "King Matfei has been struck dumb by the gods because he allowed Christians to interfere with the ways of the people."

"If the gods have struck down my father the king, why do you need to keep him under guard?" asked Katerina. "The gods need no swords. Father Lukas carries none."

"We face a terrible enemy," said Dimitri. "Do you think Father Lukas can stand against the army of the witch?"

"I know that he would stand more bravely than one who strikes a cowardly blow against his own king," said Katerina.

Ivan did not like the way things were shaping up. Words of defiance would lead to a showdown, not to reconciliation. It was for Katerina to decide, but Ivan did not like their chances against Baba Yaga, if blood were spilled here today. "Dimitri," said Ivan.

"Ah," said Dimitri. "My pupil. Apprentice swordsman."

"And I'll never be master of that weapon, as you are," said Ivan. "I beseech you to turn your sword against the enemy, and stand beside your king as you have always done before."

"I stood beside my king until the king's daughter married a man who wears women's clothing." Some of the soldiers with Dimitri snickered at that.

"I have never dressed as a woman," said Ivan. "But I tell you I would rather wear a hoose every day of my life than bear the shame of taking up arms against my king."

A murmur from the crowd made it clear that Ivan's words had struck a responsive chord.

"*You* will never be my king," said Dimitri.

"But Dimitri," said Katerina, "if you remove my father as king, then by law my husband *will* be king, and it will be you who gave the crown to him."

"It's not his if he can't keep it," said Dimitri.

"The crown," said Katerina, "is only a symbol of the love and honor of the people. You can put it on, but it doesn't mean the people will follow you."

"When the Widow comes," Dimitri said, "they will follow me because I will stand against her."

"How long did you stand against her when she came to you with her lies? I can feel her magic on you, Dimitri. You already serve her will." Katerina turned and addressed the people. "Whom does it serve, to have our kingdom divided like this? Only the Pretender. So whose servant is Dimitri, and the soldiers who stand with him? The Widow's servants."

"You lie!" said Dimitri.

Katerina whirled back to face him. But it was to the soldiers behind him that she spoke now. "You are men of Taina, aren't you? Sworn to your king as his druzhina. I know that you meant only to serve the kingdom, and so I promise pardon to every man who lays down his sword, or puts it in my service now."

"Any man who moves to obey her dies!" cried Dimitri.

"How will that strengthen Taina," shouted Ivan, "if you begin to kill our soldiers!" It was Ivan's turn to address the people. "You heard him! He threatened to kill your sons and husbands and brothers! And for what crime? For daring to obey the king they swore an oath to!"

"Enough of this!" said Dimitri. "Enough talk! Surrender now, and I keep your father alive until the war is over. Then I will return the crown to him. But that one"—he pointed at Ivan with his sword— "that one must leave! Go back to where he came from! Annul the marriage, and I'll spare his life."

Before Katerina could answer, Ivan sprang forward. "When I fought the bear and freed Katerina from her enchantment, where were you?"

"Ivan!" cried Katerina. "Come back!"

Ivan pointed at one, then another of the boys with Molotov cocktails. He made the handsign they had agreed on—light the fuses.

"Dimitri!" he shouted. "You stand alone! For Katerina's true husband is the one who commands the gate of this fort!"

"You spoke truly!" said Dimitri. "The man who rules this gate is the one who should be Katerina's husband!"

"Agreed!" shouted Ivan. "Set this *gate* ablaze with Katerina's fire!" He gave the signal to throw. The boys had heard and understood. It was not at Dimitri that they threw the cocktails, but at the gate itself. Both pots flew true and broke against the lintel. Fire blazed all up and down the wooden gate.

"Pass through that gate if you dare!" cried Ivan.

"No man can!" Dimitri shouted back.

"I can!" Ivan cried, and he ran headlong at the gap between Dimitri and Matfei.

For a moment he feared that Dimitri would seize the opportunity to skewer him on his sword. But no—the fire had unnerved him, and he only watched as Ivan ran past him, past Matfei, straight into the flames.

He knew, of course, that the fire wouldn't have time even to singe his hair; and because it was an alcohol fire, it would quickly die back to nothing. Once inside the gate, however, the real challenge came. He turned quickly, looking every soldier there in the eye, if they dared to meet his gaze. "I passed through fire for the princess Katerina. What will you do? Who stands with her? All loyal men, to the walls, and cry the name of Katerina!"

With no weapon other than his voice, his courage, and his love for the princess who they also loved, Ivan faced them and prevailed. First one, then two, then a dozen, then all the soldiers ran to the wall, climbed it, and stood there with swords raised.

"Katerina!" they cried. And again, and again. "Katerina!"

Ivan could hear the chant being taken up by the people outside. He sauntered to the gate and passed through it, with only a few flames on the wooden posts to frame him.

"Katerina," he shouted, out of the rhythm of the chant, so she could hear him. He raised his hands for silence, and the chant subsided. "Katerina, princess of Taina, I give this fort to you!"

The soldiers and the people erupted in cheers.

The action had played out the way Katerina and Ivan had hoped. Ivan now stood as the man who had taken the fort away from Dimitri, who had helplessly watched him do it.

But Dimitri still had his sword, and Katerina's father, and the two soldiers who held the king between them. It was Katerina, now, who had to control the final scene of this dangerous play.

She stepped forward, putting herself almost within reach of a lunge from Dimitri's sword. "This is your last chance," said Katerina. "I only offer it to you because Ivan pleaded with me that we needed you beside us in the war against the witch. Command these last two soldiers to release my father, and then all three of you lay down your swords and pledge yourselves again to his service. Do this, and I will plead with my father to pardon you."

Before Dimitri could begin to obey, the two soldiers, who were not fools, let go of Matfei, knelt, and laid down their swords at the king's feet.

Dimitri was absolutely alone. He had his sword, and no doubt he could kill several, could kill the king himself, and Katerina, before other swords brought him down. But he would die if he did such a thing, for no one was likely to follow him now, still less if he had the blood of Matfei and Katerina on his hands.

He knelt. He laid his sword at Matfei's feet.

Ivan walked around this tableau of kneeling men and took his place at Katerina's side.

The face of King Matfei was filled with rage when he looked down at Dimitri kneeling at his feet. The king bent down and picked up Dimitri's own sword. He raised it over his head.

"Father," said Katerina. "I beseech you to spare the life of this man. His crime was grave indeed, and no one here has the power to restore the power of speech that he took away from you. He diminished you at a time when we needed you whole. And yet I plead with you—do not weaken Taina by one sword arm, not even his. Accept his vow of loyalty again, though he has broken that selfsame vow before. I beg you, Father, for the sake of your daughter, and of the grandchild that grows in your daughter's womb."

It was the first Ivan had heard that Katerina might be pregnant. And even now he wasn't sure, for she hadn't actually said that she had conceived a child—she might have been speaking of a child that would someday grow within her.

But her words had the desired effect. Matfei's rage turned to thoughts of his daughter, of his grandchild. What she asked for, he would give her.

For a moment Ivan felt a stab of regret. Things would be much simpler if Dimitri died right now.

Then, ashamed of the bloodthirsty thought, he stepped forward. "Matfei, my father, my king, and my lord," said Ivan, "may I have Dimitri's sword?"

Matfei lowered the sword, then laid it across Ivan's hands.

Ivan made no effort to put his hand on the hilt. Rather he kept the sword as he had received it, lying across his hands. Ivan turned back to face Katerina. "May I give this sword to the king's true servant?"

"You may," said Katerina. "When we hear his oath and his plea for pardon."

Dimitri did not hesitate. Weeping, he gave his fervent oath of loyalty to King Matfei, and to Katerina and Ivan too, for good measure. Then he begged for pardon for his dire offenses, and swore to be true to Christ as well, whose atoning sacrifice would make him clean again, if only the king would pardon him.

King Matfei, speechless still, nodded gravely.

"Let my husband, Ivan, return the sword of a true knight to you," said Katerina.

Ivan knelt before Dimitri, so their eyes were nearly level, though Ivan had the advantage of height, even kneeling. He held out the sword.

Dimitri took it from him. Tears flowed down his cheeks. He looked sincere. But beyond appearances, Ivan had no way of measuring Dimitri's heart. He had been humiliated here today. If he was a good man, he would now be the most fervently loyal soldier in Taina's army, the most faithful of King Matfei's druzhina. But if he was not a man of honor and goodness, he would already be plotting his revenge for this humiliation. Someone would die for this day's work. There'd be no more talk, if he betrayed the king again.

But for now, the appearance was all that counted. The king reached down and raised Dimitri up. Katerina did the same for Ivan. The four of them together turned to face the crowd. Only one more step was needed. Katerina reached out her hand to Father Lukas. The priest came forward and took his place between Katerina and her father, with Ivan on the other side of her, and Dimitri on the opposite end of the line, beside the king.

Katerina raised her voice and let it ring out across the crowd. "In the holy name of Christ our Savior, the kingdom of Taina is whole again!"

The cheers were deafening, as the people shouted. Taina! King Matfei! Katerina! Dimitri! Even the name of Ivan could be heard.

Their first victory together. And Katerina had chosen to heed his counsel. Now Ivan could only hope that his counsel had been wise, or, if he was wrong, that the price of Dimitri's pardon would not be too high.

BABA YAGA

"It's so good to be home, my love," she said to Bear. "Did you miss me?"

"I felt your absence every moment you were gone," said Bear.

"How ambiguous you are," said Baba Yaga. "But I'm content, for here you are, and here I am, and this is our happy home."

"I see a familiar thirst for blood in your eyes," said Bear.

"But not *your* blood, so you shouldn't mind," she said. "The pretty little princess and her husband have just defeated my puppet."

"You always said that he was just a toy to you," said Bear.

"Oh, I know. I didn't expect much. But I thought at least he'd go out with a splash of blood. That he'd kill the king, or at least that annoying Ivan, before he went down."

"It's always tragic when you don't get your way, my love," said Bear.

"Never mind. No loss. The fools haven't even killed him. They've given him back his sword—because he promised to be loyal. Don't they know that once I've won a man's heart, he's mine forever?"

"You know, you haven't actually tested that proposition," said Bear.

"Do you doubt it?" she asked. Her temper was ready to flare, for despite the unconcern that she affected, Bear knew that it bothered her very much to have been defeated in the first skirmish of the war.

"I merely point out that in order to know a man is yours forever, you would have to wait an infinitely long time."

"Not infinite," said Baba Yaga. "Only until the man is dead. That's forever as far as *he's* concerned."

"Ah," said Bear. "I see your point."

"And I see yours, don't think I missed it. Let me assure you, my dearest darling swatch of fur, that the spells that helped you discover your deep abiding love for me will never dim with time, and there is no one alive with the power to break what I have bound."

"Technically speaking," said Bear, "*I* have that power."

"But since I have bound your power to my will, and I don't will you to be free of my binding, I can't think how your power could ever be used to break those bonds of affection and devotion and humiliating servility that make us such a perfect couple. So the word *forever* seems to apply in your happy case, as well. Aren't you glad?"

"I am as happy as you wish me to be," said Bear.

She cackled with delight at the deftness of his answer. "Oh, Bear, the best thing I ever did was give you speech! Only you are worthy of me! I shall be entertained forever, because I have you!"

"No doubt you'll strive to keep me entertained as well."

"Why yes," she said. "For instance, I have all these useless people that came along with my flying house. I have no interest in feeding them. They're not good at any service I require. So you may sport with them however you like. In fact, I resolve not to feed you again until you've rid me of them all."

"I don't require food to live," Bear pointed out.

"But you *like* to eat. And winter will come, and you'll wish to be nice and fat, won't you? Be a dear, and kill at least a few of them tonight."

"Do you really, truly want me to?" asked Bear.

"Oh yes, I do."

"And may I really, truly choose whether to eat them now or not?"

"Of course! It wouldn't be entertaining otherwise."

"Then I choose to take a nap. If you want to eat them, go ahead, but I'm not interested in doing your bloody-handed work right now."

She almost said the words that would compel him to obey. But instead she laughed. "Play your games with me, my pet. There's one enemy I think you'll *want* to kill."

"Which one is that?" he asked.

"Why, the one who took your eye," she said.

And she was right. That one he would gladly tear to bits. "When will I have him?"

"As soon as their little army moves against us," said Baba Yaga. "Soon. Now take your nap, my dear."

17

WAR

hey held a council of war that night, all the soldiers, all the elders of the villages of Taina, Father Lukas, and King Matfei and his family. No one questioned Ivan's right to be there, but he was wise enough to speak only when spoken to. His prestige was high right now, but few would take him seriously when it came to any aspect of war but bombs and Molotov cocktails and the ungainly hang glider they were already building.

It was unnerving to have the king so silent. But every word he did not say was a reminder of Dimitri's treason, so Dimitri, at least, was not the one to fill the gap. Instead, Katerina quietly led out in the conversation, calling upon each man for counsel who seemed to want to speak, and then deferring to her father whenever a question was raised. He wrote his answers to her in a tray of dirt that rested before him on the table, but his writing was slow and inaccurate, for literacy was only somewhat within his grasp.

Of course the command was reorganized, with those most loyal to Dimitri replaced by those most loyal to the king. Everyone understood, and beyond that there was no punishment or recrimination. It's not as if the peasant portion of the army would be expected to stand against anything but other peasants, while knights would fight only other knights.

Then it was time for Ivan to explain what his new weapons could do. To his surprise, there was vehement opposition to the use of fire against men. At first Ivan thought it was some misguided notion of chivalry and fair play that was causing the druzhina to object. Then he realized that the problem was using peasants to attack knights. They didn't like the precedent.

"The weapon is terrible," Katerina admitted, "but remember that we're outnumbered greatly. Our hope is that the grenades and cocktails will terrify the Pretender's peasants into running away. They have no love for her anyway. And as for their knights, putting his weapon in the hands of boys and old men helps redress the balance between her swordsmen and ours. I will give you spells and charms, and so will she, but hers will be more powerful. Shouldn't we use whatever magic we have to counteract her strength?"

When they saw it as magic against magic rather than peasants against knights, the opposition melted away.

The next morning, Father Lukas led the women in carefully loading gunpowder into as many canisters as the smithy could produce. Sergei supervised the boys in making Molotov cocktails, which did not require as much care to avoid blowing off a finger or a hand. And Katerina and Ivan worked with several of the more skilled woodworkers and seamstresses to make the hang glider.

By afternoon, they had something that would fly; but it would not bear much weight. This meant it could only be Katerina who would fly in it, and not in the voluminous clothing she normally wore, either. She carefully announced to the women that in Ivan's world, there was special clothing for those who flew. She would have them make the women's version of that clothing—which consisted of slender trousers, which differed from a man's only in not having an opening through which a man could urinate. Since trousers were not widely accepted as a part of the male costume yet, no one questioned her declaration.

It was this mission that most frightened Ivan, for many reasons. Katerina would be alone, with no one to help her. And while she would be fenced around with charms and spells—many of them patterned after Mother's—there was no possibility that in a face-to-face encounter she could withstand Baba Yaga. Yet someone had to get inside her house to free the captives who were imprisoned there—if any of them survived—and perhaps to do some other mischief, even if it was nothing more than burning down the house with whatever charms and potions the witch might have stored there. What they had going for them was surprise—Baba Yaga had seen airplanes fly, but never an individual person in a hang glider—and also Baba Yaga's well-known custom of riding into battle on the back of an ass, so she could trot from place to place, screaming orders and casting spells.

If only they could be sure that Katerina would even reach Baba Yaga's house. They were counting on warm updrafts to keep the hang glider aloft, that and dumb luck, for it had a long way to go, and not that high a hill to launch it from. It was downhill, generally, all the way to Baba Yaga's lands, but her house itself was in the middle of a fortress high on a hill. To arrive so low that Katerina couldn't get over the wall would be a disaster.

And Ivan wouldn't know whether she had succeeded or failed. If he died in battle, then the question was moot; but if he lived, if they were victorious, only to learn that she had died falling from the sky before ever reaching Baba Yaga's house, it would be unbearable. Why had he ever thought of a hang glider? Damn that little brat Terrel and his kite!

Yet the thought *had* come to him, and they knew of no other way to get someone over the wall, and once inside Baba Yaga's house, there was no one with a better chance of getting out again alive. So Katerina it would be.

Ivan's part in this battle might be crucial, but his role would still be small. He had command of the boys with grenades and cocktails. Not that they really needed a commander. Their job was to dodge in and out among the fighting men; they were counting on the men to ignore them as unarmed children until it was too late. Each boy would be on his own in this. Ivan's role would be little more than telling them to fire.

Not that Ivan had not volunteered for more important work. A soldier he was not, but he could read, and so he asked to be the man who would stand beside Matfei, reading his instructions as he wrote them during battle and shouting them out for others to obey. In the end, though, Ivan knew that it was impossible. It could not be his voice that the men heard ordering them into battle. Instead, Father Lukas would read out the orders, shout the commands. Even though his proto-Slavonic wasn't as good as Ivan's, his voice was more familiar here, and he hadn't earned the resentment of every man who had ever dreamed of marrying Katerina.

Katerina, of course, questioned whether it was right for a man of God to be so centrally involved in war. Father Lukas only laughed sharply and said, "If Baba Yaga wins, then all my work here is undone, and the name of Christ might not be heard again in this land for centuries.

Besides, I carry no weapon, I harm no man. I will do nothing more than read in a very loud voice, which is what I do in church."

There was appreciative laughter at that bit of sophistry. Everyone understood that it was not hypocrisy but exigency. Father Lukas hated war, but the wolf was coming, and these were his sheep.

In the morning, it was agreed, they all would march to war. They knew where Baba Yaga's army was gathered—not far from the large meadow where scouts reported that a big white house on chicken legs was moving back and forth at her command.

Even after the council ended, Ivan and Katerina had no time alone, not for hours; instead they settled into a candlelit room with King Matfei, Father Lukas, and Sergei, telling all that had happened to them in Ivan's country. They had not told a word of it to Sergei and Father Lukas back in the forest, and it was only at the king's insistence that they told it now, for they did not expect to be believed.

"Ivan's mother is a witch?" Father Lukas sharply asked.

"I never knew till now," said Ivan.

"Bad enough when she was just a Jew," Father Lukas grumbled.

"She saved my life a dozen times," said Katerina. And then she held up the dozens of charms that she had made during those long days in the woods. "Our soldiers will also wear these, of her design, but with my power in them. Aware will make them quicker to recognize their enemy's intentions. Baffle will confuse the enemy, while this potion, which they must drink just before going into battle, will make their movements faster, their aim more accurate. You can be sure that the Widow will have her own charms on every soldier in her army— but her designs are not as deft as Mother Smetski's."

It didn't reconcile Father Lukas to this whole business of relying on witchcraft, but he was a practical man, and there would be time enough to stamp out charms and potions after the war was won, the witch defeated. Someday when a woman gave a gift to a departing soldier, it would be nothing more than a token of her love, and not an amulet with powers in it to protect him in the fight.

As for the tales of flying across oceans, no one seemed to doubt them because no one understood what they really meant. What was an ocean to them, who had seen only forest in their lives? What did it mean for a huge house to fly, when there was no house that they had seen as large and heavy as a transcontinental jet? They had never heard a noise so loud as the engines of a plane. They had never seen anything move as swiftly as a car on the interstate. So whatever mental picture they received from Katerina's account, it could not be very close to what had really happened.

What interested them was the soap opera—the jilted lover, coming with charms to win Ivan back or punish him, only to discover that the witch had tricked her, and both the potions had the power to kill. And then the adventure of detecting the witch in the flying house, and their departure just before it flew away and disappeared—that one, too, was sure to be added to the fund of folklore.

I have already changed the future, thought Ivan. There will be different folktales now, to take into account in my dissertation. The lists and charts will be altered.

And then he wondered: What if the folktales I studied already included what we added here? What if the Ivan of the Russian folktales—Ivan, who was as common as Jack was in the English tales—was really Ivan Smetski, a Jewish boy from Kiev?

Now that he thought about it, he could see that he was right. For he had proof. He knew the origin of the tales of Baba Yaga's house that stood up on chicken legs and ran from place to place at her command. In all his years of study, he had never seen a single speculation from a folklorist or literary historian that the original of the witch's walking hut might be a hijacked 747. Yet there were the stories all along.

So everything that is happening now had already happened before I was born, thought Ivan. The hijacked jet. The coming of a common peasant named Ivan, untrained in battle but blessed with magical charms and gifts from his mother. The man who marries the princess, but then finds himself in mortal danger. He had read these tales before, never guessing that he would live through the originals.

What, then, of the tales that Sergei had written down at his behest? Those were the pre-Ivan tales, the stories from the time before Baba Yaga got her walking house. The lore of the folk before being corrupted by his backward passage through the centuries.

But what did the stories say the outcome would be? Ivan won in most of the tales Ivan knew, but that didn't guarantee a victory in this case, for not one of the tales told of Ivan commanding a group of grenade-throwing boys in the midst of battle. Did the silence mean that they would lose today, their exploits forgotten because everyone who witnessed them had died? Then only the women of Taina would be left, to tell the tales that they already knew before the battle's start.

No, no, he could not reach any conclusion from the silence. Besides, there were more Ivan stories that were nothing like the things that he'd already done. Couldn't he live to have more adventures? Only if they had a victory today, for it was certain that in defeat there would be no escape for him.

Of course, those other Ivan stories might be more embellishments, told about a legendary figure who was dead.

Russian fairy tales were the only ones he'd read that were so grim, even the princess sometimes died.

Why couldn't I have been born a nice Protestant boy from Omaha or Sacramento? Why couldn't Katerina have been the unattainable girl that somehow agreed to let me take her to the prom? Why couldn't I have been the track star with the letters on my jacket, instead of making bombs and Molotov cocktails, and sending my wife into the air to face a dire enemy alone?

Lost in thoughts like these, Ivan let the conversation drift around him until someone called him back. Misunderstanding his inattention, Sergei whispered to him, "Don't be afraid. I believe God has chosen you for a great work." To which Ivan, just as quietly, replied, "He chose his own son, too, and look how that turned out."

At last the councils and the conversations ended. Ivan and Katerina slept then, their first time together on the straw mattress of her bed in King Matfei's house. They did not make love, but only held each other, whispering their happiness over the time they had together, plus a few hopeful comments about the baby that yes, indeed, Katerina carried in her womb.

It was a fine morning for a war. They set out with songs and tears—the songs of men putting on a show of bravado, the tears of women mourning in advance while protesting through their sobs that they knew God would protect him—husband, son, brother, father. It was a scene that had played out ten thousand times already, and would play again ten thousand more.

They marched that day and slept that night, consuming half the food they carried with them. What more was needed? If they won, they would have Baba Yaga's lands to pillage; if they lost, there would be no need for food at all. The second half of their supply was only to feed them if by some chance the battle lasted until a second day.

Somewhere behind them, on a high hill, Katerina would be launched at dawn, the few men she had with her watching her out of sight, then rushing to bring their report. Ivan tried not to think of that, but rather to concentrate on the task at hand. A dozen match boys, including Sergei, who—though a good throw—could not possibly dart in and out among the fighting men. Four times as many who carried a half-dozen grenades and cocktails each. The grenades, they knew, were to throw once at the start, to frighten the peasants of Baba Yaga's army, and then to hold in reserve, for they were too dangerous to use among the soldiers, where the shrapnel could kill a man of Taina as easily as his foe. For the close-in work, the cocktails would do the job, and when a boy had run out of his supply, he was to flee back behind the line of battle, to wait. If the worst came, and they lost the day, then these boys were to be the rear guard, using their grenades to cover a retreat, delaying the enemy long enough that there might be hope for some, at least, to get away.

Get away, yes, but not back to Taina, for that would be Baba Yaga's land, and the women would be given to her followers. Any man found there after a defeat would be killed or enslaved and sold far away. To Constantinople, perhaps, where they might live as Christians despite their slavery, to weep the remainder of their days, remembering their wives and daughters, now belonging to other, crueler men; remembering their sons and brothers who were lucky enough to die in battle rather than living out their lives in such despair.

None of this was said aloud. But all of them knew what lay ahead, if the day were lost. But what made it possible for them to fight was the knowledge that if they did not struggle against Baba Yaga, the outcome would be the same, except that all the men would be sold as slaves, and without even the comfort of knowing that they fought for their families, their God, and their king.

The battle would be fought where it had to be fought—the self-same meadow that was large enough to land a plane. Baba Yaga's army hovered in the shelter of the trees on the eastern side of the meadow, with the morning sun at their backs. King Matfei emerged from the wood and arrayed his army almost exactly as Baba Yaga's men were organized—peasants to the left and right, the druzhina in the middle, to guard the king and lead the push into battle.

The same, but with two important differences. Baba Yaga's army was larger, at least double the size of King Matfei's. And as the armies moved forward, ready to collide, young boys darted out from among the men of Taina, carrying something burning in their hands. Were they such fools as to think that they could set such a green meadow on fire?

Then they threw their canisters, some of which burst open in midair with terrifying noise, right above the heads of the peasants. Tiny shards of metal were flung out at such speeds that they could cut open a man's face or throat as he raised his head to see what this strange weaponry could be. Many fell; the rest, seeing the hideous wounds on their comrades and deafened by the booming noise, cried out in panic and ran away.

In three minutes of chaos, Baba Yaga's army became nothing but her druzhina and a handful of peasants, who now bunched up as close to the knights as they could manage. In moments they were under-foot, the druzhinniks screaming at them to get out of the way, and fi-nally lashing out at their own peasant soldiers to get clear of them.

Again the boys ran forward with fire in their hands, but this time Baba Yaga's knights only laughed, for they had seen how the shrapnel from the grenades did not penetrate their helms and mail and heavy leather garments. These loud noises might scare away peasants, but there were still three knights of Baba Yaga for every knight of Taina.

Then the little pots of alcohol began to strike them in their armor and burst into flames. The well-oiled leather under their mail took to the flame and burned merrily; faces, too, caught fire, and men flung down their weapons and ran screaming from the field.

Baba Yaga, from her vantage point on donkey-back at the forest edge, struggled to find what spell of fire was being used so she could quell it with a counterspell. But there was no magic in it, not that she could detect. Her knights, too, were being defeated, and while she hurled curses at the matchboys, tripping them or blinding them, other boys took up their matches and the flames continued to fly.

"Attack!" cried Baba Yaga. "They can't throw flame on you if you're close to their own knights!"

Fully half her knights remained, and hearing her command—for they all wore charms that attuned them to her voice—they saw the wisdom of what she said, and plunged forward, hacking at the boys to get them out of the way. It was the knights, it was the king of Taina that they wanted, whose blood they had to shed. The boys could taste the pain of fiery vengeance later.

And in the meantime, Baba Yaga saw, to her fury, who it was who gave commands to these fire-bearing urchins. Ivan. The man who should have died at his mother's house, who was now defeating her spell-protected army with a troop of boys.

Well, Ivan Smetski, I have your measure. You will cease to cause this havoc.

As the knights at last came together and the clang of sword on sword rang across the field, Baba Yaga herself rode onto the field.

"Ivan Smetski!" she cried. "Ivan Smetski, why do you send boys out to be killed!"

As far as she knew, not one of his boys had yet been harmed, but all she wanted was his attention, so his ears would hear her voice. What she wanted, she received: Ivan turned to look at her, his face alight with triumph as the peasant army of Taina swirled around him, rushing forward to pick at the Widow's knights with their javelins and pitchforks, distracting them, knocking them down so King Matfei's knights could slaughter them.

Look at me. Yes.

She called out to him again, but this time it was another name she used, and it was her voice of command, her hands moving in a spell of binding. "Itzak Shlomo! Thou art mine today, and mine always! Obey!"

She felt the connection between them form, and now she made the handsigns of command. Ivan stood helpless, motionless.

"Watch this, Itzak Shlomo. See the price of mercy."

She turned toward the main body of knights, and waved her arms over her head. At once her appearance changed, to the face that she had worn in Dimitri's dreams. "Now!" she cried. "Now is the time to strike the cowards and the weaklings down, so Taina can be strong again!"

Dimitri heard the command and smiled. He tipped his head back and cried out the agreed-upon command. Only a half-dozen knights were with him now, but they would be enough, for in the heat of battle they had all maneuvered to be closest to the king. They turned as one, their backs to the enemy—but Baba Yaga's command stayed their enemies from killing them as they raised their swords to strike against the king.

In that moment, Father Lukas, grasping at once the treachery at hand, stepped forward between the king and his would-be assassins. Holding his testament before him, he cried out, "In the name of Christ, forbear!"

Dimitri's answer was to sweep Father Lukas's head from his shoulders with a single blow of his sword against the unarmed man.

King Matfei stood alone, except for the cripple Sergei, who held his pathetic little fire-in-a-box. Dimitri laughed and held up his bloody sword. "You dared to shame me by giving me this sword from that girl-man's hands! See what happens to you now!"

Beside the king, Sergei held six fuses into the flame at once. They all caught. Sergei flung the match away. "Matfei, fall to the ground right now or die!" he cried. Then he tossed the grenades under the feet of the circle of treacherous knights and leapt back himself. The bombs exploded, some in the air, some on the ground; some before Sergei had fallen atop the king, and some after. The grenades that exploded at their feet tore their groins apart or shredded legs. Those who faced a bomb in midair were blinded and deafened. Either way, they had no chance to resist the true knights who struck them down at once, then turned again to face the witch's men.

Having seen the traitors torn apart, the foe had no more taste for this affray. Baba Yaga's screams to kill, kill, went unanswered now, for fear of the bombs was stronger than the fear of the witch. The battle was lost to her.

She saw it as the last of her army melted away, turned into individual frightened men fleeing across the meadow, trying to outrun each other so the following swords would not hack them down. The only man who stood still on all the field of battle was Ivan, who was still frozen in his place by her command.

She thought of killing him on the spot, but had a better idea. At the far end of the meadow stood her house-that-flies. She kicked at her donkey and raced for it; at the same moment, Ivan, obeying her will, also ran—faster than her mount, so he arrived before her and mounted the ladder into the metal structure. Leaving her donkey on the ground, she clambered after him, then pulled the ladder up from the inside.

Ivan stood helpless inside the airplane, watching as the witch climbed up, then dragged the ladder in. He wanted to move, to speak—more than anything, he longed to push her as she leaned over the edge, so she could break her neck on the ground outside.

But he did nothing, for his body did not respond to his will.

"Close the door!" she commanded him.

Now he *could* move, but only to comply. He tried to resist, but his efforts didn't even slow him down. He had seen the flight attendants as they tried to close the door with him inside; he had little trouble doing what they had done, and closing the door.

Maybe there was someone outside who could figure out a way to break into the airplane. But he doubted it. He was alone here with Baba Yaga, unable to raise a hand or speak a word to defend himself. Whatever Mother's spells were supposed to do, they were useless against this spell of binding she had cast upon him.

"Face me," she said.

He turned and looked at her. She was hideous—not just old, but her face deformed by the malice that had driven her for years. And now her face burned with hatred for the defeat he had just inflicted on her.

"You think you beat me?" she said. "This army is nothing. I'll have Taina tied in knots, husband slaying wife, mother killing babies, till no one is left alive, except the ones who wish that they were dead. All because of you and what you did today, with your vile magic from your terrible, mechanical land."

Of course he could not answer.

"Ah, he wants to speak, he longs to speak. But I don't want to hear your voice just yet." She walked around him in a slow circle, looking him up and down. "You're not much. What does she want with you?" Then she laughed mirthlessly. "Oh, that's right, she didn't choose you. Who did? That's the question, isn't it? Who chose you?"

Ivan wanted to answer defiantly, to utter some witticism that would prove his courage and give her something to remember and resent after he was dead. But then again, if he *could* speak, chances were his voice would tremble and betray his fear, giving her something else to mock.

"Don't be frightened," she whispered. He could feel her breath as she pulled herself up to get her mouth closer to his ear. "Don't be so afraid that you piss on yourself like a baby."

At her command, he felt his bladder release his pent-up urine down his leg.

Do you think this bothers me, Baba Yaga? It's no worse than what happened to poor Sergei. Besides, it isn't me doing it, it's you.

"Whoever chose you knew how to send you to where the little bitch was napping. *I* couldn't go there, not even with all the power of Bear. Was it that walking windstorm, that fart in a bottle, Mikola? I don't think so. He knew, he *sensed*, he stayed near the place, but no, he didn't find you, did he. Someone else. Someone who could look past the frailty of your body and see something useful. Something that could un- . . . do . . . my . . . army." Her fingers clenched tightly on his arm.

"There *is* muscle there, after all. Not a swordsman's muscles. Not even a peasant's. But lithe. You throw things. Like those boys. You throw things."

She was in front of him now. She slapped his face. Again. Again. Each blow staggered him, but he suddenly had enough volition, enough reflexive control, to regain his erect posture before losing control to her again. His face stung from the blows, and under the stinging on his skin, he felt a throbbing ache in his nose, around his eye. Thus it begins.

And thus it ended. She leaned back against the flight attendants' station and contemplated him. "Finally rutted with her, did you? I heard you. I was listening, just across the street, in the house of the woman whose beloved puppy died. You were humping like bunnies. If there's a baby inside her, I'll show it to her before she dies." She leaned closer, a little more alert. "That bothered you, didn't it. You see, there's pain . . . and there's pain. But your pain is nothing to me. You were a tool all along. But not *my* tool. And whatever it was that whoever-it-was saw in you, I don't see it, and I don't have a use for you. So I don't care what happens to you."

He felt a relaxing in his throat. He could speak. But the words she just said gave him hope that she might let him go. And if she let him go, he might find some way to help Katerina. With that hope came silence—he didn't want to say anything that would damage whatever chances he might have.

Of course she knew that, counted on it. She was just toying with him, of course she was. But *maybe* there was a chance.

She laughed. "You can speak, and yet you say nothing."

All at once he felt the need to speak well up in him; he was going to say something. Anything. So to keep from saying what was in his heart, he said the first thing that came to mind. "You'll never get this thing to fly again."

She was interested in that. "What do you mean?"

"It needs fuel to fly. It hasn't got much left."

"The man who thought he was in charge said that before I let Bear eat him. Keep talking."

"The meadow isn't long enough. It will crash into the trees before it gets into the sky."

"What makes you think my powers won't be enough to make it fly? I can send it straight up in the air if I want."

"If you could," said Ivan, "you already would have."

"Shut up!" she shouted. "I'm not accountable to you. I can make this house do anything I want. Do you doubt me?"

Suddenly the plane moved under him. Unable to control his body, he lurched to the floor, swiping his head against the metal face of the attendants' station as he fell.

"Careful," said Baba Yaga. "It's dangerous to be standing up when this thing moves."

The plane turned, moving this way and that, yawing left and right like a ship with a madman at the tiller. Which was more or less the way things were.

"Into the air!" she cried.

The plane sped up, but the wheels were still bouncing along the ground.

She waved her arms, again, again, each time making the movements more flamboyant.

"Careful you don't bump into the trees," he said.

She brought the plane to a sudden halt. "I have all the time in the world to work on this. There's always a way to do anything I think of. Bear just isn't strong enough. I'll have to find somebody else to bind to me. Maybe I'll use your princess for a while. No, someone much stronger. What about Mikola? Bind him along with Bear, and maybe then I'll make it fly. Or . . . here's a thought . . . I'll go back to your country and take your mother. She's a clever one. She'll help me. Or I'll pluck off pieces of your father and feed them to her. Of course, I'll do that anyway. She caused me enough trouble to deserve much worse than that. You think I'd ever let you go? The only thing I regret is, I won't be able to kill you myself. I promised that privilege to another. He's waited such a long while for me to let him have you. Killing you won't get him his eye back—but maybe he'll feel better about having only half his vision after he's persuaded you to pry your own eyeballs out of your head and offer them to him in your open hands."

She waved her hands over her head, uttered a couple of incomprehensible words, and disappeared.

I wonder what language *that* was, he thought. And then wondered why he would think of such a useless question at a time like this.

18

UNBINDING

aterina did not like to fly. She had already discovered this on the airplane flight from Kiev. She liked it little better on her other commercial flights. But she did not discover the depth of her distaste for it until she inserted herself into the hang glider and soared out over open air. It filled her with bottomless fear; she clung to the handgrips, her body more rigid than the frame. And then, in each trial flight, forced herself to remember what Ivan had said, what he had shown her, what she had seen. She leaned, she pulled, and soon she learned to find the air currents, to stay level. Nothing fancy—no swoops, no sudden curves. Steady. So she wouldn't die. So the terror would end.

She spoke not a word about this to anyone, least of all to Ivan. For she already knew that the only mission to be accomplished with this contraption was to enter Baba Yaga's fortress, and the only one who had any hope of accomplishing anything there was her.

For even though they counted on Baba Yaga being with the army, Katerina knew she would not stay forever. She would be back, and there would be a showdown, and then it would be the strength of all of Katerina's kingdom against Baba Yaga and the power she had harnessed from a god.

So when Baba Yaga seduced Dimitri all those weeks—or was it months?—ago, she had more in mind than whatever mischief Dimitri might accomplish on his own. Whether he lived or died, one thing was certain: In her confrontation with the witch, Katerina would be weaker because her kingdom was less unified.

She had only one surprise: the child inside her. Mother Esther had taught her how to use that magic. "I used it when I had my son inside me," Mother said. "As he grew, his power was part of me. For those months, I felt like the goddess of creation. And then he was born, and became his own man, and I was just myself again. But for that time—I pray that it's enough to make a difference for you, Katerina, if you are pregnant by the time you face the Widow in her den."

Yes, well, I'm pregnant, all right. I only hope the power that the baby brings to me will compensate for the greater fear I have now, the fear of something happening to harm the child.

The day of battle. She had bound herself thrice over to her people, in ceremonies among the women before she left. So she could feel it, like a vague unease in the back of her mind, the fear of the men as they prepared for battle. She felt the sudden sharpening of alarm, the rush of anger and dismay as the enemy appeared.

"It's time," she said.

As they had practiced, the strong young men picked her up, glider and all, and ran together down the slope until the wind caught the wing and she rose above them, gliding away over the treetops. Behind them, she heard them wanly cheer.

Then it was just her, the fragile kite that held her aloft, and the space below her—a distance far too high, so a fall would kill her, and far too low, for she had little faith that she could glide as far as Baba Yaga's fortress.

At least she had no fear of the glider falling apart, however jury-rigged the thing might be. She had bound it together with spells, each knot and joint and seam and stitch, so that the natural forces that pried at things could not tear this thing apart, not as long as she was in it, gliding over the forests of Taina.

It was all Taina, for even the lands that Baba Yaga had long called her own had once been part of her father's kingdom, though it was before her father was ever king. If they defeated the witch, it would be Taina land again; if not, then Taina would cease to be. Some other name would come upon the place. As in fact it would no matter what. She thought of the history that Ivan had told her about, the names this land had borne. Great empires had washed across this land—the Golden Horde, Lithuania, Poland, Russia. And now in Ivan's time, Ukraine. But all were foreign names here, in the end. The land was Taina, underneath it all. The place of her people.

What would she do in Baba Yaga's stronghold? She did not know. Destroy, that's all the plan she had. Find the spells, the potions, the supplies she used, and utterly destroy them. Burn down the place, if it would burn, if she could counteract the protective spells. She had learned much from Mother Esther about the art of protecting a house, and by implication therefore the art of unprotecting one. She knew what to look for. She would find it. But would she find it soon enough?

And before she burned it down, she had to find the people from the airplane, and any other captives Baba Yaga might have. It wouldn't be right for the freedom of Taina to be bought at their expense, not without at least trying to free them first.

The updrafts that she needed were all there. She found them and circled slowly, rising, rising. She felt the progress of the battle. How much longer? Not long at all. Pain. Triumph. Terror. How could she make sense of this?

The walls of the hilltop fortress loomed. Earthen walls, with palisades on top, but not a soldier watching. There were other sentinels that never fell asleep. But none were looking up into the air. Katerina passed over the walls in silence.

Then there were the desperate moments of maneuvering to land within the narrow confines of the stronghold. If there had been archers on the walls, she would have been pierced a hundred times as she descended—no, plummeted—to a brutal landing in a rick of hay. The hang glider crumpled around her, but she had let go in time, and none of her limbs was broken. Or perhaps that was a testimony to the power of the charms she learned from Mother Esther.

She struggled from the hay, gasping, coughing, then stood in silence to get a feel for the magic around her. There would be few traps inside, she knew, because even Baba Yaga wouldn't want to be bothered with her slaves constantly getting caught in her defenses. Still, there might be talismans that betrayed her presence, calling out to Baba Yaga: Come. An intruder has passed this way.

Or perhaps Baba Yaga was so confident she didn't need such things. She would sense an intruder herself, would never be taken by surprise as long as she was home. And if she was away, then upon arrival she would sense that someone wrong was here.

No use speculating. If she had any traps or warning talismans, Katerina did not detect them. Either she would be caught or she would not.

What mattered now was to find the heart of the magic in this place. Even that was easy enough. There was nothing subtle about the layout of the place. Baba Yaga's house was the central building; her most precious places were below the ground.

The halls were lined with shelves of charms and amulets and talismans, stored to be able to equip an army—and these were only the extras, after the army had been equipped! So grandiose were Baba Yaga's dreams that she imagined someday she'd need all these devices.

Katerina was tempted to take some, to study them. But no, the artifact would always serve its maker, so if she tried to use one, it would work against her. These would burn when the house burned.

Where did she make these things? Where were her ingredients? And where were all her prisoners?

She found them together, in the most obvious place. A large round room, with a fire and a cauldron and many pots, for mixing what she mixed; tables, mirrors, and a large bed. Around the room, chained to the walls, the passengers of the hijacked flight, sleeping as best they could, though only those chained to the lowest rings on the wall could lie down to sleep, and many had to stand. Some of them eyed her incuriously as she came in. She could see that they had eaten little during their confinement.

She hurried to the nearest set of chains and tried to see how they were fastened. Soon enough she saw that powerful spells of binding had been used, so powerful that she could not see a way through them.

How were they made? The spells had to be constructed here. Some of it was done with voice and hands, and there was no hope of guessing the word of unbinding; but if she could see how the spell was made, she could figure out a way to unravel it, or at least could try.

Someone spoke to her, but she didn't understand him. It was English that he spoke. So she answered him in her own language, lacing it with every Ukrainian or Russian word that Ivan and his parents had taught her. It didn't work for the man who had spoken—apparently he knew only English—but several others understood and translated for her. "Watch out," they said, in Russian. "Watch out for the bear."

A bear? Ivan's bear from the chasm?

She turned to see the hulking animal shamble into the room on all fours. Seeing her, it rose to its feet, a huge beast that had to be at least twice the height of even as tall a man as Ivan.

So here she was, having accomplished nothing, already caught.

But the bear did not roar or threaten her, unless simply standing there was something of a threat.

"My wife is not at home," the bear said.

Said! In human speech! She had heard old tales, of course, but had never heard real language from an animal before.

"You'll have to come again later if you wish to kill her," he said. "You *are* here to kill her, aren't you? You didn't come all this way just to rattle these people's chains."

This was not at all the tone that she expected from Baba Yaga's husband.

"Speechless?" said Bear. "I understand. The sight of me can take a woman's breath away. Baba Yaga fell quite in love with me the first time we met. I was here to kill her; she thought I had come because she called me. I found, too late, that here was one human who knew spells that could bind even me, who had never been bound. So if you happen to fall in love with me as well, be sure to unbind me from Baba Yaga before you expect me to run away with you."

"I don't love you," Katerina said.

"Ah, she talks after all. I'm a bear, and I was talking more than you!"

"I'm not here for you. I'm here to free these people."

"Now, that's too bad. She's got them rather permanently fastened here. I expect she plans to keep them on display for years and years, until she sweeps away the bones and brings in a new set."

"She loves death so much?"

"It's not death she loves, my dear. It's victory. Power over the vanquished. She can get an amazing amount of gloating time out of each of these poor corpses."

"They aren't corpses yet," said Katerina.

"Well, they will be soon enough. She tried to get me to kill them for her, offered them to me for sport, but I don't kill for sport. Well, usually not."

"You're missing one eye."

He growled, turning the blind eye away from her. "Thanks for reminding me."

"You hate her, don't you?"

"I'm sure I would, if I were at liberty to do so. But you see how it is—I'm ecstatic with devotion for my beloved hag. No husband was ever more faithful. I only have eyes—or rather, *eye*—for her."

"How can I stop her? How can I undo her magic? How can I break her power and make my people safe from her?"

"If I knew, don't you think I would have slipped a hint to someone long before now? No, you're on your own. Fortunately, though, I won't be here to watch."

"Why not?"

"Because at this moment, my dear girl-wife has got an enemy of mine pent up in her house-that-flies. She promised me that I could kill him, and I rather think I will, since he cost me this eye."

"Ivan," she whispered.

"The very one. He kissed you once, I think. That *was* you, wasn't it? Did that develop into anything? A relationship?"

"You know it did."

"Oh, yes, I remember now, my crone mentioned it to me. She was entertained by it all. Young love. Anyway, she wants me to go there and kill your husband as repayment for this eye. And she wants to get back here to deal with you—because of course she knew you were here the moment you arrived. I, for one, planned to sleep through the whole business, but she made me get up to come and deal with you. In fact, she was quite specific, she wanted me in the room with you."

"Why?"

"I rather imagine it's because the fastest way to get me to your husband and get Baba Yaga here to you is for her to do that little trick she does where the two of us change places. It's almost instantaneous. For a moment or two, there's nothing. And then, there where Baba Yaga was standing, there'll be me. And where I was standing, there she is."

"So she'll be here, and you'll be there."

"What a bright girl you are."

"How can I prevent that?"

"You can't."

"Then why are you telling me this? What can I do about it?"

"I think it should be plain by now that I can't tell you anything directly. Nothing but what she wants me to say. Well, maybe I slip in a little more information than she wanted. But it's entirely up to you what you do with it. I'd do it quickly, though, if I were you."

What was she supposed to do? Run? There was no escape from this place, and that wasn't what she came for, anyway. Nor could she hide, not from Baba Yaga.

She looked at Bear, who was now standing in the middle of the room, motionless. In one place. Very still.

And then she understood. Bear and Baba Yaga would change places *exactly*. Where he was standing, she would be standing. So if Katerina did something to that space, and Baba Yaga arrived inside it . . .

She set to work at once, snatching up a stick from the fire and marking a pentagram in charcoal on the floor around Bear's feet. The beast stood very still while she drew it. He stood just as still as she carefully but quickly went through the spells of containment. From this place you shall not wander, of your own power these five walls are made, and so on, and so on.

And then she was done.

"Well?" she said. "Enough?"

"We'll see," he said. "I've been trying very hard not to know what you've been doing, and I think that I succeeded. You'll soon find out, though, won't you?"

And with those words, he disappeared.

For three infinite seconds, the pentagram was empty.

Then Baba Yaga stood there, looking even more hideous than Katerina remembered from the few times her father had taken her to the court of the high king in Kiev when Baba Yaga was also in attendance there. She turned immediately to face Katerina—the witch had arrived knowing where she was.

"How long do you think your husband will live?" she asked. "I think it will be a long time. Hours and hours. I wonder if he'll still be thinking of you, at the end. Or if he'll just be wishing Bear would finish up so he can die."

Katerina had expected some such boast; she barely listened. She was much more concerned about whether her binding would hold. "When you look in the mirror, old woman, do you like the face you see?"

"Of course," said Baba Yaga. "But I don't see the same face you do."

"I'm not surprised," said Katerina. "Won't you step over to the mirror and let me see you as you see yourself?"

Baba Yaga laughed. "You're hoping that I'll try to step outside this foolish pentagram and I'll be stopped and then I'll scream and rail against you and finally plead for you to release me, which you'll do only after all these nice people are free, and your husband is safely delivered from *my* husband's wrath, and I've renounced my claim on Taina, and . . . oh, what else is it you want?"

"I expected nothing of the kind," said Katerina.

"You drew this pentagram for exercise?" asked Baba Yaga. "This sort of thing is useless against me, you know. I unmake such spells a hundred times a day, and make others twenty times as strong that I can still unmake with a flick of my fingers."

"And yet," said Katerina, "you stay within the pentagram."

"Why not?" said Baba Yaga. "It's as good a place as any to stand and watch you writhe. I'm only deciding whether to make these good people tear you limb from limb and eat you raw, or make you watch while I dismember *them*. Which would be more fun to think back on? If only I had one of those marvelous little boxes from Ivan's country, that remember things for you so you can see them later, as often as you want to watch."

"You talk and talk," said Katerina, "and yet you continue to stay within the pentagram."

"It amuses me to stay here, so you can hope that the spell you cast might be working."

"You don't know what spell I cast."

"You think I can't smell a binding from a hundred miles away?"

"I'm sure you can."

"Well, here." Baba Yaga waved her hands and clapped. "The binding is undone."

"Well, that was easy, wasn't it," said Katerina.

"Everything you fret over and sweat over is easy for me."

"And yet there you are, within the pentagram."

Emboldened, Katerina walked over to Baba Yaga's mirror and looked in it. "It didn't turn me ugly," said Katerina. "So it can't be the mirror's fault you look the way you do."

"Get away from that table."

"Come and make me," said Katerina.

"Don't think I won't, if you provoke me."

In answer, Katerina began opening boxes and bottles, jars and bags. She took a few of them to the fire and emptied them over the flames.

"You shouldn't play with things you don't understand," said Baba Yaga.

"I'm sure you're right. Though I do recognize some of these things. This is what you used to make the cloth that brought the airplane here, right?"

"Oh, now look what you've done. It will take me *minutes* and *minutes* to get more of that."

But Katerina knew otherwise. These things were rare and hard to get, dearly bought when they could be found, and treasured by those who had them. Soon all of them were empty.

"Let these people out of their chains," said Katerina.

"Not likely," said Baba Yaga.

"If you do, and give us safe passage out of here, I won't burn your house down over your head."

"But, foolish girl, that's precisely the only time you *could*. For as long as I leave them chained here, you won't do anything to harm my house."

"I would be sad to see them die," said Katerina, "but everyone dies eventually."

"Even your husband," said Baba Yaga. "I wonder if Bear has taken his eyes yet, or if he's saving them for last."

"And still you stand within the pentagram."

Katerina dashed a chair against the mirror. The glass shattered.

"No!" cried Baba Yaga. "What kind of monster are you! Don't you know how many slaves I had to kill to give that thing its power?"

"If only you could step outside the pentagram, you could stop me." She set the ornate chair onto the fire.

"Don't burn that chair! It has so many spells of comfort on it that—"

"Set these people free, and I'll let you out." Katerina was opening larger boxes now, and found one that was filled with books. She walked to the fire, ripped a page from somewhere in the middle of the book, and dropped it into the flames.

Baba Yaga shrieked. But she did not move.

And then she calmed down. "I see," she said. "I see. You didn't just cast a spell of binding. You cast a spell of desire. Very clever."

"So if you'll just release the captives—"

"I must be tired, for it to have taken me so long to see it. I can't *want* to leave this space, which holds me far more firmly than if there was more physical restraint."

"Very good," said Katerina.

"Clever of you."

"And yet you stand within the pentagram. Will you release the captives? Start with one, just to show you're paying attention."

Baba Yaga glared at her. "No, no, that's too easy. There's more to it than that. Perhaps a spell to make it so I can't even desire to break the spell that keeps me from desiring to leave the pentagram. That's very circular, isn't it? But then there might be a spell making me forget how to break such spells, and on and on, when there's a simple thing you just don't understand."

"And what is that?" asked Katerina.

"This is my house," said Baba Yaga. And with that, the whole section of floor with the pentagram on it dropped out from under her. The witch fell through the trap door, but rose again almost at once, climbing up a ladder. "Oops," she said. "No pentagram. Even though I never wanted to leave it, now that I'm outside, I can't understand why I ever wanted to stay. Or why Bear stood still for you while you drew it on the floor. But that's between him and me, later. Now your precious captives start to die, one for each box of precious powders and each bottle of precious liquors that you ruined. That should take us more than halfway through this crowd, don't you think?" Baba Yaga strolled over to where the pilot stood, half-dead from the beating she had given him. "For instance, I told poor Ivan a lie—I said I killed this one. I think it's just about time I made it true, don't you? We wouldn't want Ivan to die believing something that isn't so!"

On the airplane, Ivan did not wait to see where Bear would appear. The moment Baba Yaga was gone, he sprang for the door, tried to open it. But it wouldn't budge.

A voice behind him said, "Of course she bound them all closed before she switched with me."

Ivan turned. There was the bear on all fours, his head tilted to one side as he studied Ivan's face.

"That missing eye," said Ivan, "I didn't mean to do that."

"The eye's gone anyway, whatever you meant."

"But it was my job, to save the princess."

"From what? It seems to me she's in a lot more danger now than she ever was on that pedestal."

Ivan sidled away from the door, then began backing down the aisle. "On that pedestal she was as good as dead. Now even if she dies, at least she lived first."

The bear shambled easily after him. "Same goes for you."

Ivan slid along a row of seats, then ran headlong up the other aisle toward the front of the plane. Into business class. Into first class.

Bear was singing to himself as he meandered up the aisle. The song was one Ivan had never heard before, in a language that he didn't understand. "If the old hag thinks she gave you the gift of perfect pitch," said Ivan, "she was wrong."

"Singing goes along with speech. I tried it out, I learned a song or two."

"What language was that?"

"My language. The language of bears."

"But bears don't speak."

"That's why you never heard it before." Bear half-stood in the far doorway of the first-class section, his paws leaning on the backs of the last seats. "Baba Yaga thinks I'm going to torture you, but I'm not a cat. I'm just going to kill you, because it isn't right for someone to put out the eye of a god and walk away."

Ivan remembered something, trapped as he was. For he happened to be trapped in a particular place. Standing right where he had stood when he first boarded this plane, to put his carry-on bag of books in the overhead compartment.

He opened the compartment door. He pulled down the bag.

"Are you going to read to me?"

As he opened the bag, Ivan knew what he was looking for. What this whole business had been orchestrated in order to accomplish.

He had a message to deliver.

He pulled the slip of paper from the bag. It still said what it had said before. Ivan was disappointed. He had half-expected that when it was in the presence of the one who was supposed to receive it, new words would appear. But it didn't happen.

Still, this was his last chance. If it wasn't for Bear, Ivan wasn't going to live to deliver it to the intended recipient anyway.

"I think this is for you," he said.

Bear cocked his head to look at it. "I don't think so."

"I think it is," said Ivan. "A message from someone in my time to someone here. The old hag didn't know it, but she brought this plane here solely so that this note would travel back in time, eleven hundred years, so you could have it here today."

"What good is a note like that to me?"

"I don't know," said Ivan.

"Give it to me."

Ivan held it out toward one of Bear's huge paws.

"What, are you blind? Do you see thumbs on my paw? How exactly am I supposed to take that tiny piece of paper?"

"I don't know," said Ivan.

"My mouth," said Bear disgustedly.

Ivan raised his hand, offering the note to the open mouth of the bear, knowing that if he felt like it, Bear would take his hand as well.

Instead, Bear took it between his lips. Then a bit of his tongue came out, tasting the corner of it.

"Delicious," said Bear.

He sucked the paper into his mouth, chewed it slowly, and swallowed.

Now I'll never deliver the message, Ivan thought.

Then Bear stood up so suddenly he hit his head on the ceiling of the plane. He roared, and roared again. And again. And again.

Why didn't he speak?

Bear began slashing the upholstery of the chairs. He rampaged through first class, then back into business class, seemingly oblivious now to Ivan, who followed him, fascinated and appalled by what seemed to be rage. Yet through it all, though Bear roared again and again, he said not a word.

And then, suddenly, he turned toward Ivan and clambered deftly over the seat backs and in a moment he had Ivan pressed to the floor in the aisle, looming over him. He opened his mouth and lowered it toward Ivan's head.

Katerina, if only you survive, it's all been worth it.

It was not teeth that touched him. Only a huge tongue lapping his cheek, almost pulling half his face up with it.

And another lick.

He's saying thank you. He's thanking me because . . . because . . . the note wasn't a message at all. It was the spell of unbinding. It was the spell that set Bear free of Baba Yaga. That's why he wasn't speaking— he had lost her gifts as well as her chains.

"You're free, aren't you," Ivan said.

Bear roared triumphantly in response, then overleapt him on the floor and began pawing at the airplane door.

Ivan got up, wiping the bear slobber from his cheeks, and made his way to the door. The spell on it was gone. He opened it, but before it was even a quarter of the way up, Bear shimmied out through the opening and landed on the ground, rolling in the meadow.

The door opened the rest of the way. Ivan could see a campfire, then another. Dozens of them in the meadow.

Whose? Baba Yaga's army? Ivan had seen them run away.

Ivan lowered himself from the airplane and dropped to the ground. Just in time—the moment he got to his feet, he heard a rush of air and a clap of thunder, and the 747 was gone.

He walked across the meadow to the fires. As soon as people saw him, they began coming up to him, touching him, greeting him. We saw you go into the big white house with *her*. We thought you were dead. How did you get away? Is she still there? Where did it go?

"No, she's not there. She's back at her fortress now, and Katerina's there, and we have to go and finish the job, we have to rescue Katerina."

Now that Ivan had said it, it was the obvious thing to do, no time to waste. They searched for their weapons, picked them up.

"The day's work isn't done here yet," Ivan said, speaking louder and louder. "Not while Katerina is in the witch's fortress! We drove away the witch's army! Now let's have done with her ourselves! Her power is broken, Bear is free, her spells are coming apart—now is the time to strike!"

Then he realized that one of the bloodstained faces that was peering at him was King Matfei, holding Sergei in his arms.

"Look what he did for me," Matfei said. "It was the crippled one who saved my life!"

Ivan looked with grief on the body of his friend. "Oh, God, no. Sergei."

"He isn't dead," said King Matfei. "But he's dying."

"Then that's all the more reason for us to hurry to the fortress and bring back Katerina. She'll know how to heal him, if it can be done at all. Where's Father Lukas?"

"Dead," said King Matfei.

And then, in unison, because they both realized it at once, Ivan said, "You're talking!" and King Matfei said, "I can talk!"

That was the final proof, for any doubters, that when Bear was set free, all the spells the witch had created by his power were undone. King Matfei had his tongue. And therefore there was hope that somewhere in that stronghold, Katerina was alive.

They ran along the road, unhindered by any enemy. They all ran, casting away armor, clothing, bucklers, clinging only to their swords and bows and spears and axes. Yet for all their strength in battle, none of them came close to keeping up with Ivan. He approached the gate of the stronghold before any of the others were in sight.

Baba Yaga was in the midst of the spell that would doubtless kill the pilot in some gruesome way, when she was interrupted by a surprising sound. The thud of metal on wood. And then the clinking of metal on metal.

The links were falling from the chains that bound the prisoners, tumbling into piles on the floor.

The captives began rising to their feet, rubbing their wrists, watching warily. But before they could say much of anything, or take even a few steps, they began disappearing with a loud popping sound—the cracking of air rushing in to take the place of the person who had disappeared. Within a few moments, with a crackle like a string of firecrackers going off, the entire complement of passengers was gone.

Katerina looked at Baba Yaga and smiled. "Bear is dead," she said.

"Don't be an idiot," said Baba Yaga. "He's immortal. No, he's not dead."

"Then somehow Ivan set him free."

Above them, the great timbers of the house began to groan. In the distance, Katerina heard the sound of a beam cracking.

"Even the house is sustained by magic, isn't it?" asked Katerina. "By his power."

Was that fear on Baba Yaga's face?

"In fact, everything you've done for years depended on having him as your slave, didn't it? And so now all your vicious little works will be undone."

Baba Yaga raised her hands slowly. "Gloating is a great joy, isn't it?" she said. "To have your enemy in your power—there's nothing sweeter, is there?"

Her words stung Katerina to the heart. She *had* been gloating. In that, at least, she was no different from Baba Yaga. It was an unbearable thought.

"But you gloated just a little bit too soon," said Baba Yaga. "For I was a witch before I ever fell in love with Bear. And I was powerful enough on my own to capture him and use him as I wished."

"A dreadful power," said Katerina, suddenly humble again. "But haven't you learned anything today?"

"If I think of it before you're dead, I'll mention it," said Baba Yaga. "There'll be nothing refined about your death, I fear. A simple, ordinary one."

Katerina felt a pulsing of one of the amulets she wore.

Baba Yaga cursed. "Where did that woman learn these things?"

"I believe she said her teacher's name was Baba Tila."

"Never heard of her," said Baba Yaga. She walked to the fire, took out a longish piece of wood, about two inches thick, and came back toward Katerina. She raised the wood over her shoulder and swung it like a battleaxe at the princess.

The wood shattered and fell in shards and splinters to the floor.

Baba Yaga cursed again. She stood staring at Katerina, as if measuring her, searching her, probing her. And then, to Katerina's horror, she felt the strings that held the charms around her neck come loose.

Baba Yaga lunged for her, tore the talismans away. Katerina clung to the last few of them, but by brute strength—no doubt augmented by magic—Baba Yaga got them all and tossed them in the fire.

"Now let's have at it," said Baba Yaga. "You without your helper, me without mine. Witch to witch."

Baba Yaga made a motion in the air.

Katerina tried desperately to interpret it, but then realized that it was futile, Baba Yaga wouldn't reveal herself so easily. Whatever it was, Katerina needed protection. No, deflection. She cast a Turn-Away, expecting it only to deflect the witch's spell a little, to weaken it. Instead, when Baba Yaga cast the spell, nothing happened to Katerina at all.

"What?" said Baba Yaga. *"Nothing?"*

She tried again, a different spell, and again Katerina cast a Turn-Away. This time, though, the Turn-Away was so powerful that it turned the spell back on Baba Yaga herself. The old witch bent double in pain and screamed in agony, then dropped writhing on the floor.

"Who is it!" she howled. "Whose power are you drawing on! Answer me! How are you so strong!"

But Katerina did not see why Baba Yaga deserved to have an answer of any kind. All that mattered now was to get out of Baba Yaga's house before the timbers gave way and the whole thing collapsed on top of her.

If there were other captives in the building, Katerina could only assume that they had been set free when the airplane passengers were loosed, and had made their own way out of the house. There was no time to search for them. Katerina cast only a couple of spells, to hold some roofs in place until she had had time to leave the room. Behind her, the building tore itself apart.

She came outside just as Ivan ran up to the gate. They saw each other, ran to each other and clung, laughing and crying, as Baba Yaga's house collapsed upon itself, burying the witch beneath it.

"We did it," said Katerina. "But how did you break her power over Bear?"

"I gave the message to him," Ivan said. "He ate it."

"And that was it?" She laughed. "That note was it? We accidentally left it on the plane, so it was there for you to find?"

"Accidentally," said Ivan wryly.

She understood, and asked the question that was also on his mind. "Who sent it?"

"I don't know," said Ivan. "But Sergei was injured badly, saving your father's life. Have you strength enough to come to him? Do you know how to heal him?"

"I know some healing arts," said Katerina. "Tetka Retiva and Tetka Moika taught me a little, before they stopped visiting. Whether it's enough, with all the power of Taina inside me, with the power of our child as well . . ."

"Let's go find out," said Ivan. And they set off at a weary run along the road.

19

HEALING

ergei was in bad shape when Katerina got to him, and some around him were already whispering, "He's dead." But King Matfei greeted his daughter with a fierce hug, then pointed to Sergei and raised his eyebrows questioningly.

"I thought you could talk again," said Katerina.

"I forgot," said King Matfei. "He's still alive. Can you help him?"

She knelt beside him, put one hand on his forehead, the other on his chest. "The wounds are many, but none of them are grave. It's the shock of it that's killing him." She began to call for herbs, and some of the men, who had gathered herbs of healing for their wives, went in search of them. Not all were found, but she had enough, along with the great power that surged through her now, to stop the bleeding and to still the panic that was making his body withdraw into itself.

He slept.

"Take him back home," she said. "But the rest of us must go and burn down the ruins of her house."

"Where is the Pretender?" asked her father.

"At the bottom of the ruin. But perhaps not dead. And she'll make her escape if we don't destroy her now."

Only Ivan and Katerina and a handful of others remained with Sergei, making a sledge to carry him home. Before they were half-done with it, Ivan said, "Never mind, there's no need for this. I'll carry him."

"In your arms? You'd never make it all the way—a day's march!"

"You have the power to make him lighter, don't you? And he won't be in my arms, he'll be on my back."

"You can't do that unless he's awake to help hold on."

"He *is* awake," said Ivan.

"I feel like my arse is on fire," said Sergei.

"That's where the bits of bronze from the grenades hit you, as you were falling on the king."

"Is the king all right?" asked Sergei.

"He watched over you like his own son until Katerina came to heal you."

Sergei looked at Katerina, then at Ivan again, and smiled. "You're both here. That means you won."

"Bear is free, so her power is broken," said Ivan.

"All that she did with his power is undone," said Katerina. "Father can speak again."

Sergei suddenly sat up, then put his hand to his head. But still he persisted—he had to look at his deformed leg. "Well, Mother was wrong," he said. "She always claimed that it was a curse of the Widow's that crippled me."

"Not all the ills of the world began with her," said Katerina. "I'm sorry."

"With all the magic in the world, you'd think there'd be some power to make me whole."

"The spells I cast on you just now," said Katerina. "I've never had more strength in me, with the love and hope of all the people inside me, and it worked to start the healing of your injuries of today. But if I had the power to heal your leg, it would be healed right now."

"I know," said Sergei. "Father Lukas always said that I was crippled to show forth the greatness of the works of God. I never understood how a crippled leg did *that.*" Then, suddenly, a sob burst from him. "I hated him, but he died so bravely."

He started to get up. Ivan helped him, and he and Katerina supported Sergei between them, bearing him to the body of Father Lukas. "We can't leave him for the vultures," he said.

"We won't," said Katerina. "When the Widow's house is a beacon light, then the king will return, and rewards will be given, and bodies buried, and punishments meted out."

At the word *punishment*, Sergei began looking for Dimitri's body. The whole lower part of it was shredded by the bomb. From the rictus of his face, it seemed that he remained conscious long enough to feel the pain as his lifeblood slipped away. "After all his mockery of me, all his life," said Sergei, "it was the crippled boy who finished him."

"Don't gloat," whispered Katerina. "I did it too, but it's wrong. He's to be pitied, not triumphed over."

"He never had pity for me, or anyone," said Sergei. "It took longer for the king to know it, but I knew what he was from childhood on."

"He was the twisted one, Sergei," said Katerina. "Compared to him, you have always been whole."

In his weakened state, in his grief for Father Lukas, the kind words were more than Sergei could withstand. He burst into tears. Katerina held him, and Ivan's arms encompassed both of them.

The search for survivors or for wreckage of the plane ended when the crew and passengers of the missing 747 wandered out of the woods in western Ukraine. The airplane was found soon after—in the midst of dense forest, where it could not possibly have landed. It was as if some giant hand had gently set it down amid the trees. Closer examination revealed that trees that had once stood where the plane now was were sheared off to fit the exact contours of the plane's body and wings.

The passengers were debriefed for two days while frustrated relatives clamored to see them. When the families were finally reunited, the passengers were reluctant to speak about their ordeal, and government spokesmen in Ukraine endlessly repeated the mantra "We are taking all appropriate measures" as if it meant something.

Rumors flew. Every group of terrorists was suspected, as was every government with a conceivable interest and many without. The tabloids were full of stories of alien abductions (how else could the airplane have appeared where it did?) and speculations about whether a new Bermuda Triangle was forming farther north, or whether the old one was merely beginning to give up its captives.

Every comedian got three days' worth of jokes out of it, including Sam Kinison, who, after reciting all the theories, burst into his trademark scream. "It was the Wicked Witch of the West! They got back because there's no ——— place like home!" He got a pretty good laugh.

BABA YAGA

The house collapsed, but none of the beams could fall on her. The worst that happened to her was a mouthful of dust. Then she began to climb through the wreckage. No doubt they'd burn the place, and she'd rather not remain inside.

Everything lost. Everything broken. And that princess—who could have guessed the power that she'd have? No more head-to-head competitions for Baba Yaga. She had met her match, more than her match. In a way, the falling of the house had saved her life. It was only a matter of time before that little bitch would have destroyed her.

So let her have the kingdom. What good was a kingdom anyway? Whining people to govern, rents and taxes to collect, which everyone tried to steal from her at every step in the process. What good had any of it done her? She'd played at it, but the game wasn't worth the cost.

She was still Baba Yaga, though, wasn't she? Her books might be buried and soon burned, her spells might have been broken, but she could still do magic.

That house-that-flies, for instance. She could make another one like that. Maybe smaller, so it didn't take so much strength to get it off the ground. And come to think of it, it wasn't the flying that was so important, it was the mobility. In the forest here, a huge building that wouldn't fit between the trees was useless—of course it had to fly, and then where would it come to land? No, what was needed was a tiny building, a simple hut, but with legs on it, like those chicken legs, which would pick up and move where she wanted it to go.

That way no one would ever be certain where she was. She might stay in a place for years, harvesting pleasures large and small from the surrounding countryside, then give the command and let her house carry her away to another place. And, come to think of it, the house could stand up on its legs whenever she was gone, and spin around so its door would face away from any intruder. No one could get inside. That way her possessions would be safe. No more nasty little princesses undoing centuries of work.

It was a good thing she had never relied on Bear's power to sustain her life. She never trusted her life itself to anyone. No, the spells that held her body together were paid for in long-shed blood. But she would need more, soon.

More blood, but none from Taina. She didn't want that princess looking for her. She'd move eastward, deeper into the forest, where they'd never heard of her, where she could take the occasional child gathering berries in the wood, and then move on. And someday she might run into Bear again. He'd be more careful, of course. But wasn't it just possible that he'd miss her, just a little bit, and want her back? Trade a little power for the gift of speech? She'd been using him, of course, but she also enjoyed his company. It was good to have someone to talk to now and then. Even if it was a gruff old bear who probably betrayed her.

How *did* that Ivan break the spells of binding?

Oh well. There'd be many centuries to ponder that.

The bonfire lit up the sky behind her. Ahead of her, small nocturnal animals fled from her approach. Inside her, the flame of malice burned as bright as ever. As bright, but smaller. Her reach was smaller, too. But so were her needs. She was retiring from public life. Simplicity was what she wanted now. Simplicity and someone's skull to crack between her hands.

Ivan! Katerina! She thought of them and almost choked on rage. To think of the happiness that lay ahead of them, after all the harm they'd done to her! Was there no justice in this miserable universe?

20

SUMMER VACATION

he school year was over in Tantalus. Children threw papers out of bus windows and ran shouting over the lawns and meadows. But none of them was happier than Matt, Steven, Luke, and Little Esther Smetski, who knew that something more than mere summer vacation awaited them.

Father and Mother already had their bags packed—but there weren't many, only a few days' worth of clothes, just enough for the visit they always had with Uncle Marek and Aunt Sophia. Father always spent some time in Kiev, because he was the hero of the literary community there, having discovered the most amazing trove of ancient writings in Saint Kirill's own hand, on parchment which had been filled by another ancient, anonymous writer, who recorded the earliest known versions of the folktales of the Russian people. In America, he was respected at the university and among colleagues, but in Kiev, he was known to the people on the street. Indeed, there was a street named after him, one which had once been called by the name of a Russian Communist who slaughtered millions of Ukrainian kulaks, but now was named for the scholar who had opened up the Ukrainian past.

But what did that matter to the children? Father had his fans—he'd be busy with them for a while. What mattered to Matt, Steven, Luke, and Little Esther—or, as they were called all summer, Matfei, Sergei, Lukas, and Tila—was the other place, the faraway place, the place they never spoke of to their friends. The land where they were princes and princess, where Mother was queen, where Father was king and counselor to her.

Matfei was old enough to be learning history in school, but he had to laugh when he read about kings. He knew what kings and queens were. In at least one kingdom, nestled up against the eastern reaches of the Carpathian Mountains, there was a kingdom once where a queen ruled over her people, while her bookish husband played with his children, worked alongside the people, argued questions of philosophy with the priests, and gave whatever counsel his wife might want. He was a foreigner there, but with only a trace of an accent, and the people loved him, partly because Queen Katerina loved him, but mostly for himself.

It was the children they adored. But when it seemed they might be pampered to death, Mother and Father always drew them back, put things in perspective, reminded them that it was the kingdom-in-them that the people loved, and that they had to learn to become worthy of the devotion of the people. "It's not yours by right, this power," said Mother. "It is earned, by service, by loyalty, by sacrifice." Just one of the many lessons, the thousands of lessons that they had to learn. Of kingship, soldiering, farming. This year, Matfei and Sergei would be taken along to Kiev to be presented before the high king and have their first lessons in political maneuvering. They could see that Mother and Father feared this more than anything, but that only made it more exciting for Matt and Steven to look forward to.

Grandma and Grandpa came along with them to the airport in Syracuse, so they could drive the minivan back, as they did every summer. Grandma, as always, had a new charm for them to wear. Luke begged her to teach him how to make such things, but Grandma wouldn't do it. "The need for magic isn't so great anymore," she said, "and besides, the power that sustained it all is fading. It was the old gods who were behind it, and as their power weakens from the unbelief of the people, their power also fades." Luke had no idea what she was talking about, but Matt and Steven did. They knew how the people of Taina came to their mother for healing, and how she was able to do less and less for them, and how it grieved her. What they didn't understand was Mother's and Father's refusal to take modern ideas back with them. "Why not find the penicillium mold and use it to fight infections?" Matfei asked Father once.

"Because it isn't time yet," he said.

"But people will die from simple cuts and injuries," said Matfei.

"People all die eventually," said Father, sounding utterly heartless.

But then he hugged his son. "I love your compassion, Matt. But here's the thing. In our own time, after just a few generations of using anti-biotics, the bacteria are developing resistance to them all. If penicillin were put into use in 905, what would happen then? The whole history of the world would change, and we don't know how, and so it would be wrong of us to change it."

"But you took gunpowder back, Father. And alcohol."

"I kept the secret of gunpowder from the others," said Father. "A few know the ingredients, and they've promised not to pass the in-formation on. I did it because the need was great. Because that was what I was sent to do. But we haven't needed it since."

"What about when I'm king, Father? What if I need it then? Will you tell me?"

"No," said Father. "And if you haven't the heart to rule without it, if you need the modern world, then you don't have to stay here. You don't have to be king. One of your brothers will, or your sister. Or none of them, and the people can elect another, or the high king will take the land. History will move on, whatever you decide. You don't have to take the burden on you."

"I will, though," said Matfei.

"If you do, then that will be good, it will be the life you chose. But if you don't, it won't mean that you failed. You're a child of both worlds. With any luck, the choice won't be forced upon you too soon."

Father and Mother could be so inscrutable sometimes, full of mysterious wisdom. Didn't they know how much children were able to guess? How much they could understand if only someone would ex-plain it to them? When we're parents, the children told each other, we'll tell our children *everything.*

They got to the airport, they kissed Grandpa and Grandma good-bye, they flew to Kennedy, then on to Vienna, then to Kiev. There were the days at Uncle Marek's farm. And then at last it was time to cross the bridge.

They never took the same way twice, for fear of making a path. The clearing opened before them. The chasm yawned. Then all joined hands and the bridges both appeared. They crossed to the middle and stopped, for this was a tradition that they never broke. There on the pedestal in the middle of the moat, Father and Mother sat on the slab where Mother had slept the deep enchanted sleep of centuries, and he kissed her, once, a sweet and simple kiss.

This time it was Little Esther's turn to finally understand. "Mama!" she said. "*You're* Sleeping Beauty!" Her brothers laughed and praised her for figuring it out. Mother and Father hugged her and let her lie on the slab herself. She closed her eyes and then said, "Kiss me, somebody, and wake me up!" And her father knelt down, and bent over her, and kissed her, while Matt and Steven and Luke all growled and roared like bears.

Then they joined hands again, the bridges appeared, and they crossed into Taina.

No one waited for them—that was what they asked for, not so much for privacy as because the day of their arrival was never certain, for the calendars of the two places fit together unpredictably. Why should someone waste his life waiting and watching for a queen and king who could find their own way through the woods?

This time, though, they didn't rush away from the chasm. The children were told to play—"But stay away from the edge!"—while Mother and Father stood beside the pit and talked.

"What if one of us dies?" Ivan said to her. "A car crash. An accident at harvest time. Everyone will be stranded then, on whatever side of the bridge we're on."

"If only the children had been born with the power to use both bridges."

"But they can't use either of them without us, and they need both of us to cross at all. We can't leave this to chance, can we? Don't we want the children to be free to choose?"

"They're too young to divide the family."

"I don't want to divide us either," said Ivan. "I want us to live to be a hundred. But life is fragile."

"Someday we'll make them choose, and settle them on whichever side they want, and then we'll choose ourselves, and stay together in the world we want to grow old in. But not yet."

"So if one of us dies . . ."

"We plan what we plan, and if it doesn't work out, then that's the way life will be. What else can we do? Divide the family now, and guarantee unhappiness, for fear of a different misery later?"

"You're right," said Ivan. "You're right, of course. But having children makes a man afraid."

"Afraid, yes, and also very brave."

"Did we really do the things the stories say?" asked Ivan.

"We did."

"And tell me, Sleeping Beauty, are you living happily ever after?"

"Yes, I am."

They called the children then, and as they made the trek through the wood, Matfei joked that Father ought to take his clothes off so people would recognize him when he arrived. "We should never have let people tell those stories to the children," Ivan said to Katerina.

They got to the village and the cheering started, the crowds following them, the parade. They sat down to a feast and heard tales of the winter past, and who had babies, who died, who got married.

It was nearly dark before Ivan and Katerina slipped away and went to the church, where Bishop Sergei was waiting for them, greeting them with a kiss and an embrace. Together they walked into the graveyard, where King Matfei's body had been buried five winters before, and where Father Lukas had a little shrine. "He'll never be a saint," said Sergei ruefully, "and in truth he didn't deserve it. But he was a hero all the same."

"And a great missionary," said Katerina.

"So are the children Jews or Christians?" asked Sergei.

"In Ivan's country, they are Jews," said Katerina. "And here they're Christians. Two worlds. Two lives. Someday they'll decide. Or God will decide for them."

"Doctrinally, there are problems with that," said Sergei. Then he laughed. "But I'm glad you're here."

"So are we," said Ivan. "We miss our dear friends when we're away."

They left the graveyard then, and returned to the royal house, where they had to speak sternly to the children before they'd finally go to bed. Then they, too, lay down on mattresses stuffed with straw, hearing the music of the flies to buzz them to sleep, holding each other's hands as they dozed, thinking of the miracles by which love works its will in the world.

Acknowledgments

Since this novel is set in milieux that are unfamiliar to me, I have relied on various sources, especially:

Pinhas Sadeh, *Jewish Folktales,* trans. Hillel Halkin (New York: Anchor, 1989; 441 pp.). For stories and motifs used in *Enchantment*, especially the story of the Sky, the Rat, and the Well.

Charles Downing, *Russian Tales and Legends* (H. Z. Walck, 1968; 215 pp.). For stories and motifs used in *Enchantment.*

Vladimir Propp, *Morphology of the Folktale,* trans. Laurence Scott (Austin: University of Texas Press, 1968; 158 pp.). The pivotal book whose conclusions Ivan is testing.

Hillel Halkin, "Feminizing Jewish Studies," *Commentary* 105:2 (February 1998, pp. 39–45). For the rhetoric of Jewish feminism.

Jerome Blum, *Lord and Peasant in Russia: From the Ninth to the Nineteenth Century* (Princeton, N.J.: Princeton University Press, 1961; 656 pp.). For a rough idea of how the Russian people were governed before the dominance of the Rus'.

Marjorie Mandelstam Balzer, ed. *Russian Traditional Culture: Religion, Gender, and Customary Law* (M. E. Sharpe, 1992). Many articles were very helpful in grounding my speculations about religion and law in the imaginary kingdom of Taina.

Bruce Cockburn, for the album Ivan listens to in chapter 14. Sharp-eyed readers will note that *The Charity of Night* was released in 1997, rather too late for Ivan to listen to it in 1992. But my opinion is that if you can accept the idea of Ivan and Katerina passing back and forth between 1992 and 890, there should be no problem with Cockburn's music traveling only four years back in time. Think of it as the sound track for that scene.

Sam Kinison, whose screaming comedy is sorely missed, died only a few months before the 747 returned from Taina. But this novel is a fantasy, and in that fantasy Kinison is still alive.

Alexander Pushkin, *Eugene Oregin,* trans. James E. Falen (Oxford University Press, 240 pp.). The best of the translations, I found it with the help of Douglas Hofstadter, *Le Ton Beau de Marot.*

I owe thanks to many individuals for helping me create this novel or prepare it for publication, particularly:

To Derryl Yeager, for the idea of Sleeping Beauty waking up today, and to Nik Gasdik, for putting the story in Russia.

To Krista Maxwell, for details and corrections in my depiction of Russia in several centuries, and for everything in this book that is correct about my use of Old Church Slavonic and proto-Slavonic; the errors that remain are my own, despite Krista's best efforts. Ivan is especially in Krista's debt for the wonderful food Sophia served to him; I had no reason to change Krista's list, so there it stands in her words.

To Linda Bass for the correct spelling of *mohel.*

To D'Ann Stoddard, for research on making gunpowder.

To Clark and Kathy Kidd and to Mark and Margaret Park, for once more opening their homes to me, and for countless other helps, only some of which can be repaid.

To Kathleen Bellamy, who reads my novels last, to catch those pernicious errors that have evaded all other eyes.

To Scott Allen, who keeps the tools of my trade cleaned and oiled.

To Kristine Card, Kathy Kidd, Peter Johnson, Jay Parry, and Robert Stoddard, who read the chapters as they came along.

To Lisa Collins, for a superb and sympathetic job of copy editing.

To Amy Stout and Kuo-Yu Liang, whose patience passes understanding.

To Barbara Bova, who makes it possible for me to live from the proceeds of this hobby of mine.

To Erin Absher, for Baba Tila's real identity and for being our help in all good things.

And, above all, to Kristine and to our children, Geoffrey, Emily, Charlie Ben, Zina, and Erin Louisa, whose lives are the meaning of my life, and who have made me, not yet a virtuous man, but one who knows what virtue is and yearns for it.

About the Author

ORSON SCOTT CARD is the first writer to be awarded both the Hugo and the Nebula in two consecutive years for science fiction novels. He is thus far the recipient of four Hugo Awards, two Nebula Awards, one World Fantasy Award, and four Locus Awards, among others. Also, a dozen of his plays have been produced in regional theater, his novel *Saints* has been an underground hit for several years, and he has written hundreds of audio plays and a dozen scripts for animated video plays for the family market. He is the author of two books on writing: *Character and Viewpoint* and *How to Write Science Fiction and Fantasy*. Card has conducted writing courses at several universities and a number of renowned workshops. In addition, Card is a partner in Fresco Pictures, a movie production company. He lives in Greensboro, North Carolina, with his family.

ABOUT THE TYPE

This book was set in a digitized version of Garamond, a typeface designed by the French printer Jean Jannon. It is styled after Garamond's original models. The face is dignified, and is light but without fragile lines. The italic is modeled after a font of Granjon, which was probably cut in the middle of the sixteenth century.